MORE PRAISE FOR MARIANNE MANCUSI!

A HOBOKEN HIPSTER IN SHERWOOD FOREST

"Mancusi's tongue-in-cheek wit and clever take on Robin Hood and his Merry Men is enjoyable."

—*RT BOOKreviews*

"Steamy romance blends seductively and seamlessly in *A Hoboken Hipster in Sherwood Forest*....a tantalizing tale that will appeal to a wide range of romance readers."

—A Romance Review

WHAT, NO ROSES?

"A romance that's fast, funny and as bubbly as bathtub champagne...Mancusi's witty, tongue-in-cheek remarks and sprightly dialogue make for a joy ride of a read with an ending that's as surprising as it is original."

—*RT BOOKreviews*

"Humorous and sexy."

—*Booklist*

A CONNECTICUT FASHIONISTA IN KING ARTHUR'S COURT

"Sassy...a cute hoot...Talented author Mancusi clearly knows her Arthurian lore."

—*RT BOOKreviews*

"A sparkling debut...a nice twist on the modern girl's search for prince charming."

—*Publishers Weekly*

"This is not your mother's Camelot!! Spicy romance, hilarious thrills, and a heroine who kicks butt in her stilettos—this book is a definite keeper."

—Alesia Holliday, Author of *American Idle*

"Marianne Mancusi's debut is super-snappy, pure fun, fast-paced, and even educational—in more ways than one!"

—Melissa Senate, Author of *See Jane Date*

A ROUGH-CUT GEM

"You know, I meant everything I said," Chase remarked, suddenly earnest. "And you're still a diamond, no matter what anyone else thinks. If anyone's dumb enough to not realize the truth beneath your implants."

She could feel his breath on her face, once again doing crazy things to her insides. She knew she should resist, get up and walk away while she still could. After all, there was no use in starting a relationship. It would distract her, and she had a mission. Maybe when and if everything was over and fixed, when she'd done what she needed...

Against her will, she was trapped by his kryptonite-colored eyes. They were so brilliant in the firelight, they glowed. Molly's traitorous body moved forward instead of away. Her traitorous heart pounded in her chest and her traitorous lungs struggled to take in air almost too thick to breathe.

Chase drew her hand to his lips, kissed Molly's palm with an unbearable softness. She squirmed as impossible sensations coursed through her, too hard and fast to catalog. Six years without being touched by a man. Six years when her body's drive for that was strongest.

He smelled like the earth: rich, dark, delicious. She wanted nothing more than the opportunity to taste him.

"Kiss me," she whispered.

MARIANNE MANCUSI

RAZOR GIRL

LOVE SPELL

NEW YORK CITY

LOVE SPELL®

September 2008

Published by

Dorchester Publishing Co., Inc.
200 Madison Avenue
New York, NY 10016

ISBN 10: 0-505-52780-4
ISBN 13: 978-0-505-52780-6

Printed in the United States of America.

10 9 8 7 6 5 4 3 2 1

Visit us on the web at www.dorchesterpub.com.

ACKNOWLEDGMENTS

Thanks to:

My editor extraordinaire Chris Keeslar. I've learned so much from you, I can't even begin to thank you enough.

My agent, Kristin Nelson, who is ridiculously good at her job. I feel lucky to have you looking out for me.

My Rebels of Romance partner in crime Liz Maverick. May our adventures continue! Where to next year?

The SWAT Writers. For constant encouragement and bottomless cups of Starbucks. (Even if you guys do like McDonald's better...)

Jacob Beach for zombie-zapping stress relief on the Wii and sooooo much more. <3 u!!

My awesome readers. Thanks for your e-mails and My-Space messages! They keep me going— even on the hard days!

And finally, George Romero. For all the zombie awesomeness you've given us all.

RAZOR GIRL

She turned suddenly, bloodshot eyes zeroing in on where Chase stood in the shadows. Forcing himself to keep his breaths slow and regular, he lifted his rifle, trying not to make any sudden moves that would set her off. His hands shook, making it difficult to line up the female creature's head. The money shot. The shot he'd need to take her down for good and protect his family with the least risk to himself. How had she gotten so close without him realizing?

The woman let out a muffled moan, her hairless, bony arms outstretched like something from an old George Romero movie. But this was no film set. The world in 2036 had become a true horror flick, and Chase was one of its stars. He was the one who'd done the drugs, had sex with the girl and uttered the words, "I'll be right back." In other words, he was the one who was about to wind up dead.

It was more than a bit tempting to run. To get as far away as possible from this pus-dripping creature formerly known as a human. But she was too close to the campsite where Molly and the children were sleeping. And while Chase had failed before—failed whenever it counted, in fact—things were different now. For the first time since the plague erupted, there was hope. And no dumb, oozing, post-apocalyptic monster was going to take that away. Not on his watch.

He blew out a breath and steadied his gun, eyes narrowing to slits. Steady as she goes, he told himself. This was a matter of protecting his family: both what was left of it and what he'd rebuilt. It was a matter of doing good, and not the simple rehash of senseless violence that once had been so popular on the silver screen. Shoot-'em-ups and *slasher films . . . It was so different in reality—tougher to summon the courage to fire, to engage, to set in play the sequence of events that he knew had to follow.*

In an instant it happened. The creature lurched forward and Chase fell back a step, squeezing the trigger of his rifle. Its recoil bruised his shoulder. A gout of blood spurted from the woman's chest—he'd missed. Only a flesh wound. And she was still coming. And two other shadows had appeared behind her. Three . . . no, four? How much ammunition was left in his gun?

He fired again at the Other, twice more, and her head exploded in a mass of red and grey pulp. At the same time he reached around his neck and pulled free a whistle. Sometimes this worked, as the creatures were sensitive to high-pitched noises. He blew as hard as he could. Sure enough, the shadows that had risen behind the first Other stopped moving. There came a cacophony of inhuman screeches and then the shadows dissipated. The creatures had turned and fled, hands over their ears.

Chase watched them go, breathing heavily. The whistle fell from his bloodless lips. "Yeah, I thought so," he said, shaking out his arms and trying to regain some composure. "I thought so! Run, cowards!" He nodded to himself and stepped out from the shadows.

Only to find himself thrown backwards.

He crashed hard onto the asphalt of the street, the impact knocking the breath from his lungs. His vision blurred and, for a moment, nothing made any sense. Then he looked up and saw what had struck him. An Other towered above, clearly not scared away by his whistle. It was growling and spitting.

It was a huge male, and it lunged forward, hands finding Chase's neck, encircling and squeezing tight, cutting off his breath. Desperate, Chase kicked out and slammed his foot into the creature's groin. The monster bellowed but didn't let go. Chase struggled harder, panic slamming through him as he used one arm to brace himself, fighting to keep away from the monster's mouth. He reached for his boot with his free hand, feeling for the knife he always kept there. It took what seemed like forever to wrap his fingers around the hilt. The creature's grip tightened, and Chase saw blackness swimming toward him.

Pain seared through his shoulder. Then, in his final moment of consciousness, he managed to yank the knife free and drive it into the creature's heart.

The zombie recoiled then fell on top of him, crushing Chase with his weight. But the fingers loosened and Chase was able to breathe. He sucked in a huge breath and pushed the creature off. It rolled back onto the pavement, staring up at the sky and whimpering. The heart was always a weak spot.

Chase surged to his feet and stared down at the monster. It looked a lot more human lying there now, vulnerable and bleeding. This was something he always hated. He wondered who it had been before the change. A doctor? A lawyer? Maybe a humanitarian who built houses for poor people.

It didn't matter. It was none of those things now, he reminded himself. Just a monster. A monster that needed to be put out of its misery.

He grabbed his rifle and pressed the barrel to the zombie's head. Closing his eyes, he pulled the trigger. The shot shook his arm and echoed in his ears. He let the sound fade away before looking. The body was twitching, the head disintegrated.

He forced himself to look away, but as he did, a piercing pain found his right shoulder. Startled, he glanced down, his mouth falling open as he saw where his leather jacket had come open, where the shirt below was ripped and bloody. Teeth marks. He'd been bitten. He'd been bitten.

"Chase! Chase, are you okay?"

He looked up. Molly. She was running toward him, her face white.

"Chase?"

"I'm okay," he said, turning at an angle so she couldn't see his wound. "I got him."

She stopped a few feet away, looking down at the remains of the two dead zombies. "God, what happened?" she asked.

"One got the jump on me. No big deal. It's all fine," he lied. The pain gripped his shoulder like a vise and it was all he could do not to fall to his knees. But if he fell, she'd know. He couldn't let her know.

She took a step forward but he held out a hand. "I'm all slimy," he said. "Zombie gook. You know. I'm going to go find a fountain or something to wash off."

"Are you sure you're all right?" she asked, peering at him, confusion and worry warring on her face.

He felt sick to his stomach but nodded. The last thing he wanted was to lie to her. But what choice did he have? He had to think of Molly and the kids. She was too weak to get where she needed to go on her own now. Wonderful Molly. Tough Molly. His beloved. She needed his help to find her father. To complete her pilgrimage. To save the world. And who knew how her priorities would change once she learned the truth?

Well, he had two weeks. Two weeks before the virus could work its way fully through his system, mutating his cells, destroying his brain and turning him into one of them: a diseased, merciless monster with an appetite for human flesh. An Other. He had two weeks to get Molly where she had to go. Then he'd use his rifle one last time—to put a bullet in his own head.

CHAPTER ONE

Several weeks earlier

"Ashes to ashes, dust to dust," Molly Anderson murmured as she laid the rose on her mother's unmoving chest. The silk petals had faded over the last six years from their original crimson to a dull, orangey pink hue, and they were curled and frayed. Over the years the flower had been a decorative mainstay—a centerpiece for Molly and her mother's dried food dinners, a beautiful hair ornament to complement one of their gowns at imaginary parties they'd throw. Now it would serve its final purpose: an undersized funeral bouquet. It seemed wrong, somehow, that an object that had once brought such happiness was now reduced to a symbol of Molly's loss, but that didn't change anything.

She fanned herself as sweat dripped between her breasts. Walking to the far end of the fallout shelter-cum-underground apartment complex, she checked several gauges. The ventilation system hadn't been working properly for months now, and she wondered how long it would be before it conked out altogether. Not that it mattered. And lately everything down here seemed past life expectancy.

Except her mother. Ashley Anderson should have lived longer. *Could* have lived longer, had she maintained the will to do so. Though, truth be told, she had held out longer than Molly imagined she would. Long enough to see July 1st, 2036, the day the time-locked titanium shelter door finally clicked open and allowed access to the outside world for the first time in six years. It was as if she'd been waiting for just that moment, not wanting to leave her daughter stuck alone in the shelter, going crazy with solitude. And yesterday, as soon as freedom greeted them with that cheery computerized hello, her mother had taken more pills than Molly had ever seen her take, said a half-hearted good-bye and checked out.

So now Molly was alone. But she was also free. Sort of. She still had to accomplish her mission. She still had to find her dad. Oh, and of course she still had to save the world.

She glanced over at the door. When it unlocked itself yesterday, she'd been too wrapped up in caring for her mother to push it open and see what was outside. Who had survived? Who had died? What had happened to her friends? And most importantly, what had happened to Chris? Had he and his brother found a way to stay alive? Were they out there somewhere? Did he remember her?

She shook her head. In all honesty, whatever remained out there, it was likely she'd never find out what had happened to the Griffins. With the entire world as she'd known it ended, it wasn't like she could just Google them. And perhaps it was better this way. At least she could imagine he and his brother were alive somewhere, living a happy, safe life in a brand-new world. Whatever was out there, she could avoid the most likely scenario: that they, like almost everyone else, had died.

Molly twisted the air-conditioning temperature gauge to its coldest setting, then headed back to her mother's bed, swallowing the lump in her throat as she looked down at Ashley Anderson's fragile frame. The woman looked so peaceful now, lying there as if she didn't have a care in the world. And maybe she didn't anymore. Maybe she was dancing, right this very second, waltzing with the angels. Socializing with all her old friends and family who had preceded her into the afterlife. Wasn't that what she'd always said would happen?

Come to think about it, heaven was likely bursting at the

seams these days. Her mother would have a lot of people to socialize with.

Feeling tears threaten, Molly leaned over to kiss her mother's forehead, then went to the makeshift gym and pulled on her boxing gloves. She raised her fists and smacked the punching bags as hard as she could, trying to exorcise the pain and anger welling up inside her. To get it out of her system so she could move on. Because that's how her father had trained her. He didn't have time for weaklings who focused on emotion when there were things to be done, people to save. To focus on emotion was to be self-involved and short-sighted. And Molly was, at the end of the day, her father's girl. He'd made sure of that. Even before the apocalypse.

After a few rounds versus the heavy bag, Molly realized she was only prolonging the inevitable. Putting her gloves away, she reconciled herself to going. There was nothing to hold her back now, nothing to keep her in this sterile place, this sanctuary, this prison. She had her mission, after all. She didn't have any time to waste.

"Good-bye, Mom," she said, leaning over to kiss her mother's cold forehead a final time. "I'll see you in heaven or phone you from hell."

God knows how'd she'd gotten here, but she had somewhere else to go.

CHAPTER TWO

"I wouldn't go out with Chris Griffin if he were the last man on Earth!"

Fifteen-year-old Molly Anderson tossed her long blonde hair over her shoulder and smoothed down the pleats of her cheerleading skirt as she watched the gawky sophomore dribble the basketball down the court. He turned and caught her looking and gave a goofy grin. She rolled her eyes and looked away. God, it was tough being a sophomore in 2030, especially when the biggest geek in the school had a crush on you.

"How many times has he asked you out now?" Erin, Molly's best friend, asked. She turned and stretched against the closed bleachers, smoothing down her own cheerleading outfit. When the holographic scoreboard above them blinked—someone from the opposite team had stolen the ball from Chris and scored—she effortlessly launched into a triple backflip, ending with a twist, then cheered their team on. She was never dismayed by little setbacks and was eternally optimistic, which was one of the reasons why she was so good at this. And maybe that's why she and Molly were friends: in some ways they were completely opposite. Of course, they came from completely different backgrounds, and Erin didn't have a father always spouting words of doom at her. "Six?" she asked after she was done.

"Try sixteen. Maybe sixty, if you count first grade when he moved down the street and first started stalking me."

"Aww. That's kind of sweet, don't you think?"

"Kind of sick is more like it. What do you think he's doing here? You think Basketball Dayz is a natural sim for him? If it was like the old days and you had to try out for a team, there's no way he would have made it." She laughed. "I'm sure he's better at other things, though—like that Knights of the Living Dead VR all the nerds are in love with. That seems more his style."

"Swapping sims just for you? You gotta admit, that's some dedication," Erin declared. "He's like your Ducky!" The two girls had been on a 1980s movie kick lately, downloading the old stuff their grandparents had grown up with, 2-D stuff that you didn't even need VR goggles to watch. Crazy! The John Hughes films, including *Pretty in Pink*, were undoubtedly their favorites. The cheesy, poufy 80s outfits alone were worth hours of cracking up.

"Where's my Andrew McCarthy?" Molly moaned, leaning back against the bleachers and staring at the ceiling. "I at least deserve an Andrew McCarthy if I'm stuck with Ducky the dork."

"Please. You've got Drew. And Drew totally trumps Andrew McCarthy."

Of course Erin would say that. She was dating his twin brother, Todd, and had set the two of them up to begin with. And in some ways, Molly saw her point. Popular, hot, and ridiculously rich, Drew was the envy of every guy in the school and the heartthrob of every girl. He'd done wonders for her status. Still, she couldn't very well say the relationship itself was stellar. For one thing, Drew was shallow as hell, unlike Erin's dreamboat, who evidently had scored all the humility genes in the womb. At seventeen Drew had already had three plastic surgeries, whereas most guys his age only got the one. (Yes, penis enlargement. Did you really have to ask?) Truth be told, he wasn't exactly the sharpest tool in the shed. Maybe Todd got all the brain cells as well. Whenever she tried to talk to Drew about real things—stuff that was bothering her, stuff that her dad was always citing, like the economy and ongoing famine

and seemingly never-ending war—he'd always laugh her off
and change the subject back to sports, virtual or otherwise.
She'd wanted a popular boyfriend to draw her out of the social
black hole her family's oddity had bequeathed her, but was
Drew the right choice?

Still, it was better than dating a pathetic geek like Chris
Griffin. She was sure of that.

Chris waved to her from the court again then tripped over
his feet and went sprawling to the ground. The crowd went
wild. Molly groaned. You wouldn't think they'd allow that
sort of incompetence in here. Wasn't that the whole point of
sims and why they'd gotten popular?

"I'm exiting," she declared. "I can't stand him staring at me
for a second longer." She blinked her eyes twice.

The signal to exit worked. A moment later the gym disappeared and she was back in Erin's basement. Molly pulled off
her VR goggles and leaned over to switch off her deck plug-
in. She watched her friend do the same in the armchair across
from her.

"I gained a level with that last flip," Erin said, bouncing excitedly in her seat. "Unlocked the NCAA courts!"

"Stellar," Molly muttered. "I'm thrilled for you."

Her friend looked a bit embarrassed. "Yeah, well, you'd be
just as high if you had your own copy and didn't always have
to play at my house. I get a lot of late-night practice once my
parents go to bed. That's when the real action on the court
happens anyway." She winked.

Molly sighed. "Yeah, well, that'll never happen. Not as
long as I live at home."

"You know, the fact that you don't have your own sim deck
in this day and age is almost criminal. Someone should report
your dad for child abuse, denying his kid virtual reality."

Molly sighed. Never mind the sim deck—the virtual reality
video game system that every three-year-old kid was given by
his or her parents—at her house they didn't even have a Smart
TV. There was just a small, thirteen-inch black-and-white television sitting on a stand in one corner of their living room. It

was the kind of TV they'd made last century, when television was first invented. It was almost as bad as having no TV at all. It got thirteen stations from bent, rabbit-ears antennae her dad had jury-rigged from a coat hanger. And none of the thirteen ever had anything worth watching, just crackpot broadcasts by old technology enthusiasts and something called "I Love the Aughts" reruns by a station called VH1.

When she was younger, she'd begged her dad for a Smart TV like all her friends had hanging in their living rooms, the ones where you could inject yourself into the show, become a character. But time and again her dad had explained that those kinds of televisions were dangerous. After all, there was no way to tell what programs the government had put inside of them, what the interactive devices were doing to your brain. Weren't the higher-ups involved enough in their lives? he would ask her. Molly supposed he was right.

"I've got to kick you out," Erin said apologetically. "Gotta hit the doctor's office this afternoon. I'm . . . I'm getting my LTF! Can you believe my parents finally said yes? How rocking is that?"

"Lucky you," Molly said.

An LTF. A License to Fuck. It wasn't the official name, of course, but that's what all the kids—and, Molly knew, quite a few adults—called the Copulation Conditional. Kind of a stupid name, but what did the government expect when they started legislating people who could have sex and requiring you get a license?

The AIDS vaccine had been the biggest scientific break-through of the 21st century, if also the most controversial, especially after the United Nations exerted their newfound global legislative powers and made it mandatory for everyone in their majority. It made sense, after Africa was decimated by the disease's resurgence in the early twenties. The virus had mutated, rendering the formerly effective drug cocktails use-less. And now, from the richest Upper East Sider in New York to the poorest bushman in Australia, everyone over eigh-teen was required to be vaccinated. Not that anyone sane would want to have sex with a partner who might be infected. Everyone knew how virulent the disease was, and how gruesome its effects. How could they not know with those UN Biological Division advertisements playing 24/7 on every media outlet? Even if you didn't agree with the laws against unlicensed fornication, it was safer to stick to those partners who had their CCs.

The vaccine was available for those younger than eighteen, too, but because of certain complications with children in early tests—as well as moral objections across the more religious sectors—it eventually had been left up to the parents to decide about inoculating their families. And Molly's dad had said "no way" without even offering a reason why. Not that Molly had argued with him over it much.

"Does Drew have *his* license?" Erin asked.

"Yup. And he's not happy about me having to wait, let me tell you." Molly slid her VR goggles into their protective case and handed them back to her friend. "He thinks we should just hook up anyway."

"You mean, break the law?" Erin asked.

It wasn't too likely they'd get caught. Molly knew that there'd been problems like this through the ages for youngsters in love and ready to do the nasty. It wasn't exactly like the sex police were going to come and get her, though the penalty for people caught having sex without a license was pretty severe: extended quarantine to make sure you didn't have a disease or unauthorized pregnancy, and exposure through the media for ridicule and contempt. But that wasn't her biggest issue. She just wasn't in love.

Erin shook her head. "What's your dad's deal, anyway? I mean, he's a doctor of some sort, right? He should be all for vaccinations and stuff."

Molly shrugged. Her dad was a medical researcher/scientist whose early claim to fame was the invention of special cybernetic implants used to turn a platoon of human soldiers into robotic murder machines. The implants had made them stronger, faster, and better at killing. Which they'd proceeded to do for three years, he'd told her. Deployed by the government to sweep into conflicted territories and murder men, women, and children without effort or remorse, they'd killed and killed and killed until finally those opposing governments waved their white flags and gave in to all demands. They'd been used in the Middle East and Africa, mostly. Wherever they went, things changed. Mission accomplished.

Ian Anderson hadn't taken this quietly, of course. Learning of some of the shadier situations his soldiers had developed, about the devastation his inventions caused, he'd quit his job and joined a militia group, rallying against the government for which he'd once worked. It hadn't helped when the platoon of soldiers went mad and killed each other, either. Breaking into his former labs, he'd destroyed all of the prototypes and plans and then set fire to the building itself in order to ensure these creatures could never be built again.

"What had he expected?" one prosecutor had asked at his trial, as well as a number of newspaper reporters. What had he thought would be the use of super-powered soldiers? He hadn't answered, but Molly knew that her father had expected the creations to protect the people. He'd been trying to help, and the government had turned his inventions against him. He still muttered about it while he was working.

His years in prison hadn't helped his anger, either. Molly was embarrassed to admit it, but her father's cellmate had convinced him that the end of the world was near. Ian talked about it often, and had decided he needed to start making arrangements. Armageddon was on its way, and the Andersons would be ready. Not even his wife had been able to dissuade him from preparing. Molly was torn between admiring her father's genius and horror at what the rest of her school would think if they knew him. She never brought up that her father's lawyers had used his mental instability to eventually have him released back into the world. He'd been going to the court-appointed therapy, even if he never talked about it.

"Well, I'm sorry," Erin said, patting her friend's shoulder. "It will suck not to fuck." She cracked up at her accidental rhyme.

Molly rolled her eyes, having one of those moments where her friend seemed like a character out of one of the old movies they watched—and not one of the "good" kids. But she knew better. Erin *was* good, and she was the odd one. Everyone wanted to have sex these days, and there wasn't much reason not to, as long as you were safe; it was one of the few physical outlets people enjoyed. Erin was a good friend. Molly didn't know what she'd do if they didn't have each other.

"Meh. No biggie," she said with a sigh. "Drew and I will manage. It's not like it's the end of the world or anything. Talk to you later."

"Later, girlie."

Molly tried not to think about Drew pressuring her for sex as she headed up the basement stairs and into the main house—and then she tried not to think of the differences between her family and everyone else's. Erin's family wasn't rich by any stretch, but they had all the latest gadgets: the refrigerator that reminded you which groceries you needed, the music system that sensed who was in the living room and adjusted its music accordingly. Of course, Molly didn't have an iChip like everyone else and so it remained on "Sounds of the Twenties" classic electronica that had been all the rage in Erin's parents' generation as she passed through. It had no idea of her secret love for music from the 1980s . . . which was perhaps for the best. Hearing "I Want Your Sex" would have just depressed her.

Walking out the front door, she squinted into the bright afternoon light and gazed around Monroeville, their suburban South Carolina subdivision. The sun was high in the sky and a slight breeze was the only relief from its heat. Still, life could be worse and she knew it. She had friends and a boyfriend. She was liked at school. Her grades were good. There were people much worse off than her, and all she had to do was look in the news to see them. She should be thanking her lucky stars every day.

She headed down the street, passing Chris Griffin's house

and wondering if he was still playing virtual basketball in that sim or if he'd quit when she exited the game. His silly crush was getting very annoying. She'd have to talk IRL to him sometime soon. In Real Life talks were important. *Everything* in real life was important, her dad was always reminding her, which was another of the reasons he was so down on sims. She knew he was right. She would have to face Chris eventually. He just wasn't getting the hint, kept insisting they were meant to be together. But they weren't. After all, she had Drew. He was just going to have to accept it.

She arrived home to find her mother sitting at the table looking through some mail.

"Hey, Ashley," she said with a wink. "What's going on?"

Her mother looked up. "Not much, sweetie," she replied. "Just answering some party invitations. The Nixons are having a huge bash this year. But they waited forever to send out the notes. I'm going to have to go shopping *this nanosecond* to find something to wear."

Molly smiled. For as long as she could remember, her mother had always been a social butterfly, flitting from party to party, happiest when she was around people. That was how she and Ian met, many years ago, when he was still a dashing government employee and she was the child of a state senator. Molly's grandmother had been ecstatic that her socialite daughter had snared such a great man and a patriot. She'd become less than pleased since.

But Ashley Anderson was a woman who stood by her man. During the rough times, during the prison sentence . . . even afterward, as the years went by and Ian became stranger and more antisocial, Molly's mom continually defended Ian to friends and family. It was hard on her, Molly knew, to have the neighbors whisper about the crackpot she'd married. He'd stopped going to parties with her and eventually withdrawn from society altogether, spending his days down in the basement with his weird experiments, but Molly respected her mother's stubborn sense of loyalty. Ashley had time and again rejected her parents' pleas to just walk away from the marriage altogether. That was why Molly loved her mother and father equally and intensely, no matter their individual flaws.

Molly looked down at the invitation. "Sounds fun," she said. "Can I come?" She didn't really have a strong desire to go, but she hated to see her mom attend alone.

"Of course. If it doesn't interfere with your training schedule," Ashley said, reaching over to brush a lock of hair from her daughter's eyes. "You know how your dad is about that."

"Yeah," Molly said, rolling her eyes. "Believe me, I know. If I bring it up, he'll probably tell me that I shouldn't bother to buy a dress. 'No, no!' he'll say, 'The End of Days is right around the corner, and there won't be any parties ever again!'"

Her mother smiled and rose from the table. "Yes," she said. "He probably would. But I'll tell you what, sweetie." She leaned over and planted a kiss on Molly's head. "Come with me. If the world does end, I want you dancing by my side. I'm not going to die alone."

CHAPTER THREE

As Molly stepped from her family's underground bunker, she was immediately struck with wonder at the outside world. She'd forgotten how vast it was, how beautiful. There was the sky, a vibrant blue sprinkled with puffy cotton-like clouds. Wildflowers tumbled across sagging porches and poked defiantly through cracked pavement. Her favorite oak tree was still standing, strong and majestic in the center of their front yard, its branches stretching up to worship the heavens.

The scent of honeysuckle tickled her nose and Molly sucked in a large breath, delighting in the fresh, clean air that was so much sweeter than the stale re-circulated stuff she'd been breathing for the last six years. Strange. Back in the shelter, she'd always imagined the outside world to be a gray wasteland with stormy clouds that would mirror the death of humanity below. She'd expected a graveyard, a desolate landscape, a world with acrid winds and a sepia palette. But it seemed nature didn't mourn man's destruction after all. If anything, it appeared to be relishing its freedom from gardeners and landscaping, this once tamed suburbia becoming a feral forest full of magical emerald life. Or maybe she was overdoing it in her excitement.

She stuck out her arms, feeling the warmth of the sun on her skin for the first time in six years. She wanted to skip down the street, dance, cartwheel. Run for ten miles without stopping. Enjoy a world without boundaries after years in a cage.

After doing a little shimmy of joy on the front porch, she stopped herself, looking around, self-conscious, even though she knew there was no one to see her. That thought sobered her a bit. This beautiful world would be empty. Or practically so. How many would have survived? Not many, according to her father. A new emotion gripped her heart: sadness, the beauty of the world fading as reality sank in. Though she'd mourned her world for six years, it was different to suddenly experience its loss firsthand. Back in the shelter this reality had seemed unreal, distant. Like something in a film. Actually stepping out into the world and seeing the empty, debris-filled streets, the houses crumbling from years of abandonment, made the whole situation a lot more real and a lot harder to swallow.

It was the silence that felt eeriest. Not that her middle-class suburb had ever been a bustling metropolis, but there had been sounds all the same: the droning of lawnmowers pushed by banker or doctor dads on their days off, the screams and laughter of kids playing wild games of tag, cars streaming down the nearby interstate and beeping away their road rage. Normal, everyday, take-them-for-granted sounds. All were now swept clear by an overwhelming, almost suffocating silence. There wasn't even birdsong.

A realization she had half-suppressed for too long rose up and choked Molly. Everyone and everything she knew and loved was gone. Her friends, her teachers—now even her mother had succumbed. Only her father was left. Out there. Waiting for her. Waiting for her assistance in rebuilding the world he'd known would fail.

She focused on her dilemma. How was she going to get to where Ian was? His destination had been far, hundreds of miles away, and she truly doubted she could get the rusted old car in their driveway to start. Not that she had any idea how to drive; after the Highway Congestion Act of '24 you had to be eighteen to take drivers education in South Carolina, and she'd been way too young when they'd gone into the bunker. Besides, with no working gas stations and the streets filled with debris, as she could clearly see they were, it was probably better not to depend on cars. Maybe she could find a bike or something.

First things first, though. She should find supplies. And while it was tempting to just hit a few of the nearby houses to see what they had in their pantries, it was also too morbid an errand for her to face. She didn't want to see the remnants of her former neighbors tucked into beds or lying sprawled on the floor, thank you very much. She'd try to find a store instead.

Steeling herself, she stepped from her porch and set off. Something in the middle of the pavement a short distance away made her pause. A small figure, more than half decayed, lay in the street, its skeletal hands clutching something shredded and pink. It was . . . a teddy bear. Molly fell to her knees, bent over and threw up.

"God, Molly, get a grip," she muttered to herself a moment later, wiping her mouth, embarrassed by her weakness. She'd known it was going to be like this, after all. That she'd have to be strong and push all the horrors to the back of her mind. She didn't have time to mourn humanity. She couldn't be distracted by the past. What was done was done, and it didn't do any good to cry about it. After all, a Razor Girl didn't cry. When they were sad, they spit.

Molly did exactly that. She felt a little bit better, wiped her mouth again, this time with her sleeve.

A voice cut through the dead air, surprising her where she crouched on the ground. A human voice. She looked up, mouth agape. Was she hearing things? Was it only the wind? Was it some old holo broadcast?

She heard it again.

"Dude! Where'd you go?" the voice cried. "Hey!"

People? Real-life people? Had her father been wrong? Had humanity survived, or at least more of it than expected? Considering the shout sounded like it had come from someone her age, or at least someone who shared her way of speaking, she felt a surge of hope. Were these people who could help her? Kids, like her—or like she'd once been? Or would they be savages, brigands and people generally unworthy of her trust? It was difficult to know what to expect when the entire world had changed and she'd been locked underground for it.

Well, wondering wouldn't answer any questions. Molly staggered to her feet and set down off down the street as fast as her legs would carry her.

Chase swore under his breath as his brother's shout filled the otherwise still air, echoing through the neighborhood. "Way to be subtle," he muttered. "Why not just call them down on you?"

Crouched on the rooftop of a dilapidated garage, he inched forward, careful not to make any sudden movements. As he'd climbed the weather-beaten structure, it felt like it could collapse at any moment; still, it was the best vantage point for seeing any Others wandering the nearby perimeter, and Chase wanted to know the area was clear before making his score. It wasn't like they saw Others every day, but it seemed the creatures always appeared when you least expected it. Whenever you let your guard down, *bam*, that was when they got you. Wasn't that what had happened over and over to their little group?

"Chase! Dude! If you don't come out I'm going back!"

His brother's voice again. Louder, more urgent. Did the idiot really think he was lost? That he hadn't slipped away on purpose? Probably. Tank wasn't known for his brains. Just his foolhardy protectiveness of those he took under his wing—which was practically anyone and anything these days. Nonetheless, Tank wouldn't have approved of Chase going off on his own, and he certainly wouldn't have approved of Chase's intended goal.

Whatever. At the end of the day, a man had to do what he had to do, older brother's approval or not.

"Hey! Over here! I'm over here!"

Chase's head jerked around and he almost lost his balance

on the roof. What was that? Another voice? And not just any voice. It sounded like a woman. It came in the other direction from his brother, and it was faint.

He squinted as he peered down the street, the setting sun making it difficult to see. But then his eyes found movement. Something—some*one*—was running down the street with wild abandon.

At first he feared it might be one of the Others, but it didn't move like one. They could be quick, but he'd never seen one run. And the air didn't smell like them, either. Their putrid rot often caused a stink that gave plenty of warning—although not always.

Just to be safe, he lowered himself onto his belly, flush with the garage roof, pulled his thick leather gloves over his wrists and drew the steel blade from the sheath at his waist. Once properly prepared for any potential fight, he peered over the roof edge again.

At first he thought he must be hallucinating. The girl came around the corner and he blinked his eyes a few times, rubbed them, then took another look. She was still there. Wearing a white tank top and jean cutoffs, of all things. Miles of skin— milk-white skin—completely exposed. His first thought was that she must be truly stupid to walk around like that. His second thought was how truly happy he was that she did.

His eyes roved her body, drinking in the first live adult female shape he'd seen in years. The curve of her waist, the flare of her hips. Full breasts, tempting and teasing under the thin fabric of her white tank top. Her long neck, high cheekbones and beautiful golden hair, pulled up in a casual ponytail. She wore some sort of mirrored sunglasses, leaving Chase with an inexplicable curiosity about the color of her eyes, though he wouldn't have been able to see the irises from here anyway.

He watched as she ran down the street in his direction. She was beautiful, to say the least; it became clearer the closer she came. But there was something else. Something weirdly familiar about the—

He shook his head. *Impossible. And pay attention*, he told himself. *Distractions will get you killed.*

As if on cue, the breeze suddenly shifted and a smell caught his nostrils. A putrid stink. He tensed, shoving all thoughts of lust to the back of his mind. The Others were near. One of them, at least. And this girl was a sitting duck.

Something stirred inside him, some weird, knight-in-shining-armor bullshit that compelled him to jump off the roof and go down to rescue her. The notion went against his grain, and he didn't obey it, but he did scramble to his feet and wave his arms. "Hey, up here!" he hissed. "Quick!"

She looked up, surprise mixing with joy on her face. She really was beautiful. And as she practically bounced over to the garage she cried, "Oh my God. You're a person. A real person. I was beginning to think I was the only—"

"Behind you!" he cried, realizing he was likely too late. The Other had shown up out of seemingly nowhere, appearing from behind an overturned Smart Volvo, and was inches away from the girl. Dressed like that, with all that skin exposed and perfect for biting, she didn't have a chance of escaping infection. Of course, she wasn't even going to avoid becoming the monster's dinner. Yup, she was a goner for sure. And since he'd made himself known, he was likely in for a battle himself.

Shoulda just stayed hidden and let her die, he berated himself. He knew as well as anyone it did no good these days to help people. Or even animals for that matter. Look what happened to Spud when he'd tried to save that puppy he found in the alley two weeks ago. Picked up the little wiggly thing and *bam!* Zombie gets the jump on him.

Yes, these days, it was every man—and dog—for himself. That was the only way to really survive.

CHAPTER FOUR

"Molly, where have you been? You're late. And you know how I feel about tardiness." Ian Anderson raked his hands through his graying hair and scowled as his daughter entered the basement where he had set up their training center. There were two punching bags—one heavy and one speed bag—a weight bench, a treadmill and some jump ropes. It was all last-century tech, like everything else in their house. Except her dad's lab, that was. Beyond the gym, a locked door held more equipment than most government research facilities, all illegally firewalled and creatively routed to avoid unwanted scrutiny. All totally off-limits to Molly.

"Sorry, Dad," she apologized, setting down her bag and grabbing some workout clothes. She stepped into the bathroom and closed the door behind her. "I got tied up."

"Tied up?" he repeated through the wall. "You wouldn't happen to be using those sims again, would you? With your friend Erin? You know how I feel about them."

"They're just games, Dad."

"They're all connected up, linked to the system. Meaning, everything you say in there is monitored by Homeland Security—or worse. We don't need any trouble with the feds."

Molly sighed as she pulled a tank top over her head. "Dad, we're in there chatting about boys and clothes. I hardly think the government is interested."

"It's always better to err on the side of safety," came the

reply as she next pulled on her shorts and leaned over to lace her sneakers. "Besides, if nothing else, they're also a terrific waste of time. Especially when they start interfering with your training. We've got a lot to get through and not a lot of time. We need your body strong and fit."

"I know, I know." Molly opened the door. "Because the end of the world is near."

Her dad handed her a set of boxing gloves. "Go ahead and laugh," he said, nodding serenely. "Everyone does. But you will all see for yourselves soon enough."

Molly donned the gloves. It was pointless to argue with him when he got on this track. He didn't care that the rest of the world thought he was crazy; he believed what he believed. And, at the end of the day, she gave him some props for that. Even if it was a big pain in the ass to be his daughter sometimes.

"So, what have you been up to today, Dad?" she asked, ready for a subject change. She tossed a few punches at the heavy bag, warming up. Mostly she enjoyed these training sessions. There was something about breaking a sweat that no one else in her world seemed to understand. Her classmates were too into their injections and surgeries to find any joy in building muscles the old-fashioned way. In the same way Molly liked fitting in at school, she was glad to be different at home. She mostly understood what her father wanted her to be.

"Reading," her father replied. He walked over to his desk and held up a paperback book.

Molly resisted the urge to roll her eyes. Ian Anderson was the only person on Earth who didn't own an e-reader. Even she had one: he'd had to allow it, for the technology was the only way to access school texts. But her dad always claimed he preferred the good old days when books were made of paper and the government couldn't check up on what you were reading. He hunted flea markets constantly, looking for rare, out-of-print treasures and banned books.

She swung a few times at the speed bag, then glanced at the cover. "*Neuromancer*," she said. "What's it about?"

"It's brilliant," he replied. "The author completely predicted sims and the Internet and the dangers of artificial intelligence. And this was back in 1984—before most people even had a computer! If you read this book you'd never use a sim again, I bet. At the very least you'd want to know who was controlling it."

"Sounds interesting," Molly said, feeling sweat bead on her forehead as she continued her speed training. "I'll have to take a look when you're done."

"There's even cybernetics in it," her father continued. Though he was officially out of the business, he admitted to continued fascination in the art of enhancing man by machine, and he was constantly tinkering with parts in his lab. "A girl named Molly Millions. A razor girl."

Molly stopped punching. "What's a razor girl?" she asked.

"A cybernetic ninja, of sorts," Ian explained. "Sort of like those soldiers I worked on but . . ." He broke off, stared at the wall for a moment. "She has four-inch razors under her fingernails that she can slide in and out at will. Deadly. She knows half a dozen forms of martial arts. And she has these ocular implants with infrared and a bunch of other functions. She can see better, move faster, react quicker . . . She's amazing. If I had everything from my old lab . . . Well, she'd be the perfect creature to survive the apocalypse."

"I don't know. Sounds pretty weird to me." Molly grabbed a towel and wiped her brow. "Besides, how would this person survive *before* the apocalypse? Imagine what that'd be like. Would she be chopping apples with her fingernails?" Molly laughed. "I'd hate to see her forget while she's picking her nose."

Her father shrugged, set his book down and pulled the gloves off her hands. He handed over the jump rope, saying, "She'd manage. She'd have to be tough to survive the operation, anyway. You wouldn't want to choose someone who wouldn't be able to use the enhancements." Picking up the book and flipping through it, he said, "People adapt. The good ones, at any rate. They take their hardships and make them strengths. Because of her implants, the heroine of this book can't cry. Her tear ducts were rerouted to her mouth."

"Er, okay," Molly replied.

"In other words," her dad said, "a razor girl doesn't cry. When she's sad, Molly Millions says, she spits."

"Now that's just plain weird."

Her father held up his hands. "Again, mock if you will," he told her. "But what's the use in crying? Molly Millions has it right. My bet is that when the end of the world comes, it won't be the ones who cry who survive, but the ones who spit."

"Right." Molly shook her head and started to jump rope. "Well, I guess when the end of the world comes knocking we'll see."

CHAPTER FIVE

"Behind you!"

Instinct from years of training kicked in as Molly heard the warning. The strange guy on the roof pointed, and she whirled. A kick of adrenaline slammed through her body, activating her body's cybernetic offense. The razors shot out from under her fingernails, flashing in the bright sunlight, and she held them in front of her face, ready. She was coiled in a fighting stance.

Her eyes widened under her ocular implants. Oh God, it was one of *them*. For some reason, some stupid reason, she'd imagined they had gone away by now. Died out. Become extinct or something. But no. Evidently they had survived. Perhaps they even ran things these days; she had no idea.

They sure were as ugly as she remembered. This one was naked, save for scraps of tattered clothing clinging to its glowing yellow-green skin. It had too many fingers, too many toes, a third eye growing out of its forehead. It was covered in festering, pus-filled wounds. And it smelled like—well, she couldn't think of anything foul enough to compare it to.

But while they might still be ugly, she wasn't still defenseless. And she sure as hell wasn't about to let anything kill her on her first day back in the real world. What would her father say? What would Molly Millions say?

"Stay back, Pus-head," she growled. "Unless you want to be sliced and diced."

Sadly, though she hadn't expected him to, Pus-head didn't seem to have a good grasp of the King's English. Either that, or it underestimated the martial arts training and nano-enhancements of its intended dinner. With a bellowing roar the monster lunged toward Molly, fleshy arms outstretched, clearly preparing to grab her by the neck and chomp on her face. She leapt away and lashed out with her razors. Those caught the thing's left shoulder, sliced across its chest, and the creature squealed in pain and fury, blood gushing everywhere. It lunged again but Molly ducked, avoiding a spray of gore and bodily fluids.

Looking at the ooze on the ground, Molly almost hyperventilated. Returning to her basic defensive stance, arms up, razors out, she focused and forced herself to breathe. This was what she'd trained for, she reminded herself. She could do this. She *would* do this. She spat on the ground.

The creature made a grab for her. She swung her leg out, slamming the thing in the stomach with a well-placed kick. It made her stomach turn, the sickening thud of her boot meeting rotten flesh. Good thing she'd left the flip-flops at home. But the creature staggered backwards, losing its balance for a few precious seconds. This was just the opportunity Molly needed. She swept her arm out, blades flashing, aiming at its face. The blow didn't miss. All three eyes were blinded at once, and the creature bellowed in pain as Molly yanked her hand free and retreated.

Had her attack been enough to stop it? She wasn't sure how many more rounds she could take. *Only a flesh wound*, she imagined it saying, forcing her to slice off its arms and legs. And maybe she should cut off its head.

Evidently Pus-head hadn't had a chance to see Monty Python, because instead it made the logical choice: to turn tail and run blindly down the street, still sobbing in pain and rage. Molly couldn't blame it. She wouldn't be happy either if she'd spent her whole life missing Monty Python and then been turned into a zombie.

She sucked in a breath, her heart pounding a mile a minute.

CHAPTER SIX

"Hey, geekazoid, what are you doing?"

Chris reluctantly pulled off his VR goggles at the sound of his older brother's voice. When Trey plopped down uninvited on the couch beside him and punched him in the arm, he grunted, "What does it look like, shit for brains?"

"You know, too many video games will make you sterile," Trey volunteered. "I read that once somewhere."

"You read somewhere that you won the Space Station 13 lotto, too," Chris retorted. "And that you'll die if you don't forward that note to ten of your friends."

"Oh, you're such the clever little man. If you're so clever, though, why don't you have a date tonight like I do?"

"Because that stuff isn't important to me. Not right now at least. I've got better things to do."

Trey could barely hide his mirth. "Oh? Did your Knights of the Living Dead guild just take down Fiddler's Green?"

"No. I'm using Basketball Dayz now," Chris snapped. "And just 'cause I use my time to enhance my basketball skills instead of cracking into that Playboy House of Love sim you jacked doesn't mean I'm some social reject. There are girls in B-Dayz, too. Real girls from our school. Not computer-generated sexpots."

"Yeah, well, I hate to break it to you, little bro, but you'd have a much higher chance of scoring with a sim star than anyone at our school."

Sadly, Chris knew Trey was probably right, but he wasn't about to admit it. The last thing he needed was more teasing from his older brother. He understood the reality: Trey was über popular. Everyone loved him. Trey was the life of the party, and Chris was the dweeby little brother no one ever noticed, including the person he was most desperate to have notice him—Molly Anderson, the most beautiful girl at school. Ever since his family first moved down the street from her, Chris had known she was the girl for him. But she'd turned him down time and again, this year going for that stupid meathead Drew Barry. Chris had no idea what she saw in him. He had a brain the size of an amoeba and even less personality.

But hey, Drew was tall and built and had a flashy smile. And Chris was just a beanpole who couldn't manage to put on any weight if he tried. If only he'd gotten Trey's genes, maybe he'd have had a chance.

"Hey . . . Trey, Chris . . . will you guys play Barbies with me?" a little voice begged.

Chris looked over to see that his sister Tara had entered the room. Back when she was a baby, his parents had adopted the six-year-old girl from an African country all but wiped out by the resurgent AIDS epidemic. Sometimes he wished they'd traded his brother for the privilege.

"Yeah, *right*," Trey said, rolling his eyes. "I've got to get ready for my date with Anna Simmons."

Tara's face fell, but Chris knew how to fix that. "I'll play with you, Tara Bara," he said, pulling on his VR goggles. He didn't have much else going on. "What address are you at?"

His sister chirped in joy. "Dreamhouse Fifteen, on the Blonde and Beautiful server." She grabbed her own sim deck. "Thanks, Chris. You're the best!"

"You just remember that come dessert," he teased as he activated the sim. "I want your portion of Mom's banana cream pie."

"Anything!" Tara promised. Of course, he knew she'd deny it all when it came to actually giving up her sweets, but he didn't really mind.

Just before putting on his goggles he glanced out the window. Molly was there, talking to their neighbor, Mrs. McCormick. The old woman was his favorite person on their block. She was a sweet, cookie-baking, grandma-type who'd been his babysitter when he was younger, and they'd found an unlikely bond over romance novels, of all things. Something Chris could never in a million years admit to Trey. She was always around to listen, even when his parents were late coming home from work, which they usually were. He'd never seen Molly talk to her, though. He wondered if Mrs. McCormick was putting in a good word for him. He hoped so.

After a moment he squinted. Was Mrs. McCormick okay? The older woman swayed then stumbled, and Chris rose to his feet. He turned back to his sister.

"Meet me in the Glow Cat area," he told her. "I need to make sure everything is okay outside."

Molly, late for her training session with her father, had been rushing home from a fight with Drew at school—he hated how she had to rush home to train every day instead of spending time with him—when she came across her elderly neighbor hobbling down the street. The woman was coughing so hard that at first Molly was worried she was going to die. She ran up, placed a hand on the old woman's shoulder and peered into her eyes. "Are you okay, Mrs. McCormick?" she asked.

The old woman grasped her with a bony hand. "I don't know," she said, her voice cracking. "I felt fine this morning. But now I can't seem to stop coughing." She opened her hand, revealing a tissue clotted with scarlet-flecked phlegm. Molly recoiled. "A few minutes ago I started coughing up blood."

"We need to get you to a hospital," Molly said, glancing around for a neighbor. She needed someone with a SmartCar, because it was unlikely they'd make it to a hospital otherwise; the old lady was never going to be able to walk. Making it tougher, unlike everyone else in the universe, Molly didn't have an iComm. The tech that had replaced the cell phone was yet another modern convenience her dad forbade, and if she used her outdated phone to call home, she doubted he would answer. He never did.

Molly led Mrs. McCormick to the curb and helped her sit down. "I'll go try to find someone to help."

"Hey, what's going on?"

Molly turned to see none other than Chris Griffin approaching. After a brief spasm of discomfort, relief washed over her. Maybe he could get his mom to drive them or something, or just call the hospital. She doubted he'd take this opportunity to make a pass. She prayed he wouldn't. "Mrs. McCormick's sick," she explained. "Do you have an iComm? We need to get her to an ambulance."

Chris pulled his longish hair back from his ear, revealing the tiny headset. He pressed the silver button at its tip. "Dial 911," he commanded, then waited. "Hello?" he said. "Yeah, I'm at 23 Mulberry Lane. We need an ambulance." He listened for a moment. "Yeah, she's an elderly woman. Name's Mandy McCormick. She's coughing up blood." Another pause. "Okay, thanks. Yeah, we'll be right here. No, we won't leave." He pressed the button again and turned back to Molly. "Okay, they're sending an ambulance."

"Just hang in there, Mrs. McCormick," Molly said, patting the coughing woman on the back. "They'll come for you in a minute."

Mrs. McCormick looked up at the two teenagers, appreciation in her watery blue eyes. "Thank you, kids," she said. "You're good to help me." She was overtaken by another wracking cough.

Chris sat down beside her and took her hand in his. "Are you kidding, Mrs. McCormick?" he asked. "You know I'd never let anything happen to you."

The older woman blushed like a schoolgirl, and Molly couldn't help but notice. "Such a sweet boy," she said. She looked up at Molly. "You know, he comes by twice a week after school to visit me."

"He does?" Molly was surprised.

"Oh, yes. He reads me all my favorite romance books," the

woman explained. While she was smiling at him like he was her own personal savior, Chris was beginning to look uncomfortable. "Of course, we skip over the sexy parts. He's just a baby after all. Can't have him reading about blowjobs and boinking."

Chris's face turned instant tomato red. "Mrs. McCormick!" he cried, sounding absolutely horrified. Molly didn't blame him. She was blushing pretty furiously herself. And Chris looked like he wanted to be anywhere but there at that moment. Suddenly she wondered if he'd applied for *his* LTF yet. Probably not. He did seem really innocent. But then, so was she.

Mrs. McCormick reached out and pinched Chris's cheek then turned to Molly. "See, this is why we have to skip them," she confided in a stage whisper that everyone in a ten-block radius could probably pick up. "But don't worry. I go back and read them after he leaves. They are the best part, you know." She giggled, prompting another coughing fit.

Chris instantly snapped out of mortified mode and reached over to pat her on the back. "Relax, Mrs. McCormick," he instructed in a voice so authoritative you'd never know a moment ago he'd been blushing about boinking. "You're going to laugh yourself sicker." He handed her a clean tissue he'd pulled from his pants pocket. She blew her nose. No blood this time, at least.

Mrs. McCormick turned to Molly. "You're a very lucky girl," she said.

And here Molly had thought she wasn't capable of blushing more than she already had been. "Oh, we're not . . . I mean, we're just friends." She didn't want to say even that was pushing it.

Mrs. McCormick was taken by another coughing fit, but when it quieted, she squinted up at Molly. "Maybe for now, dear," she gasped. "But I have a good sense of these things. My kids call me psychic."

For a moment Molly wondered if Chris had paid the woman to say that, then she scolded herself for even thinking it. He wasn't *that* bad. In fact, despite his unwanted crush, he was kind of sweet. Wasn't that what Erin was always saying? The way he was caring for his elderly neighbor . . . well, she couldn't imagine Drew or any of her other friends doing it.

"Sorry, Mrs. McCormick," Chris said. "It'll never happen. Molly's got a better boyfriend than me." He said it completely seriously, without sarcasm, and Molly felt her face burn.

"That's not—" she started.

Before she could finish, an unmarked van careened down the street, seeming to come out of nowhere. It screeched to a stop before them. Two men, each wearing a brown uniform and a respirator, jumped out and ran to Mrs. McCormick.

Chris jumped to his feet. "What are you—?"

"Get out of the way, son," interrupted one of the men. His respirator made him sound like Darth Vader from those ancient *Star Wars* movies Erin loved. "You need to get home. We'll take care of your friend."

The two grabbed Mrs. McCormick by her arms and dragged her somewhat ruthlessly toward the van. She screamed in protest, surprised, then broke into another coughing fit.

"Stop!" Chris demanded. "Where are you taking her? We called for an ambulance."

"Yes, we got the report," said the second masked man, pausing. "We're taking her in to get treated. Mount Holyoke. She'll be back in a day or two."

Molly stared at the men, her brain awhirl with her father's many conspiracy theories. Instead of reacting, she forced herself to stay calm and catalog the details. The masks. The uniforms. The seal on the van. It looked like a government seal, and there was no way this was a normal ambulance.

"Mount Holyoke? Well, Westview's not too far away. Can you tell me when and where I can visit her?" Chris asked. Molly had never heard him sound anxious before, but she understood his fears. She also knew Mount Holyoke was in Monroeville, not Westview. Was he testing them? "Or maybe you should tell me your names."

The two men looked at each other. "Perhaps we should take them, too," the first said. His voice was amiable. "Just as a precaution."

The second man turned back to look at them and nodded.

"Take us?" Chris repeated, looking scared. "Take us where?"

"We're not sick," Molly added, in case it wasn't obvious.

"Well, why don't we just find out for sure," suggested the second man, still smiling that weird smile that didn't quite reach his eyes. "Get in the van."

Get in the van? No effing way. Not with all her father's fears and stories whirling through her head. And it didn't take a paranoid nutjob to see the red flags waving in this situation.

Mrs. McCormick broke into another coughing fit. Molly took the opportunity to glance at Chris. He caught her eye, looking as freaked out as she felt. *Shit*, he mouthed. *I don't trust these guys. Run.*

Molly didn't need a second invitation. She and Chris both took off at the same time, as fast as their legs could carry them. She was surprised they shared an instinct: neither headed to their respective homes.

When she glanced back, Molly saw the brown-suited men had gotten Mrs. McCormick into their van and had turned it around, likely to give chase. "Go through the yards!" she cried, pointing. "They won't be able to follow."

Chris hung a sharp right and dove through a neighbor's yard, dodging clotheslines and wading pools, avoiding a snarling dog. Molly followed, her heart pounding wildly in her chest. What the hell was going on here? Who were those men? Why had they just all but abducted a sick old woman in the middle of the street? Why were they now giving chase to a couple of kids?

More running, less thinking, she reminded herself, picking up her speed to keep pace with Chris. Together they leapt another fence and ran into the woods behind a nearby elementary school dodging trees and stumps and fallen logs. Finally

Chris stopped, in a clearing, leaning over, hands on his knees, panting heavily. He looked behind him and then at Molly. "I think we lost them," he said.

"Yeah." She plopped down on a stump, sucking in breaths. "But what the hell was that about?"

"I don't know. But that sure wasn't a normal ambulance."

"No. They were government, I think. I saw the seal on their van. They must have intercepted your call. My dad always says the government monitors all transmissions. That's why I'm not allowed to get an iComm."

"What do you think they'll do to Mrs. McCormick?" Chris asked, looking worried. "I don't want anything to happen to her."

"You really like her, don't you?" Molly mused. She couldn't help adding, "Do you really . . . read her romances?" *Do you really skip over the sex scenes?* she wanted to add, but didn't.

"She used to babysit me and Trey when our parents went away. She's like my grandmother. I think she's a bit lonely now. And since she can't really keep up with all the technology changes—they confuse her—I try to stop in after school a couple times a week. Try to take care of her like she once took care of me. Read to her or whatever. And yes, romances. You probably think that's weird, but there's some good stories out there. Action, adventure, history. They're not all about sex like some people think." He blushed again. "I actually . . . enjoy reading them, too." He paused, then added, "You probably think I'm a complete freak, huh?"

"Actually I was thinking you're more like a saint," Molly marveled. She couldn't imagine any of her friends doing that. Especially not Drew. He'd probably rather commit hara-kiri than spend two minutes with someone over forty. And if he were reading romances, it'd only be for the sex scenes.

Chris blushed. "Thanks," he said. "It means a lot coming from you."

He was sweet, she'd give him that. And a real nice guy. But she had a boyfriend. And Chris had to get it through his head that there could never be anything between them.

"Why do you always do that?" she asked, feeling bad about having to break his heart. She reminded herself that it was better in the long run. The sooner he could get over his crush, the sooner he could move on to another girl—one who would appreciate how nice and sweet he was.

He cocked his head in confusion. "Do what?"

"Say things like that. Flatter me."

"'Cause I like you," he said. He gave an embarrassed little shrug.

She groaned. "Well, can you like me a little less, maybe?" she asked. "Please? At least just keep it to yourself. It can be embarrassing."

"Oh. I'm sorry. I . . . I didn't realize . . ." He sounded astonished, shocked that his unrelenting puppy love would bother her if he didn't mind her continued rejections. "Yeah, sure. I'll leave you alone."

He looked so wounded, she felt a moment of remorse. "No, you don't have to . . . I mean . . ." Now it was her turn to stutter. "You're nice. I like talking to you. I just don't like you like *that*. Like a boyfriend. I have Drew." She realized it sounded like she was trying to convince herself as much as Chris.

Chris screwed up his face. "You sure do. And you can keep him."

Molly found herself laughing, thinking of the fight she and Drew had just had. Of how she'd thought about getting rid of him. "He's not that bad, you know."

"Sure. If you say so."

"Really! He's a good guy."

Chris held up his hands. "I believe you. You don't have to prove it to me." But he wouldn't look her in the eye.

Molly found herself a little annoyed. "I mean, I know he's not the brightest. And sometimes he can be kind of bossy . . ." She trailed off, realizing what she was saying, how she was defending herself, and for no good reason. "Anyway, he's cool. I like him. We're going out. End of story."

"Okay, then," Chris replied. "Understood."

But Molly couldn't let that be the end of the conversation. "If you want to be . . . friends, though . . . I think that would be okay." It was, wasn't it? Yes. As long as she wasn't encouraging him in any way, making him think they'd ever be more.

"Friends," Chris repeated. "I'd like that."

CHAPTER SEVEN

Molly stared at the man in front of her, hardly able to believe her eyes. Chris Griffin. *Her* Chris Griffin? Okay, not hers exactly. Not anymore. But still! Of all the apocalypses in all the world, he had walked into hers. What were the odds? What were the chances?

He'd certainly changed since she'd seen him last. It was no wonder she hadn't recognized him. His once scrawny, gangly body had filled out. He now had broad shoulders and an impressive chest, narrowing to a trim waist. He was . . . handsome. Hot, even. Chris Griffin had grown up into a hottie. It was almost odder than the zombie she'd just fought.

"I can't believe it," she whispered, still not able to look him in the eyes. After the initial shock wore off, she managed to remember that he might not be all that thrilled to see her. Not after what she'd done to him. How they'd left things between them. She thought about the diamond still burning a hole in her pocket. She'd carried it around with her for years. And now here he was, the diamond-giver himself, standing not two feet in front of her.

Had the stone somehow worked as some kind of talisman, drawing him to her? That was stupid. Ridiculous. But still, what a coincidence.

"I thought you were dead," she said.

"Yeah, well, I guess you never bothered to find out," he growled.

She stopped, reeling a little. She deserved the biting comment, and she knew it, but that didn't diminish the sting.

"No," she said simply. "I guess I didn't."

"Anyway, it'd take a lot more than an apocalypse to kill me," he said with a laugh. His smile didn't quite reach his eyes.

Molly wanted to ask a million questions: where he'd been, how he'd lived, how anyone had survived. But she didn't know how to do that without bringing up the obvious. And she wasn't ready to do that. Mostly because she didn't want to see the pain in his eyes and know how much she'd hurt him by her actions. How long had he waited for her? When had he finally realized she wasn't coming? What had he done then?

"We headed up to the mountains," he began, answering her unasked question. "As you might remember, that was the plan. We found a refugee camp set up by a group of former Boy Scout leaders, hung out there while the shit all went down. Not exactly cushy quarters like your daddy's fallout shelter, I'm sure," he added, and she winced a little at the dig. "Way too many people, not nearly enough food. Still, it got us out of the line of fire, which was good, I guess."

He trailed off and Molly thought about her own experience. Sure, she'd had blankets and food and medicine, but it hadn't exactly been easy living, stuck inside an 800 square foot box for six years, dealing with a manic-depressive mother. It wasn't exactly the Ritz. But she knew better than to bring that up. Chase wanted to hate her, and she had little right to convince him otherwise.

"That must have been rough," she said.

He glared at her, and she realized her tone might have been misinterpreted as patronizing. She began to speak again, but Chase cut her off. "It's no big deal," he said, then fell silent and shuffled his feet.

She watched him, a wave of sadness washing over her. He was not only different on the outside, but on the inside as well. The years had hardened him, and the man before her now was cocky, confident and had a dark edge. He scared her a little. Which seemed ridiculous. How could sweet, geeky Chris Griffin scare her? Easy. When he had become Chase.

She considered again if she should apologize for standing him up, leaving him in the lurch, choosing her father and not being able to let him know. But was it really worth going there? What good would it do, opening up old wounds—and all to what purpose? She was only going to have to leave him again. She had her mission, after all. She'd made her choice long ago and she had to stick with it. Now more than ever. So much was riding on her.

"What's with the new name?" she asked, trying to change the subject to something safer.

He snorted. "Oh, that. Yeah. Well, my friend Stephen was bored one day and came up with tribe names for all of us as a joke. And well, they kind of stuck, I guess. Trey's called Tank—'cause, well, he's built like one, what with all the bench-pressing he does. We call Stephen Rocky 'cause stuff around him never goes smoothly. Spud's our resident gardener . . ."

"And they call you Chase because . . . ?"

He beamed with bravado. " 'Cause there ain't no zombie out there who can catch me."

She offered him a half-smile, considering this. He certainly was cockier than she remembered. "What made you come back here?" she asked, looking around. "Why not stay up in the mountains?"

"Ran out of food," Chase replied—too quickly. A dark flicker in his eyes also made her wonder if there was more to it than that. "Trey and I and a few others headed back here to see what was left to salvage."

"Makes sense."

"Problem was, when we got back, we ran into the Others. They'd pretty much taken over the town by that point. They attacked immediately and killed most of our little group. We weren't prepared back then. We had no idea."

Molly thought back to the monster she'd fought, and she

shuddered. She didn't want to imagine fighting off a group, didn't want to picture what he'd gone through. "But you escaped," she concluded. She was feeling an urge to spit.

Chase nodded. "Yeah. Most of the credit goes to Trey. He's a born leader, that guy. After we fought our way out . . . well, he dredged up all the survivors and herded us to the local Wal-Mart. He even collected others who'd been hiding around town."

She raised an eyebrow, half-amused. "You all live in a Wal-Mart?"

"Hells yeah, we do," Chase declared. "And it was a good idea, too. Wally's world has everything you need to survive an apocalypse—canned food, camping supplies, first aid, bedding, even toys for the kiddos. You can live in a Wal-Mart for a long time. We even grow our own vegetables in the Garden and Patio section."

"You grow your own food?" She'd been wondering how they were eating. How many years' worth of canned food could a Wal-Mart hold? She supposed it depended on the number of survivors.

Chris nodded. "Sure. In addition to the stuff in our building, we have some corn growing out in Washington Park. We also hunt. Neighborhood's overrun by animals these days. Deer, rabbits—we even keep a cow around for milk."

"Nice," she said. And she meant it. She hadn't had a glass of milk in years. "So . . . what about the others?"

He looked annoyed. "Oh, yeah, we have to compete with them for the deer and stuff. But they really aren't into the whole vegetarian thing, so they don't mess with our corn. And they're lousy at opening cans."

"No, no," Molly corrected. "Not the *Others*. I mean the other survivors."

Chase shook his head. "I told you, we all live in the Wal-Mart. Or do you mean others outside of the tribe? There aren't any. As far as we know, we're the last. Everyone else either died, was eaten or . . . well, you know—became one of *them*." He looked ill for a moment then shrugged it off.

"That's why I was so surprised to see you today. I haven't seen anyone new for probably three years."

Molly spat. Everyone was gone. "How many are you?"

"Not that many anymore," Chase said, looking at the ground. "We've had a lot of casualties over the years. And not just from the Others. We have no doctors. No hospitals. Two years ago there was a bad flu going around. We lost seven with that." He raked a hand through his hair. "So that leaves twelve of us. There's an even dozen of our tribe, holding on, waiting to die. Nice, eh? You'd make thirteen. Lucky."

She wanted to cringe at his bluntness. His bitterness. She didn't blame him, but it hurt all the same. She wondered if she should invite him to come with her. It'd be nice to have the company and maybe safer to travel in a group. Still, she had to get to her destination quickly. Before her nano-enhancements broke down and she was weakened.

Chase looked up at the sun, which was setting, and shook his head as if clearing it. "I can't believe we've been standing out here talking all this time. Stupid. We've been lucky. Why . . . why don't you come back with me?" he asked. "I'm sure Tank would love to see you. And you can meet the rest of the tribe."

Surprisingly, there was no warmth in his voice. No softness. He might as well be extending the offer to a stranger. In a way, she guessed, he was.

She glanced at her wrist. It was a crazy habit, since actual time had lost its meaning long ago and she hadn't worn a watch in years. "Well, I'm actually in a hurry," she hedged. "I've got to start a journey down to Florida."

She caught a flicker of emotion in his eyes, felt a mixture of pleasure and angst. Had he thought she would just stick around? Pick up where they'd left off? She supposed that made sense. After all, how would he know about her mission? She'd never told him her father's plan, so he couldn't know how important it was. How it had to take precedence over everything.

"You're not going anywhere tonight. It's almost dark," Chase reminded her. "Trust me, you don't want to be out alone in the dark these days. And you've got to be hungry, right? We've got plenty of food. And sanitizers for those . . . fingers." He looked down at her razors and she wondered why he didn't ask her about them. "We can hook you up with supplies for your trip, too. And tell you about what we know of the area."

He had her there. There was no way she could embark on the journey without some basic necessities: food, a sleeping bag, maybe a tent. Stuff to make a fire. That sort of thing. Items Wal-Mart would have in high supply. And she'd been planning to collect them anyway. And hearing whatever information the survivors had to offer would probably be a good idea.

"Okay," she relented. "But I need to leave first thing in the morning."

"Not a problem." Chase smiled. "So, um, I've got to go . . . grab something. Some . . . stuff. And then we can go on our way, okay?"

"Okay. Want me to help?"

"No. Stay right here. I'll be back in a flash."

Molly Anderson. Molly fucking Anderson. Chase couldn't believe it. How many nights had he thought of her as he lay on his old creaky cot in that overcrowded, filthy, stinking refugee camp? Where she was, why she hadn't shown up on that last day. Wondering if something had happened to her, if she was dead. But, no. Here she was, alive and well. And mostly unfazed, too, by the looks of her. While he and his brother had suffered, while they'd watched their friends and family die, she'd prospered, living it up in some cushy hideaway set up by her crazy father.

He wanted to be furious at her, to abandon her to the darkness and the zombies, to leave her to fend entirely for herself. But at the same time, he was just so goddamned happy to see her alive. To know she'd survived. It was all he could do not to grab her and pull her into his arms and kiss the life out of her, to finish what the apocalypse had so rudely interrupted.

But he couldn't do that. She'd betrayed him. She'd left him

high and dry without a thought. She hadn't even apologized after seeing him again! He remembered waiting in the rain until dark, waiting until Trey finally returned and dragged him away. The thought was like a knife in his guts.

And so, while, sure, he was happy to learn she was alive and well, he knew in his heart there could never be a happily-ever-after for the two of them. He'd let her stay the night at the Wal-Mart and get her what she needed; then tomorrow he'd see her on her way and try to forget he'd ever run into her. It was better that way—would be better that way even if they were the last two people on Earth.

Anyway, he had more pressing things on his mind at the moment.

He stole down the street and slipped into the vacant house he'd originally been casing. Fading light filtered through its half caved-in ceiling, allowing him the luxury of not wasting the precious battery power remaining in his flashlight. He stepped over a decomposing body sprawled out on the floor—he hated when they weren't tucked away in their beds—and made his way up the creaky stairs to the master bathroom.

Man, the way Molly had taken on that Other was un-fricking-believable. Sure, he'd seen people turn and fight be-fore. Most of those people were dead. Molly had made it look effortless. She'd sliced through the creature with razors that appeared to be fused to her fingertips: some kind of cy-bernetic enhancements, he guessed. Her dad had been into that stuff. It looked like he'd messed with her eyes, too. Upon closer inspection he'd seen the sunglasses she was wearing looked almost permanent. Weird. Hot, too, but definitely weird. He hadn't dared bring it up.

He hadn't been prepared for his body's betrayal, the tight-ening in his pants as his eyes roved her scantily clad body. The reaction wasn't surprising, he supposed. He couldn't re-member the last time he'd seen a grown woman, never mind an attractive one, never mind an attractive one who was his first-ever love. He involuntarily remembered her curvy hips, long shapely legs, her baby-powder scent. God, how did she smell like baby powder six years after the apocalypse? She was too much. It was a good thing she wasn't sticking around.

He shook his head, desperate to get sex off the brain. He had to grab the stash quick and get out of there. Leaving Molly alone had been a stupid, selfish idea. What if that injured Other came back, this time with buddies? Not that they were usually very organized, but you never knew. And while she'd done a great job taking on one, how would she fare against four or five? It'd be better to get back to safety, especially with darkness coming on.

He considered turning back, returning tomorrow alone, but the raw need churning his stomach wouldn't let him. He couldn't play protector, not even to Molly Anderson. Not that she needed it. She'd abandoned him, all those years ago, and she looked like she could take care of herself now. And nights were long in the Wal-Mart. Nights without medication were even longer.

Just grab the goods and get the hell out.

He reached the upstairs bathroom, pawing away the cobwebs across the medicine cabinet. A disturbed layer of dust filled his lungs and he coughed. Yanking open the cabinet, he checked the contents.

Score. Total score. He grinned. Well, this made things a little better.

A bottle of Vicodin. Another of Oxycontin. He'd been thinking about it all yesterday, and figured old Mrs. Gardner with all her aches and pains would have a good stash in her bathroom. And he'd been right! Of course, he had no idea if the stuff was still good. It likely wasn't going to be the same as the government surplus he'd scored from that military base a few months ago, properly stored and sealed for an extended shelf life. But that base was a day's journey away and he needed some short-term relief, at least until he could think up an excuse he could give Tank for another journey.

He stuffed the bottles in his pocket and hurried back to Molly. Squinting as he stepped into the fading sunlight, he let out a sigh of relief. She was waiting for him, untouched, unharmed. Another wave of protectiveness washed over him. It was strange. She looked so vulnerable standing there, studying a small clump of daisies. But, he reminded himself, she wasn't what she appeared.

Which was a good thing, he reminded himself.

He waved to her. She waved back. "Got the supplies?" she asked.

"Yup." He stuffed his hands in his pockets and felt the drug bottles. "We're good to go."

CHAPTER EIGHT

"Don't look now, but he's behind you again," Erin whispered to Molly a few days later at school. "Your stalker." They were pushing their way through the crowded halls.

Molly glanced over her shoulder and saw Chris fast approaching, fighting just like a salmon in the stream of students going the other way. She waved then turned back to Erin. "He's okay, actually" she said. "I don't think he's going to do that anymore."

Her friend rolled her genetically altered purple eyes. "Whatever you say, girl. He looks shiftier to me."

"How'd the vaccine go?" Molly asked, changing the subject before Chris caught up. She didn't want to hurt his feelings. "Did you get it?"

"Hells yeah, I did. LTF, here I come. Second I got the shot, I logged in and signed up. It takes a few weeks for everything to process. You know the government. But, I can't wait! Me and Todd are planning a trip to the mountains when it's all official. We're going to rent some cabin in the woods that doesn't even have sim decks and never get out of bed."

"Sounds dreamy," Molly said, even though it actually sounded like a nightmare. Thinking of Drew . . . well, she really had no idea why everyone was so excited about sex. From what she'd seen in health class, it was messy, sticky, and often embarrassing. And with what she and Drew had already done, well, there were times it was nice to have a father who was old-fashioned and a life that was over-regulated.

"Yeah. It will be. You know, you should totally talk to your dad again about getting the shot," Erin remarked. "I mean, Drew's not going to wait around forever, you know. Almost everyone in the senior class has their license."

Molly fought back annoyance. "Yeah, well, if he's not willing to wait then he's not worth having." But even as she said the words Molly knew they were kind of ridiculous. Drew was only asking for something every other kid was doing. And he could have any girl in school. What made her think she was so special that he should wait on *her?* Wasn't that what he kept saying?

Erin snorted and verbalized her fears. "Yeah. You keep telling yourself that. But it's just as easy to fall for a girl with an LTF as a girl without one. And a lot more fun."

Chris caught up, saving her from some lame reply. "Hey, Molly," he said.

"Here you go!" Erin teased in a whisper. "I bet Ducky would wait decades for you. Maybe even millennia."

Molly punched her in the shoulder. "Yeah, yeah. Don't you have a class to go to or something—like our English class? Mrs. Adams's going to have your head if you're late again."

"Yup," Erin replied, laughing. "Later, 'gator. See you inside." She gave a wave and hurried off down the hall.

Molly turned and looked at Chris, who appeared to be studying something in his deck. She supposed he was letting her and Erin finish their conversation. "What's up?" she asked.

He shook his head, looking dazed. "Have you seen Mrs. McCormick yet? I went by her house yesterday and she wasn't home. I figured that maybe she'd be back by now."

Molly shook her head. "I actually went by there myself this morning," she admitted. "No answer."

"I called Mount Holyoke. All of the hospitals in the area, actually. None of them have even heard of her," Chris said. He shuffled from foot to foot. "I'm worried. I mean, what do you think happened to her? You said those men were from the government, but . . . I don't know."

Molly swallowed the fears she herself had been fighting. She'd decided not to tell her father about the incident the other day, as she didn't want to raise his hackles. She knew how he could be about the feds. And she'd felt so odd that day after she'd left Chris that she hadn't wanted to think about anything involving it. If anything weird started happening, she'd tell her dad—or that's what she'd told herself. But nothing weird had happened. The brown-suited men had not reappeared.

"I don't mean to be harsh, but . . . maybe she just died. It sucks, but sometimes that happens," she said. Not everything was a conspiracy.

"Yeah." Chris raked a hand through his curly blond hair. "I thought that too at first. Then I did some more digging, went to some unauthorized Web forums and . . ."

"And?"

"She's not the only one who's been taken away in a brown van with that seal. I found almost a dozen similar stories from around the country. And then there are a few international cases, too. It doesn't make much sense, but the descriptions all seem so similar, and . . ."

Molly's mouth went dry. "Are you serious?"

Chris nodded. "Yeah. I think something's going on."

Molly fought with herself for a moment. At last she said, "I should ask my dad. He's up on all this. It's his thing. Conspiracy theories. If anyone would know, it'd be him. I should have mentioned it the other day but . . . I'll ask him after school."

Chris nodded. "Good idea. I'll come with you."

At his self-invitation, Molly narrowed her eyes. She couldn't help but feel a moment of suspicion. "Are you telling me the truth? You're really only interested in Mrs. McCormick here, right?"

"You mean, did I make all this up for an invite to your house?"

Molly shrugged, not sure what she meant.

"Don't flatter yourself," he snapped. "I just want to know

what's going on. If your dad's the one who'd know, I want to talk to him."

"Fine," Molly said, resigning herself to the plan. She knew Drew wouldn't approve of her new friend, but she supposed this visit was for a good cause. Who could object to two teenagers looking into their neighbor's disappearance?

Suddenly a new fear crossed her mind. "Um," she said. "About my dad. I warn you, he's a little . . . intense."

Chris laughed. "That's okay. So am I."

The bell rang and Chris darted off. Molly hurried down the hall, too, only to find the door to her class swing shut in her face. Great. She'd made a joke to Erin but their teacher, Mrs. Adams, didn't tolerate any latecomers, and this was her own third tardy in three months. She considered pushing the door open and braving the teacher's wrath, but then she thought better of it. A happier solution would be to head to the nurse's office, feign being sick, and get a pass.

On the way, she decided to swing by the cafeteria to grab a snack; she liked having food while she was thinking, and she wanted to think about Mrs. McCormick—and about Chris and her dad. She could only swing by without penalty because, unlike the old days, which she saw in all the old movies, everything here was automated. Lunch ladies had been phased out. Her school cafeteria was all machines, and it would be empty right now. Insert ID, press button, remove food. Fast and easy. She wondered if the old food tasted better.

As she entered the caf, her eyes fell on two figures at the far side of the vending area. The pair were curled into an embrace. Molly quickly looked away, not wanting to spy. Then, curious, she took another peek.

Her stomach dropped like it was on a roller coaster sim, and her world spun off its axis. Drew. Here was her super-popular boyfriend and the trashy president of the student council, Brenda Booker. They were sucking face. God knows what else they'd done. Brenda had gotten her LTF back when she was fourteen years old and was legendary for her STD-free exploits.

A mixture of self-disgust and righteous rage filled Molly. Erin had been right; Drew had decided she wasn't worth waiting for. All that stuff he'd said about love and loyalty—even if it had been when they were making up, after he'd been pressuring her on and off for the past few months—it was all bullshit. He was just like every other horny guy in her high school, looking for one thing and one thing alone.

She tried to take a step back, to flee the scene, but her legs felt like they were stuck in mud to the knees. She tripped over a chair and crashed to the ground.

Swift. Real swift.

They hadn't noticed her before, but they did now. Drew and Brenda looked over, startled. Molly scrambled to her feet, her face burning. She would never say it to her dad, but now would be a great time for the end of the world to commence.

"I-I thought you had English class this period," Drew stammered.

Anger at him overcame her embarrassment. "Is that all you can say?" she demanded. "I catch you making out with the school slut in the middle of the school cafeteria, and all you can say is that I should be in class? Since when did you become hall monitor?"

Drew didn't even have the good grace to look sheepish. He whispered something to Brenda, who nodded, giggled, gave Molly a dirty look and took off. Molly glared at her back, wishing she could shoot daggers out of her eyes. Then she turned back to her cheating boyfriend.

"How could you?" she demanded, feeling tears well up in her eyes. "I thought . . . I thought you loved me." God, it sounded so lame and stupid when she said it aloud, and she'd known the relationship had problems, but . . . well, it didn't matter. Everything you knew went right out the window when you were in the situation. "I thought . . . Oh, never mind."

"I *do* love you," Drew said, walking over to her. He took her hand in his. She yanked it away. "I love you so much, baby."

"I see," Molly said through clenched teeth. "You have a weird way of showing it." She squeezed her hands into fists and forced herself to stay calm. "You love me, but, let me guess—you want to be with someone who has their CC. You're tired of waiting."

"We've talked about this," Drew said. "I mean, everyone and her mother has one. You're one of the last hold-outs in your entire class. I'm even willing to do it illegally for you, Molls. That's how much I love you. But if you won't say yes to that . . . how much can you love me?"

So there it was. Erin was right. It all came down to sex. That's how her peers saw things. Lame. So utterly lame.

"I'm not going to break the law," she protested.

"No, you won't, will you? 'Cause you're too afraid of your crazy daddy and what he might do if you live a little. You're trapped in a cage, Molly," he told her. "Living half a life. All because some Armageddon nut who should be locked up keeps telling you that the end of the world is near." He shook his head. "Well, let me tell you something: when the end of the world comes, I'm going to have lived my life. How about you? You still going to be waiting around with Daddy?"

Molly snapped. Her fist found Drew's nose in a millisecond. There came the sound of crushing bone and a scream of pain. Her boyfriend's perfect proboscis—the one that his parents had paid, well, through the nose for—was now a shapeless, bloody mess.

"Don't talk about my father like that," she said, lowering her bloodied hand. Then she turned and stormed out of the cafeteria, leaving Drew bawling like a baby and shouting for the nurse.

As she left the cafeteria, she fought the urge to spit.

CHAPTER NINE

As Chase and Molly traversed the Wal-Mart parking lot, they wove through abandoned cars and shopping carts, many of which still contained plastic bags stuffed with decomposing goods. The car windows were mostly broken, and shattered glass on the asphalt caught the failing sunlight, sparkling like a field of scattered diamonds. Molly fingered the object in her pocket and wondered if she should show it to Chase. Would he even remember giving it to her? It was a lifetime ago, after all. And he'd changed. He wasn't that boy anymore. She had to remember.

She withdrew her hand from her pocket and took a look around, shivering at the sight of the barren landscape. Everything was so still, so dead. What had it been like for these people whose rag-clad skeletons now stretched before her, littering the parking lot? One moment they were blissful, happy-go-lucky Wal-Mart shoppers, ready to enjoy an hour or so of discount commerce, the next they were collapsing where they stood, their lungs seizing up, their hearts failing—and those were the lucky ones. What went through their minds as they fell to the hard, cold pavement? Had they pled for some kind of last-minute divine intervention? At what moment had they resigned themselves to the fact that none would come?

As she stared at a car that looked vaguely familiar—was it the Smart Nissan of one of her teachers?—a lump formed in her throat that she struggled to swallow down. She was supposed to be tough now, after all. Her father had trained her for this: to be strong, to not let overwhelming emotion wash her away. So there were some dead people here. So it went. After all, she was a razor girl. Like Molly Millions. And Molly Millions didn't cry.

She faltered, unable to go on. Her dad would be ashamed.

Suddenly a strong grip found her shoulder, spinning her around. Chase cupped her chin in his hand. His fingers were warm—and when had he grown so big? He forced her face to look at him, and she suddenly remembered the kaleidoscopes that were his eyes. Those greens and yellows and blues. That sympathetic gaze.

"Are you okay?" he asked. She realized she was trembling. How embarrassing. The last thing she wanted was for him to see her weak.

"I'm fine," she retorted, shaking her head to free herself of his hand. He gripped her chin tighter, running a finger along her jaw. That touch sparked an ache deep inside—one she found she couldn't will away. Like everything else in this world.

"Sure you are," he said, giving a nod. "That's why you're white as a sheet."

She slumped her shoulders and sighed. "Okay, fine. It's . . . a lot to take in. I admit it."

"Duh," he said, bitter amusement in his voice. "When we first got back, after being in the mountains for so long, we couldn't believe it." He let go of her chin and she felt a weird emptiness inside, then scolded herself for feeling it. Whatever had been between them, it was long over. The sooner she recognized that, the better. "I threw up like three times when I saw the first bodies."

"I did, too," she admitted. "Outside my house, I saw . . . a child." She shuddered.

"You get used to it after a while," he said, staring around the parking lot. "I know that probably sounds crazy, but trust me, it'll happen. One day you'll be out and about—hunting for food or whatever—and something will strike you as funny.

You'll start laughing just like you would have before." He turned back to her, his face earnest if sad. "You'll be standing there alone, smack-dab in this mass graveyard we call Earth, surrounded by cannibalistic zombies and cackling like a loon." He smiled for a moment, a cocky grin she never remembered him having before, then grimaced. "It's that moment you realize life goes on. And it really does. Until you bite it."

She exhaled, not sure what to say. She wanted to believe him, but at the moment she couldn't imagine ever laughing again or treating this reality with such nonchalance. It was all too grim. "If you say so, dude," she finally replied, choosing bravado over sincerity, mostly because she was too frightened to show anything else.

"It's okay, don't believe me," he said with a smirk. "I wouldn't believe myself either." He ushered her through the parking lot. "Now, come on, let's get inside before we lose all the light."

They walked up to what had once served as the front of the store. The normal glass-windowed entrance was boarded up with large sheets of metal, roughly fused together with a combination of bolts and solder.

"The Others aren't too shy about jumping through glass windows," Chase explained, gesturing to the makeshift barriers. "Hell, it's practically an Olympic sport for them. But they can't see for shit and aren't too smart, so the metal here keeps them out. Tank rigged it up a couple years back, and so far we've managed to keep a low profile. We've killed those who've come around so . . . well, we think they assume the place is abandoned."

He gave a cursory glance around the parking lot, Molly assumed checking for zombies, then went to a door cut out of the metal plates. He opened its lock with a key that hung on a silver chain around his neck. Beyond was a smashed-in glass door.

"Careful," he said as he motioned for Molly to step inside. "Don't cut yourself. A single scratch could be lethal these days."

She hadn't thought of that. With no physicians, an untreated infection could be as dangerous as a zombie. Stepping through, she took care to avoid any sharp metal edges or glass shards.

Chase entered, locking the metal door behind them. "Here we are," he said, ushering her forward. "Home sweet home."

The normally bright overhead fluorescent lights were, of course, no longer functioning in this superstore, and the darkness was shocking compared to the sun outside. Otherwise, in what light there was, coming from a skylight to the northwest, the place seemed much as she remembered it. The shelves nearby were stacked with discounted electronics, yellow bouncy ball signs declared which products were currently—or in 2030, in this case—on special. A long row of checkouts, manned by silent cashier sentinels, stretched into the distance. In short, it was a barren wasteland of dust-caked commercialism, a vivid reminder of how the world once was.

Molly sneezed.

"Maid's day off," Chase quipped, beckoning her to follow. "Come on. I think the gang's in Toys."

"Toys?"

He laughed. "You'll see."

He reached into his bag and pulled out a flashlight, flicking it on. A weak beam did its best to pierce the darkness, but as they walked briskly through the aisles and farther from the skylight, she wondered how Chase could even see. Her own implants compensated, switching to night vision. Thanks, Dad.

At the back of the store a much brighter light appeared, if localized. As Chase promised, they were nearing the Toys section, and a minute later Molly caught high-pitched giggles accompanied by a loud whirring. They turned the corner and came upon a small circle of children all sprawled out on the floor. The light, she realized, came from a couple of lamps powered by a generator that was producing the whirring noise she'd heard.

Molly took a closer look. Toys she remembered from her childhood were scattered everywhere: beautiful Barbies with long, flowing hair, dashing Ken dolls with their anatomically correct parts. (She and Erin were scandalized to learn they hadn't always been manufactured that way, though in some ways Molly thought she'd prefer the old way.) These kids had every toy except the electronic ones, and sim decks, which were likely too expensive to run with limited battery power. Molly had to restrain herself not to scramble down onto the floor and play with the group.

She did a quick count. Eight children, ranging in apparent ages from six to fourteen. The oldest two, a girl and boy, were arguing in a corner, while the younger ones contented themselves with play. There were boy triplets with shocks of carrot-colored hair and matching pug noses, but what seemed strangest of all was their outfits. In fact, all of the kids were outfitted the same way: a total mish-mash of colors and patterns, not a single one of which matched. Even stranger, the kids all wore makeup—even the boys. Or was it war paint? she wondered, because the swirling cheek and forehead designs appeared almost tribal. The whole thing reminded her of a book her dad had once made her read. *The Lord of the Flies*. Of course, Wal-Mart was no jungle, and these kids had no hope of a rescue plane swooping down anytime soon.

"So they're all orphans?" she asked Chase, keeping her voice low. "And you brought them all here?"

A laugh sounded behind Molly, making her jump. "Chase? He would have let them be killed if it was up to him."

Molly whirled around to see a good-looking, barrel-chested man approach. He had long dark hair tied back in a ponytail, and a trim beard. He walked up to Chase and Molly and held out his hand. "I'm Tank," he said. "Chase's brother." He looked her up and down. "I wondered where my little brother had gone. Ran off like an idiot. Now I see why."

"He always thinks the best of me," Chase grunted. "Tank, this is Molly. Remember the Andersons? From down the street?"

Tank gave her a double take. "Molly Anderson?" he repeated. He looked her up and down and whistled. "*Damn.*"

"Don't mind him," Chase snapped. "He's a bit desperate. Six years without a chick, you know."

"Hey, what about Anna Simmons?" Tank protested. "When we were still at the refugee camp."

"Yeah, right. That happened."

"If she told you otherwise it was only to keep you from getting all jealous."

"As if I'd want that skank."

Molly shook her head at the banter. It was kind of nice, in some ways, to be back among humanity, and among humanity that was acting so casual. She'd been away for too long— even if the men were still idiots fixated on sex. "So, you're the one responsible for all of this?" she asked Tank, gesturing to the kids.

"Yeah, he is. Tank's a regular Pied Piper," Chase spoke up. "I swear, he must have some kind of flute stuffed in his pocket."

"Nah, man, I'm just happy to see you."

Raising an eyebrow, Chase stared at his brother.

Tank turned back to Molly. "Yeah, I'm the leader of this here motley crew. When all the adults started dying, I realized someone had to step up to the plate. And I was the oldest."

"And the dumbest," Chase snorted.

Tank smacked him in the shoulder. "Pot, kettle, black, Chasey," he said. "Anyway, I combed the city for survivors and brought them all back here. We have a pretty good set-up going on. Sleeping bags, food, water, toys. Even rigged up some electricity."

"Limited electricity. Which you are currently wasting," Chase remarked, motioning to the lights.

"Hey, the children wanted to play."

"Softie."

Tank shrugged, not denying it. "I try to make it as good for them as possible," he said. "I mean, it's not much of a life here, but it's better than being out there."

Molly thought about the zombie she had fought and how it

had come out of nowhere. She couldn't imagine a child being able to cope. "I can see that," she agreed.

Tank studied her, and his eyes grew a bit cold. "So, what's your story?" he asked. "Last I remember, you were standing up my brother on judgment day. Get a better offer? Not that beggars can be choosers these days. We're happy to have you."

Molly cringed. This was so not the conversation she wanted to be having. "What happened? It's a long story," she mumbled. "My dad needed me and . . ." She trailed off. What good would it do to explain? In their eyes, she was a traitor. That's how it'd always be. "Sorry to leave you guys hanging."

"No skin off my back," Tank said. He shrugged. "In fact, I should thank you. Because of you bailing, there was room in the van for Anna Simmons." He paused, then asked, "So, what happened to your old man? He was one of the few people who was probably prepared for this, considering who he was."

Molly bristled, waiting for an insult. One didn't come, so she forced herself to relax. "I believe he's down in Florida," she said. "That's where I'm headed."

"What's down there?"

"Disney World."

Tank laughed. "Disney World? You mean, like, Mickey Mouse and all that shit?"

"Well, I doubt Mickey's still around, but yeah, that's the place."

"Y'all got a sudden urge to ride Space Mountain?"

She laughed and shook her head, though the joke wasn't funny. "My father and his scientist buddies are—I hope—holed up there. They're working on rebuilding society. When things started getting bad, they made a pact to meet. It was meant to be the Eden of the new—"

"Hey, Tank, you've just survived the apocalypse. What are you going to do now?" Chase interrupted.

Tank erupted in a howl of mirth, gave his brother a high-five, and the two men cracked up. "I'm going to Disney World!"

The kids stopped playing and stared at them.

Molly rolled her eyes. "I know it sounds silly," she said. "But Disney makes perfect sense if you think about it. The way my father talked, his friends were planning to make the place completely defensible, underground service tunnels and all. Also, there are a ton of hotel rooms—localized residences with their own power and water plants. And Florida is warm year-round, so no worries about anyone freezing to death."

"I guess that could work," Tank said. "Sort of like what we did here in the Wal-Mart, but on a larger scale."

Molly nodded. "Right. So my dad made me promise that once the doors of the shelter in which my mother and I were living all this time opened, I'd head down to find him. They opened yesterday, and so I'm on my way."

"Your mother?"

"She . . . was sick. She passed on yesterday." Molly felt her throat tighten as she pictured her mother's unmoving body and the plastic rose. She fought the urge to spit.

Tank shook his head, giving a little snort. "Well, nice idea or not, sorry, sister, you'll never make it to Florida. Not with how things are. The Others will have you by breakfast. There's too many of them. You can never predict where they'll appear or when. It's smarter not to travel, to hole up and keep hidden. To stay in places of strategic advantage. Otherwise, we don't stand a chance."

"We'll see," she said, refusing to let his pessimism soak in. She was, like it or not, a razor girl; she could do things normal humans couldn't. That was the whole point. "I mean, I'm not entirely helpless," she explained, holding out her fingers, displaying her blood-encrusted razors. Ew. She really needed to clean those.

"Yeah, check it, Tank. You should see what she can do with those bad boys. She took on one of the Others when I first ran into her. Big guy, too." He mimicked her martial arts movements with an exaggerated flair. "Hiiii-yah! Bang! Boom! The thing didn't know what hit it."

Tank let out a whistle, staring at the blades. "Damn. Your daddy make you those?"

Molly nodded then looked down at the ground, suddenly feeling self-conscious. "It's another long story," she said at last. "I've got ocular implants, too." She pointed to her sunglasses. "They allow me to see in the dark, have GPS navigation linked to an old-time satellite and allow access to special databases he left up and running."

"Nice," Tank said, taking her hand and examining her fingers. "I could use a set of those myself." He dropped her hand. "So, have you talked to your father lately?"

She stared at the ground and shrugged. "No. Not for a bit."

Tank nodded. "I thought not. You, girly girl, should face facts. With all those things running around, your father's probably dead. I hate to say it, but it's true. And you're not going to make it to Florida. Consider hanging out with us instead. We could use someone like you to pick up the slack for my lazy-ass, no-good brother over there." He gave Molly a charming smile.

Chase gave his brother the finger. "Please," he said, rolling his eyes. "Who catches half the deer? And who's the better cook?"

"Me, of course," Tank replied.

"The last time you tried to boil water you nearly burned us out of here!"

"Lies," Tank said. "If there were any lawyers left I'd sue for slander." He turned back to Molly. "So, what you do say? How about you skip Disney and join our little tribe?"

She shook her head. It was nice of them to ask, and she was tempted, seeing as they were the best company she'd had in years—even if she had a guilt complex around Chase—but she couldn't forsake her mission. She had to find her father and help him, just as she'd promised. There was also the change going on inside her, which she didn't want to mention. She had that fast-approaching expiration date. If she didn't get down to the Magic Kingdom pronto, things weren't going to get easier. "Thanks for the offer," she said, "but I have to do this."

From the corner of her eye she noticed Chase scowling, his snarky good humor all but disappeared. *Was* he still mad at her? After all this time? Did he hate her for not showing up at the eleventh hour? For choosing her dad over him? Would he understand if she explained? Would it do either of them any good?

No. Probably not. And in the long run, what did it really matter? What was done was done. She'd made her choice, couldn't take it back. And she was leaving in the morning. Probably would never see him again. Which was best. Really. Even if the sight of him did make her heart ache a little, seeing how he'd grown. The closeness they'd once shared was now a gaping chasm of regret.

Tank sighed. "Okay," he said. "But at least stay the night. We'll hook you up with some supplies."

Molly forced her thoughts back to the issue at hand. "Right," she said. "I'd appreciate those. But I do need to head out first thing in the morning." She wanted to be clear.

"Big hurry to save the world, huh?" Chase asked.

"Something like that." Molly stared down at her feet. She wished there were one sentence she could say, one short speech that could make him and his brother understand who she was and what she'd become, but it just wasn't going to happen. She was on her own until Florida.

"So, it's decided," Tank announced, obviously wanting to change the subject. "Maybe if you're lucky, Chase, chef extraordinaire, will cook you up some of his special five-star grub. Hope you like reconstituted beef stroganoff. It's his specialty," he added.

Molly threw Tank a small smile. "Right now, I'm so hungry I could probably eat a zombie."

The big man took a step closer. He put his arm around Molly and said, "Hey, Chase, why don't you make yourself useful and get some disinfectant for her hands?"

Chase gave him a look, but skulked off to obey. Molly watched him go, trying not to notice how the taut leather of his pants perfectly molded to his backside. Stupid frustrated libido, she thought. The sooner she got away from Chase Griffin, the better.

She turned back to the children, who'd gone back to playing. Molly wondered why they seemed uninterested in her, but maybe they'd seen a lot of people come and go. Maybe they weren't anxious to meet new people who were just going to die.

"Why are they dressed like that?" she asked, needing to change the subject.

Tank laughed and took his arm from around her shoulders, glancing off in the direction his brother went. "We gave up trying to dress them years ago," he explained. "It was way too hard to convince them of the whole matching concept, and we eventually realized it didn't make a difference anyway. No one's gonna see them who'd care, right? So we just point them in the direction of the children's department and tell them to go nuts. The older ones sometimes try to recreate what they see in the fashion magazines up front, and the little ones try to mimic the older ones, but basically none of them have any fashion sense whatsoever. Hell, half of them would run around naked if we let 'em."

Molly laughed. "Little savages, huh?"

"You said it, not me." Tank grinned. He still had that easy smile he'd been known for in high school, a smile that made Molly feel comfortable and at home. Unlike Chase, who made her feel completely on edge. The sooner she got away from here, the better.

"And the makeup?"

"Ah, that's courtesy of my man Rocky. When we first started gathering up the kids, they were all freaked out and scared. None of them would talk to one another; they just huddled in corners, practically catatonic with fear and grief. So Rocky came up with this idea to tell them that we were a special tribe. He came up with a whole story about us and told them all members of the tribe needed war paint." Tank smiled at the memory. "He hit a Halloween costume store downtown and brought cases and cases of makeup back with him. Painted all the faces of the children, one by one. They loved it. First time we saw any of them smile." He looked down at the kids lovingly. "Half the time I forget they're wearing it nowadays, I'm so used to seeing it. Probably looks pretty silly to you."

Molly shook her head. "I think it's cute," she said. "You guys are really good to them."

"Well, I try to teach 'em stuff," Tank continued. "We set up a little school in the café and meet for a couple hours a day. I hit the library down the street and got a bunch of books for them to read. I'm not the best teacher in the world, for sure, but I figured it was better than nothing. Right?"

She was impressed. "Definitely. They are the future, right?"

"Damn straight." After a moment he added, "Gotta take a leak. Be right back." Then he walked off down a nearby aisle.

She watched him disappear, thinking that here was a good guy. Her father could use people like him down at Disney World, she'd bet: dependable leaders who could get a job done. Once she joined her father and got settled in, she'd have to see if there was a way to bring this entire group down. She'd get the kids in school, give Tank a real job in whatever new society was being built. And Chase would come, too, she supposed. As long as he was living on the other side of the park, far away from her.

She felt a tapping on her leg and looked down. A scrawny little girl, about six years old, with big brown eyes and straw-colored braids, looked up at her with a curious expression on her war-painted face. She was joined a few moments later by a similarly painted Asian boy who had crimson streaks in his otherwise white-blond hair.

"I'm Darla," the girl declared, pointing to herself. "And this is Red. Who are you?"

Molly crouched down, getting to eye level. Kids always made her nervous, and it didn't help now that she hadn't had any to deal with in six years. But she'd do her best.

"I'm Molly," she said. "Nice to meet you." Should she hold

out her hand? No, her razors were still flared and covered with goo.

Darla squinted at her. "What's wrong with your eyes?" she asked, pointing at Molly's glasses. "They look freaky."

Molly tried not to bristle. Darla was just a kid, and kids were blunt about that kind of thing. Still, it was more than a bit unsettling. Back in the shelter it had been easy to pretend everything was normal. Here, out in the world, she was a total freak.

"They're special lenses," she explained. "They help me see better."

"Well, they're weird," Red pronounced, reaching up to try and touch them. Molly dodged so that she wouldn't have to wipe away the smudge marks later on.

"Weird," Darla agreed, nodding. "Very weird."

"Hey, don't you rugrats have anything better to do than pester our guest?" Tank demanded, reappearing. She hadn't heard him return. "If not, I suggest you start peeling potatoes for dinner."

"What*ever*," Red retorted, sticking out his tongue.

"Whatever," Darla repeated like a parrot.

"Oh, yeah? Is that how we speak to our elders?" Tank dove for the two children, grabbing one in each arm and whirling them in a circle. They squealed in protest. "You know what the punishment is for 'whatevering' me, don't you?"

"No!" Darla pleaded. "No, Tank!"

"Oh yes," he said, grinning wickedly. He set them down. "Tickle torture!"

They both screamed.

"You've got three seconds to eff off and spare yourselves my wrath," Tank said. "One, two . . ."

The two children scattered. Tank nodded. "Thought so," he said. He turned back to Molly. "Little cowards. Sorry about that. No manners. Little *savages*, just as you said."

"Who are little savages?" Chase asked, making Molly turn again. She hadn't heard him approach, either. He handed her a few wet naps.

"Who do you think?" Tank replied.

Molly rose to her feet, ripping open a wet-nap packet, trying to regain her composure as she wiped down her blades. How much had Chase and Tank overheard of the conversation between her and the pair of children?

She wasn't sure what bothered her. It wasn't as if they didn't already know how freaky she looked. Hell, she could see it herself in a mirror. But it was easier when she was alone to convince herself that her appearance wasn't a big deal—that it was kind of geeky cool, almost superhero-like. But here, back in society—or what was left of it—with people who didn't understand the intended purpose of the lenses and razors, Molly definitely felt like a freak.

"You need to teach those brats some manners," Chase declared. "If I hear one more of them 'whatever' me, I swear to God . . ."

Tank laughed. "Reminds me of Tara, you know," he said, watching Darla and Red wrestling in the corner. "Every time one of them says it, I feel like she's back with us."

Chase scowled at his brother. "I thought we decided not to talk about her anymore."

"Come on, Chase. Ignoring her death won't bring her back. We should celebrate the time we had with her. After all, she was—"

Chase held up a hand. "Whatever, man. Do what you want. Say what you want. I'm going to get Molly her supplies and then go play ball."

"Oh, no you don't. It's your turn to guard Spud," Tank corrected. "Rocky's been on guard duty since early this morning."

"Oh God, you still got a guard on him?" Chase cried, rolling his eyes. "That's ridiculous. It's been two weeks. He hasn't changed a hair on his head. He's clean. He's fine."

"We don't know that. He could still change."

"Change?" Molly asked, not able to help herself from asking. "What do you mean?"

"Spud got a tiny bit knicked up by one of the Others a couple weeks ago when we were out gathering food," Chase explained. "So Tank here put him in jail."

"Quarantine," Tank clarified. "Not jail."

"The dude's been in the supply closet for two straight weeks," Chase argued. "And he's totally fine."

"What about that infection on his inner thigh?"

"It's just an ingrown hair. Or a boil. You know Spud never bothers to use soap when he bathes. He's dirty. But that doesn't mean, he's . . . you know."

"He's what?" Molly asked.

"Infected."

"You don't know that," his brother insisted. "It hasn't been long enough to tell."

"What could happen?" Molly asked.

"Infection. The Others like to eat people, right? Well, sometimes they only get a bite in before we kill them. But that bite is bad news. Some people . . . change."

She shook her head. "It's just like an old zombie flick."

Chase nodded. "Yeah, exactly like that. Who knew it was real? Although, I guess it's not like any one zombie movie. Sort of a mix of a bunch.

"Anyway, some of us are immune. Tank here is for sure. He's been bitten by Others about three or four times now, and he's completely fine. But you never know who's going to be okay and who's not. So we put anyone bitten in quarantine. Monitor them."

"And your friend was bitten two weeks ago?"

"Yes. About that. And he's fine. Totally immune," Chase claimed. "I saw him this morning and he was doing crossword puzzles."

"I want to keep him two more days," Tank said. "We're better off being safe than sorry. I don't want him transforming in the middle of the night while we're asleep and eating the other children."

Molly shuddered. Monsters that ate children. Monsters that were children eating children. And here she'd been in a hurry to leave the fallout shelter? The sooner she got to Disney, the better.

"What about you?" she asked Chase. "Are you immune?"

He grinned. "I don't know. Never let one get close enough to find out. I'm called Chase for a reason."

"You've been lucky," Tank reminded him. "But luck doesn't hold out forever. Especially for people as foolhardy as you."

"Whatever."

"See? You're as bad as the children."

Chase stuck up his middle finger, then grabbed a nearby shopping cart and whirled it around. The wheels squeaked in protest. "Come on, let's go get your supplies," he said to Molly. To Tank he said, "I'll relieve Rocky when I'm done."

"Fine. Just don't come crying to me when he rips you a new one."

"It's cool, Tank. I'll deal. We'll only be a few minutes anyway."

Chase made the cart do a wheelie and then pushed it down the aisle. Molly followed, a little disconcerted. She didn't get him. He acted angry one moment then completely blasé the next. What was up with him? Neither personality fit what she remembered. He'd been a sweet, earnest boy who'd sacrifice everything if only someone asked.

Of course, in a way she had asked. And he'd sacrificed. And then she'd rejected that sacrifice without ever offering an explanation. It was no wonder he acted a bit resentful. She'd likely feel the same way.

He turned left, pushing the cart in front of him. Away from the laughter and light, the store started seeming a bit spookier. With only Chase's dim flashlight working, Molly activated the night vision option on her implants in order to drive away the imagined ghosts. It was then that she realized Chase was looking at her strangely.

"What?" she asked. Did he think she was a freak like Darla and Red had but was too polite to say it?

He shrugged. "I don't know. I guess I can't believe you're actually here. I never thought I'd see you again." He tossed a large backpack into the cart, followed by a water purifier and some bottles. "You know, after you stood us up and all."

She stifled a sigh. Here came the anger. She deserved it, she guessed. But that wouldn't make the feelings easier to handle. She wished there was a way to move on without a discussion. She wished . . .

"I never thought I'd see you again, either," she said, realizing the comment sounded lame and patronizing. After all, it'd been her choice. Sort of.

He stopped the cart and looked at her. She couldn't read his expression. "You know, I waited for you," he said.

She hung her head, guilt gnawing at her insides as she pictured the scene. "I didn't mean . . . I didn't mean for that to happen."

He stayed still, staring at her so hard she felt naked. "What happened?" he said at last. "Why didn't you come, Molly? After all that we talked about, why didn't you show?"

Gone was all the arrogance, the cocky grin. In its place was vulnerability, an old hurt he'd probably tried to bury for years. Anguish flickered across his handsome face. It made her want to answer. To explain it all away. But she knew that he wouldn't understand, and her explanation would only hurt him further. What was done was done and there was no taking it back. Better to move forward.

"Does it really matter?" she asked. "I mean, will it make any difference?"

He sighed, looking disappointed. After a moment he made up his mind. "I guess not," he said. "Forget it. Sorry I asked."

She forced herself to turn away, unable to bear the pain radiating from his body like heat from a fire. But she was a razor girl with a mission, not just Molly Anderson from his past. She was the worst person in the world and knew it. She'd hurt him before and here she was, hurting him all over again. She could lie to him, try to smooth over the past, but what would that help? Every answer led to his continued pain. It would have been better had they never reunited.

"Can we just concentrate on the supplies?" she suggested.

He nodded and switched gears abruptly, turning off his emotions. He'd probably had to do that a lot over the years.

Just like she had. She fought the urge to spit as he led her down several more aisles.

"Okay," he said, throwing a few last things into the cart. "We've got you a backpack, dehydrated food, a water purifier, a solar flashlight, a sleeping bag and a tent. What else do you think you'll need?"

"How about a mule to carry it?" She groaned, looking at the almost full cart. The realities of the trip were beginning to sink in, and it wasn't looking pretty.

"Mule, no," Chase said. "We might be able to score you a horse, though. Ever ridden one?"

She raised an eyebrow, surprised. "Yes," she said. "I had lessons when I was a kid. Are horses still around, though—I mean, somewhere we could get one?"

"Sure." He nodded. "We rounded some up after we came out of the shelter. They're great for transportation now that cars don't really work. You must have noticed how the roads are all blocked up. We have like five or six in a makeshift stable. I'll see if Tank's cool with you taking one. I doubt it'll be a problem."

"Thanks, that'd be great." She felt an overwhelming relief. Trekking to Disney on horseback would be a heck of a lot easier than on foot or bike. "I owe you, man."

Chase gave her another look. "Before we head back," he said. "There's something I want to show you, okay?"

"What?" she asked, wondering what on Earth it could be.

He beckoned for her to follow. "Follow," he said. "And you'll see."

CHAPTER TEN

Chris passed his own house that afternoon, his step light and his mouth involuntarily quirking. He couldn't help a half-grin despite the weightiness of the problem he'd set out to solve. He couldn't believe his luck! Molly Anderson had invited him over after school. Sure, it was just to help investigate Mrs. McCormick's weird disappearance, but he'd take what he could get. He'd been looking for an excuse to talk to her since first grade, when she'd yelled at him for pulling her braids, and not even the solemnity of this occasion could dispel a small thrill of excitement.

He approached her house, his heart pounding in anticipation. Maybe after they'd talked to her dad, she would invite him to dinner. Or maybe they could go out for a soda. They'd start talking and she'd see that he was more than just the dork she assumed. He knew that, just given an opportunity, he could be the perfect guy for her. He just *knew* it. All he needed was a chance.

She was turned away from him in her driveway, a basketball in her hands. There was a hoop above her, and she shot at it. He squinted, surprised. She was playing basketball? Real-life basketball? He couldn't remember the last time he'd seen anyone play an actual sport. Then he remembered the rumors he'd heard. Her dad was some kind of crazy conspiracy theorist who didn't even let her own a sim deck. Chris hadn't believed it, though. Honestly, who didn't have a sim deck in this day and age? And besides, he'd seen her cheering on the virtual sidelines of Basketball Dayz plenty of times. So maybe it wasn't true. Still, there she was, outside and playing real-life basketball, which was weird to say the least.

He stood at the end of the driveway for a moment, mesmerized by her agility and strength. Her arms stretched above her head as she aimed again. There was a tiny flash of flesh between her shirt and her shorts, and it was more desirable than any of the full-frontal nudity sims Tank had shown him. The fabric of her shorts pulled tight across her butt, and Chris gulped. As she took her shot, effortlessly hopping on one foot and watching the ball swish through the hoop, he fought the urge to clap. Impressive. He barely managed to score in the sim.

The ball rolled down the driveway and she turned to chase it. Stopped as her eyes fell on him. He grabbed the ball before it could roll into the street.

"Um, yes?" she said, her voice cold. "What do you want?"

He was taken aback. "I thought . . . You said . . . We were going to ask your dad . . ." Had he misheard? Had she changed her mind? Disappointment washed over him. Had he made a bigger fool of himself than ever?

"Oh." Some flicker of recognition lit her eyes. He squinted at her, noticing for the first time that her cheeks were blotchy. Her eyes were bloodshot. She'd been crying!

How dare someone make his goddess cry? A wave of protectiveness mixed with anger washed over him, and he wished more than anything he could just walk up and hug her, fix whatever was wrong, no matter what it was. Of course she'd probably rather hug a muddy pig, so he decided against following through.

"That's right," she said, rubbing a hand against her cheek. "Sorry. I forgot."

"What happened?" he asked, walking up and handing her the basketball. He might not be allowed to touch her, but he could still sympathize. "You okay?"

"I'm fine," she said. The words were too quick to be

believable. She grabbed the ball. "Listen, do you think you could come tomorrow or something? This isn't a good time for me."

What was the deal? Had she learned something more about Mrs. McCormick? But no, she barely knew the woman and would simply tell him. It had to be something bigger, something more personal, something that had nothing to do with him. Had someone she knew died? Had she gotten in trouble with her parents? Failed a test in school? What? It was driving him crazy, and she obviously wasn't going to tell him.

Why *should* she tell you? a voice inside his head jeered. After all, Molly had no reason to love him like he loved her. He was a geek. A nerd. A nobody. Hell, he was lucky she'd even let him set foot on her driveway.

Still, now that she had, he wasn't going to let her off the hook. He took the ball back and dribbled it a few times, prepared for a shot. It felt heavy in his hands, very different than the virtual ball they played with in Basketball Dayz. Holding it over his head, he threw in the direction of the hoop. It hit the backboard and bounced away. "Damn." He raced after the ball. "I suck in real life as bad as I do in the sim." Grabbing it and bouncing it back to the center of the driveway, he gave her an apologetic grin.

"Sim basketball's for nerds," Molly scoffed, grabbing the ball away and laying it up into the hoop. She was good. And so hot. As the ball bounced back to her, she passed it. Chris caught it and shot again. This time it bounced off the rim.

"Closer," she said, half-smiling. She caught the ball and bounced it to him. "Try again."

He caught the ball and looked up at the hoop. Concentrating this time, he aimed first. Pictured the shot going in. Pictured Molly being impressed.

He shot.

It bounced off his head.

As it rolled down the driveway, he rushed after it, his face burning. He swiped it up with both hands, turned and shot without thinking, wanting to rid himself of the stupid ball for good—

Swish!

"Damn!" he cried. He was so surprised and pleased, excited by his accomplishment that he'd all but forgotten it was a ploy to get her to talk.

Molly gave him a thumbs-up. "Not bad," she said approvingly. "Not bad at all when you don't think so hard."

"One more," he told her, feeling all warm inside. "And if I make this one, you have to tell me why you've been crying."

Molly considered. "Okay," she said at last. "You'll never get two in a row anyway."

Oh, wouldn't he? They'd see about that. He bounced the ball twice then caught it. Aimed again, sucking in a breath but also trying not to think . . .

The shot bounced off the rim.

"Damn," he said again, but this time with less joy.

Molly laughed, collecting the rebound. "Ha!" she said. "Too bad, so sad!"

Chris sighed. "Oh, come on," he said. "You want to tell me regardless."

She stopped the little victory dance she was doing, her expression sober. "Oh, fine," she said. "You're going to probably find out tomorrow in school anyway." She walked to the stone wall dividing her house from the neighbor's and sat down on it. Chris joined her, his heart beating as fast as he could ever remember. He was so close he could reach out and touch her. Of course, that would end any chance of her talking to him, so he managed to resist the urge. If only she wasn't so damn pretty. That gorgeous, long blonde hair and those beautiful blue eyes. He could barely stand it.

"It's Drew," she explained. "I caught him . . . He was kissing Brenda Booker."

Chris made a retching noise before he thought. "Gross!"

Molly turned, slight amusement coloring the sadness in her eyes. "You don't approve?"

"Of Brenda Booker? I wouldn't fuck her with your dick

and Trey pushing. Didn't she have her LTF revoked?" Then he had a brief moment of horror at what he'd said to her.

Molly just gave a half-smile. "I don't know," she said. "I guess you'll have to ask Drew."

"Well, he always was a bit of an idiot." Chris knew he was being too daring, but he didn't care. That Drew had hurt Molly made him furious inside.

She stared down at her feet, looking so sad that Chris once again wanted nothing more than to reach out and hug her and tell her everything would be okay. That she didn't want to date such a loser anyway. But he didn't know if any words of comfort would help. Also, sadly, he was pretty positive she'd reject any physical comfort.

"I'm sorry," he said. "You don't deserve that. It'd be better not to sleep with anyone than Brenda Booker."

She looked at him quietly for a moment, her mouth still quirked in a half smile. Then she said, "I punched him in the nose."

Chris's eyes widened. He couldn't imagine punching Drew, because he knew what would happen to him if he did. "Nice," was all he said.

"I think I broke it, actually. I've been training a ton, and I'm pretty strong."

Chris couldn't believe his ears. His day couldn't have gone better. "I can't wait to see him in school tomorrow. He's going to be so embarrassed! To be shown up by a girl! Lawlz!" He caught himself too late. "Um, not that there's anything inferior about girls."

For the first time, Molly laughed. He'd made her laugh! "Yeah, don't worry. I know what you mean," she said. "And thanks. For listening and stuff. And for shooting hoops with me. Basketball always makes me feel better."

His heart was pounding again. "I'll listen anytime," he said. "And shooting hoops was fun. I'd love to try it again sometime."

"It's a deal," she said. When she held out her hand, he took it in his and shook, shocked by the tingle of electricity that passed between them. He wondered what it'd be like to hug her. To hold her. To feel her body against his. He'd probably go into cardiac arrest.

She dropped her hand quickly, and he wondered if she'd felt the jolt, too. Her expression was unreadable.

"Anyway," she said. "Let's go find my dad."

CHAPTER ELEVEN

Molly followed Chase down the aisles toward the Garden and Patio section. He pushed open a door and led her into a large, colorful greenhouse. The walls of the house were blocked off with metal, but the glass ceiling was still uncovered and let in the last of the evening light. Lush emerald vines loaded with plump tomatoes and shiny yellow peppers climbed brightly painted trellises in the center of the room. Fresh herbs sprouted from small planters lining one wall. Carrot tops poked through the dirt in a trough.

She twirled around, impressed, taking it all in. "This is amazing," she remarked. "When you said you grew your own food, I figured maybe you had a few raspberry bushes or something."

"With all the mouths to feed we needed more than that," Chase explained. "So Tank rigged this up a few years ago. Spud's our resident gardener—when he's not stuck in a cage and waiting to morph into a monster, that is." He laughed.

Molly wandered over to a tomato plant, salivating. "Can I . . . ?" she asked. "I haven't had any fruits or vegetables that didn't come from a can in six years."

"Be my guest."

She snapped a small tomato off the vine and bit into it. The juicy sweetness filled her mouth and she practically moaned with pleasure. "Oh, God. This is so good," she said with her mouth full.

Chase laughed again. "When you're done with your orgasm, come outside and see what I really wanted to show you." He walked to the far side of the greenhouse and unlocked a metal door. Curious, she followed, still munching on the tomato.

Outside, she found they were in a small section walled off with cinder blocks but open to the night air. Chase pointed. "Basketball," he said. "Just like old times."

"Wow," Molly marveled. It was a portable pole and hoop that he'd clearly relocated from the Gaming section inside. She took the last good bite of her tomato. "I haven't seen one of these in six years. Virtual or real."

He grabbed a grungy ball off the ground and tossed it to her. She caught it and dribbled a few times. The synthetic leather slapping against her palm brought back memories of days outside her house. She remembered Chase joining her that first time, right after Drew broke her heart. She hadn't had any true feelings for him then; he'd just been a boy with a crush. But afterward . . .

It was best not to think of such things.

"No? Well, then that gives me the advantage," Chase boasted, and he lunged at her. She dodged quickly and dribbled around him toward the hoop. Raised the ball over her head and laid it up.

"Damn," she swore, as the ball bounced harmlessly off the rim and into Chase's awaiting hands. "There was a day I'd never have missed that."

Chase shot the ball into the net with ease. "I've been practicing," he said. "Not much else to do once the chores are done." He dribbled twice then passed. She took another shot. This one went in.

She cheered, feeling a moment of happiness. Chase gave her a high-five then chased the ball, which was rolling away from them and into the greenhouse. She watched him go, a flush warming her cheeks as her eyes found his tight butt. Damn, he looked good in those leather pants. And it was nice to feel normal, to think about how things might have been, if only for a few minutes.

How odd it was, thinking about the repercussions of choices you made. What would have happened if she had gone with Chris and the gang instead of into the shelter? They might have had a chance romantically, but would she have survived? Trey and Chris had left with a bunch of other students. Molly hadn't seen any of them here.

Chase returned with the ball, checked it to her. She bounced it back. He dribbled toward the hoop. She stayed in front of him, anticipating his path. He stopped just under the backboard, lifted his hands to shoot . . . She knocked the ball from his hands, sending it bouncing away.

"I'm starting to remember," she said.

"Guess I should stop taking it easy on you then."

They played for probably a good half-hour, the lead always changing. Chase's jump shot had really improved, Molly noticed, and she was impressed that he played well though there was little light. Throughout the game, they traded verbal jabs. For a brief period there was no apocalypse, no betrayal; they were just two friends playing one-on-one.

Until they heard the scream.

Molly and Chase looked at one another. Chase's face was white as a ghost under the sheen of sweat. Molly was sure she looked similar. He dropped the ball and started toward the door. "Come on," he said.

Molly didn't need a second invitation.

Chase darted down the aisle, not looking back to see if Molly was following. His heart pounded and adrenaline pulsed through his veins. On the way through the Sporting Goods section he used his flashlight to find a golf club—not exactly the perfect weapon, but it was the best thing in reach.

Another scream. Oh God, what was happening?

He could feel Molly behind him, her footsteps echoing his. They swung around a corner and burst into the Toys section. What once had been an oasis of children's laughter and games was now a horror show. The lights were tipped over. Toys were strewn everywhere. The children were all running and screaming.

At first Chase couldn't figure out what the hell was going on. Then his eyes fell upon the monster: Spud. Or, more accurately, what had once been Spud.

No, this was no longer his goofy, geeky friend. In Spud's place stood a horrifying monster with red eyes, razor-sharp teeth and bleeding, pus-filled sores. His clothing was shredded—it must have torn in the metamorphosis—and only scraps still clung to his body. A Rolex dangled from his wrist—the one Spud and Chase had stolen from Neiman Marcus one day when they were bored. Spud was one of them now. An Other. And somehow he'd gotten out of his cage. The cage Chase was supposed to be guarding instead of playing basketball with Molly.

There was only a moment to hesitate, to mourn the loss of yet another friend, because Chase knew what was coming next, what had already begun. His friend was now a destroyer and needed to be destroyed. There was no alternative.

He sprang into action, swinging his golf club at the creature with as much force as he could muster. The nine iron struck Spud's head with a sickening thud, sending the zombie sprawling. But that wasn't going to stop him. Spud righted himself quickly and charged forward, bellowing an inhuman cry. He grabbed the club from Chase's hand and snapped it in two.

Oh shit.

Chase leapt backwards to avoid the creature's arms, his eyes darting around and searching for another weapon. Luckily for him, Spud didn't pursue him. Instead, his old friend turned and went for Darla, who was cowering nearby. Chase screamed in rage, hoping to distract it.

Suddenly Molly was there, right in between Spud and the little girl. Blades shot from her fingertips with an elegant violence that took Chase's breath away. Without pause she engaged, striking Spud in the chest. Chase's former friend screamed as blood soaked what remained of his Gothic Robots from Hell concert T-shirt.

Molly wasn't finished. Her foot found Spud's groin, and the Other keeled forward. Chase felt a moment of relief that the monsters weren't true Hollywood zombies and still felt pain. Molly didn't pause; she took the opportunity to grab Spud's head and twist, snapping the neck. Spud fell to the ground, dead. *Really* dead. Chase let out a sigh of relief, forcing himself to forget that the creature she'd just killed was one of his best friends, trying to focus on the fact that Darla was safe and unharmed.

Molly leaned over and vomited. Chase didn't blame her. He was pretty sick to his stomach as well. Seeing one's friend morphed into a monster and trying to chomp little children could do that to a guy. He forced himself to look away from the mayhem, remembering all the stupid pranks he and Spud had pulled back in the refugee camp.

Stupid old Spud. Stupid, stupid Spud. He felt bile rise in his throat and forced it back down.

"Chase, Chase!" Red cried, appearing out of nowhere. The little boy tugged at his pant leg.

"What is it, Red?" When Chase looked down, he saw that the child's normally brave face was stained from tears.

"Tank. You gotta help Tank."

Chase's heart leapt into his throat. "What do you mean?" he asked. In the chaos, he hadn't processed that his brother was missing.

"Spud hurt him," Red said, yanking at his hand.

Chase left Molly where she was puking and let the boy lead the way down an aisle, fear slamming his heart against his chest. A moment later his eyes fell on his brother lying motionless in an ocean of blood. Chase flew to Tank's side, on his knees, peering into his brother's face. Tank's eyes fluttered open. He was alive. Thank God.

"He got me," Tank said, his voice strangely gurgling. "He killed Rocky and then came after me."

Chase glanced over and saw Rocky's body a little ways off in the darkness. He felt tears welling up in his eyes and a lump clogging his throat. His best friend and his only brother. "God," he said. "How bad?" At least Tank was immune to the infection. He'd be okay. He had to be okay.

"Chase, I need you to promise me you'll look after the kids."

Chase struggled to understand. "What? What are you talking about?" he asked, the lump in his throat now threatening to choke him. "You're going to be fine. We can stitch you up. Get you some antibiotics and—"

Tank reached out and brushed a lock of hair from his eye. "Chase, I don't have much time. I need you to promise me. I'm not kidding."

Chase squeezed his eyes shut, trying to block out the pain. This couldn't be happening. First Tara, now Tank. It wasn't right. It wasn't fair. And, once again, it was all his fault. If he hadn't been so distracted he could have done something.

"You're going to be fine!" he said, trying to sound cheerful. "What hurts? We'll fix it!" His hands roved his brother's body, seeking out injuries. It was then that he saw the wound in Tank's lower back and side. It had been concealed by the way he was lying, but it was grievous. Chase felt the gorge rise in his throat and leaned over to let it out.

"Chase, focus!" Tank commanded, his voice weak but determined. His skin was very white. "The kids need you. I need you to promise me you'll look after them. You're all they have now."

"But . . . I can't!" Chase cried, his life flashing before his eyes. "I'm not like you. I can't take care of them. I can barely take care of myself. Look what happened to Tara! I couldn't save her!"

"No, you couldn't save Tara. But you can save *these* children. Do it for Tara. And for me."

"But I'm not like you. I can't lead them," Chase said.

His brother's face twisted in a combination of anger and hurt. "Grow the fuck up, man," he growled. "*There's no one else.*"

Chase paused, anguished. Then he swallowed. "I promise," he said. "God, Tank, what will I do?"

"You'll manage." Tank's eyes rolled up in his head for a moment, then he drew a deep breath and forced himself to look at Chase. "You're stronger than you think. You're not a fuckup—or you don't have to be. I have faith in you. And I love you, man."

"I . . . I love you, too."

But he'd said it too late. His brother's eyes were closed, and Tank's final breath had just escaped in a long, torturous wheeze. He was dead.

Chase threw back his head and screamed.

CHAPTER TWELVE

Chris followed Molly down the stairs.

"Dad, this is Chris. Chris, this is my dad," Molly called as they entered the basement. Her father was sitting in a lab off to one side, working on some kind of metal gizmo. He set the device down, came out of the workshop and shut and locked the door behind him. Off limits to tourists, Chris guessed.

"Ian Anderson." Molly's dad introduced himself, putting out a hand. The guy looked like a mad scientist with his shock of graying hair and wild blue eyes. Hard to believe he was Molly's father. "It's nice to meet you, son. I saw you two playing basketball outside. It's great to see kids enjoying real sports in this day and age. Everyone's always inside on their sims twenty-four-seven. Missing out on what the great outdoors has to offer."

"I thought it was awesome," Chris agreed. "I'd never played before. Of course, I'm kind of sweaty and gross now." He sniffed his armpit and made a face.

Ian slapped him on the back. "Nothing wrong with a little sweat," he proclaimed. "It'll put hair on your chest. Now, what can I do for you kids? I'm kind of busy at the moment."

"I know, Dad, I know. But I figured you'd be interested in this." Molly paused. "I should have come to you before, but . . . well, I wasn't sure if it was important and didn't want to bother you. Have you heard anything about weird disappearances related to illness? Anything to do with the government? A few days ago Chris and I came across Mrs. McCormick from down the street. She was acting all sick, coughing up blood. We called for an ambulance, but instead this strange brown van showed up. It had a government seal. They took her away."

Chase noticed she didn't add anything about them being chased. He guessed she just didn't want to worry him.

"That was a few days ago, and she hasn't been back to her house since," Molly said. "I figured she might have died, but—"

"I called all the nearby hospitals," Chris spoke up. "They said they were taking her to Mount Holyoke, but the guys in the van didn't really even know where it was—and no one there's heard of her. And when I went searching some of the Internet forums about this, I found similar things are happening other places." He crossed his fingers that he wouldn't get the usual lectures about accessing unauthorized sites; adults seemed to think that what the government banned really shouldn't be talked about. He figured Molly's dad, if anyone, would feel differently. After all, he was about as anti-establishment as anyone could get. "Molly thought maybe you would have read or heard something else."

Ian looked distracted. "Sorry," he said, shaking his head. "No, I haven't heard anything."

"Is there . . . is there any way you could take a look?" Chris pressed. He didn't want to be rude, but he was worried about Mrs. McCormick, and Molly's dad seemed the only option for information. Rumor had it that he knew all sorts of people in high places, although not all of them were friendly.

"That woman was like a grandmother to me," he explained. "I'm worried something really bad might have happened to her, and she's got no one else who'd care."

Molly's father sighed. "What did the van look like again?"

"Brown," Molly said. "And like I said, there was a government seal on the side."

"The men had brown uniforms, too?"

"Yes," Chris said, remembering. "They did."

"Cleaners," Mr. Anderson said. "Government cleaners.

They're called the DNP, the Department of Natural Progressions, but basically they get paid to get rid of messes."

"Messes? What mess could an old lady like Mrs. McCormick be in?" Molly spoke up. "That doesn't make any sense."

"Look, our government has its own agenda that we can't even try to understand. You two are very lucky they didn't come after you," her father said sternly. He waggled a finger at Molly and Chris. "The next time you see a van like that, leave the area immediately. I don't care who they're taking away. Do not get involved, whatever you do."

"But—" Chris started.

Mr. Anderson glowered at him. "No buts," he said. "It's dangerous and stupid for you to mess with government operations. They don't care that you're just kids. If they think you know something, they'll remove you without a second thought."

For the first time, Chris felt true fear crawl through his stomach. He'd been nervous when he and Molly were chased, but that had just felt like something from a Smart TV show or a sim. Was this guy right? Would the government actually do something like "remove" him? It was tough to credit.

Of course, they had given chase, and Mrs. McCormick really had disappeared.

"Okay, Dad, we got it," Molly said, grabbing Chris's hand. She began to drag him upstairs. "Government agents are bad. We'll stay away."

"Mock me if you will, daughter!" Ian called after them. "But mark my words. This is the End of Days we're living in. Many will fall. Only a few will rise like phoenixes from the ashes. These will create a new heaven and Earth."

Wow, the rumors were right, Chris marveled as they reached the top of the stairs. Molly's father was out of his goddamned mind. End of days, indeed! How ridiculous was that?

They stepped out into the living room, and Molly closed the door behind them. Chris noticed her face was flushed. Was she embarrassed by what her dad had just said? She shouldn't be. He didn't judge her by her parents. He tried to avoid judging anyone by anyone else.

"Hey, kids, come in here!" cried a woman's voice from the kitchen. "I want you to try my cookies." It was like jumping from an Operation: Terror sim into a Mrs. Rogers's Kiddie-time sim, but Chris found he didn't mind the transition.

They entered the kitchen to find Molly's mother setting down a plate full of delicious-looking cookies. The room was warm and smelled like chocolate. The creepy feeling Chris had felt down in the basement started to dissipate. At least one member of Molly's family was normal.

"I need your opinion," Molly's mother told them. "Are these good enough to sell at the church bake sale this Sunday?"

They obediently tried the cookies. "Mmmmm," Chris said. "These are delicious." And he wasn't exaggerating to get into her good graces; he hadn't tasted such a wonderful cookie in forever. "Thanks, Mrs. Anderson. Can I have another?"

Molly's mother beamed at him. "Of course," she said. Then she turned to her daughter. "I like him," she mouthed, but Chris caught it.

Motherly approval? Nice.

Molly didn't know what was more embarrassing: her crazy father talking about the end of the world or her matchmaking mother. Her mom had never liked Drew; she was going to be psyched when Molly informed her of the breakup.

First she had to get rid of Chris, though. Grabbing another cookie and motioning for him to follow her outside, she hoped he'd take the hint and go home. Not that she minded his company; it'd been good to have someone to play basketball with today. But now she was ready to wallow again in the pain of the whole Drew situation. Why hadn't she walked away when she'd had a chance? Why hadn't she broken up with him before this? And why had she thought it was a good idea to break his nose? Now everyone in school was going to think she was crazy like her dad. That was just the reputation she'd been trying to avoid.

"Sorry my dad wasn't more helpful," she said, wandering

over to the nearby stone wall. Chris followed, evidently not interested in saying good-bye yet. What a surprise.

"It's okay." He shrugged, hopping up on the wall. "I mean, he's right in a way. Not about the end of the world or anything, but he's probably right that it's a good idea to stay away from government agents. I'm glad we ran."

She half laughed. "Me, too. And I'm glad I didn't tell him what really happened. He probably would have locked me in my room for the next six years."

"Well, he just wants to protect you," Chris said. "Which is nice."

"Yeah, real nice," Molly snapped. "Do you know I'm stuck every day after school doing martial arts training with him? It's so I'll be prepared for the coming apocalypse."

Chris looked surprised. "Really? That's hardcore." He paused then added, "Though, maybe it's a good idea? Just in case?" He was trying to be nice. She'd give him that.

"Whatever." She shrugged. "Personally I fail to see how martial arts will help if we're talking Armageddon." She sighed, feeling suddenly old. "The world will either end or it won't. There's nothing we can do about it. There's nothing we can do about anything."

"You're still upset about Drew," Chris observed, picking a piece of broken glass off the top of the wall. Their neighbors liked to have rowdy barbeques and, try as they might, the Andersons were never able to get rid of all the after-party evidence.

"That obvious, huh?" she said with a small snort. "I guess I just feel stupid. Like such a loser."

Chris shook his head. "Please," he said. "Because of *him?*"

He was sweet. But he had no clue. "You don't understand," she said. "I punched out the most popular kid at school. My family's kind of weird. Tomorrow I'm going to be a total social outcast, some leper that everyone will go out of their way to avoid. I'd kind of hoped . . . Well, this is what I'd wanted to avoid. Drew was—"

Chris grabbed her hand with a suddenness that startled her, pried open her fingers and deposited in her palm the shard of broken glass he'd picked up. She looked down at it then up at him.

"Um," she said. What was this about?

"Tell me. What is that?" he asked.

Was he for real? "A piece of a broken beer bottle?" she said.

"No." He shook his head. "You're wrong. What you're holding in your hand is a diamond."

She rolled her eyes. He was too much. "Excuse me?"

He took the shard back and held it up to the sun. Molly had to admit, it did have a beautiful sparkle from that angle. But it was still no diamond.

"Sure, this may look like something busted off a beer bottle, but it's not. To me it's a diamond. That's what *I* say it is—and who are you going to believe?" He handed it back to her. "You see, I know it's a diamond because I found it when I was with you, and when I'm with you wonderful things happen. Why couldn't I have just found a diamond? It's Drew's problem if he can't see the precious gems in his driveway. Don't you make the same mistake."

His words hit her just right, and Molly's breath hitched in her throat. This was without a doubt the sweetest, nicest thing anyone had ever said to her. The logic was a little iffy, but his heart was in the right place. She stared at the diamond, seeing it clearly now as a precious gem. Doing so made her smile.

"Thanks," she said, closing her hand around the offering, wanting to keep it close. "I'll try to remember that."

"Good," Chris said. His voice was breathy. Suddenly she realized how close he was to her. His leg was brushing hers. His face was only inches away. She shivered. What was *wrong* with her? Wasn't she trying to get rid of this guy? After all, she couldn't possibly be attracted to him. Geeky, dorky, Chris Griffin? Surely she'd never want to . . . kiss him?

He leaned over, a deadly serious look in his eyes, and for the first time she found herself noticing their color—green with swirls of blue and yellow. Kaleidoscopic eyes. Beautiful. Maybe she was wrong about him. Maybe she'd been ignoring something deep inside of her. Maybe she should kiss him, just to see what it'd be like . . .

Just before his lips could brush hers, she heard her dad's voice calling her name. It called her back to reality. She remembered all the reasons she hadn't wanted to date Chris in the first place, and she realized what an act like this would mean. She'd be leading him along, allowing him to build hope where there shouldn't be any.

She leapt off the wall, putting as much distance between them as possible. "Coming, Dad!" she called. Shooting Chris an apologetic look, she shrugged and motioned to her house. "He needs me," she said, feeling awkward and lame. But what had she been thinking? Chris Griffin? The breakup with Drew really must have thrown her.

Chris stared at her for a moment, glassy-eyed. "Oh, no problem," he finally said, recovering. He hopped off the wall. "Thanks for the basketball and letting me talk to your dad. I'll catch you at school." And with that, he turned and walked down the drive. He didn't look back.

She, on the other hand, found herself watching him all the way down the street until he turned the corner and disappeared from view.

CHAPTER THIRTEEN

Molly had been busy comforting the crying children and cleaning off her razors when she heard the scream. More danger? But no, this wasn't a cry of pain. More like a cry of anguish, amplified to a shocking decibel level. And it sounded like Chase.

"Stay here," she instructed the children. Then she ran to investigate.

Around a corner she found Chase crouched over Tank's blood-soaked body, tears streaming down his flushed cheeks. "Oh God," she murmured. Tank wasn't moving and she was pretty sure he wouldn't move ever again. Spud must have gotten him before going after the children. This was not good. Not good at all. Tank was the one who had saved all these children. Set up the shelter. Run the group. What would they do without him? And how was Chase going to deal with losing yet another member of his family? It was like Tara all over again.

Chase turned to look at Molly, his eyes wild and unfocused, his face a storm of rage. She took a step back, frightened suddenly of what he might do. Remembering how little she knew him now. Remembering how much he'd changed.

"Oh, Chase, I'm so sorry," she said, feeling useless and stupid. What could she say? What should she do? There seemed no practical way to provide comfort at this point. No words were going to help ease this pain. She felt saliva fill her mouth.

"You," he growled, his lips curled back. "This is *your* fault."

Her heart plummeted as she realized what was going on. He needed someone to blame for his brother's death, and she was the only one left who wasn't a child or a monster. She was the interloper here. Everything had been going fine until she returned to their lives.

The logic was ridiculous, of course, but Chase didn't exactly appear at his best.

"No, Chase, I—"

"If I hadn't been forced to help you gather your stupid supplies, I would have been here," he raged, not listening to her attempted protests. "I could have gotten to Spud before . . ." He made a sweeping gesture over his brother's corpse. "Before he did *this*." He slammed a fist against the floor. "I could have saved him. I could have stopped this!"

Part of her wanted to remind him it had been his idea to play basketball, but that seemed counterproductive. Why make him feel worse than he already did? His brother had just died; there was no need to play the blame game. And, besides, there was no way to predict alternate scenarios had there been no basketball. If Chase had been guarding Spud like he was supposed to, Spud might have killed him *and* Tank.

Still, it hurt to see the rage in his eyes. He was blaming her for everything. And there were things in the past that she was guilty about.

"Chase . . ." she began. She should have never come here, never have allowed herself to be distracted from her mission. But it had been so good to see him. She'd missed him over the years. Wondered what had happened to him. If he had survived. If he was okay. If they could ever be what they had once seemed destined to be. And then, to find him alive and well . . . Well, she was only human, after all. And it had seemed so harmless to indulge in one night. To go and see what might have been, had she made a different decision six years ago.

Now she was paying for that indulgence with the knowledge that Chase would probably hate her for the rest of his life. She was no longer able to pretend that maybe, just maybe, he had forgiven her and understood deep down why she had made the choice she had.

"Get the hell out of here," he growled; then he turned back to his brother.

She paused for a moment before turning and walking away. What else could she do? Tank was dead, and nothing she did or said could change that. It was better to just leave. She would just walk out of their lives forever and get on with her mission. After all, she had so little time to make it to Disney. She couldn't afford any more distractions.

She almost made it out. She walked through the aisles to the front doors of Wal-Mart into the night, never looking back, but then, like Lot's wife in Biblical times, she turned and glanced back into the store. She thought about the faces of the children she was leaving behind, the already homeless orphans who were now robbed of their finest protector as well, clinging to one another, frightened, lost, and alone. They'd need someone to comfort them tonight, to help them get past this latest tragedy. And Chase, cocooned in his own grief, didn't look like he was going to be that person.

She squared her shoulders and resolved herself. One night. She'd stay tonight as she'd originally planned, then she'd start her pilgrimage in the morning. This way she could make sure the kids had everything they needed and she could get Chase back on track. Tomorrow she'd set off to find her father.

Pain wrenched at Chase's gut until he couldn't even think; a vise of grief was crushing his chest. This was like Tara all over again, but this time he had no older brother to share his sadness. Half of him wanted to just curl up and die. That would make the pain end. After all, what did he have left to live for? The world was a nightmare, the last of his family and friends had been killed, and he and these few children were living day to day, like sitting ducks, waiting for the next Spud to pick them off.

He fingered the knife he'd taken from Tank's boot and

thought about how easy it'd be. One single cut down his wrist—or maybe something less girly, like a stab to the gut as those samurai used to do in Japan. Either way, he could off himself. A few minutes of physical pain and it'd be over forever. He could do that.

He lifted the knife then stopped, hand frozen by the memory of his promise to Tank. He'd sworn to stay and take care of the children. His brother would hold him to that. If there was an afterlife and the two ever saw each other again, he didn't want to be ashamed. He wanted his brother to respect him.

Kneeling beside the corpse, Chase lifted his brother's heavy, lifeless frame. He cradled Tank in his arms like a baby then staggered toward the front of the store, barely able to direct his flashlight. First he would find a place to bury his brother; he'd worry about the rest later.

Grabbing a shovel out of the Garden and Patio section, he managed to make it outside. A moon shone down in the night sky overhead. His mind was racing, filled with thoughts of self-recrimination. If only he hadn't been so distracted, had thought with his brain instead of his dick. If only he'd relieved Rocky like he was supposed to, none of this would have happened. Tank would still be alive. But, no. Once again he had failed. Just like with Tara. He remembered her broken, bruised body lying lifeless on that stage like it was yesterday. He hadn't been able to save her. He hadn't been able to save Tank or Rocky. He hadn't been able to save anyone. He was utterly worthless.

And now he had eight children depending on him, eight children more helpless and defenseless than Tara or Tank had ever been. What was he going to do?

Pushing all thoughts from his mind, he scanned the parking lot for zombies. Just after dusk was usually the quiet time—when they napped after gorging themselves with meat from the noon hunt. And sure enough, the coast seemed clear. He crossed the lot and entered the small adjacent field strewn with garbage and broken bottles. He stuck his shovel into the ground and stepped on it. Burial seemed a bit silly in some ways, what with the piles of skeletons everywhere you looked, but Chase couldn't bear to leave his brother's body exposed to the elements or to be ripped apart by feral dogs. Tank had been a good man. Noble, kind, true. He had taken good care of them all with no thought for himself. He deserved some dignity in death.

Sweat beaded on Chase's forehead as he dug. Thank goodness it wasn't winter, and the ground was soft. Even so, it took forever to create a hole big enough to inhume a large man like Tank. He finished at last, though, and wiped the sweat away with his sleeve, mumbling a little prayer to whichever god was left to listen. Then Chase dropped his brother in and started covering him over with dirt.

At first his brain entertained a wild notion that Tank would suddenly leap from the grave, claim he was just joking and he'd never leave his little brother alone in the world. But of course that didn't happen, and eventually he filled in the hole. Tank—or Trey Griffin as he'd once been known—was gone forever.

Chase dropped his shovel and sank to the ground, head in his hands. What was he going to do? Everyone his age was gone. Well, everyone except Molly, and she'd be leaving for Disney World soon. If she hadn't already. He felt horrible about yelling at her. After all, this wasn't her fault. She'd just caught him at the wrong moment, when rage had welled up inside and captured his every sense. He'd needed someone separate to blame—someone, *any*one—for the senselessness that had robbed him of his family. He now knew he was the one in the wrong.

Molly probably hated him. She'd probably wasted no time grabbing her supplies and heading out on her mission, leaving him alone with eight children for whom he had no idea how to care. He wouldn't blame her if she'd left, but it hurt to consider it nonetheless.

He sighed. What was he going to do—hole back up in Wal-Mart, wait for the next person to get bitten, the next person to die? How would he provide food for all of the kids? As much as he'd teased Tank about being a superior hunter, his brother had done quite a bit of the work himself. As had Rocky. And Spud had tended the garden. Chase didn't know the first thing about farming, and what if something laid him low?

He'd promised Tank he'd take care of them. He also had a fleeting premonition that if they stayed here, they'd die. But what was the alternative? What else could they do, and where could they go that was safe?

A light bulb went off above his head.

Disney World.

It was both a destination and hope. Molly had claimed that her father and his cronies were making it the last human outpost, a place where people could meet and rebuild the world. It was defensible, she'd said, and they would have beds enough for everyone. There'd probably be a lot of adults, too—meaning there would be people who'd know how to take care of children.

Of course, this plan would involve tagging along with Molly, the woman who'd betrayed him all those years ago, left him standing in the rain, cold and alone, risking his life for nothing. He still had feelings for her, wanted her to like him, but he didn't want to be indebted to her or ask her for any favors. He wanted to be the one in control this time. However, he didn't see any alternative. They could stay here and die or head for the one place where there might be hope.

He'd have to swallow his pride. But he'd be doing it for the children. For his brother.

"I think it's the right thing to do, Tank," he said to his brother's grave. "If we make it, we'll have a new future. The children will grow up safe. If not . . . well, maybe it's better to die on your feet than sitting on your ass."

Tank didn't reply, but Chase nonetheless felt a certainty growing inside him. This was definitely the right move. He just had to find Molly and convince her.

He felt tears welling up in his eyes again; once more he was reminded that no matter how far he'd come, he was still weak. He was still the stupid geek no one ever took seriously. Well, they'd have to now. There was no one else left.

He reached into his pocket and pulled out one of the pill bottles he'd scored just that afternoon. He was just going to take one, he decided as he messed with the stupid childproof cap. After all, he'd had a horrible day. Drugs, he'd found, did the trick of melting all the pain away.

Just a few moments of mindlessness, that was all. Then he'd go back to the Wal-Mart. He'd find Molly and convince her to take him and the kids to Disney World.

He could only hope she'd say yes.

CHAPTER FOURTEEN

"Was that one of the Griffin boys from down the street?" her mom asked as Molly walked back into the house. She was still fussing with her cookies. Not surprising. Every other woman in the world would have used a Smart Oven for perfect crispiness and flavor. Ashley Anderson did it the old-fashioned way.

Molly grabbed another cookie off the rack. "Yeah," she said, her mouth wonderfully full of chocolaty goodness. "He was just . . . helping me with some homework."

"He seems like such a *nice* boy," her mother remarked.

"I guess." Molly wasn't going to take the bait. Ashley had probably been spying on them out the window. She'd likely seen her daughter almost lose her head and make out with the school geek in the front yard. Bleh. It was bad enough that Molly could still feel Chris's fingers on the back of her hands, bad enough she still had a weird ache in her stomach, her traitorous body wanting to see where things might have led. She didn't need to hear Mom's encouragement on top of it.

But her mother wasn't the type to be dissuaded by vague answers. She continued, "His family is nice, too. They adopted that little African girl. She was an orphan, you know. We had a fundraiser for her."

"Yes, her name's Tara. I know," Molly snapped, a little exasperated. All she'd wanted was a cookie, and now she had to go see what her dad wanted. "Look, if there's something you want to say, why don't you come right out and say it?"

Her mom looked at her. "How's Drew?"

"There. That wasn't so hard, was it?" No, her mom didn't miss a trick. "Let's just say that Drew's no longer in the picture," she said. "Not that Chris is," she added quickly, lest Ashley get the wrong idea. "He was just comforting me about the whole thing."

"Oh, honey." Her mom rose from the kitchen table and walked over to give her a hug. But Molly suddenly realized she didn't need one.

"No, it's cool," she said, waving her mother off and surprised at just how okay she felt about things. "It's better this way, actually."

"Are you sure?" her mom asked, studying her. "The way you looked earlier, I was worried. I was waiting for the right moment to bring it up."

It was nice to know her mom cared, even if in this case she couldn't change anything. Molly fingered the diamond Chris had given her under the table, thinking about what he'd said. "You know what, Mom? I think it really is."

"Molly!" her dad called from the basement. "Are you up there?"

She groaned. "Gotta go," she told her mom. "Gotta see what Admiral Armageddon wants."

Her mother handed her a napkin full of cookies. "Take these down with you," she suggested. "Even the admiral himself has a weakness for chocolate chips. Maybe he'll go easy on you."

"Thanks, Mom." Molly grinned. She grabbed the cookies and headed downstairs.

Her dad was standing at the bottom, arms crossed over his chest, not looking at all pleased.

"Uh, I brought you some cookies?" Molly said, holding them out.

He shook his head. "Not hungry."

"What's wrong?" she asked. He looked really annoyed. What had she done to piss him off? Her training was going as well as could be expected, and she'd have more time to devote to it now that Drew was out of the picture.

"Molly, what was the meaning of you bringing that boy down here to talk to me?" her father asked. He spat the word *boy* as if attempting to expel poison. This was certainly a one-eighty from her mom's reaction.

"Er, what do you mean?" she asked. "What's the big deal?"

"The big deal, as you call it, is the end of the world. The apocalypse is almost upon us." Ian Anderson uncrossed his arms then crossed them again. She got a whiff of whisky on his breath. Great. Things were going to get better. "The government has spies everywhere. And we don't have the first clue regarding whom to trust."

"Uh, Dad? Chris is just a kid from school, not to mention our neighbor. He's lived down the street since he was six years old. He's definitely no government agent."

"And you know this, how? What if he was just recruited? You say he's lived down the street for years, yet I've never seen him in our house until today. Don't you think that's a bit convenient, especially when he's asking what he's asking about the government?"

"Well . . ." She sighed. "I used to think he was a bit of a geek, if you must know. I didn't want him here. But that's not 'cause he's suddenly turned James Bond. He's not a government plant. Trust me."

"You brought him down to my lab!" her dad continued, obviously not listening. "What if he saw something I was working on and is now off to report back?"

"Report back?" Molly cried, exasperated. "He's a high school kid, for God's sake! Who's he going to report to, the electro shop prof?"

"Molly, you're obviously not taking me very seriously," Ian scolded, walking back to his lab bench. "I would have expected more from you—especially now that you've seen the first signs."

Oh God, where was he going with this? Had he drunk

more whiskey than usual? Normally he only got a bit tipsy, and then only when he was working his hardest. "First signs?" she asked, knowing she should resist the urge to encourage him.

"Of the apocalypse. You know, disease. Plague. Your Mrs. McCormick is obviously one of the first to fall. And the government's scared. They know as well as I do that more will come. God will sweep down on this world and smite those who deny His name."

"Uh, okay." Molly let out a big sigh. Thank goodness Chris wasn't still around to hear this. She loved her dad but his conclusions were sketchy to say the least. There were a lot of problems in the world, yes. There might be government cover-ups, yes. But one sick old lady, weird government van-collection or no, did not an apocalypse make.

But it was better not to argue. "Sorry," she said. "I won't bring anyone down here again."

"Actually, I think it would be better if you never saw that boy again, either."

"*What?*" She wasn't prepared for her stomach's strong reaction to that mandate. It wasn't as if she'd made plans to hang out with Chris Griffin in the near future. But it was ridiculous for her dad to forbid it. "That's stupid."

"Is it?" Her dad peered over his black-rimmed glasses at her. "He wanted to come down to the lab. He wanted to ask questions."

"He was concerned about Mrs. McCormick!"

"So he told you."

"Oh God, Dad, I can't listen to this anymore." Molly started up the stairs. "I'm going to help Mom bake her cookies."

"Fine. But remember what I told you, Molly. More will fall. And we don't know whom we can trust."

"Right. Plague, famine, badness. Trust no one," she muttered. "And the truth is out there, and I want to believe." She couldn't resist adding the old *X-Files* joke. That was another old series she and Erin had downloaded. Fox Mulder, the FBI agent, was remarkably similar to her dad in some respects. Though the actor, David Duchovny, was a lot cuter.

A shout echoed up the stairs. "The end is near, Molly. I'm the only one who can save us!"

Yes, there were times she really wished she had a normal father.

CHAPTER FIFTEEN

"Okay, line up single file so I can count you."

Back in Toys, Molly barked orders at the whimpering children, trying to gain some semblance of control over the situation. The three youngest were crying. The middle ones were standing white-faced and stoic. The two oldest were off in a corner, whispering furiously.

Molly clapped her hands and repeated her order, not sure if they'd obey her or not. After all, it wasn't as if she had any claim to authority over them, save that she was older by a few years. What she really needed was Chase to come back. He, at least, would be a familiar authoritative face.

The children at last obeyed, shuffling into line, all eyes on her. They looked so shell-shocked and sad.

Molly ran a hand through her hair. Now what? What would a normal adult do in a situation like this? Though she was technically twenty-one, she still felt like a kid. She thought back to her parents. Her father would probably start barking at them, telling them there was no use in crying. Her mother would call for a big group hug and then organize a bake sale. Not that there was anyone left to buy cookies.

She decided to try something in-between, something kind but in control. She had to make them feel safe in her charge.

"Is anyone hurt?" she asked.

Shaking heads all around were the reply. After a pause, the littlest girl in line—Molly remembered she was called

Darla—stepped forward, a single blonde pigtail stuck in her mouth. "I got a boo-boo on my knee," she announced, sticking out her left leg for observation.

Molly knelt down, taking the leg carefully in her hands, examining the wound. She let out a breath when she saw that it was just a bruise—a small one, with no skin broken in any way. She lowered Darla's leg and looked up at the little girl.

"That must hurt a lot," she said in a serious voice. "How did it happen?"

"Dude, that's nothing," butted in another kid. "You shoulda seen Tank. He had his guts ripped out. They were all over the floor."

Molly winced as Darla and the brunette standing beside her burst into a fresh set of tears. Another kid said, "Shut up, Red." Great, they were fighting.

"Thank you, Doctor," she said, turning to the first boy. "Your detailed analysis is very helpful." She guessed he was just as upset but was overcompensating with false bravado. She wanted to stop that immediately.

The oldest girl stepped forward, a teen who wore a ridiculously short skirt and had spray-painted her hair with blue streaks. "I'm Starr," she announced. "Is Tank dead?"

Molly swallowed hard, not sure what to say. Then she decided the truth was probably best. After all, the kids would find out sooner or later. And she had a feeling they were pretty used to funerals.

"Yes," she said simply, looking from face to face. "I'm sorry, but he is."

The children nodded, staring down at their feet. They looked sad but not shocked. Which made sense, really. Pretty much everyone they'd ever loved had died. They likely didn't remember things any other way.

"Rocky's dead, too. And Spud. Who's going to take care of us?" demanded one of the triplets. "Who's going to hunt for food?"

"And tend the garden," added one of his brothers.

"And keep out the Others?" added the third.

"Who's going to read us stories?" asked little Sunshine, the brunette next to Darla. She stuck a grubby thumb in her mouth.

"Oh, please," Red said, rolling his eyes. "Who cares about stories?"

"I do," Darla growled, grabbing Sunshine's hand and giving Red the evil eye.

Starr snorted. "And you do, too, Red, even though you're too cool to admit it."

"Red likes stories, Red likes stories," the triplets began chanting.

"Shut up!" With a cry of fury, Red lunged at them. The three fought back.

Molly held up her hands in protest. "Enough!" she cried. "There's already been far too much violence today. I don't need it coming from you guys, too."

The fighting subsided. Eight pairs of eyes settled back on her. Great. Now what? she thought, frustrated. Chase needed to get his ass back to help out.

"Look," she said, "I know this is difficult. I know Tank was like a father to you guys and his death is a huge deal. But bad things have happened before, right? And you've gotten through them okay. You'll get through this, too. I promise."

"Will you stay with us?" asked Sunshine, pulling her thumb from her mouth. "Will you cook for us?" Her sky-blue eyes swallowed Molly whole. "Will you tell us stories?"

Molly cringed. How did one explain to a seven-year-old that you were one of the last people in the world and had a very important mission—one that could be humanity's only salvation? How could you explain that eight children were less important than however many others had survived and needed to be rescued?

Of course, who could be sure how many others had actually survived? For all Molly knew, these eight children were the world's future. She looked over the band of ragamuffins, with their dirty, makeup-stained faces and ridiculous outfits. What would her dad say? *Stop being so sentimental! You have*

more important things to do than babysit. Or would he understand that these children were a future she could see and
should bet on? Would he give her dispensation to delay her
task a few days?

She exhaled, realizing there was no easy answer. In the
meantime, there was one thing she could do: make life go on.

"Okay guys," she said. "Who's hungry? Let's get some food
in you. After we've eaten, those of you who aren't too cool
for stories are in for a treat."

When Chase woke up, it was still night. The full moon cast
eerie shadows on the rusted cars in the Wal-Mart parking lot,
and he was lying next to Rocky's grave, which he'd dug next
to Tank's. He remembered how Rocky used to annoy Tank
with his constant silliness and hoped his brother would forgive him for burying them side by side.

He scrambled to his feet, realizing how stupid he'd been.
He'd come outside alone, his mind addled by grief, and dug
two graves right in the open where any wandering Other could
put him on the dinner menu. Then, to make matters worse,
he'd taken drugs and passed out. Fucking brilliant. He was going to make a kickass leader.

He headed back to the Wal-Mart, his body and mind still
hazy from a mixture of sleep and Vicodin. He'd been stupid to
take the pills. They'd made him even more careless than usual.
His brother had given him shit for his lackadaisical nature in
the past, but now it was inexcusable. He had children to take
care of. He had to be responsible. And that meant getting over
his pain in other ways. He had to throw out the drugs and start
over. Become the man he was supposed to be. One who had no
difficulties raising a brood of crazy children on a zombie-
plagued wilderness trek to Disney World.

Sounded great.

Still, from here on out he'd be stone-cold-sober Chase.
Starting tomorrow. Tonight he needed more sleep.

He made sure there was nothing dangerous around before he let himself back inside the Wal-Mart, then wandered

through the quiet store, flashlight in hand, looking for the kids. Finally he found them, all curled up and sound asleep in a pile of pillows and blankets around Molly's feet. They were in the Home section. And they looked so innocent lying there, as if they didn't have a care in the world. He wondered what she'd said to them.

At first he assumed Molly was asleep, although it was impossible to tell with her glasses. But then she shuffled and stirred, crawling out of her sleeping bag and motioning him to follow her away from the circle of sleeping children.

"Where the hell have you been?" she demanded, her face twisted into an angry scowl. They were out of earshot of the kids. "They've been asking about you all night."

Chase stepped back, startled. He'd forgotten they hadn't parted on good terms. To make things worse, he'd promptly gone off and passed out, leaving her stuck with the kids, a responsibility he'd had no reason to expect her to accept. Kids he'd promised Tank he would protect.

"I'm sorry," he said. "I was . . . burying the dead."

She gave him a suspicious look. Not that he blamed her. He'd been gone much longer than would be necessary for that. But he wasn't about to admit to accidentally passing out from pills. She wouldn't understand, and that'd just make things worse.

"You've been gone a long time. Must have been some funeral."

Chase glared at her, annoyed. "I needed some time. I'm sorry. It was my brother, you know."

She softened, looking embarrassed. Part of him breathed a sigh of relief.

"So, I fed the kids. And I got them to sleep," she said, motioning to the brood. "I'm going to be leaving really early in the morning. I didn't know if you wanted me to say good-bye now so I didn't wake you."

Panic slammed through him. He hadn't thought she'd leave so soon. It was true she'd had this plan beforehand, but after the killings . . . He hadn't even had time to butter her up to agree to his plan!

"About that," he said. The words sounded awkward. This was going to come out all wrong and he knew it.

She stared at him.

"I was thinking . . . I mean, with Tank gone and all . . . there's really nothing here for us at the Wal-Mart," he began, struggling to explain. "And so, I was wondering if . . . maybe, if you wouldn't mind—"

"Oh, no. No way."

He stared at her, startled. He'd figured she'd at least agree to think about it. But the look on her face made him think she'd rather eat a snake than consider what he was about to suggest.

"What?" he asked, unable to keep the irritation out of his voice. "You don't even know what I'm going to ask."

"If you and the kids can tag along with me."

Ah. "Okay, fine, maybe you do know," he replied. "But you haven't heard my argument yet as to why it'd be a good idea."

"I don't need to hear it. It's not a good idea. In fact, it's a very bad idea," she said. Her voice was quiet.

"But why?"

She made a pained face. "I have . . . a schedule to keep," she said. "I need to get down there quickly, and there's no way I can do that if I'm dragging a bunch of kids along. Maybe if it were just you . . . maybe. But even then . . ." She trailed off, and he realized she was trying not to be insulting and was finding it difficult. Did she find him to be such a pathetic tool—fine to use when she needed stuff, but easily dumped afterward? It was just like old times. She hadn't changed a bit.

"Oh, I see." He gritted his teeth. "I forgot. You're better than us. You're all cyber-chick, what with your implants and shit."

"Chase . . ." He could see the apology in her face, but he was too angry to accept it.

"Yup. Once again you've got more important things going

on, and you're going to abandon your friends." He gestured around, arms wide. "I hate to break it to you, Molly, but you might be sacrificing us for nothing. Not that it'd be that much of a sacrifice, but . . . Earth to Molly. The world's dead. It's over. The human race is struggling to survive here, and the only way we're going to do that is to stick together. Combine our strengths."

She looked a little guilty, but then her lips tightened into a thin line. "Chase, I'm not saying you guys aren't important. You don't understand—"

"Oh, I understand perfectly, don't you worry. And don't let me stop you. I can take care of these kids by myself. Maybe we'll take our own little field trip to Disney. There's plenty of maps in the Books section. We don't need you as tour guide."

She frowned. "That's a bad idea. It'd be dangerous."

"What, and staying here isn't? Or is it 'cause we don't have you to watch our backs? Please. You, Super Girl, have been out and about this world for exactly one afternoon. You may be all rawr-rawr razor girl when it comes to hand-to-hand combat, but do you know anything about surviving day to day? Do you know when they're most likely to hunt, or that their eyesight is weak and how to take advantage of that? Did you know that they hate high-pitched noises and that whistles can sometimes save your life? I make sure the kids always have them when we go outside. Are you going to take one? And how about the fact that sometimes they work together, a small one baiting you into the open before a larger one jumps out of the shadows?"

"No. I didn't know any of that," she said.

"No, of course you don't!" he said, triumphant until he realized she had just admitted it, which stole a tiny bit of his thunder. "So while you may be stronger, faster and deadlier, you're also probably going to be lunch by the third day. And then none of that cyber strength will matter."

"You're right," she said simply.

He looked at her. "What?"

"You're totally right. I'm sorry. I didn't mean to sound

insulting. I was just worried about time. I don't have much time to get there."

"What's the deal with this not-much-time thing?" he asked. "I mean, you've waited six years. What's the hurry now?"

She paused, looking pained. "It's a long story," she said. "Let's just say that I'm sick. The nano computers inside me, the ones that make me stronger and faster—well, they're not working right. They're malfunctioning. Breaking down for some reason. And as time passes I'm going to get weaker. Eventually I'll be so weak that I won't be able to walk."

Wow. He hadn't been expecting her to say that. "What about once you get there?"

"Supposedly they can fix me. They'll cycle my blood, get rid of the nanos and make me good as new. But I have to get there. And the sicker I get, the less chance I'll have to make it. In other words, I'm in a hurry."

Chase felt like a tool. No wonder she didn't want to take them along. It wasn't about her being selfishly unwilling to commit to him and the kids; it was about staying alive. He kept picturing himself standing in the rain waiting for her all those years ago, but he didn't know what had happened back then. Maybe she'd had a good reason for that. Maybe it was something he could ask her. Maybe . . . but not now.

He shook his head. "Okay," he said. "I get it. I'm sorry for what I said before. I was just . . . Well, it's been a long day, to say the least. Anyway, I think we can help each other out here. Sure, we might be a little slower with the kids, but at the same time, you're getting some travel insurance. I'd make sure, no matter what, you got to Disney World so your dad can fix you. Hell, I could carry you or something, worst comes to worst. We'll protect each other from wandering Others. I mean, on your own there's no guarantee that you'll make it in time, anyway. This way you know you'll have your own personal body-guard to keep you safe. One without a ticking time bomb inside him."

She seemed to consider for a moment. "What about the kids?" she asked.

"Well, they have to come. I mean, I promised Tank. And I wouldn't just leave them. Would you? But we'll make sure they behave and don't get in the way. And we'll grab those horses. The kids all know how to ride. We can just head down I-95 on horseback. It'll be easy." He found himself full of a new enthusiasm he hadn't felt in years. Her next words dimmed that a little.

"Easy?"

"Fine. Maybe 'easy' is overstating just a tad, but it'll work. You'll see. Seriously, I think it's the only way."

She paused, but only for a moment. "Okay."

"Okay?" He couldn't believe it. She was really going for his idea?

"Okay, let's do it," she said. "But we have to move as quickly as possible. We'll gather our supplies tonight, leave first thing in the morning. Even if I do now have you watching my back, I still would rather make it to our destination before things get bad for me."

At that moment she could have requested the moon and Chase would have agreed. He was just so happy not to be left alone with the kids. "No problem, I'll stay up all night if I have to. This will be great. You won't regret it."

On impulse, he threw his arms around her in a hug. She was a bit stiff. He remembered how once upon a time she'd melted into his kiss, her body soft and supple and willing. Would she ever be that way again?

He knew he shouldn't want it. Better to keep their relationship on a professional level. After all, she'd betrayed him once. And whether she explained herself or not, she'd made it very clear what her priority was now. Better for him to just keep away. Getting emotionally involved would just open old wounds.

Still, he thought as she disengaged, watching her walk away and curl up inside her sleeping bag, her blonde hair spilling onto her pillow, part of him believed the teen goddess he'd once worshipped might be worth it.

CHAPTER SIXTEEN

Several teachers were absent the next day at school. Some kind of flu was going around, the principal said over the loudspeaker. Chris tried to tell himself that it was all a coincidence; a sick old lady and a few ill teachers didn't equal killer plague. But something was still making him uneasy. Molly's dad's words kept echoing in his ears. The End of Days. That seemed so ridiculous. So, why couldn't he get the concept out of his head?

There was something else he couldn't get out of his head. Make that some*one* else. He hadn't been able to sleep a wink last night, tossing and turning, replaying that moment on Molly's neighbor's stone wall. He'd been literally millimeters away from kissing the goddess herself and—shock of all shocks—the goddess had seemed willing. At the very least, she hadn't punched him in the face. (He'd seen Drew's nose this morning and had a good laugh.)

But, of course, nothing had happened. Par for the course in his sorry life. Her dad had called, ruined the moment. He remembered how Molly had leapt away. That hasty good-bye—she couldn't get away from him fast enough. He'd never, ever get her in that position again and he knew it. Not Chris Griffin, super dork.

"Hey, Chris, did you see that crazy post on the forums about the Super Flu?"

Speaking of dorks. Chris looked up to see his best friend

Stephen nearby, attempting to pry a sim deck out of his over-stuffed, undersized locker.

"What post?" he asked. Like him, Stephen was a total forum troll, always looking through the lesser-known, unmonitored message boards for information. "I didn't log on last night." He'd been too busy dreaming about Molly. Sweet, beautiful, almost-kissed Molly. He hadn't even done any further research on Mrs. McCormick. He felt a brief pang of embarrassment at his selfishness.

"It's all over the place. People are sick, guy. Like, really sick. The hospitals are supposedly overflowing, especially in the big cities like New York. The government is trying to keep it on the down-low, obviously. Not wanting to start a panic, you know. But it's big news. They say you can even die from it. Especially if you're, like, an old person and shit."

Chris stared at him, his creeping worry returning with a vengeance. So, he'd been right; there was something weird about this sickness. He thought about Mrs. McCormick. The cleaners. Molly's dad's warning. "For real?" he asked, hoping that maybe Stephen was pulling his leg. "You're not messing with me?"

His friend shrugged. "Well, it's on a number of forums. Log on and see for yourself."

"Yeah, I will when I get home." The school connections blocked any kind of non-government-sanctioned forums, of course.

"It's fucking scary, let me tell you," Stephen continued, slamming his locker shut. "It's like End of Days shit, some folks are saying."

Chris started. "What did you say?"

"You know, the apocalypse. Everyone dying of some plague. The end of the human race as we know it," Stephen replied with a cocky grin. "On the plus side, maybe we'll get zombies. Usually when this kind of thing happens in the movies, they get zombies."

"Oh yeah, zombies would be kind of cool," Chris said with an uneasy laugh. He and Stephen had a special fondness for old horror movies—the old George Romero ones in particular. Still, given the circumstances, the thought wasn't as funny as it might have been.

Stephen stuck his hands out and purposely stumbled off down the hall, moaning. "Brains . . . brains . . ."

Chris laughed appreciatively. "Yeah," he said, slapping his friend on the back. "I agree. You could use some brains. Especially if we're stuck living through Armageddon. You wouldn't want zombies to kill you and find there's nothing to eat."

Molly was just about to jump on the bus home that afternoon when she heard someone calling her name. Turning, she saw Chris Griffin waving to her. Their eyes met. *Ugh.* Now she had to go talk to him. She felt really weird doing so after what had happened yesterday. What if he wanted to pick up where they'd left off? She wasn't ready to deal with that. Especially not after the day she'd had in school. Drew, as expected, had gone out of his way to make her a social outcast.

Still, Chris had been really nice to her yesterday and managed to cheer her up when she was at her lowest. And, of course, her mother had taught her not to be rude to anyone no matter what. So reluctantly she stepped off the bus and headed over to where he was standing.

He'd better have something important to say, though. She'd miss the early bus.

"What's up?" she asked.

He held out his deck. "I went home during lunch and did a little research," he said. "And I found out there's some weird Super Flu going around."

"Super Flu?" she repeated.

"Yeah. People are getting really sick all over the world. Most metropolitan hospitals are packed and there have been a ton of deaths." He handed her his device. "Look. It's all there."

She scanned the documents he'd downloaded. It certainly seemed like he was right. Things were bad if these reports were to be believed. She thought about her dad's warnings. They were starting to seem uncomfortably relevant. Why hadn't they heard more in Monroeville? Sure, they weren't a bustling metropolis, but still, she would have thought they'd have heard some whispers. Then again, with the government in control of the media, sometimes real news traveled very slowly.

She looked up at Chris. "Wow," she remarked, not sure what else to say. "Do you think that's what happened to Mrs. McCormick?"

"I'm sure of it," he replied, taking back his deck. "And I think we should investigate."

"Investigate?" Her father's warning came back to her. *Don't trust anyone.* But that was stupid. Wasn't it?

"Yeah," Chris pushed. "Like, let's go visit a hospital. See if they're really full."

"But then we'd be exposed to the disease, right?"

"Well, we were already exposed if Mrs. McCormick had it. But I also have some respirators. We used them when painting the house last year. And we won't get too close to the hospitals, just in case. We could just go and have a look."

She considered. "But what are we looking *for?* What will going to any one hospital prove?"

"Well, these reports, for one. It'll give us a better sense of what's going on around us. Don't you want to know if there's some deadly plague floating around that could kill us all? Looking up forum posts is one thing, but it's better to do some research on our own."

She did want to know what was going on, because she'd seen a million conspiracy theories in her day, none of which had ever panned out. Most non-government-sanctioned media outlets were just glorified rumor mills, after all. So, some people were sick. Some old people were dying. That wasn't exactly enough to prove a coming apocalypse. Though her father would claim it was.

"Okay," she said. "I'll go with you to check one, at least." She really would have preferred to head over to Erin's for a round of Basketball Dayz; she was going to be totally left behind if she didn't get some practice in. Erin had already told her about the NCAA level, and it sounded awesome. And tonight of course there was her nightly training with her father. But she knew Chris was really concerned, and she felt like she owed him something. So what the hell; she would go to the hospital, check things out, and she could still get back in time for training. Then she and Chris would be even.

"Cool. We'll start with Mount Holyoke. That's the one they were supposedly taking Mrs. McCormick to, right? Makes sense. I'll go home and get the respirators and meet you there in an hour, okay?"

Molly sighed. She had to be crazy to be agreeing to this. "Okay. Fine. See you there."

She watched him walk away, part of her shrieking to call the whole thing off. Her new friend was turning out to be just as crazy as her dad. But just go to the hospital, check things out, she told herself. We'll see that nothing is really going on, and I can say "I told you so" to the both of them. They were going to feel like idiots when the world didn't come to an end.

CHAPTER SEVENTEEN

Even after six years of thievery, Wal-Mart still held an enormous quantity of supplies, and Chase made good on his promise to get everything gathered for their trip. When Molly woke up the next day he had backpacks large and small, stuffed with essentials. He also had a few saddlebags packed to the brim with dried food, bottled water (Tank had demanded they collect rainwater from barrels placed outside for everyday use) and first-aid supplies.

"It's not everything we'll need," he explained. "But this will get us started. And I figure we'll be able to pick up some stuff on the way, too. Whatever wasn't looted at the beginning or eaten by the Others over the years. Even if the stores are bare, we can always try houses."

"Right." She didn't relish the idea, looking through dead people's property, but it was certainly a better option than starving, worst come to worst.

She looked over the supplies and nodded at Chase. "This looks great. Thanks."

He shrugged. "The horses are outside. I collected them earlier. I'm going to go saddle them up. Be back in a minute."

As much as she'd originally hated the idea of this group tagging along, she had to admit it was nice to have someone else take control. As Chase had pointed out, she might be a good fighter, thanks to her father's work on her, but he definitely brought other things to the table. She'd been so sheltered, living underground with her mom all these years. She had no idea what the world outside was really like. As much as she didn't want to admit it, it was a relief to have Chase on board.

The kids, on the other hand, were likely to be millstones. Chase was all gung-ho to be Disney-bound, but the others weren't exactly thrilled with the idea. They were leaving the only safe home most of them had ever known. And while Molly tried to be patient and understanding, she was about ready to strangle the lot. After all, she was doing them a favor—literally risking her life, slowing herself down in order to protect them—and there was absolutely no gratitude. They just whined and complained and demanded she allow them to take useless items. She was at her wits' end when Chase finally came back from readying the horses.

"Chase!" whined Darla. "She won't let me take my pony."

"You're getting a real pony, Darla," Chase answered, ruffling the girl's blonde head. "And if you shut up for two seconds, I'll even let you name him."

"Chase!" cried Starr. "I can't fit my makeup in my bag."

"I'll carry it in mine," he replied.

Molly marveled at how he handled them. It was almost effortless: sometimes teasing, sometimes flattering, sometimes authoritative. And the kids listened. In the time it had taken her to get them to even acknowledge her presence, Chase had them dressed, packed, and on the horses, ready to go. He was like the world's number one Scout leader. It wasn't something she would have expected from him, and she had to admire it.

"Hey, Molly, I got you something," Chase said, pulling her aside. She raised her eyebrows, wondering what it could be. He reached into a bag and pulled out a black leather jumpsuit and coat. "I hit a fetish shop down the road," he said with a sheepish grin. "It may look a bit seedy, but they have the best leather stuff. It'll protect you from Other bites if you get in a scuffle. Not that you've had much of a problem yet, but . . . well, we don't know how many we'll meet out there, or what sort of situations we'll be in."

"Thanks," she said, grateful. She wouldn't even have thought about that. Again, his street smarts were invaluable.

"I'll put it on right now." She stepped behind a shelf display and undressed, then slid on the leather pants. They felt soft and luxurious on her bare legs. She slipped into the top and zipped up before stepping into view. "Perfect fit," she announced.

Chase whistled. "Damn. That's hot."

She swatted him. "Yeah, yeah," she said. But her stomach fluttered. "I'm roasting actually."

"That is so not what I meant."

"Chase! My backpack's too heavy!" cried one of the triplets.

"Take out the toy trucks and you'll be fine," Chase replied. He threw Molly a rueful smile. "Duty calls."

She watched him walk off to deal with the kids. It was pleasing—if surprising—how upbeat he seemed. Perhaps the demands of their trip were taking his mind off his brother's death. Her own quest had certainly forced Molly to stop thinking about her mother. She and Chase had both lost people they were close to, but there would be time for mourning later. As her dad said, it wasn't the people who cried who survived, it was the people who spit and went on. Right now, this group had a pilgrimage to begin. A world to save.

She followed Chase and the kids out of the Wal-Mart. Six horses stood in the parking lot, looking very out of place amidst the abandoned cars. Chase boosted Darla and Red up first, then instructed the two oldest—Starr and Torn—to ride with them. (Red protested loudly that he could ride his own horse, but Chase refused to let him have his way.) Molly got her own white mare, and Chase shared his mount with the littlest child, Sunshine.

"We're off," he proclaimed, once everyone was seated and ready to go.

Molly looked around, nervous. Before, nothing had seemed very real. But here they were, heading out into the unknown with no clue as to what they'd encounter. Of course, that didn't matter; they were committed. What other hope was there, other than this journey? Once again, Molly felt a pang of relief that she wasn't on her own, despite everything else she'd said or thought.

And so the journey began, Chase leading the way, Molly taking up the rear. Single file they rode down the trash-strewn streets, the clomping of horse hooves filling all of their ears. No one talked.

According to the databases accessed by her ocular implants and built-in GPS—which, thank God she had, since old-fashioned paper maps were few and far between, just like real books—she'd decided the best way to take was old Interstate 95. The highway ran north-south along the entire eastern seaboard. It'd get them to Daytona, Florida, where they'd pick up Route 4 for the remainder of their trek. Molly had hoped the highway would be relatively clear, making for an easy journey. But she'd been deluding herself. I-95 was much like the Wal-Mart parking lot: a graveyard of rusted-out cars and debris. Broken glass, downed trees and power lines, unidentified objects strewn here and there—it looked as if a hurricane had swept through. Maybe one had.

After a bit, Chase stopped his horse. "God," he muttered, as Molly came up beside him. He surveyed the scene, hand over his eyes to shield them from the sun. "This is going to be a long trip."

"I got to go the bathroom!" whined Darla.

Molly raked a hand through her hair. She felt a little like Pilgrim, in John Bunyan's *Pilgrim's Progress*, one of the only books her mother had brought down into the shelter. In that book, a guy named Pilgrim had made his way from the City of Destruction to the Celestial City, undergoing terrible hardships and traps all along the way. In the end, he'd managed to get to his destination. She hoped she was as lucky.

Of course, Pilgrim didn't have eight grumpy children in tow. And though it had been a hell of a journey, there were no zombies after his ass. The damn guy had had it easy when all was said and done.

Molly shook her head, remembering what Erin had always said back in the day. Negative people were doomed to fail. If she wanted to survive, she'd have to become Mary fucking Sunshine. Pollyanna incarnate. She'd have to shut down the side of her that was like her father and be more like Erin.

Poor Erin. Optimism hadn't gotten her very far.

"This is stupid. I want to go home!" cried Red. Molly squeezed her reins in frustration. Rose-colored glasses were easier to talk about than find. She should have had her father build a setting into her implants.

"Okay, that's it. Everyone dismount," Chase commanded. She glanced at him, a little irritated. They'd already wasted too much time. She wanted to get some miles in today, feel like they'd made some progress.

The kids slid off their horses. Chase jumped off his own mount and reached into his bag. He pulled out a bunch of sunglasses and started passing them around. "Okay," he said. "Make sure you all put these on." One by one the kids slid the glasses over their eyes. Molly watched, curious.

"These are magical glasses," Chase said. "Just like Molly's there. And they're going to help us see Disney World."

She fought the urge to roll her eyes. Surely the children weren't going to buy this.

"Do you see it?" he asked, when each had donned their glasses. He pointed down the highway. "The trail of pixie dust? Isn't it beautiful?"

"I think I see it!" cried Sunshine. "I think I do!"

Sure enough, the rest of them chimed in. Molly couldn't believe it.

"That's the path we need to take to get to the Magic Kingdom," Chase continued. "Some very smart magicians are building a new society there, and we'll all get to be a part of it. Just like the princes and princesses in the storybooks."

"I see it, too," the teenager Starr said, obviously playing along. A big smile broke out across her freckled face. "Way out there."

"Yes. It's very far," Chase agreed, serious. "But we can make it. Right, guys?"

"Yeah!" they chorused, completely under his spell. Molly shook her head. He was amazing. Absolutely amazing, the way he handled them. Hadn't his brother been calling him a fuckup?

"Okay, guys, let's do our tribe dance and then we'll start our journey," Chase commanded. "Remember the one Rocky taught us when he gave you your war paint?"

The children cheered, and Chase broke out into a wild dance, twirling in circles and kicking up his feet. He looked so damn ridiculous, Molly smiled. Soon the children joined in, giggling and cheering. They were a group of mad whirling dervishes on a lost highway.

She suddenly felt a tug on her leg and looked down. Darla was standing beside Molly's horse, looking up at her with her big eyes. "Come on, Molly," the little girl said. "You gotta do the tribe dance."

It was a waste of time. It was stalling the journey. And everything inside of her said she should just say no, force them back on their horses and move things along. Instead, she found herself slipping off her horse and kicking up her heels. She grabbed Darla's hands and twirled her around. The little girl squealed in delight.

"You're one of us now!" Darla said, grinning from ear to ear. "You're part of the tribe."

Molly was secretly pleased at the idea. Maybe there was a chance she could fit in after all; she just needed to relax a bit and go with the flow. She needed to not expect everything to be timely and perfect, had to channel her mother rather than her dad.

A moment later, Chase was next to her. "D'you mind if I cut in?" he asked Darla. He took Molly's hands and, pulling her close, began a waltz. She allowed him to lead, following his steps and wondering where he had learned. His hand was firmly planted against her back, the other grasping her hand. Forward, back. Side to side. She felt his hot breath on her cheek. Breathed in his musky scent. Felt his thigh move accidentally up against hers. She sucked in a breath and—

—stepped right on his foot.

"Ow!" he cried, dropping his hands and hopping up and down. "Forget the razors. Your feet are deadly weapons."

"Yeah, yeah." She laughed, then caught herself. Put a hand over her mouth.

He grinned. "See?" he said. "I told you you'd laugh eventually. Life goes on." He turned back to the children. "Okay, mount up, Mouseketeers," he commanded. "It's a small world after all!"

CHAPTER EIGHTEEN

Mount Holyoke Hospital was a tall brick building originally built in the 1800s and it had survived the Civil War. Over the years there had been additions, but the main structure still stood. It was a full-service facility, but one of their main operations was delivering babies. They had a reputation for kind nurses, beautifully decorated private rooms, and the best epidurals around.

Thus, it was surprising that when Molly and Chris got off their bikes and approached the place, they saw armed, uniformed guards flanking the sliding glass doors of the entrance. Guards who stopped them from entering.

"We're sorry," said the one on the left, a giant in full beard and brown uniform. "We're full."

Molly cocked her head. Full? Since when did a hospital turn people away? Didn't doctors sign an oath to help everyone? Or at least those with good medical insurance . . . "We don't need to see a doctor," she informed the guard. "We just want to find out if a friend of ours was admitted."

"No visitors," said the one on the right. He was clean-shaven but just as big.

Molly and Chris looked at one another. "Since when?" Chris asked.

"Kids, we're going to have to ask you to leave," said the guard on the left. He rattled his machine gun.

Molly shivered. None of this was helping her case against the apocalypse.

"Come on," she said, grabbing Chris by the arm. There was no need to mess with soldiers. "Let's go."

Once out of earshot, Chris turned to her, looking puzzled. "We're giving up that easily?" he asked.

Molly shook her head. "No," she replied. "We're just going to have to be more creative. Let's walk around back and see what we can find." She was curious now, to be honest. Were her dad and Chris actually onto something? She wasn't leaving until she got some answers.

They headed to the back of the hospital, ducking under barbed wire fencing that pronounced the area off limits. Since when did a hospital use barbed wire?

"We have to be quick," Chris whispered. "They've probably got a billion security cameras and motion detectors. And maybe guards patrol here, too."

Molly nodded, peering around the back lot. At the moment the place was desolate, and it gave her the creeps by being overgrown and trash-strewn. She pointed to a window and motioned for Chris to follow. Wiped off the grime with her sleeve and peered in.

She drew in a quick breath. The guards hadn't been exaggerating when they'd used the word "full." Packed like a can of sardines would have been more accurate. The room had row upon row of cots with very little space between. A patient lay upon each, many looking weirdly green or yellow. The close ones had bloodshot eyes, drool at the corners of their mouths. Some lay still, eyes staring wildly into nothingness. Still others thrashed in their sleep, as if they were living a nightmare from which they couldn't wake. And perhaps they were.

Molly backed up, horrified, and bumped into an enormous trash compactor directly behind her. She hadn't paid it much attention before, because it looked like it was used for industrial construction work. She wondered now what it was doing here. "Ow!" she cried, rubbing her arm. "That hurt."

Chris abandoned the window to give her his full attention. "You okay?" he asked.

"Yeah." She nodded. Then she peeked back inside the hospital. "God. There's so many people in there. And they look . . . awful."

He nodded. "And if this is happening here, maybe it really is happening everywhere around the world. . . ."

She shuddered. "Maybe those rumors weren't exaggerated after all."

"I wonder . . ." Chris absently flipped open the compactor door, peering inside. He went dead silent. Molly turned from the window and squinted at him. He looked horrified.

"What did you find now?" she asked, almost afraid to know.

He banged the door shut. His face was white as a sheet. "Nothing," he said.

"Let me see." She reached over to pull open the lid.

"Molly, no—"

But it was too late.

The first thing she noticed was a horrific smell. An overwhelming odor of rot assaulted her nose. But that smell was only a precursor to the true nightmare.

"Oh God." She felt her knees wobble and she stumbled.

Chris caught her, steadying her. His hand felt warm on her suddenly freezing-cold skin.

"Those . . . those . . ." She found she couldn't finish. It was too awful. All those bodies, thrown out like common trash. What about their families? Their friends? Their chance at a proper burial?

"Come on," he commanded. "We need to get out of here. Now!"

She nodded, and they started back the way they came. Suddenly they heard a sound: a low, guttural moan. They looked at each other.

"It sounded like it was coming from the trash compactor!" Chris observed in a shaky voice.

Molly felt her stomach heave. It was all she could do not to throw up. "Do you think . . . Oh God, what if the doctors made a mistake? What if one of them is still alive?"

The moan grew louder, accompanied by a thrashing noise. Someone was clearly trying to get out.

"Should we check?" she asked.

Chris glanced at the compactor and then back at her. "I don't know."

"I'm going to take a quick peek," Molly said, inching over to the compactor. Everything inside her said it was a mistake, but she just couldn't bring herself to walk away from a living person trapped in there with corpses. Her heart was beating a mile a minute, and it was difficult to take a breath. She swallowed the bile bubbling up in her throat. "Here goes," she said, reaching for the door.

She lifted it then jumped back, her heart stopped from shock.

"Oh, my God!" she cried, dropping the door closed with a bang. "Run!"

CHAPTER NINETEEN

"Another marshmallow, m'lady?" Chase said, pulling his stick from their makeshift fire. Of course, he didn't really have a toasted marshmallow on the end. If he did, it'd likely have been stale and hard as a rock. Molly giggled at the gesture all the same.

"Why, thank you, good sir," she said, miming acceptance. She popped the fake sweet into her mouth and rubbed her stomach. "Mmm. Delicious."

"What's a marshmallow?" asked Darla, the only child still awake. The others were mostly sacked out a few feet away, exhausted by their trek.

"Only the best food on Earth," Chase declared, reaching over to tickle her. "Soft and squishy, just like you." The girl squealed in delight and jumped onto him, knocking him backwards. They tussled for a bit before Chase finally let her pin him to the ground in victory.

They'd set up camp in a small motel courtyard off of I-95 for the night. Chase had scouted out a room for them to sleep in and collected blankets from other rooms. Those blankets were all now spread across the floor inside, making a cozy little space to sleep and an easy position to retreat to. But first he'd said they should cook dinner. They did so right in front of the room he'd chosen, and there was a good view of all their surroundings, no way for someone to sneak up on their position. And by cooking outside they were saving their precious supply of gas in their portable stove for rainy nights.

He'd made one hell of a fire, a roaring blaze circled by big stones he'd collected from nearby, then cooked their feast: something he'd teasingly called Stone Soup in front of the children. It was watered-down chicken broth with some vegetables from the Wal-Mart garden thrown in. He'd added a little whiskey and some other spices, too. Not the most filling or delicious meal in the world, but Molly applauded his efforts all the same. Alone, she probably would have only managed to crack open a can of string beans.

"What was that old movie that had the giant marshmallow guy? Remember?" Chase asked Molly, eyes shining, as he lay back on the grass. Darla had gone back to her dolls. "Something about ghosts?"

"*Ghostbusters*," Molly replied, laughing as she thought back to the silly movie. "My dad loved it." She smiled at the memory. "I used to sneak out of bed as a kid and slip downstairs to the living room. He and my mom liked to watch old movies on our ancient DVD player, and that was one of their favorites. 'I ain't 'fraid of no ghost.'"

"That's it!" Chase exclaimed, pointing at her. Then he sighed. "Ah, movies. I would give my right arm to watch another movie right about now—on an ancient DVD player or anything. You wouldn't believe what I used to love watching. Ironic."

Molly was thinking about her own past. "Well, maybe someday there will be movies and TV again. You never know, right? When we find my dad . . ."

"Yeah, I'm sure those will be the first priority when rebuilding our world." Chase fell silent, then turned to her. "Do you ever think about that—where we can go from here?"

She turned, surprised by the question. "All the time."

"Yeah, I guess you would. Not me, though. Until we started on this little adventure, I'd pretty much given up on things," he said, poking the fire with his stick. "Figured we were destined to live out the rest of our lives in the Wal-Mart. I never in a million years would have predicted being out traveling again."

"Life doesn't always turn out the way we plan," Molly said. Then, blushing, she added, "Well, I guess that's obvious."

"What did you want to be when you grew up?" Chase asked suddenly. "You know, before, back when you *could* be something? Feels funny that we never talked about things like that. I wanted to be a video game designer myself. Talk about a useless career nowadays."

She laughed. "Why am I not surprised? Anyway, I wanted to be an actress. Also useless, I guess."

"Well, like you said, maybe there will be TV again some-day. Or at least plays."

"Yeah, right. I could never be an actress now," she said, gesturing to her eye implants. "Unless the new Hollywood is all about casting freaks."

"Don't say that," Chase said.

"Why not?" she snapped, feeling annoyed. He was trying to be nice, but she knew how she looked and didn't need to be patronized. "I've got mirrored plates fused to my skull, covering my eyes."

He shrugged. "The better to help you see in the dark."

"And four-centimeter razors under my fingernails." She released the blades, and they glinted in the firelight before she retracted them again.

"The better to fight with."

She rolled her eyes. "Okay, Mr. Big Bad Wolf. Whatever you say."

Chase caught her hand in his, ran a thumb up the inside of her palm. "I'm serious," he said, his voice becoming a husky whisper. "You may not look how you once did, but life didn't turn out like either of us expected and those razors saved us from Spud. He was about to eat Darla when you stepped in and smacked him down. You should be glad you're alive, not worried about how you look."

She sighed. "I know the razors are useful," she admitted, not wanting to enjoy his touch as much as she did. "But I can't help looking at them and seeing . . . well, seeing how things might have been. Seeing what the world has made me—or at least my father. Seeing what a freak I've become."

"Well, not that it matters what I think, of course, but to me you're still as beautiful as you were in high school," he murmured. "A goddess."

Her heart fluttered, and she was plagued by a score of memories. Chris Griffin had always been sweet. In some ways he'd changed, like she had, but in other ways . . .

Inspired, she reached into her pocket and pulled out the gift he'd given her so long ago, held it out in her palm. "Do you remember this?" she asked. The tiny bit of broken glass caught the firelight and sparkled.

He stared at it for a moment, then recognition lit his face. "The diamond?" he said.

She nodded. "You told me I needed to look beyond the surface. To see the beauty deep inside."

"I sure was wise for a kid."

She chuckled. "I guess so."

"Pretty damn romantic, too, I must say." He looked at her and grinned.

"Well, you know you won me over."

"You know, I meant everything I said," he remarked, suddenly earnest. "And you're still a diamond, no matter what anyone else thinks. If anyone's dumb enough to not realize the truth."

She could feel his breath on her face, once again doing crazy things to her insides. She knew she should resist, get up and walk away while she still could. After all, there was no use in starting a relationship. It would distract her, and she had a mission. Maybe when and if everything was over and fixed, when she'd done what she needed to . . .

Against her will, she found herself trapped by his kryptonite-colored eyes. They were so brilliant in the firelight, they glowed. Molly's traitorous body moved forward instead of away. Her traitorous heart pounded in her chest, and her traitorous lungs struggled to take in air almost too thick to breathe.

Chase drew her hand to his lips and kissed her palm with an unbearable softness. She squirmed as impossible sensations coursed through her, too hard and fast to catalog. Six years without being touched by a man. Six years when her body's drive for that was strongest.

He smelled like the earth: rich, dark, delicious. She suddenly wanted nothing more than the opportunity to taste him.

"Kiss me," she whispered.

He needed no second invitation. Taking her head in his hands, he pulled her forward, pressing his lips against hers. Softly, almost reverently. Then harder. At first she was convinced she was going to pass out from excitement, but she managed to stay conscious.

His tongue invaded her mouth. It was awkward at first—neither of them had had very much practice at the whole kissing thing—but good all the same. He explored with soft, cautious strokes, and she soon met his tongue with hers.

"Oh, God, you feel so good," he groaned against her mouth. He trailed kisses down her jaw and neck. She reached up to his face, scraping her fingers across the light stubble on his cheeks. "I missed you so much."

She breathed him in, wrapping her hands around his neck. His scent, leather mixed with something muskier, invaded her senses and clouded her thoughts. At that moment there was no apocalypse. No zombies. No mad dash to Disney World. There was just a man and a woman—a 21st-century Adam and Eve—in a brave new world.

His hand wandered from her neck down her shoulder to the curve of her waist, then it made its way up again, searching for and finding her breast. His fingers tweaked her nipple gently, sending shockwaves to her core. It was only a slight touch, but it was enough to spiral her back to reality. What was she doing? She'd promised herself she wouldn't get involved. And yet here she was: first night on their journey, necking like a teenager.

She struggled to push Chase away, reached out a hand to

back him up. He resisted at first, probably too confused and dazed to realize what she wanted. So she pushed again, this time pushing at his face. She had to stop the kiss before it paralyzed her and convinced her to do something she was very likely to regret.

Unfortunately, in her dazed state, dosed with a combination of adrenaline and hormones, her body's cybernetic defensive mode activated. Her razors slipped out. She felt them sink into flesh.

Chase gasped and backed off, clutching his cheek. Blood streamed through his fingers. "Jesus, Molly. You cut me!"

CHAPTER TWENTY

"Can you stop for a second and tell me what we're running from?" Chris asked breathlessly, grabbing her arm. They'd fled the hospital and run off into the woods, Molly looking like she'd seen something a lot worse than a ghost. He leaned over, hands on his knees, and tried to catch his breath.

"Oh God, oh God, oh God," Molly sobbed, sinking down to the forest floor.

He joined her, concerned. He put a hand on her back and peered into her eyes. She looked terrified.

"What did you see?" he asked. He wasn't sure he wanted to know. What could be worse than the pile of corpses in a Dumpster?

"A . . . it was like a monster. I mean, it was sort of like a person. But . . . different. And it wasn't dead. It really wasn't dead."

He rubbed her back, trying to calm her. He needed her calmer so she would start making sense. "A monster. Are you sure?" he asked.

She looked up sharply. "I know what I saw."

"Okay, okay." He held his hands up. "I believe you. I'm just trying to get all the information. What do you think happened?"

"I don't know. I've never seen anything like it. It was like . . . a zombie or something."

Chris remembered his earlier jokes with Stephen. They'd

seemed a lot funnier at the time. But it was also ludicrous to believe in zombies. Molly had apparently been watching the wrong types of movies herself. "Er, maybe I should go back and take a look."

She grabbed onto him, her knuckles white and her eyes wide. "No!" she cried. "Please don't! I don't want to be alone!"

Instinctively he pulled her into a tight embrace. She responded, her body pressing against his so close it seemed she was trying to push inside of him. He desperately willed himself not to get too turned on, though this was like a dream come true. God, she'd feel him growing hard and think he was taking advantage of her, and he didn't want that. Still, it was next to impossible not to be aroused, what with her breasts smashed up against his chest and her shaky hot breaths against his earlobe. She smelled so sweet. Like honeysuckle and mint gum. It was all he could do not to kiss her.

But no, she didn't think of him like that. She was only clinging now out of fear, not desire. He would end up, once again, in the role of friend. And he'd have set himself up for disappointment.

He could enjoy the physical contact now, though. And he'd protect his goddess from whatever came after them. At the very least, maybe she'd be grateful.

"Shhh," he whispered, stroking her head. "I won't let anything happen to you." He liked saying that. It made him sound manly and brave. He wondered if she'd buy it.

"Thanks," she sniffed. She pulled her head away from his shoulder and looked him in the eye. "I really appreciate that."

"Of course," he said. He gave her a little wink. "You know I'd do anything for a diamond."

She chuckled a little and sank down on the forest floor, leaving his arms. He felt lonely, rejected. But he fought it.

"All those dead bodies," she mused. "And that one . . . What does it all mean?"

Chris shook his head, forcing his thoughts back to the hospital. "I have no idea," he said. "But it seems to me that the

Super Flu rumor is very real. And obviously the government isn't telling people the truth. I mean, you'd never know from watching the regular news that this is going on. And it's happening right under our very noses."

Molly picked up a stick and broke it in two. She looked at Chris. "I'm scared," she admitted. "I'm really scared."

Chris sat down next to her and took her hand in his. He squeezed it. "I'm scared, too," he said. "But we're in this together, okay? If things get bad, we'll figure something out."

"Like what?"

He wasn't sure. Thinking for a moment, he suggested, "We could leave town. Go someplace safe up in the mountains."

"Away from the Super Flu?"

"Yes. Where we go . . . well, up there the air will be cleaner. There won't be any people. We'll be safe."

She nodded. "That may not be a bad idea," she said. "If things get really bad."

"Yes. But hopefully they won't. Who knows? By this time next month we could be laughing about the whole thing."

She smiled ruefully. "I hope you're right," she said. "But for some reason, I just don't think it'll be that easy."

Choking back vomit, Chris pulled her close and kissed the top of her head. Truth be told, neither did he.

CHAPTER TWENTY-ONE

"Oh, my God, I'm so sorry!" Molly cried as blood streamed from between Chase's fingers. She'd cut him. How badly? "I didn't mean . . . I didn't mean . . ."

Her mind flashed back to what he'd said as they first walked into Wal-Mart. No doctors. No hospitals. A single scratch could be a death sentence.

"Fuck!" Chase swore under his breath. "Damn, that stings."

"Let me see," she commanded, retracting her razors. "I need to know how bad it is."

Chase obediently removed his fingers from the wound. It was impossible to tell how deep the cut was with all the blood. Molly looked around at the children—they were asleep, thank goodness; she didn't need to deal with freaked-out kids as well as everything else—then rushed quietly inside the motel room behind them. Grabbing a couple washcloths, she came back and pressed one against Chase's wound. He twitched but didn't cry out.

After a moment, she pulled the bloody cloth away. "I think you might need stitches," she said, eyeing the cut. It was long, though thankfully not deep. Apparently the razors had been at a shallow angle.

"Great." His face was pale. His lips trembled. Obviously he was in a lot of pain, even if he wasn't comfortable showing it. "Just great."

"It's okay. My mom taught me how to stitch wounds. She

was a nurse before she had me. I can sew you up," she assured him. "Where's that first-aid kit?"

He motioned to one of the supply bags a few feet away. She handed him back the washcloth and he held it against his face. "Be right back," she said.

Scrambling to her feet, she headed over to the bags and began her search for the med kit. What an idiot she'd been. This was exactly why she shouldn't be playing around like she was. Molly Anderson wasn't some innocent little girl anymore; she was a soldier, a killing machine. And anyone who came between her and her mission ran the risk of bodily injury, whether by her choice or not. This was the price people paid when she allowed herself to be distracted.

She shot a mental promise up to heaven: she wouldn't touch Chase again. He was better off without her, even if he didn't realize it.

But, oh, that kiss. That kiss.

Her lips still felt a bit bruised, and she was sure her face was flushed bright red. She licked her lips, remembering how it felt to have his mouth on hers, tasting her as if she were some gourmet treat and he'd been banned from the dessert bar for a thousand years.

Come on, Molly! The guy's bleeding to death over there, and all you can think of is kissing him? What would your mother say? What would your father *say?*

She found the first-aid kit and headed back to where he sat. Pulling out her supplies, she handed him a vial of antiseptic and some gauze, then instructed him to clean the cut. He complied, cringing at the sting of alcohol on the wound. In the meantime, she threaded her needle and, grabbing a stick from the fire, brushed the flame across it: a makeshift sterilization, the best she could come up with on short notice.

"How are you doing?" she asked, half-afraid of his answer.

"Fine," he replied through clenched teeth.

He didn't look fine to her. In fact, he looked like he was going to pass out at any second. He was paying big time for her stupid mistake. A part of her wondered if he'd thought the kiss was worth it, but then she scolded herself for being ridiculous. More than likely he was regretting he'd ever run into her.

"God, I'm so sorry," she found herself saying again. As if repeated apologies would make the skin meld back together and magically heal. "I never meant to . . . Oh, never mind." She quit talking. What good would it do anyway? And besides, there would be time for apologies later. Right now she needed to focus. She needed to get him sewn up before he lost any more blood.

"Um, one second," he said as she readied herself to start stitching, reaching into his pocket. She watched as he withdrew some kind of prescription bottle. What were those pills, and why did he have them? But he didn't say anything by way of an explanation, only "This should help," and he popped the cap with his teeth and tossed back a few pills. Swallowing, he removed the bloody washcloth from his cheek. "Fix me," he said, closing his eyes.

And so she fixed him. Carefully, so as to not hurt him any more than necessary, she stitched the cut closed. Each time she jabbed the needle into his flesh, his body trembled a little. But through it all he stayed silent, brave, solid, only his clenched jaw and the beads of sweat on his forehead giving any indication as to his pain.

It didn't take long, and the bleeding subsided. The cut looked nasty and he'd probably have a scar. But as long as the cut didn't get infected, everything should be okay. Maybe they could find a hospital in a neighboring town, find some heavier-duty antibiotics than the ones in the first-aid kit, the topical salve she was currently applying.

"I'm done," she informed him, then realized he couldn't hear her. He was out for the count, completely passed out. Was it from the pain? Or the drugs he'd just taken? Either way, she guessed it was probably for the best. She dabbed his sweaty forehead with another washcloth then sank down beside him, wondering what she should do now. They had talked about sharing night watch duties, but she doubted he was in any state to handle them at the moment. And he wasn't going to be much help moving the kids into the motel room.

Chase groaned and shifted, his head dropping onto her shoulder. Lost in sleep, he looked like a little boy, his mouth twisted in unconscious anguish.

She wondered if pain was chasing him through his dreams. Against her better judgment, she reached over and stroked his head, trying to soothe him into a more restful sleep. She shouldn't have cared. She should have risen to her feet and left him there, stopped herself from getting emotionally involved. She should have carried each of the children inside the motel to a better-protected spot. But she found she couldn't, and instead she ran her fingers through his hair, feeling each silky smooth strand. Chase thrashed a final time then fell still, unconsciously cuddling against her, wrapping an arm around her waist.

It was too tender. Too poignant. She should remove his hand. Stand up. Walk away. But she didn't. She just sat there, willing herself to stay awake, praying they wouldn't have any unwanted visitors. Some tough girl she was. Her father would be so proud.

Trapped in the strong grip of Oxycontin, Chase swam from nightmare to nightmare, chased by flesh-eating zombies who'd soon catch him and tear him apart, limb from limb, only to put him back together and have the process start all over again.

At last he woke, suddenly, dripping in cold sweat, and for a moment he wasn't sure where he was. Then it all came back to him. Molly. The kiss. The searing pain that interrupted that kiss as she'd sliced his cheek open with one of those razors.

He couldn't help laughing, albeit hysterically. He supposed he knew now how the Others felt. Reaching up he touched the cheek in question, surprised when his fingers found tiny stitches striping the cut. Then he remembered the rest. She'd sewn him up. She'd stopped the bleeding and likely saved his life.

"You're awake," she remarked. He looked over, surprised that she was sitting beside him, awake. His little Florence Nightingale. The moonlight reflected off her ocular implants, and her face was illuminated. He hadn't been lying when he'd said she was beautiful, and he had to fight the urge not to start kissing her all over again, to remind himself that beauty was also a beast.

"Yeah," he said, stretching his hands over his head. "Barely."

"I'm so sorry," she said. "I didn't mean . . ."

He waved her off. "My fault," he said. "I got carried away. Pushed you too far. You were just . . . you were just saying no—in your own special way."

She snorted softly. "That's one way to look at it."

He wanted to explain, to tell her it wasn't her fault that she moved him as she did. She was just too delicious. The way she'd pressed her body against him, kissing him, her little tongue darting greedily in and out of his mouth. Her soft breasts crushed against him—he'd dared touch them only for a moment. But that had obviously startled, perhaps even scared her. She'd just been defending herself.

Truth be told, if he had to do it over again, he would have done the same. It was worth the scar.

Part of him recoiled at how pathetically overpowering her draw was to him. He'd only had sex once, when he'd turned eighteen years old. Tank had taken him to see a woman who lived near the refugee camp and turned tricks in exchange for food and medicine. She'd taken Chase to her dilapidated cabin and showed him how it was done. He still remembered the damp, musty smell of the bed. It was built to vibrate if you inserted a quarter, but things like that no longer worked. Which was probably just as well, since Chase had been vibrating a whole lot on his own at that point.

She hadn't been particularly attractive. Stringy hair, cratered face, jutting hipbones on a scrawny frame. But she'd been a woman willing to fuck, which was what Tank had thought he needed. And his body had responded to her touch, despite her appearance. He'd taken her against the wall and lasted about two seconds. He still remembered how she'd laughed—a witch's cackle—as he pulled out of her, wet and spent and mostly relieved to have the thing over with. She'd scolded him for his impatience and suggested that if he ever had a chance with a real lover, he'd better learn to take his time. After all, the act was supposed to be about the woman's pleasure, too.

He hadn't really thought about it at the time, but now, looking at Molly, he felt ashamed. As much as he wanted to have sex with her, as much as he liked the idea of taking her roughly against a wall, fast, hard, and quickly coming inside her, the idea of caressing her slowly was much more enticing. He wanted to peel off each layer of clothing one by one, touching and tasting every millimeter of her skin. And then, when he could bear it no longer, he'd guide himself into her, fill her and take her to the same point of ecstasy he would experience himself.

He shook his head. *Fucking dumbass*, he rebuked himself. *You're gonna get yourself hurt, just like before.* She was playing with him. Once they were down at Disney World it'd be sayonara. If and when they found her father, he was certain she'd leave him. She'd find better things to do with her time, guys who had their shit together—if there was anyone left. He'd waited for her once like a fool. He shouldn't put himself through pain like that again. This kiss had been a mistake, pure and simple. But Chase never planned on making the same mistake again.

CHAPTER TWENTY-TWO

"Dad, Dad!" Molly cried as she took the basement steps two at a time. "Dad, are you down here?"

The workshop door swung open and Ian rushed out, looking concerned. He closed and locked it behind him. "What's wrong, baby?" he asked, studying her. "What happened?"

She buried her face in his chest, searched for comfort and reassurance from the man who'd sired her. Her mom hadn't been home. "Oh, Dad, it was awful," she said, tears filling her eyes. "I still can't believe it."

He led her over to the weight bench and sat her down. "Take a breath," he instructed. "Then tell me everything."

"We went to Mount Holyoke Hospital," she said. "And there were guards with machine guns. They wouldn't let us in. So we snuck around back and looked in the windows. There are so many sick people, Dad," she said, choking on the lump in her throat. "The place is overflowing."

Her dad nodded. "Yes," he said. "This Super Flu is a big deal. The government's not going to be able to contain word of it much longer, no matter how they censor the media." If Molly didn't know better, she'd think he looked pleased.

"But that's not the worst of it," she sniffled. "There was this . . . trash compactor, I guess. And we looked inside. And there were bodies. So many bodies." She broke down again.

Her father pulled her close and she sobbed into his chest. "Shh," he said. "Remember what I told you. When the apocalypse comes, we'll be safe. I've taken preparations. Every day I'm taking more. We're going to be fine. You're not going to get sick. I can one hundred percent guarantee that."

She wasn't sure how that was possible, but she was too concerned with the next part of her story to get off track. "That's not the worst thing," she said, pulling away and looking her dad in the eye.

He scrunched up his face. "What do you mean?" He sounded concerned for the first time in their conversation.

She took one deep breath, swallowed, then another. "There was something else in the trash compactor," she said. "Some kind of . . . I don't know. You're going to think I'm crazy."

He grabbed her shoulders with his hands so hard that she cried out, startled. "Tell me," he said, his eyes wide.

She shook her head. "I don't know exactly. It was like . . . like . . . a monster."

Her father dropped his hands, released her and turned. "Where was this again?" he said. "Mount Holyoke?"

Molly nodded weakly. "But I don't know if it's a good idea to—"

But her dad was already unlocking the door to his lab and disappearing inside. A moment later he returned, pistol in his hand. Molly's eyes widened. She'd had no idea her dad even owned a firearm. It certainly wasn't legal. Not after the Firearms Act of '18.

"I'm going to check it out," he told her. "You stay here. No matter what happens, do not leave the house until I get back."

If she'd been scared before, she was petrified now. "What is it, Dad?" she asked. "Do you know?"

"No," Ian said, heading up the stairs. "But I'm going to find out."

"Trey, dude!" Chris said, touching his brother on the shoulder, trying to rouse him from his sim-induced torpor. "I gotta talk to you."

Trey pulled off his VR goggles and looked at him, annoyed. "Dude," he said. "You know better than to interrupt a guy in a sim. I was in the middle of . . . Well, I was in the middle of that sim I loaned you. You never checked it out, and damn if you shouldn't be sorry."

"I *am* sorry," Chris said. He sat down on the floor. "But I gotta tell you something."

"Something more important than the Paperdoll Ms. March 2030?"

Chris just stared at him. "You know Mrs. McCormick, right? From down the street?" When Trey nodded, he quickly related her disappearance. "And I found some other reports, too. So me and Molly Anderson decided to go check out Mount Holyoke Hospital to see what was going on."

Trey looked bored. "And?"

Chris related the rest of the story. About sneaking around the back of the hospital. The sick people. The Dumpster. "And Molly thinks she saw some kind of creature like a zombie!"

Trey started laughing.

"Dude, I'm serious."

"I'm so telling Mom to force her to take your media player away," Trey said. "Those old movies you watch have obviously warped your fragile little mind."

Chris frowned. "I'm trying to tell you there's something really wrong going on. People getting sick. And dying. And I think the government is trying to cover it up."

"You're beginning to sound like Molly Anderson's dad. Is she like this, too? 'Cause, man, she is kinda hot, but if she's spouting end of the world bullshit she's likely to be a drag in bed."

"*I don't care about that.*" Chris slumped into an armchair, realizing he'd never be able to convince his brother to take him seriously. Not when he lacked any evidence. "I just wanted to make sure we're all safe."

His brother patted him on the back and went back to his sim.

CHAPTER TWENTY-THREE

The wasteland that was once the Eastern Seaboard of America stretched endlessly before them. Interstate 95 was the least depressing part, just a parking lot of rusted-out cars, broken glass and debris. Molly supposed most of the people had gotten out of their cars and staggered off into the wild to die and be disposed of by nature. It was when her group left the highway that they truly felt the horror of the apocalypse. Ghost towns with nothing but wind whistling down the vacant main streets and skeletons lying everywhere.

They'd been traveling for three days, and everyone was starting to get cranky and saddle sore—though they were relieved they hadn't had any difficult situations. Molly knew at some point they'd have to take a day off to rest and recover, and maybe even have a little fun with the kids. Somehow. Otherwise this little band of travelers was bound to mutiny.

When they'd started out, she'd been hopeful they'd run into more people. Other pilgrims, perhaps. Maybe ragtag refugee camps. Small makeshift societies built up from the rubble. But so far they'd seen nothing. Absolutely no one. The only signs of life anywhere were occasional mutilated animal corpses, likely compliments of roving bands of Others.

So far they'd been lucky and hadn't had any run-ins with zombies, but Molly knew that luck couldn't hold forever. The creatures were out here. She'd seen glimpses out of the corner of her eye, only to have them disappear when she turned her head. It was disconcerting to say the least. For what were always depicted as brainless creatures in the movies, these seemed awfully patient.

Since that first night, she'd tried to keep a distance from Chase, riding far behind him during the day and pretending to fall asleep early at night when it wasn't her watch. He seemed to sense her stepping back and had done what he could to respect her space. Their conversations were stilted, dealing only with necessities. The two made sure never to be alone together—and to never ever touch.

Sadly, instead of this making things better, Molly felt pretty lonely. Watching Chase in the lead, trotting on his horse, she wanted nothing more than to go talk to him. For one thing, he was the only person in their ragged band who really remembered much of the world before the catastrophe, the world they'd lost. The children barely had any idea. The oldest ones had only been eight or nine years when the plague hit. Their memories were pretty limited to sim cartoons and video games. The youngest hadn't even been born.

Still, even with her loneliness, Molly realized it was best to keep a distance from Chase. Anything else would only lead to an attachment that spelled trouble. She'd let them both down once again. She couldn't do that to him. She couldn't do that to herself.

"Hey, Molly, can I ask you a question?"

Molly glanced over. In her musings she hadn't realized that fifteen-year-old Starr had ridden up alongside her. Darla sat in the front of the saddle, playing with her doll, and the older girl sat behind.

"Sure," Molly said. She hadn't had many conversations with the children. They probably thought she was either a loner or a snob.

"How do you know when you're in love?"

The question took Molly by surprise. She looked at Starr, raising her eyebrows. "Is this a rhetorical question, or do you have someone in mind?"

"I don't know what rhetorical means," Starr said, blushing furiously. "But I think I might be in love with Torn."

Molly almost laughed. Of course it was Torn. There wasn't anyone else Starr's age. And he was indeed cute, what with that shock of brown hair that refused to lie flat, his bright blue eyes and lanky frame.

"Well, I'm not really an expert on love," Molly confessed, wondering if she were blushing a bit herself. "I was still pretty young when I had to go into the fallout shelter. And I was stuck inside with only my mom."

"So you've never been in love?" Starr said, wide-eyed. "But you're so *old.*"

Old. At twenty-one. Now Molly knew she was blushing. She tried to figure out the best response. "I was," she said at last. "Once."

"Did the person love you back?"

"I believe he did."

"How did you know?" Starr asked, sounding anguished. Obviously her crush had been raging for some time. Molly was surprised the two kids hadn't acted on it. She wondered if Tank had taken him aside and given the boy a lecture, or if Torn was simply clueless. She remembered an old crush of Erin's being that way.

Molly next considered Starr's question. How had she known Chris loved her, all those years ago? Part of it was what they'd shared during the turbulent times. "It wasn't what he said, necessarily," she explained slowly. "It was more . . . what he did. Words are just words, you know," she added. "It's everyday actions that show if someone cares." She had a brief flashback to Drew.

Starr rode along quietly. Then she grinned. "He gave me his apple yesterday," she said, her voice full of pride. "Without me even asking!"

Molly smiled. "That's a good sign," she said to the girl. "A very good sign."

Darla suddenly perked up. Molly had assumed she wasn't

paying any attention, but she'd clearly been wrong. "I think Chase loves you, Molly!" she cried.

Molly turned tomato red. "Um, I don't think so," she said.

Starr grinned, quickly latching on to the idea. "I do," she exclaimed. "And I think, from the look on your face, that you love him, too."

"Stop it! Both of you!" Molly hissed, hoping Chase couldn't hear. "It's not like that at all."

"Chase and Molly, sitting in a tree, K-I-S-S-I-N-G!" sang the two girls. Molly swatted at them. They erupted into giggles.

"Everything okay back there?" Chase called out, evidently hearing the ruckus. This only caused the girls to laugh harder. Molly sighed.

"We're fine," she called up to him. "Definitely fine."

"Aw, your boyfriend's worried about you!" teased Starr.

Molly rolled her eyes. She had a flashback to being a teenager herself and growled, "If you don't cut that out, I'm so telling Torn about you. I'll tell him you want his bod."

Starr's eyes looked like they were going to bug out of her head. "No, no, no!" she cried. "I'll be quiet. Really!"

Molly smirked. "Thought so."

That night they set up camp at a rest area off the highway. It wasn't the most secluded, safest spot in the world, but darkness had fallen before they'd come to any better place, and they'd decided to make the best of what they found. So they pitched tents, built a great bonfire and settled in for the night as best they could.

The kids passed out early, even the older ones, exhausted after the day's journey. It was Chase's turn to stand watch. He was tired, too, but wasn't about to admit it. Not to Super Molly, who never seemed the least bit worn out. It was thanks to all her enhancements, he was sure. Must be nice to be half robot.

He stifled a yawn as he poked the fire with a stick. He'd rise to the occasion, of course; he needed to prove to her that he was useful, needed to make her glad she'd brought him along. He didn't want her thinking she'd made a mistake.

"It's been a long day," she remarked, coming up beside him. She must have seen his yawn. "Maybe we should split the watch tonight. I'll take a shift, too."

Chase shook his head. She was always trying to get him to admit weakness. "Nah," he said. "I'm fine."

She frowned. "There's no need to be all macho," she reminded him. "If you start feeling tired, just wake me up. I really don't mind."

Of course she didn't. "I will, I will," he said. "Now go to sleep."

She finally complied, curling up in a sleeping bag under the stars, refusing a tent just in case. Chase watched her close her eyes and waited until her breathing became regular to get up and begin his patrol.

He walked the perimeter of the camp, frustrated. Did she really see him as so pathetic? So weak? He'd bent over backwards trying to make things better for all of them, and it was as if she didn't even notice. And no matter what he said, he couldn't seem to get through to her. After that first kiss, she'd completely turned off. Radio silence. It was like traveling with a robot. She avoided him, preferring the company of the damn kids. He could hear them laughing behind him on the road, making inside jokes that only they understood. It wasn't fair. They were *his* kids. Well, sort of his kids. He'd certainly known them longer. But lately they all seemed to prefer Molly to him.

Maybe it was the pills. He'd started upping his daily dosage to deal with the pain in his cheek. He figured when the pain went away he would quit taking them again. Still, they left him groggy and lethargic and not a hell of a lot of fun to be around. Some days he could barely stay on his horse. Luckily, with everyone ignoring him, he could get away with it.

If only Tank were here. Chase missed his brother like crazy, and every day it got worse. He missed their casual banter. Tank's amazing way with the kids. If there were any justice in the world, Tank would be here now, leading everyone to Florida, not stupid, irresponsible Chase who was flying by the seat of his pants, making it up as he went. No wonder the kids didn't talk to him.

He'd promised to protect the children, to get them to somewhere safe. Now he had to make good. And he had no idea how that was supposed to happen.

After all, he'd never been able to save anyone else.

He thought about his adopted sister. Her gap-toothed smile. Her high-pitched giggles. He was supposed to protect her from all the danger. Instead, he'd left her alone. It had just been for a few minutes, but that was all it took. A vision of her broken body, lying on the stage, blood seeping out of her thousand cuts, slammed through his brain. He swallowed a lump in his throat that felt attached to his heart.

Yes, Tara had believed in him and he had let her down. Now here he was again, thrust into another position where he was expected to protect the innocent. What if he failed? Tara's face faded and in its spot he saw Darla. Then Sunshine. They were bloodied and bruised and it was totally his fault.

He shook his head, a feeble attempt to keep the inner darkness at bay. He fingered the pill bottle in his pocket, desperately wanting another pill. But the score had been a small one, and he'd had to take more and more medication these days to get results. He needed another score like the government lab one he'd once found. The high-grade stuff that was built to last for years.

A sudden thought occurred to him. What if he couldn't find another batch? What if what he had in his pocket was everything? His hands shook as he pulled the bottle out to look. Was this his last pill? Would he have to stop taking them? How was he going to function sober?

Panic throbbed through his veins as he popped open the top, and he felt like he was going to throw up. It would be fine, he told himself. He'd make up some excuse tomorrow to have the party wait for him while he went "hunting and foraging." Molly would never know, just as Tank had never known. He'd travel until he hit some pharmacies or houses, stock up good and then he'd be okay. When he came back he'd just say he hadn't been lucky finding game. The plan would work.

And for now, he'd just take one. Just one pill wouldn't do much. After all, these were super weak. One pill would calm him down and he'd be able to stay up and guard the group without feeling so freaked out. It was in everyone's best interest.

He upended the bottle. Two pills fell out. He'd only take one. Except, he took two. But they were weak. No big deal. He dry-swallowed them, feeling a sense of peace wash over him as they scratched down his throat. He'd be okay. He'd find more tomorrow. And tonight he'd keep Molly and the children safe. Tank was gone, and Chase was the main man now. But that was okay. He could do it.

No big deal. He'd just close his eyes for a second, then make another circle of the perimeter.

CHAPTER TWENTY-FOUR

"Hi, honey, how was school?"

Molly's mom's smile seemed strained as she set colorful plates down on the dinner table in preparation for supper. Dad was down in the basement again, not surprisingly. He'd been down there almost constantly for the last week, ever since Molly told him about the monster in the Dumpster. When she'd questioned him later, when he came back from checking it out, he claimed to have seen nothing. Nothing but dead bodies, stacked high. He said perhaps the shock of that nightmare itself was enough to make Molly's mind go a little crazy. To cause her to see something that wasn't actually there.

But Molly knew what she'd seen and it was no hallucination. And the fact that her dad wouldn't meet her eyes made her suspicious that he knew more than he'd tell. But try as she might, she couldn't get him to say anything more on the subject. Eventually she dropped it. But still, she found herself every day looking in the shadows, searching. Just in case. It wasn't something she could just forget about.

"Good, I guess, considering half the teachers are out with the Super Flu," Molly sneered, plopping down in a chair. "They combined all our classes in the school auditorium with the one healthy guy left teaching. The sim-gym teacher! It's ridiculous. I don't know why they're bothering. They should just shut down."

"Well, you still need an education," Ashley Anderson said, carefully placing each fork, spoon and knife in its place.

"What good is an education if we're all going to keel over and die?"

Her mother dropped a spoon, and it clattered to the floor. She squatted to collect it and walked to the sink. After tossing the utensil in, she reached for her pills. Molly sighed. She'd noticed her mother's hands were shaking and wondered how many happy pills she'd already swallowed that afternoon. It had been a disconcerting development the first time she'd seen her mother take the medication, but gradually it had seemed more normal. A lot of people were running scared these days and overmedicating.

The Super Flu hadn't stayed a hidden epidemic for long; it was too deadly and spread too quickly for any government intervention to help. By the end of the week it had been all over the news. People were urged to stay home and lock their doors. Close their windows. They'd been assured this would help keep the disease from spreading.

What people had done instead was either: a) pretend nothing strange was happening, b) dose like crazy on psych meds, or c) take the opportunity to stick it to the Man. News of looting was becoming more and more common. Shopkeepers—those who were still actually going to work—had taken to keeping loaded guns behind their counters. Last week three people had been shot.

Oh, and then there was the d) option: preparing for the worst. Some were stockpiling food and water and medicine in a desperate attempt to keep their families safe. Food prices had gone through the roof, as no one was driving the delivery trucks. Many stores that had once boasted overflowing shelves were now closing after running out of stock.

Molly didn't know which option was smartest, but she knew going to school and packing into a gym to be taught by the sim-sports coach was something of a joke. Of course, she supposed the government had to keep the children busy somehow. While adults were dying in droves, very few people under the age of eighteen had been reported as sick.

"I need you to go to the store, Molly," her mother said, rummaging through the kitchen cabinets. "Debbie told me they might be trucking in some fresh produce today."

Molly groaned. After a long day at school, the last thing she wanted was to stand in line for three hours, waiting for a delivery that probably would fail to show. But what else could she do? Fresh fruits and vegetables were the one thing you couldn't stockpile. Her mother had taken to canning them and drying them whenever she could, and her father had brought home several batches for just that purpose. Molly didn't want to ask where he'd gotten them. She was also jonesing for a nice ripe tomato.

"Okay," she agreed, grabbing her bag. "I'll be back in ten hours."

She headed outside. The neighborhood was quiet. No kids were playing outside. No cars were leaving driveways. But she could feel eyes on her from behind drawn curtains. The people here were home. Waiting. Watching. Too scared to leave.

Molly decided to swing by Erin's house on the way to the market. Maybe she could convince her friend to come with her. Having someone along would cut down on the boredom of waiting in line at the very least. And Erin's family likely needed some produce as well.

She walked up to her friend's front door and rang the bell. No answer. Frowning, she rang a second time.

"It's me!" she called loudly, just in case they were worried about thieves. "Molly Anderson."

The video-monitoring system clicked on, and unseen eyes stared down at her. A moment later she heard a click and the door swung open. Erin's mother stepped out, closing the door behind her.

"You shouldn't have come here, Molly," she said.

Molly cocked her head in confusion. "What? Why? I just wanted to see if Erin wanted to go get some produce with me. Supposedly there's going to be a big delivery today."

Erin's mom shook her head. "Erin's sick," she said, her voice shaking. "We . . . we think she's infected."

Molly stared. "But . . . I thought kids weren't getting it," she said, confused. "I thought it was just an adult thing." Chills ran down her spine. It was now affecting kids, too? This was terrifying. Not that she hadn't been scared before, but . . .

Erin's mother shrugged wearily. "I don't know. But she's been running a high fever since she got home from school and . . . well, she's coughing. It's coming up blood. They . . . they say that's the first sign." The woman was clearly near a breakdown.

"Oh, God." Molly shook her head and blinked away the tears that were flooding her eyes. "Can I see her?"

The woman shook her head. "No, sweetie," she said. "I don't think that's a good idea. You don't want to get sick, too."

In a daze, Molly nodded. She knew the woman was right, even if avoiding the Super Flu at this point seemed next to impossible, no matter what her father claimed about her being immune.

"Well, tell her I said . . . hi," she murmured, not sure how else to end things. "And . . . and that I hope she feels better soon."

She could see the tears welling up in Erin's mother's eyes, and the woman nodded, and Molly suddenly realized that Erin wasn't *going* to feel better soon. She wasn't going to feel better ever. She was going to die. Like the rest of the world was going to die.

"Take care, dear," Erin's mother said. "And be careful."

Molly trudged down the front stairs of the house, tears streaming down her cheeks. Before this, she hadn't really known any of the victims. There was Mrs. McCormick, who'd begun it all, and her teachers had called in sick, but after that everyone who'd fallen ill was a stranger. All her friends at school were still fine. Her parents were fine—apart from her mother's sudden attraction to opiates. But now, to be best friends with someone who had the disease . . . Suddenly everything was a lot more real.

Erin. Fun, sunshiney Erin. Champion virtual cheerleader. All-around great person. Sick. Probably dying. Just like everyone else.

Her dad was right. The end of the world was coming. And not with a bang but a whimper.

CHAPTER TWENTY-FIVE

The annoying chirps of hungry baby birds waiting for that early-morning worm drew Molly out of a deep sleep the next morning. She pulled her sleeping bag over her head and sat up, stretched and lamented the sore muscles she suffered from sleeping on the ground. Tonight they'd have to find a location that was safe from Others but also had beds.

The children had risen with the baby birds, and they were presently running around the rest area in what appeared to be a wild game of tag. Their laughter and high-pitched squeals pierced the air—not exactly the best way for their group to keep a low profile, and Molly hoped there were no hungry Others nearby. She noticed, with amusement, that Starr and Torn were huddled next to one another, whispering. Young love. So sweet. It gave her a tiny bit of hope for the future.

She glanced over at Chase, wondering if he felt the same. Instead, she realized he felt nothing. He was asleep.

Yes, her fearless all-night watchman was curled up in a fetal position and snoring like a trooper. How long had he lasted before succumbing to sleep? And why hadn't he woken her up? Annoyance gnawed at her gut. She should have never let him insist on taking the whole night. It was too dangerous for these kinds of screw-ups. What if one of the Others had wandered through their camp last night looking for a midnight snack?

Worried, she did a quick head count, just to make sure it

hadn't happened. Eight kids. Phew. They'd caught a lucky break. No thanks to Mr. Watchman.

She shook Chase awake. "What are you doing?" she demanded. "Why the hell didn't you wake me up when you got tired?"

He looked at her groggily, eyes still sleepy and unfocused. If she wasn't so angry, she would have thought he looked cute.

"Sorry," he muttered, sitting up and rubbing his eyes. "I don't know. I was fine and then . . ."

"Look, Chase. This isn't your protected Wal-Mart anymore. We're out in the wild. Anything could happen. We have to stand watch at all times." She was practically shouting at him, though she was also trying to keep her voice low so the kids wouldn't hear.

He scowled, looking uncomfortable. "I know, I know," he grunted. "I get it. You can stop nagging. So I fucking fell asleep. It won't happen again."

"Damn right it won't. I'll be taking the night watch from now on. After all, I—"

"You're not human. Right, I get it. You and your robotic implants. You're beyond screw-ups and better than me. I get it. I gotta go take a leak." He scrambled to his feet and stalked off toward a copse of trees to the northwest.

Molly watched him go, feeling shrewish. She shouldn't have been so harsh. After all, nothing had happened. They were all safe. It wasn't that big a deal. And he had been trying his best. They both had been working very hard, traveling, baby-sitting. It wasn't like either one of them was born to this sort of . . .

Her eyes fell on a prescription bottle lying next to where he'd fallen asleep. She picked it up, turned it over and read the label.

Oh, no.

Molly knew the prescription well. It was the same as one of her mother's. This had been a bottle of the little happy pills that had succeeded in sucking away Ashley Anderson's personality, her consciousness, and finally, her life. She'd zoned out and become completely useless, as if she were a ghost. For six years she'd haunted their shelter until she finally floated away, her body atrophied and her mind all but destroyed.

And now it seemed Molly had somehow attached herself to a guy with the same addiction. The person who was supposed to help her get to Disney, the one she was forced to depend on, was nothing more than a pill-popping junkie just like her mother. Thank goodness she hadn't allowed herself to fall for him. To start a relationship. That would have been a disaster.

In any case, this stupidity had to stop. Now. And how was she going to be able to trust him?

Chase walked back over and grabbed his sleeping bag, rolling it up. "I fed the horses," he said, his voice overly cheery, probably trying to get her to forgive him. "We're good to go when you're ready."

She held up the prescription bottle. His face turned bright red, proving his guilt.

"What?" he asked.

"Pills, Chase? Is this why you fell asleep?"

"I don't know what you're talking about."

Oh, he was going to play innocent? "I found them by your bed," she said, trying to keep her voice flat and emotionless. "It's the same bottle you had when I was stitching up your face."

He dropped his sleeping bag. "Fine. They're mine. What of it?"

"Chase." She drew in a breath. She had to get this all in the open. "Do you have a drug problem?"

"No!" he retorted, looking horrified. "How can you ask me that?"

She held up the pills. "Um . . ."

"Okay, I get why you'd ask," he relented. "But no, I don't have a drug problem. Look, my face was killing like a mother last night. You know, 'cause of the stitches. I thought maybe a painkiller would help, all right?"

"Oh." The world crashed down on Molly and she cringed. Here she was, thinking he was some sort of junkie, but instead he was just medicating because of the wound she herself had given him. She'd judged before giving him the respect of an explanation. He probably thought she was a total bitch. Maybe she was. Even if she'd come from the right place, trying to keep everyone safe.

"Well," Chase snapped, "if you're done accusing me of shit, I'm going to round up the kids. After all, we don't want to disrupt your precious schedule."

"Look, Chase, I'm sorry I—"

"Whatever." He stormed off.

She felt horrible. Why had she jumped to those conclusions? After all, Chase wasn't her mother. And besides the sleeping thing, he'd totally lived up to his responsibilities so far. He had rallied the children, gotten them a good distance in a not-terrible amount of time. It was a difficult situation for all of them, and they were doing the best they could. She shouldn't be so judgmental—especially without knowing all the facts.

Still . . . Her eyes fell on the pill bottle lying discarded in the grass. Picking it up, she scanned the campsite for a trash-can. The next time Chase was in pain, she decided, he should try aspirin.

Self-righteous bitch. Chase stole a glance back at Molly and her horse as their group clomped down the center of I-95. She thought she was so perfect and fit to judge anyone who didn't live up to her ridiculously high standards. So he'd fallen asleep. No big deal. They were all okay, right?

But, no. The way she looked at him, you'd think he'd been caught abusing puppies. The disappointment in her eyes. The judgment in her voice. Those things said it all. It had to be tough going through life so goddamn perfect. She never showed weakness. Like a freaking cyborg or some shit, intent on her mission, not letting anything get in her way. Maybe joining her on the journey had been a mistake. He'd thought she'd be different once they got to know each other; she would let her guard down. And she had done just that, briefly, when they'd kissed. But then she'd shut down again afterward. She'd gone off into her own little world, only piping up when someone dared try to slow her pace.

If this were that old reality sim, VR Island, she'd so win, hands down. Though, if it were up to him, she'd be voted off the server first.

She never used to be like this. He remembered the old Molly. Sweet, beautiful, scared. The apocalypse had changed everyone, he guessed. Forced them to put up walls and trust no one. Was the old Molly still there, deep inside? The one he'd fallen in love with so many years ago?

He realized that either way he'd better make peace. The two of them were stuck together for the time being, and he didn't think either of them could take care of the kids by themselves. So he slowed his horse and drew even with hers so that they were walking side by side.

"Hey," he said.

"Hey."

"Look, Molly, I owe you an apology. I snapped at you and you didn't deserve it."

She looked at him with cool eyes. "No problem," she said.

"It's just . . . well, I feel kind of stupid about the whole thing," he confessed. "I knew I should have woken you up when I started to feel sleepy. But you looked so peaceful, I . . . well, I didn't want to disturb you, is all. I figured I'm the *guy*, right? I should be the one to take care of you."

"So you can buy me dinner, hold the door open," Molly snapped. "You can drape your cloak in mud puddles I have to cross. I think Armageddon actually made the rules of chivalry obsolete," she added after a moment.

Chase sighed. Hers was a tough nut to crack, that was for sure. "Maybe you're right," he said. "In any case, I'm sorry."

"Don't worry about it," she replied again, and turned her gaze back to the road.

He raked a hand through his hair, frustrated, and decided to try another tack. "So, tell me more about Disney World, and what your father and his scientist friends have planned. I hope they're all down there and waiting."

She was silent a moment and he thought at first she was angry at his questions. Then she opened her mouth. "Like I told you before, they want to make Disney World the center of whatever society is rebuilt," she said. "They'll accept refugees into the many hotels there to keep them safe from the Others. They'll create a makeshift government and new laws—good ones this time, not like the past administration who did everything they could to restrict people's rights. This will be a truly democratic society, with everyone having a voice. They'll assign people to various jobs—cooks, who can use the many restaurant facilities on site to feed the people, teachers to educate the children, even an army with stockpiled weapons to keep everyone safe. After all, not everyone may be gung-ho about my dad's friends running things. There might be other groups who spring up and want to take over."

"Ah," Chase said. "Makes sense. Are you planning on joining the army? I mean, you're certainly the most amazing fighter I've seen."

She shook her head, clearly annoyed by his flattery. "No," she said. "Once I get to Disney World I want all these implants out. I can't stand them."

"Really? But they work so well! They make you so strong."

She sighed. "Sometimes I get sick of being strong."

And there it was. A shred of emotion. A thread of vulnerability spoken aloud. Chase grasped it like a precious gem. "I bet," he said sympathetically. "It must be hard to always be in control."

She turned to him. "You think I'm a total bitch, don't you?"

Her question surprised him, but he managed to keep his composure. "No," he said, reaching a hand over to stroke her forearm. Her horse whinnied in protest, but he ignored it. "I think you're suppressing your doubts and fears because you feel it's necessary to survive. Unlike me, who seems to always wear his damn heart on his sleeve."

She offered him a shy smile. "I like that about you, actually," she said. "When Tank, well, you know . . . you grieved for him. Loudly."

He nodded. "Yeah. Well, he was not only my brother, he was my best friend. I loved him."

"My mother died right before I met up with you guys," she said. "After years of sickness." She shook her head. "I still haven't been able to cry for her."

"How come?"

"Molly Millions doesn't cry. She spits."

"What?"

She shook her head. "Never mind. It doesn't matter."

"Well, last I looked, you're Molly Anderson, not this Molly Millions chick. And no one here is going to think less of you if you cry. We all have cried at one time or another. Some of us more than others. And I'm pretty sure by the time this is all said and done, we will all cry again."

She nodded absently, looking lost in thought. For a moment he thought the conversation was over; then she turned to him again. "I'm sorry about your brother," she said. "I barely got to know him, but he seemed like a good guy."

"Thanks," Chase said. "He was. He was the best." He paused then added, "And I'm sorry about your mother."

"Thanks." She started to say more, but her voice suddenly cracked. Chase looked over in surprise and saw a tear slip down her cheek. It had oozed out from behind her implants, and he wondered if it was painful or bad for the circuitry. But instead of asking, he simply reached out and took her hand in his, stroking her palm with a finger. She didn't pull away.

They rode a long while holding hands. Chase watched silently as each tear slipped down her cheek. There were five. But the ice princess was unquestionably melting.

CHAPTER TWENTY-SIX

Molly ran down the street, tears blinding her. She knew she should go to the market, should stand in line as her mother had asked and collect the food they needed to stay in good health. But she couldn't bring herself to go. Not yet.

She didn't know where she was running, and surprised herself when she ended up at Chris Griffin's house. It was weird to think that the boy she'd barely tolerated for so many years had become her number one source of comfort.

Banging on the door, she prayed he was home, home and—A crazy thought struck her. What if he was sick, too? What if everyone was sick? Everyone but her. She tried to decide which would be worse: dying, or being the only one left alive. Both options seemed beyond awful.

The door swung open. A six-year-old dark-skinned girl peered out with huge almond-shaped eyes. She was dressed in a pair of cut-off jeans, as was the fashion, and a beaded silver top.

"Um, hi," Molly said. "Is Chris here?"

"Chris!" the girl called loudly, not bothering to turn around.

"Yeah?" A voice in the distance. Molly let out the breath she hadn't realized she was holding. He was okay. He was alive.

"Some girl at the door."

"Who?"

The little girl looked at Molly with a mixture of boredom and inquiry.

"Molly," she said.

"Molly!" the girl repeated loudly for Chris's benefit.

"Be right there."

The child snapped her gum. "He'll be right here," she said unnecessarily, not unblocking the door to let Molly inside.

"Um, yeah. Thanks."

A moment later, Chris appeared. He ruffled the little sentry's hair. "You can let her in, you know, Tara," he told her. Then he turned to Molly. "Don't mind her," he said fondly. "She's just overprotective." He shuffled her away from the door and beckoned for Molly to enter.

She followed him down into a finished basement packed with sim decks and other electronic equipment. He invited her to sit down on the red plaid sofa and asked if she wanted a drink.

She shook her head. "No, thank you."

"Are you sure?" He looked down at her, concerned. "You look pale. Maybe some water?"

She nodded. "Okay."

He pressed a button on the refrigeration unit at the far end of the room. A bottle of water popped out of the slot below. He handed it to her.

"How have you been?" he asked, sitting down beside her. "Still thinking about Mount Holyoke?"

She shrugged, pulling her legs up under her. Taking a sip of the water, she tried to decide how best to answer the question. She hadn't forgotten the monster, of course. But now it seemed almost irrelevant, given the news she'd received a few minutes before. "I went by Erin's today," she told him, her voice shaking. "And she's . . . she's sick."

"Oh, Molly, I'm sorry." Chris leaned over and pulled her into a huge hug. That was all it took for her to lose her last semblance of control. Tears flowed from her eyes, soaking his T-shirt. Feeling embarrassed, she tried to pull away, but he held her tight, stroking her back with gentle fingers.

"She's my best friend," Molly sobbed. "What if she dies? What if everyone dies? If kids are now getting it, then what hope do the rest of us have?"

"Can I ask you a personal question?"

"Sure," she said, wondering what on Earth he was going to say.

"Have you gotten your AIDS vaccine?"

What? What did he just say? She jerked away, angry. "What are you asking?" she demanded. "I'm trying to tell you my best friend is probably dying and you're interested in whether or not I have my license to fuck?" She glared at him. What a mistake she'd made coming here. And to think she'd thought he was different. But no, he was just like Drew and the rest of mankind, thinking with his dick. Maybe it was better the plague wiped them all out. They were truly pathetic as a species.

Chris held up his hands in protest. "Relax!" he cried. "Jeez, it's not like I'm asking to get in your pants."

She glowered at him, not sure what to say.

"Wow, you'd really think I'd try something like that when you're crying? What do you take me for?" He shook his head. "I'm asking 'cause I've been doing some more forum trolling, and from what some scientists have gathered, it seems the flu may be some kind of reaction to the AIDS vaccine. They claim that all the victims so far have been vaccinated."

"Oh." She felt her face flame as she realized what he was saying. How stupid of her to think he wanted sex. He was Chris, not Drew. "Sorry. I didn't mean to imply . . ." She trailed off, realizing the implications of his words. "So you're saying the plague only affects those with their LTFs?" It made perfect sense. Erin had just gotten hers. Now she was sick. Molly hadn't, and she felt fine. And her dad insisted she'd be okay. He'd probably read the same research. "Are you sure? I haven't heard anything like that on the news."

"Yeah, that's 'cause the government controls the media still, and they don't want any people taking revenge. After all, they're the ones who made it a requirement to get inoculated."

"I guess that makes sense." Molly thought for a moment. "God, that's so terrible. More than three-quarters of our population have gotten the shot. All that's going to be left is a bunch of kids."

Chris nodded. "That's what it looks like. Unless other adults are immune."

She felt cold. Scared. She buried her head back in his chest, wanting his warmth. He wrapped his arms around her again, nuzzling her head with his chin. "I know it's scary," he whispered. "But I promise, we'll get through. We'll figure out a way."

She nodded against him, enjoying the sensation of his hands rubbing up and down her back. He felt warm and solid and safe. Unlike the rest of the world.

"I won't let anything happen to you," he swore. "I'll keep you safe."

She looked up at him, knowing her face was blotchy and her cheeks tearstained. "Do you really mean that?" she asked, her voice barely a whisper. Sensations she hadn't been aware existed were now coursing down her spine, tickling and tingling. He was so sweet. So brave. So caring. What had she been thinking all these years? Calling him a geek and valuing losers like Drew. He was a lot like a diamond himself. And she had treated him as a shard of glass.

"Of course," he replied, gravely serious. He reached up and brushed a tear from her cheek. The sensation gave her chills and warmed her belly. "I'd do anything for you, Molly."

Suddenly she knew what she wanted.

"Anything?"

He nodded.

"Then kiss me."

And he did. His lips brushed hers with an ultimate tenderness. The chills came harder and faster now, and she found she could barely breathe. With a soft moan she parted her lips, allowing his tongue entrance. It was hesitant, as if Chris were afraid to push lest the offer be rescinded. So Molly took the lead, pressing her mouth against his and going after what she wanted. Their tongues met and danced as they clung to one another.

She'd been kissed before. Plenty of times. But never had it felt like this. So passionate, so sweet. Maybe it was because of the situation, knowing that the end of the world as they knew it was likely near. Or maybe it was more than that. Maybe they were meant to be together. Whatever it was, it felt good. And for the first time since the whole thing began, Molly felt a tiny bit of peace.

"I love you, Molly," Chris whispered against her mouth.

And she knew right then and there, crazy as the idea might be, she loved him, too.

If the world was going to end, at the very least they had each other. And that was something.

In fact, that was a lot.

CHAPTER TWENTY-SEVEN

The sun beat down as the group followed the highway on the sixth day of their journey. By Chase's estimation, they were at about the two hundred mile point, which seemed like excellent progress until he realized that still left two hundred miles to go. And he was out of pills, thanks to Molly.

He couldn't believe she'd thrown them away. He'd asked casually, once they were back on the road, so she wouldn't yell at him more. It had been a mistake. He'd wanted to throttle her when she informed him matter-of-factly that she'd tossed away his precious pills back at the rest area. It was too far to go back, and Chase couldn't think of a reason to suggest it without sounding like a total druggie, which she already suspected him to be.

Not that he was a druggie. He could quit anytime. But his face hurt a lot and the pills worked wonders to dull the pain. They worked a lot better than the first-aid kit aspirin, which she had so helpfully suggested he try.

They were also nearly out of the food they'd packed, which meant a trip into one of the towns soon. They'd so far done their best to avoid once heavily populated areas, only stopping at roadside motels or highway rest stops. If it were up to Chase, he'd stay far away from all former civilization for good. That way he could almost pretend that just off the next exit grandmothers sat on front-porch rocking chairs, sipping mint juleps and gossiping about their crazy neighbors. He could imagine that each morning businessmen in stuffy suits were shuffling into their Smart SUVs and heading to the offices where they'd be greeted by the sexy secretaries with whom they were secretly sleeping. Soccer moms were pushing babies in strollers, and children were screaming as they played tag in the park.

He wanted to imagine that life had gone on and the whole plague was just a really long, really bad joke.

But towns were the best place to find food if they couldn't hunt game, and they hadn't seen any animals along this stretch of road. So that afternoon when they came across a sign for the town of Paradise, he'd made his offer. They could wait for him over at the Motel 6 right off the exit and he'd go in and search for food. It was safer if he went in alone, just in case something was down there. He also imagined himself returning victorious, the conquering hero with his collected supplies, Molly's smile as he presented her with a gourmet three-course meal. He'd fill her stomach with excellent things and make her grateful for bringing him along. That idea alone was worth facing the horror of the suburbs.

That and the fact that he'd get to do some exploration. He wanted to find a hospital or something, because that would have more pills. At least a few, for until his face got better. Then he could wean himself off them gradually, so he wouldn't be sick. He agreed with Molly that it wasn't a great idea to be popping opiates while on the road, but at the same time, going cold turkey was going to be disruptive to their intense travel schedule.

"I don't like it," Molly said, surveying the town from the highway. "Something seems off here. Maybe we should wait a bit."

"It's fine," Chase countered, mainly because he was itching so badly for more pills, his stomach clenching with need. That was the problem with being off drugs. You could feel everything ten times as intensely, and none of it was comfortable. "I don't see anything down there."

"I know. I don't, either. It's just I have a bad feeling. I don't know why."

"What, are you psychic as well as cyber?" he grunted.

She blushed. He had a moment of embarrassment and shame. He hadn't meant to hit below the belt.

"Sorry," he muttered. "It's just . . . I don't see what the big deal is. I'll go down, find us some supplies then come right back. You all can stay in that Motel 6 right off the exit and I'll meet you there." He threw her what he hoped was a cocky, confident, non-desperate smile. "We'll eat like kings tonight!"

"But the horses are exhausted from the trek," she said, trying a different tack. "They need rest, too. And also to eat."

"It's not far. I'll walk."

She slumped her shoulders and he knew he'd won. His stomach burned with anticipation, and he wondered how far a hospital was off the exit ramp. He'd seen a sign for one a little ways back. Of course, he'd also take a pharmacy. Or someone's house. Just a quick stop, then he'd get food and come back and no one would be the wiser that he'd added one extra thing to the grocery list.

"Be careful, Chase," Molly said. "Seriously."

As if she cared. The only reason she kept him around was that she didn't want to have to deal with the children all by herself, and she didn't want to abandon them either. She'd made it clear she wanted nothing more from him.

He waved away her fears. "I was born careful, baby," he said, psyching himself up to go. The false bravado sounded silly, even to his own ears. But really, what could happen? It was a town just like the one he'd left. The one in which he'd survived for six years. No problem.

"All right, kids, I'm out," he informed the group. "When I come back we'll have a feast."

The kids cheered. Darla stepped forward. "Be careful, Chase," she said, giving him a motherly look. It was odd, coming from a little girl.

He ruffled her hair. "I will, I will," he assured her. "You and Molly. Geez. Worry warts, both of you."

He said his good-byes and headed down the exit ramp toward the town. Looking around, he saw Paradise was a bigger city than they'd lived in back home. Not a Manhattan, obviously, but it did have its share of tall buildings. And he could see some kind of stadium in the distance. He remembered watching his beloved Carolina Panthers win the Super Bowl in 2025. Sad, there'd never be another game like that.

He walked out onto the main road, wishing he had Molly's ocular implants. She'd been able to access quite a few maps as they traveled, and thus they'd avoided some areas they thought would have a high likelihood of Others. She likely would have been able to point him to the nearest pharmacy. Of course, he hadn't been exactly able to ask.

His eyes fell on a small shop at the corner of an intersection, the only building on the street with a glass window that wasn't shattered. In the window were pictures of beautiful pieces of jewelry. Chase thought about Molly, always fingering that piece of glass in her pocket when she thought he wasn't looking. She was acting like an ice princess, but deep inside he believed she was as sentimental as he was, remembering their past. It was really too bad she was afraid to show it, afraid to be vulnerable. But she was afraid, and she lived each day hiding behind that thick wall she'd built for herself.

A thought suddenly occurred to him. Maybe he could get her something, some small token to show her what she meant to him. To show his gratitude for letting them come along, even though they slowed her down. He didn't think diamonds or jewels were appropriate, but perhaps there was something that would adequately demonstrate how he felt.

Entering the store, he scanned the glass cases looking for just the right thing. A lot had been taken, but there were a few offerings that remained. He wanted something strong but delicate, just like her. And then he saw it: a small music box, covered in layers of dust and sitting on a shelf. He opened it and turned the knob. To his surprise, a hologram of a princess appeared—it kind of looked like a Disney princess, actually—twirling in a pirouette while the box played its little tune. Was the tune "It's a Small World"?

It was perfect. After all, where were they headed but the Magic Kingdom? And Molly was certainly the princess of his fairy tale—even if things hadn't worked out quite right just yet. But maybe this gift would convince her that there was still time for a happily ever after.

Tucking the box under his arm, he headed back outside. A strange feeling came over him. The street was totally quiet. He didn't even hear any birds in the trees. Weird. And then he saw the footprint.

He stared at it, long and hard, trying to figure it out. It looked fresh. It also didn't look like a footprint of one of the Others. They usually shuffled, and this was clean, a perfect imprint. He could even see the Nike logo embedded in the sole.

He drew in a breath. Were there humans alive in this town?

Half of him wanted to turn around and run back to the kids, to get Molly and tell her the news. The other half said he should go and investigate these survivors himself. Maybe they had stashes of food. Maybe they had knowledge of other groups. Maybe they'd seen Molly's father.

He walked in the direction the footprint pointed, searching for Others but seeing none. But soon he came across something better: a small pharmacy, its door wide open.

I should just keep walking, he scolded himself. *Find the guy who made the footprint. Concentrate on my mission. I don't need drugs.*

But he did. His body ached and itched and the pharmacy drew him with an almost irresistible tractor beam. Soon he found himself walking through the front door, his forehead and palms damp with sweat.

The front of the store had something exciting: a ton of candy. Chase was surprised that it hadn't been eaten already, and he wasn't sure if it was all still good, but he knew that it would get a good reception when he returned to the kids. But as he glanced around to find some plastic bags to gather the booty up, he saw something else, just to the back of the store. The prescription counter.

Rushing over to it, he scanned the racks. Allergy medicines, stool softeners, emergency contraception. The spot where the good stuff should have been—the painkillers—was all cleared out.

Had Mr. Footprint already helped himself? Chase found himself wondering. He squeezed his hands into fists. It figured. The survivor he'd stumbled onto was just going to be competition. He wondered what he should do about that.

"Looking for something, boy?"

The scratchy male voice from behind him nearly made Chase jump out of his skin. He whirled, whipping out his knife. Sun shone through the glass storefront window, silhouetting the intruder. All Chase could tell was that he was big.

Mr. Footprint, he presumed.

"Stay where you are," he said, trying to keep fear from filling his voice. "I've got a knife."

"Yup. Can see that." The man stepped forward, evidently unconcerned. Chase could now see his wild black hair and scruffy beard. He was dressed in a pair of jean cutoffs and wearing a T-shirt that claimed pirates were way cooler than ninjas. The shirt also listed reasons why.

"I said, don't move!" Chase was beginning to wonder if coming to Paradise had been a bad idea.

"Oh, fine. Have it your way," the man said, shrugging his shoulders. "Y'all might as well put down the knife, though. Ain't aiming to hurt you none." He held out his hands, showing they were empty.

Chase lowered his knife, though he kept it in his hand. "Sorry," he said. "Just don't run into many people these days."

"Not many left to run into, I reckon," Mr. Footprint replied. "I was pretty surprised when I saw you outside. Figured I'd follow you in, see what you were up to." He scratched a pus-filled boil on his right cheek, making Chase think of the Others. But this guy wasn't a zombie. He was just . . . dirty.

"Nothing much," Chase replied, not wanting to admit his true purpose. He could barely admit it to himself, never mind this guy. "Just checking things out." The jewelry box felt heavy under his arm, and he gripped it tighter. Not that there was any reason in the world this guy would take it.

"Name's Luke," the stranger said, holding out a hand. His fingernails were caked with dirt and Chase wondered when he'd last taken a bath. Back home, Tank had made them all bathe at least once a week, and on this trip they'd washed up every time the interstate passed a river. The kids didn't like it, but Chase thought maybe they would if they saw the state of this guy. "Don't think I've seen you 'round here."

"Just traveling through," Chase replied. His instinct said it'd be better not to mention Molly and the kids, just in case. "Was looking for food." He shrugged his shoulder. "No luck, though."

Luke laughed, a little unkindly. "Think you're going to find food in the local pharmacy, do you?"

Chase felt his face heat. "Um, no, no," he said, not knowing why he'd bothered to lie. Who cared what this country bumpkin thought of him? "I was just looking for some . . . Band-Aids."

"Ah, Band-Aids. Of course." Luke snorted. "I shoulda known." He paused, shuffled his feet, then looked askance at Chase. "So, since you ain't had any luck finding food, you want to come back to my place for some grub? My girlfriend can cook you up something real nice."

"No, that's okay," Chase replied, feeling nervous. Not that Luke seemed like a bad guy, necessarily, but you couldn't be too careful. Besides, he shouldn't be hanging out, filling his stomach while Molly and the kids were waiting for him to return. And if this guy cleaned his house as rarely as he cleaned himself . . . "I've got to get going."

"Suit yerself," Luke said with another shrug. It was almost as if he had a nervous twitch. "I was just thinking I might have some of those . . . yeah, let's call 'em Band-Aids . . . back at the house." He gave Chase a knowing grin and glanced at the empty shelf of painkillers behind him. "If yer still lookin' for them, you know."

Chase actually opened his mouth to say no, but right at that moment the hunger clawed. The itch crawled up his back like a thousand spiders. What actually came out of his mouth sounded a lot more like, "Okay."

And he hated himself all over again.

Luke looked pleased. "Excellent," he said, slapping Chase on the back. He led the way out of the store. "Been ages since I had some company besides the girlfriend. And she's a right pain in the ass, always twittering away like some goddamn bird."

Chase nodded, not knowing how to respond to that. At least Luke's reasoning made sense; he was just lonely. Wanted the company. Nothing weird about that, was there? Chase's stomach flipped again, and the itch found the back of his knees. Maybe it was sweat? He then realized he didn't care if there was anything weird about what Luke wanted; he needed a fix, badly. And this seemed the easiest way to score one.

"So, where you heading?" Luke asked as Chase followed him across the street. "You got a destination, pilgrim?"

Chase shrugged. "South," he said. "Where it's warm." That sounded like as good an explanation as any. After all, he might be willing to risk his own life for drugs, but he sure as hell wasn't going to sell out Molly.

Not that he was risking his life for drugs. Luke seemed a decent enough fellow. Probably just lonely. And dirty. But everyone was lonely and dirty these days. And it was nice to converse with another adult, even if he was a little weird. Chase imagined he probably seemed a little weird himself.

Luke led the way through a narrow, brick-lined alley into what was likely once a gorgeous courtyard. Now it was crumbling and decrepit, the intricate sculpture of an algae-stained stone fountain the only remnant of its former glory. Luke pushed open a door at the far end of the courtyard, and they stepped over the threshold into a dark pit of a home.

"When we first came out after the plague, we thought we'd live in the fanciest house in town," Luke explained, striking a match and holding it to a gas lantern that had been hung by the door. "But while them things are pretty, they sure aren't easy to defend, if you know what I mean."

"From the Others?"

"The Others?" Luke chuckled. "We call 'em Knights of the Living Dead here. You know, like that old zombie sim everyone used to play."

Chase did know. Though the real-life Others—Knights— were certainly more terrifying than those virtual zombies in the old sim.

As his host turned up the lantern, Chase took a good look around the house. He'd been right about its condition: It wasn't exactly going to make the next issue of *Better Homes and Gardens*, if the magazine was still in existence. Green mold clung to the dark wallpaper. Dirty dishes were piled in an even dirtier sink. The sole piece of furniture, a faded, flowered couch, sagged in the center of the room.

"Have yerself a seat, boy," Luke suggested, motioning. Then he turned to the hallway on the left side of the room. "Helga!" he cried. "Get yer ass out of bed, you lazy bitch, and bring us some booze. We got company!"

A small blonde girl poked her head out. Her hair was dreadlocked and her face hollow, with jutting cheekbones and blackened eyes. Her sticklike arms were covered in bruises. Chase shuddered, suddenly getting a very bad feeling. He'd seen other old horror movies besides the George Romero ones.

"Helga came from the mail," Luke told him. "Mail-order bride, they used to call 'em. Though she learned English real good, so you can't even tell. The rich fat fuck she married died in the plague. So I take care of her now." He grabbed the girl roughly by the arm, gave her a slobbery kiss then pushed her in the direction of the kitchen, pinching her ass in the process. She slunk over to the cabinets and rummaged around there.

"Gotta put these damn women in their place," Luke

boasted. "I'm sure you know what I mean. You got yourself a woman, boy?"

Chase shook his head. "No. Never have," he said, doubly glad he hadn't mentioned Molly.

"You one of them queers then?"

"Er, nope." Chase shrugged. "Just aren't that many women to be had these days."

What a stupid idea, coming here, he berated himself as Helga set down three squat, cloudy glasses and a bottle of The Macallan. She poured the whisky and handed Chase a glass. He took it and watched her pour another for Luke. But her hands were shaking, and her fast pour splashed Luke's already stained jeans. The dirty man's eyes grew huge, and Helga cringed, as if anticipating his next move.

BAM! Sure enough, Luke's open palm connected with her face. She cried out and staggered backwards. "Stupid, clumsy bitch!" the man yelled, and Chase got a weird feeling he was actually trying to show off. "These are my best jeans!"

"I'm sorry," Helga babbled, tears streaming down her cheeks. She pressed a hand to her nose, which was dribbling blood. "I didn't mean to—"

"Hey, man, be cool," Chase said, feeling he should say or do something. "It was an accident."

"You *are* one of those fancy boys, aren't you?" Luke growled. "She's fine. Don't get your panties in a twist." He grabbed his glass and held it up. "To Band-Aids," he said.

One sip, Chase decided; he'd drink the toast then make his excuses and get out. It was too crazy here. Too creepy. Even the promise of drugs wasn't worth staying. But he also didn't want to piss off his host.

Oh, Chase, why did you think this was a good idea?

The whiskey burned his throat and he coughed. He hadn't drunk much alcohol in his life, and nothing like this.

Luke laughed. "All right," he said. "Let's get you those Band-Aids." He got up from his seat and walked over to some shelves at the other end of the room. He pulled down a book and opened it. Chase realized it was hollowed out. "I don't

know why I hide it. Not like some narc is gonna bust me."
Luke chuckled. "Old habits die hard maybe."

The man pulled out a syringe and a packet of powder. He
walked back to the couch and sat down. It creaked under his
weight.

Chase glanced toward the door. This was a bit hardcore for
him. Luke was pushing up his sleeve and wrapping a yellow
cord around his biceps, grabbing a spoon off the table and
pouring powder onto it. The process was mesmerizing. Chase
didn't want to be part of this scene anymore . . . but as much
as he wanted to, he couldn't get up and walk away. His eyelids
felt unbearably heavy, and the lantern light was casting strange
shadows on the walls. Demons dancing.

"I have to . . . go," he said, trying to rise. His body felt as if
it weighed a ton. What the hell was going on? From the corner of his eye he could see Luke chuckling. "What . . . did . . .
you . . . ?" His tongue felt huge and swollen, barely fitting in
his mouth.

The man shrugged, at least having the decency to look
abashed. "Sorry, man," he said. "It's sort of a deal we have.
They keep out of my domain and I find them fresh meat."

Chase collapsed, swimming in blackness. The jewelry box
fell from his grip and smashed on the floor. His last thought
was how disappointed he was that he wouldn't ever be able to
give it to Molly.

CHAPTER TWENTY-EIGHT

"Okay, you can remove the blindfold now!"

Molly pulled the rag from her eyes and looked around. She appeared to be in some kind of windowless apartment, a cozy living room with Pottery Barn furniture, a narrow kitchen with stainless steel, non-smart appliances behind a breakfast bar. Leading off the main room was what appeared to be a bathroom, two bedrooms, a pantry overflowing with food and some kind of small fitness center with weights and a treadmill. She turned to her father, confused.

"What is this?"

Ian Anderson beamed, walking to the center of the room and twirling, his arms outstretched. "This," he said, "is our Noah's Ark."

She raised an eyebrow. "Huh?"

"I bought it off the old lady who used to own it. Her father originally built it in the 1950s when they believed a nuclear war with Russia could happen at any moment. It's called a fallout shelter. We'll use it as a safe house when things get really bad." He walked over and adjusted a dial. "Of course, I made modifications to the original design. Updated everything with the latest technology. Even installed titanium so that no one can get in here. Not even government agents. We'll be safe."

"Do you really think it's necessary?" she asked, horrified. The place made her feel claustrophobic; the last thing she wanted was to spend any extended time there. "I mean, the news reports are saying they're getting the flu under control."

"Haven't I taught you anything?" her father asked. "You know the government controls the media. Those reporters are just talking heads and propaganda. Of course they're saying they're getting it under control."

"Right." She sighed. She knew her father was making sense—at least about the media. She hadn't seen anything in her town lately that made her feel any safer. She still wasn't sold on the shelter, however. "So, um, Dad . . . let's say things go down as you think. What happens?"

"In the next few days, I want you to bring down some clothes and whatever else you think you'll need," he said, not answering her question. "Then, when it's time, we can get down here in a hurry. Unlock the shelter door with a scan of your retina out front. I've set the timer for six years."

She stared at him. "Six years?" she repeated. "What do you mean, six years?" She felt panic bubbling into her throat. He couldn't be serious, could he?

"That's what my friends and I have determined to be the minimum amount of time for any airborne germs to dissipate in case the virus jumps. But don't worry, there's plenty of food and water to last you and your mother. I've been stockpiling for some time."

Food was the last thing she was worried about at the moment. "What about you?" she asked. "Won't you be with us?"

"Of course. That's the plan. But if for some reason that doesn't happen, there's a rendezvous point, a place you two can meet me after the doors open."

"Where?"

Her father grinned. "Disney World."

CHAPTER TWENTY-NINE

"When's Chase coming back?" Darla asked for the thousandth time. "I'm hungry."

"Soon," Molly replied, also for the thousandth time. "And we're all hungry."

She scratched her wrist absentmindedly as worry pricked at her brain. Soon. It'd been past *soon* four hours ago, and it was starting to get late in the day. Had something happened to him? What if he'd met up with a band of Others? Or, heck, anything—who knew what was out here, hovering in the shadows?

She should never have let him go alone. But someone had to watch the children and he'd acted so sure of himself. It seemed okay at the time. Now she wasn't sure.

She shook her head, trying to free her mind from the dark thoughts that kept invading. It was probably nothing. He probably just hadn't found what they needed yet and was too damn proud to come back empty-handed.

"When's soon?" Darla whined.

"I don't know!" Molly retorted angrily before she could stop herself. Darla stared, wide-eyed, then burst into tears, running across the makeshift campsite and into the arms of Starr. Even refusing to look at her, Molly felt the teenager's reproachful glare.

Molly felt bad for snapping. After all, it wasn't Darla's

fault. She was just stressed and scared. But there was no need to take it out on the children.

She rose to her feet and walked over to the kids. "I'm sorry," she said, feeling awkward. "I guess I'm a little worried about him, too. He should be back by now."

"D'you think the Others got him?" Starr asked. She looked like she'd swallowed something sharp and it was cutting through her guts.

"No!" Molly said, perhaps a bit too vehemently. "He probably just lost track of time or something. I'm sure he'll be back any minute."

"I think we should go look for him," Torn suggested. She hadn't realized he was nearby. But then, he and Starr had become nearly inseparable. It reminded Molly of how she and Chase had been, back in the day. They'd been so dumb and innocent once.

"It's been too long. He must be in trouble," Torn added.

Molly glanced around and realized all the kids had gathered, concerned looks on their faces. "Okay," she said. "There's no use denying it. You're right, and we need to check it out. Torn and Starr, you watch the kids. I'll go out and look for him."

"Shouldn't we all go?" Starr asked.

"Yeah, if there's Others I want to be able to fight!" Torn growled. He was fifteen. So young. Weird, to think that when the Super Flu hit, Molly and Chase had been his age. They'd felt grown up then, too.

"No," Molly replied. "I need you and Starr to look after the little ones and the horses," she said. "I'll be back as soon as I'm able." The children huddled together, looking like lost puppies. She threw them her bravest smile. "Don't worry," she added. "I'm sure he just found a toy store and is stocking up for you all or something."

But that's not what she really thought at all.

Chase groaned as he swam back to consciousness. How long had he been out? Opening one eye then the other, he tried to ascertain his surroundings. It appeared he was in some sort of jail. Lying on a stained mattress with a threadbare blanket.

Everything came back to him: looking for drugs in the pharmacy. Meeting up with Luke. The drugged drink. Him crashing to the floor.

This was not good.

"You're awake."

He whirled around, realizing for the first time that there were two cots in the cell. On the second sat a skinny blond guy in a white tank top and jeans. He had ugly welts all over his arms.

"Yeah," Chase replied. Was this guy another prisoner who'd had a run-in with Luke, too? "Where am I?"

"Welcome to the Thunderdome."

Chase cocked his head. His fellow prisoner laughed.

"The Thunder . . . ?"

"Well, that's what they like to call it. I hear it's an allusion to some old film. Mad Mack or something."

Chase scratched his head, trying to make sense of what the other man was saying. "I was drugged. By a guy . . ."

"One of their scouts, I'm sure. They hire guys around the city to bring in new recruits. Offer them protection and extra goods in exchange for the service. When people come through town the scouts offer to help them out, get them something they need. That's how they trap 'em."

Chase thought of his encounter with Luke and his own particular, rather embarrassing need, and his face burned. He was such an idiot. A prisoner to the itch, and now it'd made him a prisoner for real. He leapt off the bed and headed over to the door, wrapping his hands around the metal bars. They felt solid. Unmovable.

"No use, man," his cellmate said. "You're stuck until they decide to let you out."

Panic flooded Chase. This couldn't be happening. He couldn't be trapped like this. Not while Molly had no idea where he was. Not while she was caring for the children he'd sworn to protect. He imagined them sitting back at the campsite as the sun slipped below the horizon. Would they come looking for him? And what if they ran into Luke or another scout?

He walked back to his cot and sank down, buried his head in his hands. If only he'd just concentrated on his mission, focused on finding food and supplies. Or maybe he should have gone back right away. They'd had enough dried food for one more night, and he could have stopped in the next town, the next *empty* town. Then he could have presented Molly with her music box. He would have been a hero. Instead, he was a prisoner. And he didn't have a single person to blame but himself.

"I'm Bowie, by the way," his companion said. "Well, my real name's Mike but I like going by Bowie now. Like the old twentieth-century musician. He was great. God, I miss music."

Chase couldn't believe this guy was babbling like nothing was wrong. His life was over, and this guy was about to launch into a convo about the nice weather they'd been having.

"What's your name?" Bowie asked.

"Chase. Chase Griffin."

"Chase Griffin." Bowie appeared to consider. "I like that. Good fighting name. You should tell them. Maybe they'll let you keep it."

"Keep it?"

"Sure. If you have a boring name they'll change it. They need to impress the crowd after all. Can't draw people who aren't interested. Can't interest people with stupid names. Herbie MacMillan versus Beauregard Goldblum! Lawlz. Hardly going to get a crowd with that."

"What?" Chase was getting a worse feeling than ever.

"You don't get it, do you?" Bowie said. "You're a gladiator now."

Chase's stomach roiled. "You mean they're going to make me fight . . . ?"

"Duh. That's what they do here. The town is run by this

ex-wrestler named Brutus. He's a bit crazy—obviously. I think he must have been hit in the head a few too many times. But he brought a bunch of survivors together and formed a makeshift government. It's safer here than a lot of places. And every other Friday—if anyone really knows when Friday is these days—they have 'sports.' "

Sports. Great. Bowie likely wasn't talking about reestablishing the Carolina Panthers. "So, they recruit fighters for the ring?"

"Yup. Well, recruit is maybe stretching things a bit. They grab people passing through and make them into gladiators."

But that's barbaric, Chase wanted to protest, but knew it would do no good. "And we fight other gladiators?" he asked.

Bowie laughed. "No. You fight the Knights of the Living Dead. You know, the changed people. Brutus figures people from outta town brought them down on us; they should be the ones to do the fighting."

Chase cringed. Knights of the Living Dead. Others. The crazy people of this town wanted him to fight Others in a ring. With screaming fans watching. Awesome.

How had he gotten himself into this mess, again? More importantly, how was he going to get himself out?

"Have you fought?" he asked Bowie.

"Sure," his new companion said. "I've been in the ring three times now. Kicked those Others from here to kingdom come." He grinned. "If I win five more fights I get my freedom. I get to be one of the people who live here. Course, I gotta kick this broken leg first." He motioned to his cast. "Damn Knight cracked it last time before I knocked his head off his shoulders with my axe. It was a pretty crazy fight."

Chase closed his eyes. Crazy? That's exactly what he'd call it. And a few other things.

He wondered if Molly would come looking for him, then felt another wash of shame. He was the man; he was supposed to be the one protecting her. Now, because of his weakness, he'd fucked everything up again. He'd inadvertently broken his promise to his brother. After all, he couldn't very well care for the children if he was clawed to death by an Other in a gladiator ring.

He pictured Molly's disappointed face as she realized what had happened. How stupid he had been. She had been angry at just finding the pills; she'd never forgive him for getting himself into this mess. And she shouldn't. He sent up a vow to whatever divinity was listening: If he got out of this— someway, somehow—he'd quit the drugs. Cold turkey this time. No matter how much it sucked. Not that he had much chance of making that happen.

A rattling noise made him open his eyes. He looked up to see a tall man dressed in a tuxedo and top hat tapping on the bars with a cane. "Hey, new boy," the man growled. "Let's see how well you do in the Thunderdome."

Molly headed cautiously down the exit ramp, scanning the scene as she went. So far, no sign of life. Not any animals. Not any humans. Nothing. A completely dead town. So where was Chase? How far could he have gone? What if he'd been dragged off to some Other enclave, never to be seen again?

She shook her head, trying to clear it of morbid thoughts. They weren't productive, for one thing. Better to stay positive. To believe he was still alive.

She hadn't originally wanted to bring him along, but now she couldn't imagine the journey without him. And it would be a lie to say it was just his cooking or the way he was able to effortlessly deal with the kids. It was his quiet company that she appreciated. His smile. His eyes. His occasional laugh. Like it or not, she'd grown more attached to him than ever over the last week. She didn't want to lose him again.

She sent up a prayer, begging whatever higher power was listening to keep him safe, then did another scan of the surrounding area, trying to find some sign of life. Even with her implants, nothing. Nada.

Molly wandered street after street, searching, seeking, but always coming up empty. It was as if Chase had walked into the Bermuda Triangle, vanished, never to be heard from again.

Discouragement crept into her, and she wondered what she should do. She didn't want to go back alone, admit defeat and tell the kids that one more person they loved and depended on was likely gone for good. So she kept looking. And looking.

"Psst!"

Molly whirled around, her cyber defenses activating automatically. The razors shot from her fingers and nanos pumped hardcore adrenaline into her veins. She scanned the street. A small girl with stringy blonde dreadlocks, eyes circled by black and bruises up and down her arms had appeared out of nowhere, holding up her hands in a gesture of surrender. Molly lowered her razors. A human! And a girl! Maybe she could help.

"I'm looking for someone—" she said, but the girl put a finger to her lips and gestured for Molly to follow. Curious, Molly nodded once and did as requested.

Down a dark alleyway, through an empty building, up a hill. The girl paused in front of a small stone church and beckoned once again to Molly, then slipped inside. Molly hesitated. Should she go in after her? What if this was some sort of trap? But this girl was the first person she'd seen in this godforsaken town and thus her only prayer for finding Chase. So she sucked in a breath and stepped into the church sanctuary.

It was dark inside. Deserted. Spooky. Dust-caked pews stood empty, led to an equally dusty altar. Obviously the place hadn't been used for years—likely not since the fear-filled church parishioners made their last useless requests for divine intervention against the Super Flu.

The blonde was already at the front of the church, pulling aside a red velvet, moth-eaten curtain. Once again, she beckoned before slipping beyond.

This time Molly hesitated. "Stop," she called out. "I've followed you far enough. Talk to me."

The girl came back and frowned at Molly. "You want to know about your friend or what?" she asked, crossing her bruised arms over her chest.

Molly's shoulders sagged, realizing she was utterly at this stranger's mercy. "Yes," she said quietly, lowering her hands to her sides. But the razor blades slipped back out from under her nails. Just in case.

The blonde girl disappeared again behind the curtain. Molly followed, pushing aside the red velvet and stepping through into darkness. She adjusted her night vision, blinking twice to adjust the brightness. They'd entered a small back chamber, maybe once the domain of priests waiting to say mass. It was packed floor to ceiling with relics, and ornate crosses adorned nearly every inch of free space.

The girl was there. And she was brandishing a knife.

Molly didn't hesitate. She roundhouse-kicked, striking the girl's arm. Her attacker bellowed in pain but kept her grip, slashing out at Molly with the knife. It sliced through the leather on Molly's left shoulder.

Gritting her teeth, Molly leaned forward and head-butted the girl. The force of the blow sent the blonde flying backwards into a pile of crucifixes. If she had been a vampire, she would have been a goner for sure. But, mortal, she rallied, leaping back to her feet, and her knife slashed through the air again.

This time Molly was ready. Using her nano-accelerated re-action time, she was able to grab the girl's wrist and yank her around, pinning her arm against her back. The girl cried out but kept a death grip on her knife. So with her other hand, Molly reached out and grabbed a fistful of long blonde dread-locks, pulling backward. The girl finally dropped her knife and it clattered to the floor. Molly pushed her forward and grabbed the knife as the girl crashed face-first into the wall.

"I thought you wanted to know about your friend," the girl said sulkily as Molly stood above her.

"I do. And yet you see fit to try to lure me into a dark room and try to kill me."

"Only after you attacked me."

"Then why the knife?"

"Uh," the girl rubbed her head. " 'Cause I don't know you

from Adam and I needed protection? It's dangerous out here nowadays, in case you hadn't realized. And I'm risking my life even talking to you."

Oh. Right. Molly hadn't thought of that. She swallowed her embarrassment and offered the girl a hand up. The blonde took it, brushed off her filthy pants and muttered, "Thanks." Then, walking over to the wall, she pulled out a book of matches and used one to light a candle.

"So, why did you bring me here?" Molly asked.

"It's one of the few safe places in town," the girl explained. "One of the few empty places. Pretty much everyone here is pissed at God for the whole plague thing, so they avoid it like . . . well, you know." She gestured around. "It's become my home away from home. When I need to . . . escape for a bit."

Molly again studied the girl closely, noting the black-and-blue marks on her arms. They'd just fought, sure, but some of those bruises didn't look fresh. She wondered what exactly this girl needed to escape from. In the current world, there were a million possibilities.

"I'm Molly," she said, deciding to make the first overture toward friendship.

"Helga." The girl put out a bony hand and they shook. It seemed weird to recreate old-world formalities, but kind of nice at the same time. "You're with that Chase guy, right?"

Molly felt a surge of hope. So, the girl had been telling the truth. "You've met Chase?" she asked. "You know where he is?"

Helga nodded slowly, in a way that made Molly think wherever Chase was, it wasn't exactly good. "There's a new group running this town," she started to explain. "They rose up after most everyone died in the plague. There's a council and a sort of police department to enforce the new laws. It's good in some ways. They make sure everyone in town has enough to eat and a place to sleep. They hold regular patrols to keep the Knights of the Living Dead at bay." She paused then added, "You know. The *zombies*. I think your boyfriend called them the Others."

Molly started to correct her on the boyfriend part but decided it wasn't worth it. "Right," she said, wondering what any of this had to do with Chase. Was he okay or wasn't he?

"Anyway, another thing they do is hold pit fights. Kind of like they did in the old days with slaves."

"You mean, like gladiators?" Molly asked, thinking back to her dad's beloved movie collection.

"Yeah, that's the word," Helga agreed. "Anyway, they hold them in the old boxing arena at the edge of town. Basically they put one human and one Knight of the Living Dead in the ring and they fight." She paused then added, "To the death, of course."

Molly was beginning to get the picture, and it wasn't pretty. "So, let me guess. You have plenty of Others—*Knights*—but not a lot of human volunteers."

Helga nodded. "Right. So, the government gives bonus food and protection to those who can bring in new fighters. My boyfriend works as one of these 'recruiters.' He's a real bastard, but he's great at his job. He talks people passing through into coming home with him and then drugs their drinks. Then he turns them in to the council."

Something about this didn't make much sense to Molly. "But why would Chase go home with him?" she asked. "He knew we were waiting."

"Well, Luke always promises something. He's a master at figuring out what people need, and let's face it, people are needy these days."

"And so Chase was looking for food for . . . ?"

Helga rolled her eyes. "No. Drugs, of course. They're one of Luke's specialties."

Molly's insides tightened, and for a moment she thought she was going to throw up. She'd come here, risking everything, wasting precious time, all because of Chase's drug addiction? Just fucking great. She was an idiot to have given him another chance. He had a problem, just like her mother, and that problem wasn't going to go away. Even if he wanted to change, and she wanted to think he did, he'd likely have to fully detox first, and even then there were no guarantees. In the meantime, if she did that for him, got him out of whatever situation he was in here and put him through the process to clear him up, while she waited for him to get better, her own body would start breaking down. He'd get better—maybe—but she'd die before ever reaching Disney World.

It was her mother all over again. Except, Molly's mother had given birth to her. She didn't owe Chase a fucking thing.

She considered just up and leaving, abandoning him to the trap he'd walked himself into. She'd take the children and go, get them down to Disney, accomplish her mission. She didn't need Chase. She didn't need his bullshit. He'd let their entire group down and he deserved to pay. He deserved to get his ass chomped by a zombie in some dumbass bizarre postapocalyptic pit fight. But when she tried to take that first step toward the exit, her feet wouldn't cooperate. Nor would her mind. Instead of anger, she simply saw a vision of Chase. Beautiful Chase, who had promised long ago to protect her from all the horror at the end of the world. Even when his own world was torn apart by the horrific death of his sister, he'd still put her needs over his own. And then she'd abandoned him.

Well, things were different now. Things could be different. He needed saving, and she was the only one left to do it.

"Can you take me to him?" she asked the blonde.

Helga considered it. "On one condition," she said.

"Which is?"

"You take me with you."

"Take you with me? To rescue Chase?"

"I mean afterwards. You two must be going somewhere, right? You have a destination in mind," Helga said, looking desperate.

"Yes, but . . ." What would Molly say—that there was no room in the inn, that she didn't need any more baggage than she already had?

The girl held out her arms, and Molly saw again all the bruises. "I can't stay here any more," she said. "It's already bad, and if Luke finds out I helped you, he'll kill me."

Molly's heart went out to the girl. It was a horrible world they lived in, and the good people had to help each other out. "Okay," she agreed. "You help me get Chase back and you can come with us."

The girl breathed a sigh of relief, grinned, and Molly noticed she was missing half a front tooth. "Thank you so much!" she said. "You won't be sorry!" She grabbed her knife off the floor and pushed aside the red curtain. "Where are we going anyway?" she asked. "Afterward, I mean."

"Disney World," Molly said, though she felt a bit silly saying it.

Helga stopped and turned, surprise written across her freckled face. "Really?" she asked.

Molly nodded.

"Wow. That's so cool!" Helga turned and skipped down the church aisle. "I'm going to Disney World!" she cried. She paused for a moment and said, "I hope it's not like Baltic Disney."

CHAPTER THIRTY

When Molly got to her locker the next morning, she saw someone had crammed a note into the vents. She yanked it free and smoothed it out, studying the words with a skeptical eye. A group of kids were evidently planning a party. And not just any party—an outdoor, end-of-the-world rave. At first she was annoyed to think that people would make light of what was going on. After all, people were *dying*. It seemed so disrespectful.

She thought about crumpling the paper up and tossing it in the recycle bin. But then she had a second thought. People were scared. Stressed. Panicked. Maybe this was an opportunity to relieve some of that. Celebrate what life they had left. And maybe she'd get some more info on what the hell was going on with the world—seeing as they had all been forbidden to talk about the Super Flu at school.

Not to mention, she'd get to hang out with Chris.

Ever since last week, when they'd first kissed on his basement couch, the two of them had been practically inseparable. They'd been eating lunch together, meeting at their lockers for between-class smooches and hanging out after school. But it wasn't all about young love. They'd been developing a plan, an escape for friends in case things got really bad. They'd recruited Chris's brother Trey and some other kids from school, stealing and stockpiling supplies and non-perishable food in a storage facility just outside of town. Packing suitcases full of clothes and toiletries. The idea was simple: be ready to go at a moment's notice. Head up to the mountains and hide there until things got better.

Because, as Trey kept saying, things could only get worse. The more people who were sick and dying, the less food and necessities would be distributed. And a decrease in necessary goods would mean an increase of violence. Pretty soon the town would be under martial law, he said, and it would be unsafe to walk the streets. Much better that they avoid such a powder keg. Wait 'til it all blows over, he said. Up in the mountains they could grow their own food and hunt deer and trap rabbits. They'd live like kings, Trey said. It had sounded a lot like her father's plan, although she'd be with friends. She liked that idea.

And so they'd planned. And they'd been remarkably efficient at realizing their plans. And Molly ignored the niggling at the back of her head that reminded her she might have to choose between people she loved.

The bell rang. Molly tucked the flyer into her pocket and headed to class. This wasn't yet a done deal. The government could still find a cure. The world could still recover, and this end-of-the-world rave would just be another lame high-school theme party. She prayed that was the case. What else was there to do?

"This must be the place!" Molly said, pointing to the colored lights bursting from the woods. She grabbed Chris's hand. "Come on!"

"Are you sure you want to go to this?" he asked for the hundredth time.

"Yes," she said firmly. "It's a good thing, and I want to support it. There's been far too much anger and sadness lately. This'll be a night off. Who can't use a night off?" She turned and stared into his eyes, his molten kaleidoscopic green eyes.

He squeezed her hand. "Okay, then. Let's go party."

They headed into the clearing. The place was packed with kids from their high school all dancing around a large bonfire.

There was a tent set up in one corner, and a DJ was spinning a hard techno beat on a portable synthesizer. "Nurses" walked around with test tubes filled with "Super Flu Cures"—which, upon closer examination, contained high-octane alcohol. Molly hadn't ever had alcohol, but it seemed like this was as good a time as any to start. She grabbed two tubes for herself and two for Chris, and she downed hers quickly, feeling her mouth burn and her insides warm. Chris didn't seem to want his drinks, and he laid them on a nearby table. She pulled him onto the makeshift dance floor. He was glancing around, looking a little overwhelmed. She wondered how many parties he'd been to.

Molly let out a whoop, mindless. A weight had lifted off her shoulders, because this place seemed so far from reality and all the horror in the world. Tonight, this was exactly what she needed. Time to enjoy the fact that she was alive, time to not worry about what was to come. Dancing, sweating, laughing with friends, making out with Chris. It didn't seem right that a fifteen-year-old had to deal with plague, death, Armageddon—and what could she do, anyway? Here she didn't have to think. It was heaven.

"Come on, Chris! Dance!" she begged, grabbing him by the hands. He laughed and twirled her around.

"I suck at it!" he yelled over the music.

"I don't care!"

A few more songs, a few more tubes of "cure," and Molly was suddenly feeling really, really good. She looked over at Chris. His face was flushed. "Come on," she cried. "Let's sit for a moment."

She pulled him away from the bonfire to a spot where some makeshift tables had been set up, covered with brightly colored tablecloths. On impulse, she got down on her knees and crawled under the table, pulling Chris behind her.

"It's like a secret fort," she informed him proudly. "No one can find us here."

He laughed. "Cool," he said; then he kissed her.

She sighed against his mouth. This was the perfect night. Good music, great boyfriend, time away from—

Above the music, someone screamed. Chris and Molly broke their kiss, stared at one another. Molly cocked her head to one side. "Should we . . . ?" she asked.

Chris shook his head. "Probably just some drunk girl saw a snake or something. No need to panic." He leaned forward to kiss her again.

He was stopped by another scream. Then another. And another.

Molly stared at Chris, terrified. She made a move to leave, but he grabbed her shoulder. "No," he whispered. "Stay here."

He peeked out from beneath the tablecloth. The music had ceased but the screams continued. Molly waited, her heart beating wildly in her chest. What the hell was wrong?

"Are the cops here?" she asked, almost hopefully. "Are they breaking up the party?" She crossed her fingers for something normal, even if she'd be in serious trouble with her dad, who thought she was studying up in her room.

Chris drew his head back under the table. Even in the darkness Molly could tell he was white as a sheet.

"What—?"

He clamped his hand over her mouth and shook his head. Wide-eyed, she stopped talking. The screams, however, continued. They were louder, and there was the sound of people rushing around.

And then she heard something else. Something familiar. And then she remembered the trash compactor behind the hospital.

She stared at Chris, desperate questions in her eyes. He nodded grimly. The sounds she heard were groans and grunts similar to the monster at the hospital, the monster her father had told her didn't exist. What the hell was going on here?

She could barely breathe, she was so scared. Her whole body was trembling. Chris grabbed her and held tight, squeezing her so hard it hurt. Still, she pressed closer, wishing she could literally crawl inside of him and hide from the horror beyond their thin tablecloth shield.

The screams continued for what seemed hours but was probably only a few minutes. The dancing teenagers had scattered. At last there was silence. Deadly, horrible silence. Molly looked at Chris questioningly. He let go of her and peeked out from under the table. After a moment he leaned back inside and nodded.

"Coast is clear," he whispered. "Let's get the fuck out of here."

Gingerly, they crawled out from under the table. Molly assessed the scene before them. Carnage. Utter carnage. Tables were turned. Tents shredded. It looked like a scene from a monster movie. It *was* a scene from a monster movie.

Her eyes then fell upon the bodies, bloodied and broken and strewn around the clearing. There were a number of dead: her classmates—some she'd known since kindergarten—torn and bitten almost beyond recognition.

Molly's stomach heaved and she bent over and lost her lunch. Chris grabbed her, holding on tight. It was a good thing he did; she felt like she was going to pass out then and there. Which would be bad, she supposed, seeing as they were still at ground zero of the attack.

"Come on," Chris whispered, pulling at her arm. "We have to get out of here."

She didn't need a second invitation.

CHAPTER THIRTY-ONE

The room was dark, the walls grime-colored, and the overwhelmingly thick odor of excrement filled the air. A group had dragged Chase in here a few moments ago, ripped off his shirt and chained him to the wall with thick metal cuffs that dug into his wrists and ankles until they drew blood. In the distance he could hear the roar of a crowd, presumably cheering for his imminent demise.

He should be preparing. Mentally, if nothing else. Psyching himself up to fight an Other. He'd done it before. He could do it again. Maybe. Possibly. Or not. But whether or not his odds were good, he should be strategizing, going over their known weaknesses, his own strengths, remembering past encounters and analyzing them like a quarterback before a Super Bowl.

But all he could think of was Molly.

He was such an idiot. Such a fool. He didn't deserve her. He didn't deserve to breathe the same air as her. What was she doing right now? Waiting for him to come back? Comforting the children and promising them that for sure he would return any second? How long would she wait? How long would she hold out hope? Maybe hope was too strong a word. After all, he was nothing to her. A pain. A burden. Something slowing her down. She could have been ten times as far along if it weren't for him and the children.

And worst of all, she'd been right not to want to take him. Because of his stupidity and weakness, because of his drug addiction, he'd let everyone down. Molly might not make it to Disney in time for her tech to be salvaged. The kids wouldn't have anyone to take care of them, and they would soon be nothing more than monster bait. In the end they'd all be dead. Darla, Sunshine, Red, the triplets, Starry and Torn.

And Molly. Beautiful, determined, amazing Molly.

He yanked against his bonds, only succeeding in drawing more blood. His wrists were raw crimson bands of pain. Not exactly the best for fighting. Worse, he still craved drugs. His body burned for them, and the tickling in his stomach was a raging, all-out itch. It was like ants were crawling up and down his skin. He leaned his head over and threw up, splattering himself and his leather pants.

Well, he deserved to die. To be ripped apart and devoured by a mutated zombie. He deserved for his death to be slow. To feel every rip and tear of flesh, to hear every crunch of bone. If only it could be for a good cause instead of just the natural end to his stupidity. *Oh, Molly, I'm so sorry I let you down even though I promised I never would.*

God, you're pathetic!

He opened his eyes as a voice in his head rebuked him, the words echoing through his skull. It sounded like . . . Tank?

Be a man for once in your life, his dead brother scolded. *None of this emo pussy bullshit.*

You don't understand, Chase argued. *I'm not you. I'm not strong. And right now I'm trapped. There's no way I can escape this.*

Not with that attitude you can't. But as far as I can see, you're not dead yet. Which means you still have a chance. So buck up, stop living in your private theater of fear, and do something useful.

He swallowed hard and nodded fiercely. Imaginary Tank was right. He wasn't dead. Which meant he had a chance. And he had nothing to lose and everything to gain.

A burly man in a stained wife-beater tank top and cut-offs, carrying a whip, entered the room. He approached Chase. "You ready, boy?" he asked, then cackled to himself. "This should be a quick fight," he added, eyeing his prisoner up and down. "Pretty boy against our biggest baddie." He grabbed

Chase's face in his meaty hands, as a grandma might while pinching her grandson's cheeks.

Chase spat.

The guard bellowed in rage and struck him. The force of the open-palmed blow against his cheek almost sent Chase swimming into blackness, but he held his own and met the guard's eyes again, giving him his most defiant look. If he was going to go down, it'd be by a zombie, not some random human.

"So, we going to fight, or are you just going to give me googly eyes all night?" he said in his cockiest voice.

Another slap. It stung, but at the same time the violence was revving Chase up. The pain was spiking his adrenaline, and he was suddenly raring to go.

"Hey, what's taking so long?" another guard asked, stepping into the room.

"Little punk spit in my face," the first man growled.

"Aw, poor baby. Did he get you all wet?" The second guard scoffed. "Toro is getting impatient. Get him out there."

The first guard grunted but did as he was told. He whipped out a filthy rag and used it as a blindfold before unchaining his prisoner. Chase felt his bonds fall away, and a moment later he was pushed forward. He stumbled as best he could toward what he supposed was the main pit of the Thunderdome.

A few moments later, the blindfold was ripped from his eyes and he had to blink a few times to adjust to the light. He could hear the crowd roar before he saw them, and at first he believed they were cheering for him. Then his eyes adjusted and he saw the Other. It was the biggest, nastiest Other he'd ever seen. Snarling, drooling and smacking its lips, the creature started toward him.

Chase squared his shoulders. Okay, here went nothing. *For Molly*, he said to himself. *I'll win this for her.*

"Okay, first you need to change," Helga instructed. "They have to think you're one of them, and let's just say that leather suit is not going to cut it."

Molly looked down at her outfit. As much as she didn't want to waste any more time, Helga was likely right. The leather was practical for her purposes, but it would look out of place in a town full of people pretending things were normal. And she imagined this society didn't get many acceptable visitors.

"Right," she said. "Well, let's grab something quick so we can go."

Helga considered for a moment. "We can't go back to my place," she said. "Luke might be there. We'll hit up one of the stores. A lot of them still have clothing." She scanned the street, then motioned to a place on the corner. "Maybe there's something in there. It's one of my favorites, and not many people know it."

They crossed the street and entered what had once been a boutique, stepping through the broken glass door. Molly adjusted her lenses to compensate for the dark and looked around. For "not many people knowing it," the place was pretty ransacked, clothes ripped from racks and strewn everywhere. The jewelry counter was smashed and most of its contents were long gone.

"The Society is pretty intense when it comes to clothes," Helga explained. "So a lot of the good stuff is probably taken. But I'm sure we can find . . ." She reached down on the ground and pulled up a slinky, bright purple halter-top dress. "What size are you?"

Molly shrugged. "Four?" she said. "God, it's been a billion years since I went shopping."

Helga nodded. "Try this then." She handed the dress to Molly and gestured at a dressing room. "Don't worry, we have plenty of time. They train them before they make them fight. He's just a prisoner. In no danger for a few days at least."

"Okay," Molly said, feeling a little relieved. She still didn't like to think of him jailed, but if he wasn't in any immediate danger, it'd do better to take this slowly and surely. Also, maybe this would teach him a lesson. Stupid druggie. She wanted to be the first to smack him upside the head once he was back with her and safe.

She slipped into the tiny room behind the torn curtain that had once served as a dressing room for the boutique and slipped off her leather pants and shirt, praying this wasn't another trap. How did she know Helga wasn't just like her boyfriend: a scout, looking for new recruits? But then she reminded herself of Helga's desperate eyes and bruised body. No, the girl really needed an escape from Paradise, and Molly was likely the only one who could provide it.

Still, she kept one ear cocked as she slid into the dress. It felt creamy smooth, soft and cool against her skin. It would once have cost a fortune. She hadn't worn something so elegant in . . . well, maybe forever. After all, it wasn't like she'd gotten to go to prom. She pulled the straps behind her neck and tied them in a bow, then examined herself in the mirror. Her breath caught in her throat as she stared at her reflection. She looked good. Really good. Feminine. Even taking into account her ocular implants. The dress clung to her every curve, and it scooped low in front to show incredible cleavage. She looked like something out of an old Hollywood movie—and not a zombie movie.

Her first thought was: Wow, wait until Chase sees me in this. Her second thought was how silly she was being, how vain, caring about something so shallow and irrelevant. Who cared what Chase thought about how she looked in a dress? But Molly cared, whether she wanted to or not.

Stepping out of the dressing room, she realized Helga had also changed clothes—into a little black-sequined number, long sleeves effectively hiding her bruises. She'd pulled her dreadlocks back into a ponytail and dabbed on a little lip gloss. She actually looked very pretty. She was packing things into a big bag, and she took Molly's leather clothes without looking and stuffed them inside, too.

When she turned to look at Molly, she whistled. "Wow. You look great."

Molly felt her face heat and tried to laugh it off. "Yeah, yeah, whatever," she said.

"I'm serious. You should make sure to take that dress with

you and wear it afterward. I bet your boyfriend would love it."

Molly finally decided to correct her. "Oh, he's not my boyfriend. He's just a friend."

"Ah," Helga said. But it didn't seem like she was buying it.

Once their outfits were complete, they headed out of the store and back onto the street. Helga took Molly to a scooter and instructed she get on the back. Soon they were flying down the road, the bike's front headlight illuminating the way. Over the roar of the wind, Helga explained that one of the benefits of being a member of this society was a minimum ration of energy each month. Much of it was gasoline siphoned from stations in a fifty-mile radius and brought back to Paradise in barrels. Most people used their rations to fill scooters like this.

Molly nodded, barely listening. Her mind was focused on Chase. Even though she knew he wasn't in immediate danger, she didn't like the idea of him being trapped, especially when he had no idea the cavalry was on its way.

"So, what's the plan?" she asked Helga over the roar of the bike. "I mean, they aren't going to let us just waltz in there and let him out, right?"

Helga laughed. "Well, sort of," she said. "I know one of the guards. And I have some of Luke's shit. Some of his *good* shit."

"This guard wants drugs? And won't he get in trouble?"

"With the stuff I'll give him, he won't care."

Once again, Molly was grateful she'd run into Helga. "Thanks," she said. "I really owe you for this."

"It's cool. Just get me away from this shithole and we're square."

They turned another corner, entering a parking lot near the stadium Molly had seen from the interstate. Helga pulled the scooter into a spot and killed the engine. They got off the bike and she motioned to a police station across the way. "That's the place," she explained. "Come on, let's go."

The station was rundown but clean, evidently having been

given a good recent spit and polish, in contrast with the thick layers of dust they'd encountered in other parts of the town. There were working lights, although they looked like they ran on a backup generator. Molly assumed most of the population of this society lived on the other side of the stadium.

It was an odd feeling, to step inside a place and feel like it was lived in. Molly adjusted her implants for the indoor lighting and scanned the room. A burly man dressed in a uniform sat behind a small desk, picking his fingernails with a knife. Molly sized him up, wanting to have some sort of contingency plan if Helga's connections—and currency—weren't as good as she claimed. He was big, she assessed, but meaty rather than muscled. She would likely be okay, if push came to shove, as long as he didn't have a big-ass gun as well.

Helga sidled up to the desk and sat on it, hiking up her skirt and batting her eyelashes. Total silliness, Molly thought at first, then realized that in a small postapocalyptic society like Paradise, the ratio of pretty girls to desperate men was probably pretty low. Sure enough, the guard reacted instantly, his beefy face turning tomato red. He rose to his feet and walked around the desk.

"Hey, baby," he said, reaching over to hug Helga. Molly watched the blonde slide her body against the man's thigh. In another world, she could have been a stripper. Maybe she once was; who knew? "Where you been all my life?"

"Aw, Huggie, don't be saying that!" Helga cooed. "You know you haven't given me a second thought since I left."

Huggie looked offended. "Are you kidding?" he said, sounding incredulous. "I've thought of nothing but you for two weeks, when you last waltzed your pretty little ass in here." He smacked her lightly on the mentioned body part, and she giggled, stretching up to kiss his bald forehead.

"You're so sweet," she purred. "I thought of you, too, Huggie Bear. I thought about you a lot."

"So, who's your friend?" Huggie asked, giving Molly the once-over. She could tell he wasn't as impressed with her as with Helga. Guess he didn't like the look of her cybernetic implants. She supposed that was probably for the best, though she didn't like the reminder that she was a freak.

"Oh, this is Molly," Helga said. "She's my dear friend, and we're hoping you will be able to do us a huge, huge favor."

"Anything for a friend of yours, baby," Huggie reassured her, putting his hand on her waist. "Name it."

Helga gave a tiny grin, and hope rose inside Molly. Who would have expected this rescue to be this easy? She'd figured there'd be a fight, at the very least. Maybe a dangerous escape. But, no; it seemed like it was just a matter of making a deal. She'd have Chase back, good as new, any time now.

"You guys have a new pit fighter," Helga said. "Luke picked him up last night. His name's Chase."

Huggie nodded. "Yeah. He's sharing a cell with Bowie. Did you see the Bowster last week? That was some kickass fight. I gotta say, he's a killer. From now on, when he's back in the ring, I'm putting my money on him every time."

"Oh yeah, baby, he's amazing," Helga crooned. "But Chase. We're talking about Chase. We're hoping we can make a little deal for him. I brought you some real good shit—" She started to reach into her purse.

"Sorry, no can do," Huggie said, stopping her.

She frowned, glossy lips puffed out in a pout. "Why not?" she asked. "I thought you said you'd do us a favor, Huggie Bear."

"Baby, you know I'd do anything for you," Huggie assured her, chucking her under the chin. "But the guy's not here. They took him to the dome."

"What?" Molly cried, unable to stop herself. "I thought you said they'd train him first!" Fear pounded in her heart as she digested what was happening. Chase had been thrown into a ring and was being forced to fight a zombie while they'd wasted time trying on clothes?

Huggie shrugged. "Their originally scheduled fighter, Rumble, went and offed himself last night, so they needed a last-minute replacement. Guess Rumble didn't think too much of his odds and wanted to take the easy way out." He laughed.

"What time's the fight?" Helga asked, her face also white.

"Probably about now. If you hurry, you might catch it. Though it's bound to be quick. I heard the odds are like 1,000-to-one on the new guy. They're putting him in with Toro, after all."

Molly and Helga were out the door in a heartbeat. "Come on!" Helga said. "We'll get in the back door."

They turned right from the station, went down an alley and came to a dead end with a battered wooden door. Helga pushed it open and they entered a large smoky kitchen where cooks were preparing some sort of meal. Molly didn't even have much time to marvel at all the people still alive; she raced through, ignoring the protests, down a hall then up several flights of stairs. After one last door, she and Helga were suddenly in the Thunderdome.

Molly drew in a breath as she looked around. They were at the top of the stadium complex. But whereas many years ago this would have been full of screaming, sports-jersey-wearing fans, it was now populated by well-heeled matrons and gentlemen—Society members, Molly guessed, resplendent in ball gowns, tuxedos, and with jewels dripping from their arms, necks and fingers. There were probably a hundred of them, scattered through the stadium. More people than Molly had seen in six years.

It was as if she'd stepped into another world. One where things were still working. Where people were civilized.

Except there was nothing civilized about what was going on here at the Thunderdome: the cheering and *woot*ing and staring down into a pit that had once been an innocent basketball court. Molly followed the crowd's gaze to the center of the action. The first thing she saw was the biggest Other she'd ever seen. The second was Chase.

Without thinking or processing, only knowing she had to save him, she bolted down the stairs, taking them two at a time. She'd jump the railing, kill the Other, rescue Chase.

"No!" Helga cried, running after her and grabbing her arm. "You can't go down there," she hissed.

Molly whirled to face her. No one was going to stop her from this. "Why the hell not?" she demanded.

"Don't you see all the guards?" Helga pointed to the sidelines. "They all have guns. They'll shoot you in a heartbeat if you try to jump in."

Molly released a frustrated breath. She didn't think she could take on the Other, the guards and the whole society; there was a limit to what she could handle. "Why the hell would they do that?" she asked. "This is one fucked-up place. And what do you propose we do?"

"Pray?"

"Not funny."

"Look, it's not impossible for your friend to win," Helga suggested. "I've seen humans beat Knights before. Like Huggie said, Bowie did last week. It's not all about brute strength. The Knights are mean, but they're not exactly the brightest bulbs in the shed . . . or whatever that saying is."

Molly stared at the girl, unbelieving. This was what they were going to pin all their hopes on: that Chase was smarter than the Other? What about the zombie's razor-sharp claws, bulging muscles and appetite for human flesh? Chase didn't stand a chance against the monster. And what if he got bitten? This was a crazy and demented game to be playing with human lives!

She stared into the ring, watched as Chase approached the Other. Feeling so damn helpless. So close, yet so far. And Chase, well . . .

She tried to focus on positives, because while all her instincts told her she should dare the guards and leap frantically into the pit, she was also slightly more of a realist. If she died fighting impossible odds, who would take care of the children? Should she sacrifice herself for him when he'd put himself in this situation? She would, if it were only herself she was looking after. But with the kids . . . ?

She remembered Chase berating her back at the Wal-Mart, berating her for assuming he was helpless and weak. He'd survived for six years amongst the Others; he'd talked about how suited he was to survive. Just because he was totally human—without enhancement—didn't mean he was automatically a goner. He'd asked her to trust him. To have faith in his abilities. And, she realized, now was the time for him to prove she could.

She had to let him fight. She had to believe he had a chance to win.

"You can do it, Chase!" she cried at the top of her lungs from the side of the ring, waving a fist in the air. "I believe in you!"

Chase's legs trembled as he watched the Other approach, slowly, deliberately, as they tended to do, taking one shuffling step and then another. It was the biggest zombie Chase had ever come across, and he wondered what it'd been eating. Probably people just like him, which wasn't exactly the most comforting thought.

"Tonight is a special night for you all," came a man's voice over a loudspeaker. "Our undefeated Knight Champion Toro will take on our brand-new gladiator, Chase."

Cheers for Toro. Jeers for Chase. Evidently this guy was a crowd favorite. Jeez, weren't humans supposed to be rooting for their own? Evidently not when bets were on the line.

Despite his boasts to Molly, truth be told, Chase had killed very few Others. Well, not by himself. He'd preferred the live and let live approach, and failing that, the "run lest you be eaten" one. But here he was surrounded by guards and bars, and there was nowhere for him to go. And as well-fed as the Other in front of him had to be in order to have obtained his current size, the drool at the corner of his mouth suggested he was still hungry.

Chase swallowed hard, trying to resign himself to his fate. This was it. This was how it was going to end. And it was his fault. He'd been a fool, and now he'd pay with his life. But it wasn't his death that bothered him most. Again, it was that he'd failed the people he cared about. There was a time when he'd been a different person, a person to depend on.

No! He remembered the oath he'd just made to his brother's ghost, remembered the adrenaline that had recently seemed to ooze out of him. Thinking about the duties in which he'd failed, something inside of him, some lost bit of courage, rallied. He'd promised Tank that he'd take care of those children. He'd promised Molly he'd get her to Disney World. And he'd be damned if some sick game made up by insane people was going to stop him from following through.

He gripped the small knife they'd given him—a pathetic weapon against the monster in the ring, but the only one he had—and wracked his brain for a strategy. He couldn't best the Other in hand-to-hand combat; it had too much physical strength for that. But there had to be alternative ways of winning. He'd think of them.

He knew from experience that Others usually had poor eyesight and depended on movement to attract their attention. Picking up a rock, he threw it and struck the Other in the face. It recoiled, surprised, and closed its eyes with a roar. Chase used that moment to drop to the ground and freeze. He hoped staying still might confuse the beast, might buy him some time.

Sure enough, he soon heard rumblings from the crowd. The Other was sniffing the air, looking confused, wondering where his prey had gone. A few angry shouts of "He's right in front of you, dumbass!" fell on the zombie's uncomprehending ears. Thank God.

As the creature stood still, squinting, Chase was better able to analyze him, to size up potential weak spots. The creature wore leather armor over his chest and legs—these people had armored their zombies?—eliminating possible stab points. But his feet were bare and exposed. That was something at least.

The time he'd bought was up. The creature, clearly eager to fill its belly, was moving forward, sniffing. From his position on the ground, Chase waited until the last possible moment, then lunged forward, rolling and stabbing it in the foot. He'd chopped off a toe or two. The zombie bellowed in rage and staggered, losing its balance. Chase leapt to his feet and kicked the beast's chest, attempting to send Toro to the ground.

It very nearly worked. For a moment the Other tottered, and Chase thought maybe he'd gained an advantage. But then Toro recovered his balance and charged at him, arms outstretched. Chase had leapt backwards one second too late. The Other caught him by the neck, wrapping filthy fingers around his throat and squeezing. Chase could feel his eyes bulge out of his head.

As his air supply diminished, Chase fought the instinct to drop his knife and try to pry the hands off his neck, and instead he stabbed at the Other's chest, also making sure the creature kept its mouth away from him. His small blade was no match for the tough leather armor, however, and the knife bounced uselessly off. Chase knew he had mere seconds before he would pass out. And he'd used up all his tricks. Was this it? Was he about to be eaten, about to die for others'—and Others'—sport? It seemed so wrong: to die like this, alone, jeered at by strangers. Never to be seen again by his friends and the people he'd failed.

"Chase! Don't give up, Chase! I know you can do it!"

That voice caused him to perk up. It was Molly! He strained to look into the audience, to see if she was somehow actually there or if this was just an auditory hallucination. His eyes fell upon her, draped oddly in some sort of silk eveningwear. He *was* going crazy. But even so, the vision of her loveliness gave him strength for one more try.

He slammed his boot down on the zombie's bare foot, aiming for the severed toes. The zombie screamed in pain and loosened its grip just for a millisecond—but that millisecond was all Chase needed. He swung viciously and knocked the zombie's hands away, then followed up with a kick to the groin. The Other stumbled backwards again.

This time, Chase didn't wait to see if his opponent would fall. He charged, throwing his full weight forward, tackling the beast where it stood and slamming it to the ground. He grabbed the creature's collar and pulled that back with as much strength as he could muster, exposing its bare neck. Then he jammed his knife deep into the throat. A fountain of blood spewed from the wound, and he rolled over quickly to avoid it. He jumped to his feet, still clutching his knife, put his boot on the creature's neck and stepped. The zombie gurgled at him and died.

The crowd went insane. A fickle group; apparently he was their new hero. But he ignored them. He locked eyes with Molly, begging her forgiveness. She raised her hand in a salute of respect.

He knew then and there he would never be weak again.

CHAPTER THIRTY-TWO

Chris and Molly raced down the forest path, as fast they could, back toward town. Tears blinded Molly's vision as she ran, and her heart pounded. The plague had been bad enough, but now there were some kind of monsters on top of it? And her dad had lied to her—either that, or he'd been misled or mistaken. But what was going on? Was it really somehow the End of Days in a biblical sense? If so, what hope could there be?

Through it all, Chris gripped her hand, a silent promise of solidarity. At least she wasn't facing this alone. And at that moment she loved him more than ever. If the world was going to end, at least she had him by her side. She'd keep him there forever.

Suddenly something staggered from the trees, blocking their path. Molly screamed, startled. Chris yanked her back a few steps, putting distance between them and the creature. Because, sure enough, it was the vision of her nightmares: a yellowed, zombie-like mutation with pus-filled sores and no hair. It had blood all over its mouth, and had clearly been one of the things that had struck back at the rave.

The monster growled at them, arms outstretched, and it stepped slowly forward on wobbly legs, as if it wasn't quite sure how to use them yet. Molly stared, trying to decide if she was really seeing what she thought. Or maybe it was all the "cure" she'd drunk. Because while this definitely looked like the creature in the hospital Dumpster they'd come across weeks before, it also seemed weirdly familiar.

"Chris," Molly whispered, then trailed off, not knowing how to explain.

He glanced over at her and then back. His mouth dropped open. "Oh my God," he said. "Does this thing look familiar to you?"

Molly nodded, squinting at the creature. There was definitely something. It had no hair, and its eyes were blackened and unfocused, but beneath the tattered clothes were breasts, and the thing had obviously once been female . . .

"Erin?" she suddenly realized. "Is that you?"

The creature growled and stepped forward. But whether the growl was in any way an intended response, Molly didn't need any further affirmation. Her stomach rolled and it took everything in her power not to be sick. The booze burning like fire through her veins wasn't helping.

It was then that she realized Chris had pulled out a handgun. She didn't know where he'd gotten it, as they were super-illegal and hard to find, but she was even more shocked by what he intended.

"No!" she shrieked, grabbing his arm. His shot went wild and the creature took another step, growling. "It's Erin!" she cried. "It's my best friend."

Chris stared at her, his eyes wild. "Are you shitting me? Even if it is Erin, what are we going to do—talk her back into good health?" he asked. "Do you think she just came out to the party to dance? Do you think those 'cures' they were passing around helped?"

"But . . . look at her! It's her! She even still has that birthmark." Molly was shaking, and she pointed at Erin's arm.

The monster that was once Erin lunged, teeth bared and eyes black. Molly dodged, screamed and turned, tripped over a root and fell flat on her face. She could hear Erin behind her, jaws snapping. Lunch with a friend? Hadn't she just been wishing she and Erin could have that again? Wishes came true. Molly squeezed her eyes shut, knowing she was a goner.

A gunshot rang out. Molly's eardrums ached, and she turned to see Erin stagger backward, a bloody hole in her chest. For a brief second she thought she saw clarity come into her friend's eyes, realization on her face. A human horror at a very inhuman end. And then Erin's eyes rolled back into her head and she collapsed on the forest floor. Chris shot her again.

Molly scrambled to her feet, screaming. Chris grabbed her and pulled her into a strong embrace, shushing her. "It's okay," he said. "It's dead."

"You don't understand! That was Erin. That was Erin!"

"You're right. It was Erin," he said. His eyes looked glassy. "But it wasn't *just* Erin anymore. And you know that."

"I don't understand! How is this happening?" Molly babbled against his shoulder. It was too much. Just too much.

"I don't know," Chris muttered. "But it's only going to get worse. I think we need to start putting our escape plan into action." He released her from his hold and grabbed her hand. "Come on," he said. "We'll get you home to your father where at least it's safe."

Molly nodded stiffly, staring at the corpse of her former friend.

Safe? Ha. Nowhere was ever going to be safe again.

CHAPTER THIRTY-THREE

"He did it! He did it!" Molly whooped along with the crowd, throwing her arms around Helga and jumping up and down in glee. "He kicked that Other's ass!"

"Your man is very brave," Helga shouted over the din. Her face was alight with admiration. "I am very surprised he won. Toro—well, Toro has killed many, many men. I thought your boyfriend would be one of them."

"He's not my boyfriend," Molly said automatically, but wishing now that he were. He'd been so brave out there. So amazing.

"Yeah, yeah, so you keep telling me." Helga didn't sound convinced. "But come on, let's go bribe my buddy and get him out."

They wove through the crowd and back to the jail. Everyone seemed more intent on the next fight, getting drunk or collecting money to pay the two girls much notice. Helga led Huggie into the back room and came out fifteen minutes later. Molly didn't want to know what she'd done to win Chase's freedom, and she really hoped it just involved the drugs. In any event, she was thankful the girl had chosen to do it.

"You remember your promise," Helga said as she returned. "You're going to take me with you. I want to get the hell out of this crazy place."

Molly nodded. "Of course. We'll be happy to have you along." What was one more, anyway? Hell, it'd be nice to have a third adult around to help with the kids. And Helga had more than earned the right to come.

"Okay, Huggie said to go around back and he'd leave Chase there."

The two girls walked out of the jail and circled to the back. Sure enough, a tied-up Chase had been left there in the dirt, on his knees, covered in bruises and cuts. Molly intended to spend the night taking care of those, making sure none of them got infected.

"Chase!" she cried, not able to wait a moment longer.

He looked at her. His beautiful green eyes were almost hidden behind all the swelling on his face.

"You came for me," he croaked, his voice hoarse.

"Of course I did," she said, kneeling in front of him. It was all she could do not to throw her arms around him and squeeze like there was no tomorrow. But he was hurt. Exhausted. Affection would have to wait.

"How did you . . . ?"

"Helga helped me. She knew what her boyfriend had done to you and wanted to get you free. She has been an amazing help, and we're going to take her along with us."

Chase looked a little nervous but nodded to Helga. At first Molly wondered why. Then she remembered. The drugs. He was probably wondering if Helga had ratted him out.

As happy as she was to have him back, they'd definitely need to have a serious talk.

"We'd better get out of here before the next match is over," Helga said. "We don't want to be caught out and about. Chase isn't exactly unrecognizable now that he's taken down Toro. And the Society isn't going to be pleased at losing their new champion."

"Right." Molly nodded. "Let's go."

"Wait," Chase gasped as she helped him to his feet.

She cocked her head in question. "What?"

He looked sheepish. "Before we go, I have to . . . grab something. I left it back at your place, Helga. You think Luke is at the match?"

"He's never missed one. But what do you need?" Helga asked.

"Yeah, Chase, what do you need?" Molly demanded, narrowing her eyes, though she knew the gesture was lost behind her implants. Though why she bothered asking she didn't know. It was obvious what he needed, what he was going back for, and it infuriated her to no end: the drugs that had gotten him into this mess to begin with. Unbelievable!

The tenderness she'd felt for him just moments before evaporated, and it was replaced by fury. Stupid, weak bastard. After all he'd been through, still all he could think of was self-medicating?

"Um, I can't say," he stammered, at least having the decency to look embarrassed. "But it's important. You have to trust me."

Anger burned in her gut and swam in front of her eyes. She wanted to grab him by the hair and drag him back to camp and slap him around until he begged for mercy. After all they'd been through—after he'd almost been eaten by that monster— he still hadn't learned.

He was hopeless. Worse than her mother, even. And she was sick of saving his sorry ass. Thank God they'd never gotten involved. It would hurt too much now. It already hurt too much, to be totally honest. But at least she could manage to walk away. For good, if necessary.

"We're going back to the kids," she said flatly. "We've left them far too long and I hope they're safe. You can meet us at the camp after you do your . . . errand. We leave first thing in the morning, with or without you."

He looked hurt, and she fought the urge to feel cruel. After all, he should be the one feeling guilty, him and his pathetic addiction.

"Fine," he said at last. "I'll see you soon." And he took off, stumbling a bit, down the alley, presumably toward Helga's.

"Come on, let's go," Molly growled at the blonde, who was giving her a questioning look. She couldn't blame the woman. All this work to save Chase, and then he took off? But what could Molly say? She could only do so much. "We'll go find the kids. We're traveling with eight of them, and they've been on their own all this time."

Helga looked surprised, but then she nodded and the two of them headed for her scooter.

As they puttered up the on-ramp to the expressway, leaving Paradise and the Thunderdome behind, Molly glanced back at the seemingly peaceful town and the lights that still shone from the stadium. It seemed almost normal, compared to everywhere else. And yet the plague had changed these people terribly, made them into bloodthirsty savages dressed in Armani.

What a strange world now existed. Was there really any way anyone could ever expect it would go back, be rebuilt? Her father had always said the plague would, at the very least, get rid of humanity's worst elements, give everyone a chance to start over. But what would they be starting with? And who was starting what, and where? Molly didn't have much hope.

But then, she reminded herself, there were people like Helga. People willing to risk their lives to save a stranger. People who still held out hope for a better tomorrow. Maybe all was not lost after all.

"Where's Chase? Where's Chase?" cried the kids as the scooter pulled up to the camp in the courtyard of the Motel 6. Torn stood in front of them all, looking protective—he clearly hadn't recognized the bike. The kids moved from the bonfire they'd built to crowd around the two women, anxious faces surrounding Molly. "Is he okay? Who's this? What happened?" The questions came fast and furious.

"He's okay. He'll be here shortly," Molly assured them, feeling all the while like her heart would tear in two. They loved the stupid idiot with all their hearts. And he was just letting them down. If only they knew how little he deserved their affection. "And this is Helga. She's going to be traveling with us from now on."

The two women got off the bike and the children

surrounded Helga, asking her a billion questions, which she laughingly answered as best she could. Molly walked to the fire and sat down. This should have been a moment of triumph. Instead it felt empty, knowing Chase had once more traded his safety and the safety of them all for a quick fix.

Not ten minutes later, Chase zoomed into the camp on his own presumably stolen scooter, triumphantly carrying a big plastic bag of goods. The kids cheered and hugged him as he got off the bike. He laughed and pushed them off, protesting his injured body and promising them candy in exchange for breathing room. Then he poured out the sack like some postapocalyptic Santa Claus. They dived for the pile of sweets, not caring that the chocolate was way past its "Best If Used By" date.

He walked over to Molly, who had stayed by the fire, and looked down at her. She saw confusion in his eyes, which made her all the more furious. He really thought he was going to get away with this? He didn't know why she was angry?

"What's wrong?" he asked.

She kicked a stone, wanting to strangle him. "We have to talk," she said.

He looked nervous, but nodded. "Okay. Talk."

Molly looked at the kids, who were chomping happily away at the candy. "Not here. Away from *them*."

"Just how private do you want? Do you want to go into one of the rooms?" he asked, waving a hand at the motel. "I can grab a key from the front desk."

"Fine." Molly turned to Helga. "Do you mind watching the kids for a few?"

The blonde looked scared for a moment then smiled. "Yeah. No problem."

"Sorry, don't mean to put you on babysitting duty the second you get here."

"Don't worry." The woman laughed. "I'm just grateful to be here. I'm prepared to earn my keep."

Molly rose to her feet, realizing she was still wearing the silky dress. She'd have to change back when she had a chance;

this wasn't exactly a prime travel outfit. But she supposed it was good enough for a conversation about drug abuse. A conversation she really didn't want to have.

She walked toward the motel, her legs feeling like they weighed a ton. She *so* didn't want to have this conversation. But she had no choice. Chase was an addict, and he'd already endangered their mission on several occasions because of it. And him going back just now was the last straw. He cared more for the substances than he did for safety. And that wasn't acceptable. Molly had tolerated it too long with her mother.

Chase had taken a piece of wood from the fire and he now carried it as a torch. He also carried a bag. The key he'd collected opened one of the doors, but not before he pounded on it and pushed Molly behind him. Then he burst inside and looked around. It was empty. They could talk here.

They stepped inside. The room was musty and dank. It obviously hadn't been used in a while. Two sunken double beds took up most of the space. On the dresser sat an unplugged Smart TV.

"I know why you got caught," Molly began. "Helga told me."

Chase raked a hand through his hair and let out a sigh. "I figured she might have."

"What the hell were you thinking?"

"I don't know." He stared down at his feet. "I guess I'm an addict, okay? But I'm done. This time I'm really done." He looked up, his eyes sad. "I swear to God, Molly. I'll be a man and I'll take care of you and the kids like I'm supposed to, and I won't let you down. I won't take another pill again as long as I live."

It was all too much. She couldn't believe he was standing there, looking her in the eyes and lying through his teeth. "Don't lie to me!" she cried. "Don't you fucking lie!"

He stared at her, his face anguished, not even having the decency to look ashamed. "How am I lying?" he asked. "Can't you trust me?"

She shook her head. "Come on. I'm not stupid. I know

about your little errand just now. Even after all we went through—even though you almost died in that godforsaken town—you still saw fit to go back to the lion's den to retrieve your precious drugs!"

He shook his head, his face a mixture of horror and shock. "Is that what you think?" he asked. "Is that really, honest to God, what you think?" He slammed his fist into the wall and the old plaster crumbled. His torch smoked. "Fucking hell, Molly, you think I'm that stupid?"

She didn't know how to answer that.

He sighed. "Evidently so." Reaching into the bag he'd brought with him, he pulled out a small colorful box. "I went back for *this*," he said, tossing it down on a bed. It bounced once then settled, and she realized what it was: a music box.

"I wanted you to have something special. To show you how much I care about you. To show how grateful I am that you believe in me, that you still care about me enough to come save my life." He shook his head. "You're right, I guess. I must be fucking stupid." And with that, he stalked out of the room.

Molly stared down at the music box, her world crashing around her. This was what he'd gone back for—not drugs, but a gift for her? She reached down and gingerly picked up the music box, reaching around to wind it before opening its lid. A beautiful Sleeping Beauty twirled in a perfect pirouette, and "It's a Small World" tinkled through the air.

Her gut wrenched. Her head spun. She set down the box and ran outside to find Chase.

On the far side of the bonfire, he was grabbing a backpack and stuffing things into it. Ready to leave forever? It couldn't be. Where would he go? Would he take the kids? They had become a little family, and she didn't want to give that up. He'd made mistakes, but she would forgive him as long as he started paying attention to what was right and what was wrong. She had made mistakes in her past as well. They could forgive each other. But he couldn't go. He was hers. He'd always been hers, from before the end of time.

"Chase!" she said, running to him.

He looked up, his eyes stormy, not even pretending to hide his fury. She threw herself at him, wrapping her arms around him and burying her face in his chest. At first he was stiff as a board, unyielding and stubborn, but she refused to let go.

"I'm so sorry," she said. "I'm an idiot."

"Yes," he said at last. "But so am I. And I'm an asshole, too. But I'm not going to be either thing anymore."

She looked up at him, into those beautiful green eyes of his, and sought some sort of forgiveness in their depths. She wasn't sure if she found it. Then she kissed him, crushing her lips against his. This, it seemed, he could not resist, and he kissed her back with such passion he took her breath away.

His arms wrapped around her, crushing her against him. His fingers dug into the small of her back. Their mouths moved against one another, seeking, finding, their tongues enjoying a complicated dance of unspoken passion.

It had been too long. They'd been so stubborn. So stupid. Hanging on to past hurts and past regrets. But that was over now. The world had ended, sure. But their relationship was just beginning. A real relationship.

"Oh, Chase." She sighed against his mouth. "I'm so sorry."

"You have nothing to be sorry for," he said. "I'm the one who's proved time and again to be untrustworthy, and I completely understand why you didn't believe me. Hell, you're smart not to. But I swear to you, Molly, I'm done. I've been thinking about this nonstop since that jail cell. I'm done being that guy. I want to be better. For the children. And especially for you."

His words sent chills down her spine that had nothing to do with the physical sensation of him running his hands through her hair. "It will be hard," she said. "You may go through withdrawal."

"I don't care," he replied. "It'll be worth it."

"Well, I'll help in any way that I can."

He grabbed her face in his hands and kissed her again with a ferocity once reserved for overly dramatic Hollywood movies.

"Get a room!" called out Torn.

They broke from the kiss, laughing a bit. "You're just jealous," Chase called back to him. " 'Cause I got the girl."

"Whatever, dude." Torn slung an arm around Starr.

Chase turned to Molly. "Sorry about these clowns," he said with a laugh.

"It's okay." She smiled. "I love them, too." And she did, she realized. They really had become a little family. They all needed each other. And not just to survive, she realized, thinking back to the perversion of Paradise, but to keep alive the things about them that were good and right and human. And that was the reason they were staying alive.

CHAPTER THIRTY-FOUR

"Dad, Dad!" Molly burst into Ian Anderson's workshop, not caring about protocol or pissing him off. She was surprised the door hadn't been locked, and she found him at his computer, typing furiously. Just seeing him there, calm, normal, not a monster, filled her with an overwhelming relief. She sank down into a nearby chair, head in her hands. "Oh God, Dad, it was so terrible!"

Her father rose from his computer, his expression grave. "What is it, Molly?" he asked.

"Monsters," she blubbered, rising to her feet. "Like the one at the hospital. I didn't imagine that one, because there are more. We were out at a party and—"

Her father took her by the shoulders and pushed her back so he could look her in the eye. His face was wild with anger and she retreated, almost frightened. So much for him being calm and normal. "Didn't I tell you to stay in?" he demanded. His fingernails dug into her arms and she winced in pain. "Are you deaf or just plain stupid?"

"I'm sorry," she said, her voice quavering. "But you've got to listen to me. There were monsters. Like . . . zombies or something. And they were attacking people. They were . . ." She trailed off, unable to voice what she had seen. "It was awful," she finally said.

Her father released her. "Yes, I can imagine," he said, sounding distracted. He wandered back to his computer, staring down at the monitor as if it held the answers to all life's questions. Maybe he thought it really did.

"God, this is a disaster. It wasn't supposed to happen this way," he muttered under his breath. "Not like this."

"What?"

He straightened and turned back to her. "Nothing. Never mind."

"Dad?" She had to tell him the rest. The unbearable, awful rest.

"Yes?"

"This is going to sound crazy, but I think one of them was Erin. My best friend. She was sick. Her mom said she had the flu. But I came face to face with one of the monsters and I swear to God it was her. Or it *had been* her. She didn't seem to recognize me."

Ian nodded, not looking the least bit surprised. Probably he was the only man on Earth who wouldn't tell her she was being ridiculous. "From our research, my coalition has determined that the Super Flu is affecting different people in different ways. Some people simply die. Those are the lucky ones. The others . . . well, these others seem to have their DNA mutated somehow. They have reduced brain function and increased hunger. They lose their body hair and experience skin discoloration, get open sores. They're not zombies, per se, Molly. Far from it. They're living, breathing humans. Completely alive. But they're not your friends and neighbors anymore. They're also infectious. Their saliva . . . Well, one bite and you could turn into one of them."

Molly thought about how close she'd been to being bitten. By her best friend of all people. She sank into a chair, head in her hands. "Oh God," she whispered. "When will it all end? And how?"

"Look, Molly," her father said. "Things are likely to get worse before they get better. And I need for you to start taking things seriously. That means no leaving the house for parties anymore. And I don't want you to go back to school. I can't imagine it will stay open much longer, anyway. And no more going to the supermarket. We have enough food, no matter what your mother thinks."

"But Dad!" she protested. "I don't want to be stuck here, locked away! And I can defend myself now that I know what's going on. Wasn't that what all the training was about? What's the use of being alive if I have to spend my time in hiding, not being able to be with the people I care about?"

Ian nodded. "Indeed," he said, "that's what the training was about. I wanted to prepare you in case something went wrong. But I don't think a few martial arts lessons are enough. You need more. Humanity needs more." He rubbed his chin with his finger and thumb. "You need to be a Molly Millions."

She looked at him, confused. What on Earth was he talking about? That razor girl in his *Neuromancer* book? That was ridiculous. After all, she was tough because she had cybernetic—

Oh, no. No, no, no.

"No way," she said, shaking her head. "I'm not going to let you implant me with that technology."

He frowned, letting her know that this was exactly what he'd been thinking. "They'd help you survive," he remarked. "And I've been perfecting them."

"Survive? At what cost? Look what happened to the soldiers you created!" she cried. "Do you really want that for your daughter?" She also remembered the photos of the men her father had implanted so many years ago, their blank faces marred by metal. They were monsters, too. Just like Erin. Infected by metal instead of disease.

"That was not the cybernetics' fault," her dad retorted. "That was their inadequate government training and then their psychological response to being asked to do things outside of human nature. Sure, it's easy to blame the tech, but those soldiers would have been fine if they'd been trained as I mandated. They were unprepared for what they were sent to do." He ran a hand through his hair. "And I've even removed everything questionable from the software. Look, Molly, cybernetics don't kill people. People kill people."

She couldn't believe they were even having this conversation. That her father—her own father—wanted to turn her into a cyborg. "I'm not going to let you do that to me. I'm not a soldier. I don't want to be a soldier. I'm just a plain high-school kid!"

"There is no more high school, and just plain kids won't survive. This is the end of the world as we know it we're talking about. It's no game. And I'm offering you the best chance possible to come through on the other side. To be part of the Earth's future."

"And it means turning me into a robot."

Her father looked pained. "You won't be a robot. You'll just have . . . parts. Very tiny, non-obtrusive parts that will help you see further, react faster, fight better. Parts that will help you survive whatever may come." He paused, peering at her over his glasses. "You do want to survive, don't you, Molly?"

She hung her head, not knowing what to say, not knowing what to do. "Of course," she whispered at last. "But at what price?"

"Look," her dad said, walking back over to his computer. "We don't have to do this today. We still have some time left, and I still have some things to do before we go underground. You think about it and come back to me when you've decided. I will ultimately leave it up to you."

"Fine." She knew her answer, but at least this would buy some time. She started back up the basement stairs.

"Oh, and Molly?" her dad called after her.

She paused on the top stair. "Yeah?"

"Until you're properly outfitted to survive, I don't want you leaving the house. Not ever again."

"But Dad—"

"You want to see your friends? You want to see your boyfriend, whom you started dating against my advice? You need protection. So until you agree to the cybernetics, you are not leaving the house. Don't think it'll be otherwise."

CHAPTER THIRTY-FIVE

Chase woke to the sound of soft breathing next to him. Helga had taken the night watch, and he and Molly were able to curl up together in a motel room, snuggling close. There was little light, except what flickered in through the curtained window from the campfire, but they were both mentally and physically exhausted from the ordeal and had immediately passed out in each other's arms.

Molly was curled into him, her small body melting into his. He absently brushed her hair with his hand, fingering the smooth strands. How he'd wanted this, and for so long. Now here she was. All his. At last.

The moment should have been perfect. But he couldn't relax. Not with the itching. Low in his belly first, then crawling up and down each limb.

It had been easy to make a promise to himself to give up the drugs when he was bargaining for his life and trying to appease the girl of his dreams; it was a lot harder to act on that promise in the middle of the night when he couldn't sleep. No more pills. Not just tonight, but not ever again. The rest of his life spilled out in front of him, and it suddenly seemed very bleak.

He tried to tell himself that his love for Molly was enough. Surely she could satiate his hungers, his desires. But the gnawing attacked him like a thousand tiny midges prickling his skin, and no amount of scratching would make it go away.

Molly shifted in her sleep, moaning a bit, and he wondered if she was dreaming about him. He felt so weak, so awful, lying there with her in his arms and unable to think of anything but a hit. How was he going to kick the habit while on the road? He knew the physical withdrawal would likely render him sick as a dog, and Molly couldn't wait for him.

"You okay?" she murmured, half-asleep, turning to face him.

"Yeah, sorry," he said, brushing the back of his hand against her cheek. She was so beautiful. "I didn't mean to wake you."

"You're not sleeping. Aren't you exhausted?"

"Yeah, but . . ." He felt his face burn in shame. He was such a loser. So weak.

"You can tell me."

And suddenly he wanted to. He was sick of acting unnaturally strong. He wanted to lean on the woman he loved, allow her to see the real him. The weak, vulnerable him. "It's hard to sleep without the drugs," he admitted. "When darkness falls, they're all I can think about. I . . . ache without them. I itch." There, he'd said it. Let her take the truth as she would. Maybe she'd kick him out of bed, yell at him for how pathetic he was for having stumbled into this addiction.

But she didn't. "Oh, Chase," she whispered, kissing him lightly on the mouth.

"I'm sorry to even mention it," he said, fighting humiliation. "And I'm not going to take anything. I swore that to you and I meant it. But that doesn't make it any easier. And it doesn't make sleep come any faster."

"I know something that may," she murmured, reaching down under the covers. At first he had no idea what she was planning. Then he gasped as he felt her hand searching and finding him. His cock thickened as she ran light fingers over it through the sweatpants he wore. He groaned and squeezed his eyes shut, then opened them again. Was this a dream?

"God," he muttered. She was right. He suddenly wasn't thinking at all about the drugs. He clawed at the sheets. "Oh God, that feels so good."

She smiled gently, still stroking. Her other hand found his face and turned it so he was facing her. Leaning forward, she pressed her mouth against his, moving her lips, her greedy little tongue coaxing his mouth to part and allow her inside, all the while running her hand up and down the length of him. He met her tongue with his, stroking, teasing, way too slowly for his taste. But he didn't want to scare her away. This was her idea, and he wanted to see how far she'd take it.

Still, he wished she'd pull his pants down already, grip his cock tightly in her hands as he'd imagined her doing so many lonely nights over the last six . . . no, twelve years—nights he'd been forced to substitute his own hand. Even when they'd been kids they'd never consummated the relationship.

"It seems crazy that I've never done this," she confessed in a whisper against his mouth. Her breath smelled sweet. Like minty toothpaste. She must have found some in the motel bathroom. She laughed a little. "That *we* never did this. Of course, I never did get my LTF."

"Me neither," he said, mindlessly trying not to go cross-eyed as she finally did reach into his pants, wrapping her hands around his rock-hard length. "So I guess technically we're breaking the law."

She giggled. It was a sweet sound that sent chills through him that had nothing to do with sexual desire. God, he loved this woman so much. Since first grade he'd wanted her. In high school, for that brief time, he'd had her heart only to have her body and soul ripped away from him. And now, here she was. Both of them were adults. They were finally ready to consummate what had been so many years in the making.

He couldn't lie still anymore. He was itching again, but this time not for opiates. He reached over and trailed his fingers up and down her arm, tickling her sensitive skin. She let out a soft moan, letting him know he was doing something right. He was reminded once again of the woman who'd been his first time, how he'd rushed through sex, desperate for orgasm. Now he understood the woman's words. When you loved someone, you wanted to take your time.

Leaning over Molly, he trailed kisses down her jaw while running his hand over her breasts and hips. Those soft curves contrasted with the muscles of her stomach. Unable to control himself a moment longer, he yanked down the strap of her nightgown, exposing her breast. The nipple was puckered and taut.

"God, you're so fucking sexy," he whispered.

"You're not so bad yourself," she replied.

No so bad? Ha! Chase was the most amazing specimen of a man Molly had ever seen. Not that this was saying much. She was admittedly completely inexperienced, but she knew if she'd seen a thousand naked men none would ever compare.

His expression told her he was in no mood for silliness. His eyes roved her body like a wild lion would a veldt, assessing and choosing his prey. He caught her hands and pulled them over her head, then rolled atop her, one knee between her thighs.

"You gotta stop," he whispered. "You'll make me come."

He leaned down then, still pinning her hands above her, and began to lave her exposed breast with his tongue. Soft licks interspersed with tiny bites. Pleasure swirled with slight but delicious pain, a whirlwind of sensations she'd need a thesaurus implant to describe. It was enough to simply say he felt very, very good.

He released her hands and she went straight for his shirt, wanting to see him naked. He laughed at her efforts and yanked the garment over his head, revealing his perfectly sculpted chest. Reaching out to touch, concentrating so as to not lose control of her razors this time, she felt hard muscles encased in impossibly soft skin and fell in love with him all over again. He groaned as she pawed him, biting down on his lower lip.

"Do you want this?" he asked, cupping her breast in his hand and tweaking the nipple. "I don't want to go too fast."

She appreciated the kindness, but she was already way beyond stopping. "I want you," she said, as the romance heroines in her mother's books had been known to do. "Make love to me."

It was all the invitation he needed. He pulled down her lacy panties, exposing her core. His fingers found ways to pleasure her, rhythmically pressing against her. Two slipped deep inside. It sort of hurt, but at the same time felt indescribably good. It felt *right*.

Chase brought his fingers to his lips and licked away Molly's sweetness. She tasted better than he could have imagined. He needed more. Now. Thank God she'd said yes. He didn't know what he'd have done if she had refused. Pleasuring himself would forever again be a hollow pastime compared to touching her and being touched by her.

He got down on his knees at the edge of the bed and yanked her closer, and she lay open and exposed before him. He attacked, devouring all the sweetness he could find, alternating with tongue and fingers. It was hard to remember to be gentle. To take his time, as that older woman had directed. His erection throbbed and begged to be encased in her hot body. Enveloped, sheathed, possessed. By Molly.

But she was a virgin. And her first time would hurt. So he ignored his need and took his time, stretching her slowly, pressing his fingers in and out, preparing her for his entrance. Would she like the feeling of him inside of her? Would it bring her pleasure? Or would it frighten her? He didn't want to hurt her.

Her shallow breathing, her uneven gasps excited him as his fingers continued to thrust in and out. He leaned in again for another taste. "Mmm, you're so delicious," he heard himself say, then blushed at the words. He sounded like the star of that cheesy porn sim Tank had played before the plague.

Yet he couldn't help it. It was amazing he had any mind left to be embarrassed.

"Mmm," Molly moaned, closing her eyes and arching her back.

And that was it. He had to be inside of her as soon as possible.

He joined her back on the bed. Kissed her mouth. "Are you ready?" he whispered in her ear. His tongue darted out to lick the lobe. She squirmed in pleasure. "This might hurt a bit at first."

"I'm ready," she said, spreading her legs. "I'm really ready."

Which was all the invitation he needed. He slipped his cock against her, sliding the head up and down. She was soaking wet, which would at least make things easier. He felt himself break out into a cold sweat as he slowly pushed inside her and then even more slowly withdrew. It was all he could do not to come right then and there. Pathetic much? But he squeezed his eyes shut and concentrated as best he could to hold back. Still, marathon sex this session just wasn't meant to be.

"Oh God," he muttered, his thrusts quickening. "I don't know how I'm going to hold on."

"Hold on?" she asked with appealing innocence. "For what?"

He smiled against her mouth. "You'll see," he said. And he was very happy to show her. Happy that she'd never been with another man. It made the encounter all the more special.

He reached down and stroked her as he continued to thrust, attempting to bring her to climax before he lost himself. And thank the Lord, a few minutes later she was returning his thrusts, breaths sharp and quick, head back, back arched. And then it hit her and she cried out, grasping a fistful of sheets as he brought her over the edge.

Seeing her orgasm had to be the most amazing thing ever. He rocked against her, sweating, consumed, no longer gentle, no longer sweet. His body slapped against hers and she ground against him. He felt the tidal wave crest, the sensation consuming him, and he allowed himself to go, to be swept away, shuddering as he erupted hotly inside her. The sensation was like nothing he'd ever felt.

Boneless, he collapsed atop her. She wrapped her arms

around him and kissed him over and over again on his cheeks, nose, mouth, and ears.

"Wow," he said, his voice husky. He rolled on his side and stroked her hair, which was damp with sweat. She was so beautiful. So amazing. So his.

"I love you, Molly Anderson," he said, utterly sated. "I love you more than anything."

"I love you, too, Chris Griffin. Chase." She smiled and cuddled closer to him, her naked body pressed against his. She felt amazing. Truly amazing. He wanted to lie like this for the rest of his life.

Fuck the drugs. He had something much better now. Nothing on Earth was going to make him lose that.

CHAPTER THIRTY-SIX

Molly slipped out of her window and onto the tree branch. It was a move she'd done a hundred times before, to meet a friend for a late-night walk or to make out with Drew after midnight. But never had she felt such fear as she jumped down and crept through the bushes into the street. Her parents would kill her if they knew she was out. Well, maybe not her mom. Ashley Anderson was too zoned out to complain much these days. But her dad . . . well, her dad had made things very clear.

She didn't like disobeying him. But at the same time, she didn't see a way around it. She had to meet the gang. More importantly, she had to see Chris.

She crept down the street, ducking into the shadows as police cruisers passed. It was funny: her neighborhood seemed relatively calm considering the fact that there was a killer plague and monsters on the loose. Of course, the monster thing never made the local news; even now, the government kept a tight clamp down on the information pipeline. But people talked. They knew there was something horrifying out there, something that had killed some of their children. The police claimed they were taking care of it. But rumors of new attacks filtered down the grapevine and everyone was scared. Helpless. They hunkered down in their houses, doors locked, windows barred, waiting to see how it would all play out. Apart from increased police patrols, her suburbanite neighbors were still willing to play by the rules and not go crazy. Unlike the rest of the world, it seemed.

It took her ten minutes to reach Monroeville's center, and what she saw was another story altogether from what she'd believed. Sirens screamed, and scattered small fires flickered up and down the street. Men and women ran by, some wearing all black, some wearing masks, others in respirators, but all had their arms full of supplies from stores that had closed and barred their windows and doors. Only the Wal-Mart was still open, actually doing business. But unlike the old friendly Wal-Mart greeters that used to line the store entrance, now the place was heavily guarded by what appeared to be soldiers. There were trucks coming and going behind it, too.

The sound of what might have been a car backfiring, but was probably a bullet, rang in Molly's ears and she started worrying again about the monsters, the "Others" as her father called them. What would she do if she ran into one on her way to meeting the group at the school? She didn't have any weapon. What, was she going to karate-chop them to death? Her dad had been right; martial arts training wasn't exactly going to cut it.

But it was too late to turn back. She stole through the streets, avoiding both broken glass from the store fronts and a line of corpses littering the pavement. A terrible smell was coming from somewhere, and it was overwhelming. Apparently there was no one left to clean up.

She got to the darkened high school at last. At first she wasn't sure anyone would be meeting her, but then a flash of light flickered on and off. The signal. She followed it and soon came to a side door that had been propped open. Slipping inside, she realized she'd entered the auditorium.

"You're the last," said a deep male voice. "Go ahead and shut the door behind you."

She complied, walking into a circle of light. The school had obviously kept its power somehow. But this group was being cautious all the same. Didn't want to attract the crazies. And that meant most everyone these days.

The stage held a strange assortment of her former class-mates. The head cheerleader sat next to the biggest stoner. The math geek was next to the quarterback. Terror had made everyone equal. Go figure, it took the apocalypse to break down high school cliques.

Chris sat leaning against a wall. He beckoned her over. She complied and took a seat next to him, smiling weakly as she sat. He reached over and squeezed her hand, sending a now familiar tingle of electricity through her. He was so sweet. If only she'd discovered it earlier, when life was still innocent and normal and there weren't monsters wandering the streets.

"Okay, this meeting will come to order," announced a black-haired boy at the front. Molly recognized him as Chris's brother Trey. He rose to his feet and started pacing the stage. All eyes were on him. He swaggered like a born leader, which was funny, because mostly what Molly knew of him was his high virtual football scores, and his penchant for both blonde cheerleaders and porn sims. Of course, he had made the plan to stockpile supplies out of town. Standing there, he looked large and in charge, and he commanded everyone's respect. Guess everyone had to grow up fast these days. She was glad he was around.

"I'm glad all of you could make it tonight," Trey said. "I know it's hard to get out of the house, and certainly it's no picnic to cross town."

A few murmurs of agreement rippled through the crowd. Molly wondered what her dad would say if he knew she was here. He'd totally kill her. Maybe he'd lock her behind those titanium shelter doors he was always going on about.

"Armageddon, the End of Days, the Super Flu, the apoca-lypse. Whatever you want to call it, it's here," continued Trey. "Our friends and family are dying."

Molly glanced over at Chris, who was staring at his feet. His and Trey's parents had left for the quarantine camp out-side Monroeville two days ago, after making the boys prom-ise to take care of Tara and not follow them there. After all, no one who entered the quarantine camp ever left alive.

"The government can't control it, no matter what their stupid propaganda says. It's out of control. I know a lot of you were at the party the other night. You saw the . . . creatures, our former friends and neighbors turned into monsters. You know what's going on. And you know it's only going to get worse." He walked to the end of the stage then turned to face them. "We have to get out of town. Soon. Before it's too late."

"But where?" asked a blond boy in cut-off jeans who looked about fourteen. "They say it's everywhere. How are we going to escape?"

"Yeah, what makes you think we won't get the flu?" asked another.

Molly stood up. "Because we haven't been vaccinated," she told them. "It's the AIDS vaccine that's made people vulnerable. If you haven't gotten that shot then you're safe—at least from the sickness. It's the zombies that we have to worry about. If one bites you and you live, you can become one of them."

Several classmates shuddered, probably having been at the rave and having seen the monsters in action. She didn't blame them. Not a night went by anymore where she didn't have a nightmare herself.

"Molly's right," Trey said. "And we don't have to sit around and wait to be turned into mutants. We can leave. If we work together." He pulled out a holo-pen and pressed a button. A map of South Carolina burst to life into the center of the stage. "As a lot of you know, having helped, we've already gathered a bunch of supplies. In the next twenty-four hours, I want everyone to go home and pack suitcases. Be selective. We can't take everything. Think about what you'd need to go camping. No prom dresses," he said, looking knowingly at a group of girls to his right. "We will all rendezvous in the back parking lot. I'll have a van. We'll head up to the mountains. My parents have a camp up there, which is always empty this time of year. It's on a lake and very secluded. We'll live there until things calm down. There's plenty of wild animals and fish if we run out of packed food. We could live there a long time. Until things calm down and the government gets everything back in control. I'll bring a media deck so we can stay updated as to what's going on."

"Do you really think that will happen?" Chris's friend Stephen interjected. "I mean, what if all the adults die? What if there's nothing left to come back to?"

A good question, Molly thought as she looked around the room. And it was one, it seemed, that no one there had an answer to.

CHAPTER THIRTY-SEVEN

The next few days were so busy they went by like a blur for Chase: traveling for ten hours, setting up camp, taking care of the horses. Making love to Molly whenever it was possible, sometimes under the stars, sometimes in a motel bed. Helga had proved an invaluable asset, and Chase was thankful Molly had agreed to take her along.

It was funny. Here they were, traveling a postapocalyptic highway with only a small shred of hope there would be something worthwhile at the end, but still, Chase had never felt happier. To ride beside Molly and talk to her about everything and anything. To feel her body under his at night. This was better than anything else he could imagine. He wanted this closeness to last forever. And luckily, she seemed to want it, too.

They were so close now. He could almost taste the Florida oranges. He couldn't wait to see what they'd find at the end. Molly was so sure. She expected a new civilization, a rebirth of the world. It seemed hard to credit as they passed empty town after empty town, but he believed because she did. He believed because he wanted to.

He imagined them reaching their destination, finding a friendly home base again. Where the children could feel safe. Where he and Molly could live like husband and wife. Maybe there would even be a priest down there, someone who could marry them officially.

To have Molly as his bride—well, he couldn't think of anything he wanted more.

But thoughts of the future had to wait. Tonight he was on guard duty. The rest of the camp was sound asleep. Molly was curled up next to him after an intense session of lovemaking, dead to the world. He kissed her lightly on her forehead, so as not to wake her, and crawled out from under the covers, yanking his leather pants over his hips and grabbing his shirt.

Time to patrol.

It seemed almost a waste of time in some ways. They hadn't seen any Others in days, and even then the beasts had never attacked. They hadn't had much problem the whole trip. He wondered if the zombie curse hadn't hit southern Georgia. Or maybe the scouts of Paradise had collected them all for their gladiator games. Regardless, Molly insisted they stay watchful. Chase had to agree.

He wandered the perimeter of the motel they'd chosen, kicking rocks as he went. He tried to imagine the place before the plague. What kind of people had stayed here. Families on their way to the Magic Kingdom? Traveling salesmen without a lot of cash? Maybe a few cheating husbands and their sleazy girlfriends, never knowing, as they enjoyed their dangerous liaisons, that soon infidelity would be the least of their problems.

A sudden noise came from the bushes. Startled, he backed up, only to hit a wall that served to separate the motel from the former pool area. He reached for a rifle he'd brought out of Paradise—a lucky find when he'd stolen the scooter—praying he was wrong and it was just a raccoon or maybe one of the children up to go to the bathroom.

But it was no raccoon. And it was no sleepy child. Instead, a small Other wandered into the parking lot. A female, by the looks of it. Remnants of stringy blonde hair hung off her head and what was once a flower-patterned dress clung to her emaciated frame.

The woman let out a muffled moan, hairless, bony arms

outstretched like something from an old George Romero movie. But this was no film set. The world had become a true horror flick, and Chase was one of its stars. He was the one who'd done the drugs, had sex with the girl and uttered the words, "I'll be right back." In other words, he was the one who was about to wind up dead.

He blew out a breath and steadied his gun, eyes narrowing to slits. Steady as she goes, he told himself. This was a matter of protecting his family: both what was left of it and what he'd rebuilt.

In an instant it happened. The creature lurched forward and Chase fell back a step, squeezing the trigger. The rifle's recoil bruised his shoulder. Blood gouted from the woman's chest. He'd missed the heart and it was only a flesh wound. She was still coming. And two other shadows had appeared behind her. Three . . . no, four? How much ammunition was left in his gun?

He fired again at the Other, twice more, and her head exploded in a mass of red and grey pulp. At the same time he reached around his neck and pulled free his whistle. He blew as hard as he could. Sure enough, the shadows that had risen behind the first Other stopped moving. There came a cacophony of inhuman screeches and then the shadows dissipated. The creatures had turned and fled, hands over their ears.

Chase watched them go, breathing heavily. The whistle fell from his bloodless lips. "Yeah, I thought so," he said, shaking out his arms and trying to regain some composure. "I thought so! Run, cowards!" He nodded to himself and stepped out from the shadows.

Only to find himself thrown backwards.

He crashed hard onto the asphalt of the street, the impact knocking the breath from his lungs. His vision blurred and, for a moment, nothing made any sense. Then he looked up and saw what had struck him. An Other towered above, clearly not scared away by his whistle. It was growling and spitting.

It was a huge male, and it lunged forward, hands finding Chase's neck, encircling and squeezing tight, cutting off his breath. Desperate, Chase kicked out and slammed his foot into the creature's groin. The monster bellowed but didn't let go. Chase struggled harder, panic slamming through him as he used one arm to brace himself, fighting to keep away from the monster's mouth. He reached for his boot with his free hand, feeling for the knife he always kept there. It took what seemed like forever to wrap his fingers around the hilt. The creature's grip tightened, and Chase saw blackness swimming toward him. Pain seared through his shoulder. Then, in his final moment of consciousness, he managed to yank the knife free and drive it into the creature's heart.

The zombie recoiled then fell on top of him, crushing Chase with his weight. But the fingers loosened and Chase was able to breathe. He sucked in a huge breath and pushed the creature off. It rolled back onto the pavement, staring up at the sky and whimpering.

Chase surged to his feet and stared down at the monster. It looked a lot more human lying there now, vulnerable and bleeding. This was something he always hated. He wondered who it had been before the change. A doctor? A lawyer? Maybe a humanitarian who built houses for poor people.

It didn't matter. It was none of those things now, he reminded himself. Just a monster. A monster that needed to be put out of its misery.

He grabbed his rifle and pressed the barrel to the zombie's head. Closing his eyes, he pulled the trigger. The shot shook his arm and echoed in his ears. He let the sound fade away before looking. The body was twitching, the head disintegrated.

He forced himself to look away but as he did a piercing pain found his right shoulder. Startled, he glanced down, his mouth falling open as he saw where his leather jacket had come open, where the shirt below was ripped and bloody. Teeth marks. He'd been bitten. He'd been *bitten*.

"Chase! Chase, are you okay?"

He looked up. *Molly*. She was running toward him, her face white.

"Chase?"

"I'm okay," he said, turning at an angle so she couldn't see his wound. "I got him."

She stopped a few feet away, looking down at the remains of the two dead zombies. "God, what happened?" she asked.

"One got the jump on me. No big deal. It's all fine," he lied. The pain gripped his shoulder like a vise and it was all he could do not to fall to his knees. But if he fell, she'd know. He couldn't let her know.

She took a step forward but he held out a hand. "I'm all slimy," he said. "Zombie gook. You know. I'm going to go find a fountain or something to wash off."

"Are you sure you're all right?" she asked, peering at him, confusion and worry warring on her face.

He felt sick to his stomach but nodded. The last thing he wanted was to lie to her. But what choice did he have? He had to think of Molly and the kids. She was too weak to get where she needed to go on her own now. Wonderful Molly. Tough Molly. His beloved. She needed his help to find her father. To complete her pilgrimage. To save the world. And who knew how her priorities would change once she learned the truth?

Well, he probably had two weeks. Two weeks before the virus would work its way fully through his system, mutating his cells, destroying his brain and turning him into one of them. That was what he'd seen in the past. He had two weeks to get Molly where she had to go. Then he'd use his rifle one last time—to put a bullet in his own head. He couldn't trust anyone else to do it.

"Go back to sleep," he told her. "I'm just going to do one more round of checks."

"I'm coming with you." She was stubborn to the end.

He sighed. "Okay. But go put on your leather first. It's too dangerous to be out here in that flimsy nightgown."

She nodded and headed back to the camp. Chase looked at

his bite. It was ugly and already growing yellow. Maybe he was immune, he reminded himself. His brother had been, after all. But maybe he wasn't. There was no way he could tell.

He felt tears slipping from his eyes and brushed them angrily away. *God, Chase, be a man!* he scolded himself. But he couldn't help it. There was a time, even recently, that he wouldn't have cared much about death. In fact, he might have even welcomed it. But now, for the first time in forever, he had a real reason to live. Just figured, this was the time the Grim Reaper finally showed up.

Molly. He ached as he thought of her. Her smile. Her soft skin brushing against his. Her sweet taste. Her soft moans as he pleasured her. She was so beautiful. So precious and perfect. She'd brought him back from the darkness, showed him there could be life in a dead world. Gave him a reason to exist. To hope and pray and struggle.

He loved her. So much more than anything. He wanted to be with her forever. To marry her and have babies and grow old by her side. He wanted to spend a lifetime taking care of her, making sure she had everything she needed. But now he couldn't. Until he was sure he wasn't infected, he'd have to stay away from her. No more kissing. No more snuggling. No more making love. Tonight had been the last time.

She wouldn't understand. And he couldn't tell her the truth because she'd insist on quarantine. She'd want to stop and care for him until they knew what was going on, and there wasn't time for that. She was already getting weaker; he'd noticed it in the mornings. It took her longer to get up. She was stiff. She had headaches. He'd noticed, even though she'd taken great pains to hide them from him. He wasn't going to allow her to endanger her own life for the sake of his.

No, he had to play it safe. And that wasn't going to be easy. It involved pushing her away but not letting her know why. It would be the hardest thing he'd ever done, he realized. But it was the only way. Better to make her hate him than allow her to sacrifice herself for him. She'd already done too much of that, and he hated himself for her sacrifices. It was his time to

be a man. He would save her, even if it meant his own death.
She was worth it. Hell, she was worth a lot more.

He grabbed the first-aid kit from one of the scooters and
cleaned his wound; then he resignedly rose to his feet and
trudged back to camp. His body felt as if it weighed a ton. If
only he'd had one more night with Molly, to show her how
much he loved her. She was going to be so hurt. And he would
hate himself. But this was the only option: to push her away.

Maybe someday it would be okay. He'd find out he was immune. That he wasn't going to turn into a monster. Then he
could explain. Once she was safe and sound at Disney World.
But only then. For now, Chase had to be the bad guy—or at
least push her away so she wouldn't want to be with him and
tempt him. It was the only way to save her life. He would
make any sacrifice for that.

CHAPTER THIRTY-EIGHT

The meeting ended and the kids dispersed, leaving Trey, Chris, Molly and little Tara hanging out on the stage. Tara contented herself with her Barbie dolls, as she was too young to really understand what was going on.

"So, do you think everyone's on board?" Trey asked Chris and Molly. "I mean, they seemed to be listening, right?"

"Yeah, you did a good job," Chris said. "I think everyone's really happy to have someone come up with a real plan. Everyone's so scared, you know? It's good to have someone take charge."

Molly nodded in agreement. "You were great," she said. "And I think you totally gave everyone hope."

Trey pursed his lips. "Yeah," he said. "I just hope it's not false hope." He got up and paced the stage. "I mean, we have no way of knowing if the mountains are really any safer than here, right?"

"It makes sense though," Molly argued. "There are fewer people to begin with, and probably even fewer who went through with their AIDS vaccines. Not to mention, I doubt the monsters here are really taking many road trips, so it'll be safer on that end as well."

"True," Trey said. He shrugged. "Well, I guess we'll see soon enough. You guys going to be ready?"

Molly and Chris nodded in sync. Chris reached over and squeezed her hand. Trey rolled his eyes.

"Freaking lovebirds," he muttered. "Y'all don't even care about the end of the world, do you? Not as long as you can sit there and make googly eyes at one another."

Chris turned tomato red, and Molly could feel her face flush as well. "Yeah, yeah," Chris said at last, waving his brother off. "You're just jealous 'cause I got the hot chick." He winked at Molly then leaned over to give her a kiss.

"Argh! My eyes! Warn a guy before you do shit like that," Trey cried.

Molly and Chris pulled apart, smiling at each other. In a weird way Trey was right. It was a little easier to deal with all that was going on when they had each other. And it was good to know they always would.

"Anyway, I got some crap to take care of," Trey continued. "You mind taking Tara home?"

Chase shook his head. "No problem."

Trey grabbed his bag, said good-bye to his adopted sister, and vacated the stage. Molly glanced at her watch. "I'd better get home, too," she said. "Before someone notices I'm gone."

Chris made a mock pouting face. "Boo," he said. "I want you to stay and make out with me."

She laughed and kissed him on the nose. "Believe me, I'd much rather do that," she assured him. "But if my dad kills me then I won't be able to meet you guys for our mountain adventure." She smiled at him. "Just think, soon we won't ever have to say good-bye. We'll see each other every hour of every day."

"I can't wait," Chris whispered, leaning in to kiss her neck. His mouth tickled and she laughed, pulling away.

"Me neither. Now let's get out of here."

"Hang on a sec." Chris squinted. "Where's Tara?" In their canoodling, they hadn't noticed the little girl slip away. "Tara?" he called. "Where did you go?"

There was no answer.

Molly scrambled to her feet and scanned the darkened auditorium. She looked over at Chris, worried. "You go down each aisle," she suggested. "I'll check backstage."

They split up, Chris going down the main steps and Molly

stepping into the darkness behind the curtain. "Tara?" she cried. "Honey, you can come out now! It's time to leave."

No answer. Molly scratched her head. Where did the kid go? The place wasn't that big.

Suddenly she heard a crash stage right. Then she smelled something awful. She ran over to the area of the noise and flipped on a light. The first thing she saw was Tara, playing in a wooden box used for a stage set. Then she saw the monster.

Where it had come from was anyone's guess, but no matter what, it was here now. And it was staggering toward Tara, moaning, its arms outstretched.

Molly remembered what her dad had said: one bite and you could become infected, too. Still, she couldn't let it get Chris's sister, so she dove toward the box. But she was too late. It reached the little girl first. Tara whirled, saw the creature. Her little mouth opened up in a scream.

"No!" Molly cried. Drawing on all her martial arts skills she roundhouse-kicked, slamming her foot into the monster's side. It bellowed in rage, then reached out and knocked her away. She was no match for its strength and crashed to the floor.

"Come get me!" she cried, trying to scramble up. "Fight me, you bastard!"

But the monster wasn't interested. It already had Tara. And it wasn't going to stop.

Without meaning to, she averted her eyes. There were noises she knew she'd never forget for the rest of her life. Then a gunshot. And a scream. She turned back. The monster had fallen to the ground, its eyes bloodshot and its head blown off. It was dead.

"Tara!" Pistol still in hand, Chris ran to his little sister, throwing himself on the ground to check her.

Molly swallowed hard, unsure what to do. What to say. "Is she . . . ?"

"Oh God. Oh God, no!"

It was a definitive answer if she'd ever heard one. "Oh, Chris," she cried. "I tried. I really tried."

Her father's words came crashing back to her. If only she'd accepted his offer of cybernetics. They would have helped her battle these creatures. She would have been stronger. Faster. Better. She would have been able to overpower the thing before it stole the life of a little girl.

Chris cradled the broken body of his sister, sobbing. He looked at Molly. "I promised to protect her," he whispered, his eyes wild with grief. "And I failed. I failed her."

Molly ran to his side, putting her arms around him, holding him tight. "You did what you could," she told him. "And you saved my life. I would have been next." But she knew her words could only comfort so much. They couldn't bring Tara back.

Another senseless death. And this one was a little child. It couldn't go on. Molly couldn't let it. She thought of her father again and knew what she had to do.

CHAPTER THIRTY-NINE

"And then Sprinkles rolled onto her back. And then she swatted at the string with her paw and . . ."

Molly tried to pay attention as Darla excitedly recounted in excruciating detail the further adventures of the amazing glow cat she used to own. But the day's journey had really tired her out and it was admittedly a bit hard to follow Darla's chatter at the best of times.

They'd entered Florida that day and celebrated that night with candy and wine found in a local gas station. The kids were ecstatic about their journey finally nearing its end. Molly was pretty psyched, too. Only a few more days and they'd reach the Magic Kingdom's front gates, where she could be reunited with her father and do what she needed to help restore the world.

But her excitement was tempered by her diminishing physical well-being. Each day she felt a little weaker. A little more cloudy. The nanos were breaking down, eating her up inside like a sort of high-tech cancer. If she didn't get to her dad and the other scientists soon, she might not make it at all.

At least she had Chase. He had promised no matter what that he would get her down to Disney World, even if he had to carry her on his back. And she believed him. Even if he had been acting a little weird and stand-offish earlier today. He was just tired from being on watch all night, she was certain. Because, besides that, everything between them was great. Beautiful, amazing, loving. She'd never been happier.

He was so good to her—he had been, even when she'd refused to appreciate it. And now that they were together? It was a feeling she'd never experienced in her life, that she'd never thought it would be possible to experience. Love. Overwhelming, all-consuming, burning love. Sometimes it was desperate and passionate as they clung to one another, fighting against the hardships of the world. Sometimes it was soft and sweet, two people becoming one mind and body. Caressing, feeling, losing yourself in the other. But it was always beautiful and magical and unbearably wonderful, and she knew it would last forever.

"And then my kitty took a ball of string and . . ."

Molly stifled a yawn. Helga looked over from her spot by the fire and grinned. "If you want, I'll watch them so you can go to bed," she suggested.

Molly shook her head. "Thanks, but I'm good."

Helga looked unconvinced, and Molly understood why. She wasn't just internally exhausted and sick; she looked terrible on the outside, too. The color had drained from her face and her lips were now all but translucent. She'd lost weight, too. Muscle mass. The stuff that helped her fight.

She watched Chase pass by and gave him a small wave. He had his eyes to the ground and must have missed the gesture, because he didn't wave back. Instead, he headed into his tent and pulled the flaps closed. Concerned, Molly turned to Helga.

"If you don't mind watching them . . ."

Helga waved her off. "Go see your man."

With effort she rose to her feet and headed to the tent. All she wanted was to crawl inside and snuggle up. That always made everything better.

Chase pulled the sleeping bag over his head and closed his eyes, trying to force sleep. He knew it was futile; it was probably only around seven. The sun hadn't even set. There was no way he'd pass out for hours. But what else was he supposed to do, go hang out with Molly? She'd only want to cuddle up to him, hug him, kiss him. Press her delicious body against his. That would be too hard.

He turned over on his side, staring at the tent wall. The day had been almost unbearable as it was. Every itch, every tingle, and he was positive he was transforming into one of them. Even though he knew for a fact it'd take weeks for any noticeable change to take place. If a change took place at all, he reminded himself. It was entirely possible he was immune. Like Tank. Still, hope was little comfort. And not being able to share his fears with Molly made them all the more unbearable.

He tried to think of other things, but without much luck. Impending demise did that to a guy. Not to mention it took every ounce of willpower to stay clear of Molly. She'd noticed his avoidance; he was sure of it. He'd caught her questioning look a few times as they rode down the highway. When they'd all celebrated their arrival in Florida, he'd held back. She noticed everything.

If only he could tell her the truth: that it wasn't her, it was him. And not him exactly, either. He would tell her there was nothing on this planet he'd rather do than curl up in her arms and make love to her until the sun rose, caressing each curve, kissing each sweet inch, worshiping her like the goddess he knew she was. But he didn't want to face her questions. What was wrong with him? Why was he holding back? Questions he couldn't answer. Not when it put her life at stake.

If only she wasn't getting sick. If only she wasn't running out of time. They could have set up camp for a few weeks, put him in quarantine like they used to back in Wal-Mart. Or he could have let them go, promising to catch up if he didn't turn.

But he didn't have that luxury. She was getting weaker every day. Soon she wouldn't even be able to ride a horse without being held up. She had to get to Disney. Soon. And he had promised he'd get her there. Without him, she'd die. And he wouldn't—couldn't—let that happen.

"Chase?"

He stifled a groan as her blonde head peeked inside the tent. Great. He should have known this was coming. Next thing she'd be crawling inside, wanting him to touch her. To make love to her, as had been their habit. As he couldn't do anymore. There was no way he'd take the chance of her getting infected.

He tried not answering, praying she'd think him asleep and would wander off to play with the children or chat with Helga. But he knew in his heart she'd never do that. And sure enough, a moment later he heard her enter the tent. Felt her sitting down beside him. Her hand reached up to stroke his hair. He lay still for a moment, sad and angry at the world. Then he jerked his head away. It took effort.

He could see her in the shadow, cocking her head in confusion. "What's wrong?" she asked, her voice laced with concern. "You're acting weird. You've been acting weird all day."

It wasn't fair. He'd finally regained his true love. The woman he'd waited a lifetime for. His goddess. And now he had to push her away. Make her hate him.

Not fair at all.

"Molly, we have to talk," he said, hoping she didn't hear the trembling in his voice. There was only one thing to do, and it was likely going to kill him to do it. Kill him and crush her.

But better crushed than dead.

Her hand reached out to touch him again. His arm. It was probably okay that she was touching his arm, right? Though he didn't want to take any chances.

"Talk?" she repeated. "Chase, you're scaring me."

"It's just . . ." He struggled with a way to phrase it. One that would cause the smallest amount of pain but at the same time make her want never to touch him again. "Molly, what do you want from all of this?"

"All of . . . ?"

Ugh, he was doing a terrible job. "From this. From us."

Even in the dim light he could see her already wan face drain of color. "What do you mean?" she asked. Now her voice was completely fearful. He felt like such an asshole.

"I don't know," he said, trying to sound nonchalant. "I mean, sure, we've had some fun. But I don't see us being a long-term item, do you?"

He'd made her speechless. Her silence pierced his heart, because he knew he didn't want her hurting. He wanted nothing more than to throw his arms around her and say it was all a joke. But he couldn't. In fact, it was very likely he'd never be able to touch her again as long as he lived. It was the worst thought in the world.

"Look, you're a nice girl," he said, struggling to drive his point home. "And I'll get you to Disney. But I think it's best if we don't hook up anymore."

"Hook . . . up?" Her voice trembled, and he knew any moment she'd burst into tears. He didn't deserve to live for hurting her like this. But what else could he do? It was the only way he could think of to save her life.

"I thought you loved me," she said.

"Yeah, well, you know, we've said a lot of things and . . ."

"Chase, did I do something? Tell me what I did! Don't shut me out!"

"You didn't do anything. I just don't want a girlfriend. I want to be alone." His words sounded so stupid, so lame. Surely she could see right through them. But no, the look on her face told him she bought every last lie. His words worked. Too well, perhaps.

"Fine." She pursed her lips, obviously fighting for some control. "I'll leave you alone then." She stumbled as she tried to crawl out of the tent, tripping over a tangle of blankets. A small sob escaped her, and the sound broke his heart.

He'd hurt her. After they'd promised each other the world. After she'd freely offered up her mind, body and soul to him. He'd crushed all that in one fell swoop. She'd probably never forgive him. She'd probably hate him forever.

But what else could he do? Her life was worth more to him

than his own. He'd promised to get her to Disney World, and
he'd do so. If it took him to his last dying breath, he'd do it.

Even if she never understood why.

Molly burst from the tent, finally allowing tears to stream
from her eyes through the drainage vents of her lenses, vents
she'd demanded her father include as modifications when he
did the operations. She didn't want to be like Molly Millions;
she wanted to cry when she had to. In some ways, that was an
important part of life. Being caged wasn't living, and neither
was caging your emotions. Of course, what had indulging her
emotions gotten her?

She probably looked completely crazy. A total wreck. But
her heart was broken. Chase was gone.

She should have never gotten involved with him. She'd
been right from the start. If only she'd concentrated on her
mission, left him in Wal-Mart, or at least not fallen for him
on the road. She should have stayed strong, not let love cloud
her judgment. Her dad would be so ashamed. Thinking about
it now, maybe he'd been right.

She'd thought Chase was different. That he was the same
boy she'd loved so many years ago. But he had changed. They
all had. And there was no going back to a fairy tale.

She considered leaving. Sneaking off in the night and heading to Disney alone. But that wasn't possible anymore. She'd
put herself in the position where she needed help. She was too
weak to make the rest of the journey on her own. She'd left
herself vulnerable. Stupid her, for trusting him and allowing
herself to be dependent on another person.

That was why her father's beloved Molly Millions had always worked on her own, she reminded herself, never part-
nered with anyone for more than a brief mission. *It's just how
I'm wired*, she'd said in her good-bye note to the hero at the
end of the book. Molly should have wired herself the same
way. Trusted her dad's instructions. But she'd been emotionally weak. Allowed herself to believe, to hope, to love. And
look where it had gotten her.

She sank to her knees at the edge of the camp, choking on her sobs. She could hear her dad's words at the back of her head. *Molly Millions doesn't cry. When she's sad, she spits.*

Molly tried to spit. But her mouth was too dry.

She was a lousy excuse for a razor girl.

CHAPTER FORTY

Molly opened her eyes. Her bedroom glowed with a strange silver haze. For a moment she wasn't sure what had happened, then it all came crashing back to her. Tara's death. Her decision to get the cybnernetics from her dad so she could protect those she loved. She remembered her father's pleased grin when she informed him she'd decided to go ahead with the procedure. He had the parts all ready; he'd obviously planned on her saying yes. A slip of a needle in her arm knocked her out for the count almost before she could even ask what exactly he planned to do.

Now awake, post-surgery, she sat up in bed and thoroughly examined her arms and legs. She didn't see any obvious weird body armor, which was a relief. She looked closer at her hands. Her fingers. It felt like there was something there, under the surface of her nails. Something, somehow she knew she could control. She concentrated hard and . . .

Razors shot out from behind her nails: four-inch steel blades under each finger and thumb. Retractable. She tested one out on her silk sheets. It slit through the soft material like butter. Ultrasharp. She drew them back in. Pretty cool. Now she was armed. The next time one of those monsters tried to hurt anyone, she'd be ready.

What was with the silver haze, though? She slid out of bed and approached the mirror. Looked at her reflection . . . and screamed.

Oh God, no. Not this. What had her father been thinking? She'd told him she only wanted something small. Something to protect others. What possible use could these things on her eyes do? These ocular implants locked her away from the world.

She reached up to pull on the metal panes but they seemed fused to her skull. Blood dripped down her face as she tugged, desperate to get them off of her face. But they didn't move; this was like a nightmare from which she couldn't wake up.

"You're awake!" her dad cried, entering the room. He grinned widely as his eyes caught her face. "You look beautiful," he murmured. "Just like her. Just like Molly Millions." She realized he was still clutching his worn copy of *Neuromancer*, and she wanted to reach out and smack it from his grip. Tear it up into a thousand pieces. How dare he do this to her? Turn her into a fucking character in his favorite book with absolutely no concern or interest in what was best for her.

"What did you *do* to me?" she asked through gritted teeth. "I asked you for some small alterations. Some nano enhancers or something to make me a better fighter. What is this?" She gestured to her eyes. "You turned me into a monster."

Her father, to her surprise, merely *tsk*ed. "Molly, don't be vain," he scolded, as if she were a small child unhappy with the color of her birthday dress. "Those ocular implants will help you more than any of the nanos I injected into you. You'll be able to see in the dark—any light level, actually. You'll have a built-in GPS. Database access, life-sensors, maps, the works. I've been working on these for years. They're my life's work, culminated." He stepped forward, looking at her proudly. "I've finally built her. I've finally built a real-life razor girl."

She sank down on her bed, head in hands. What would Chris think when he saw her now, when he realized the girl he loved had transformed into a disgusting robotic monster? How could she even face him? How could she bear to see the look of horror on his face?

She was trying to cry but couldn't. "What the hell?" she said. "I can't cry?"

Her dad sat down beside her. "Molly," he said. "This isn't a bad thing. You're built to survive and protect those you love. The world has changed, but you're ready now. Together, you, me, and your mother will take part in a great and glorious rebuilding of our world. And that's a good thing, right?"

She looked up at him.

"I know it's hard to understand," he continued. "You're so young. But you must know that you were put on this Earth to serve a higher purpose. The highest of all purposes, actually." He stroked her hair. "You, Molly, my razor girl, you alone now have the power inside you to save us all."

She bit back her anger and said, "Fine. But first we have to make one modification."

CHAPTER FORTY-ONE

Everyone but Helga was sleeping when Molly slipped away from the camp that night. She stepped gingerly over the slumbering kids, careful not to wake them, and past the horses, who neighed softly but didn't give her away.

She wasn't leaving, as much as she would have liked to. But she *was* going to go out and try to find some steroids from a local hospital. She'd seen a sign on the road a ways back that her GPS confirmed, and she needed as much strength as possible to make the final leg of this Disney trip. Because, though Chase had said he'd still get her there, she realized she couldn't rely on him. He was obviously going through something odd, acting all weird, like a loose cannon. So she needed to protect herself, in case he went all crazy again. She needed to be self-sufficient. And the only way she could see to do that was to get loaded up on as much supplemental medication as possible. Her father had suggested this route if worst came to worst.

Her GPS marked the old hospital not a quarter-mile from the highway, and the faded blue signs they'd passed confirmed she was on the right track. She headed down the street, keeping a careful watch for any Others. She was pretty weak and only wanted to fight if it was completely necessary.

Luck was with her. She made it to the hospital without incident. The glass doors had been smashed and so Molly didn't have to open them to step inside. She adjusted her lenses to compensate for the low light and scanned the area, searching for signs of the living or undead. Nothing. She headed down the long, cobwebbed hallway, wondering where she should start her search. There had to be some sort of pharmacy somewhere on the premises. She just prayed that it hadn't been stripped entirely bare by looters.

The hallway came to a dead end, turning to the left and right. She chose left and headed down the passageway, creeped out by the eerie silence. Maybe she should have brought Helga with her . . .

But just as she neared freaking out, she noticed a sign for the pharmacy and followed it, coming eventually to a door. Wrapping her hand around the knob, she tried it. Locked. She'd need to break it down. Hopefully she still had enough strength to do that.

But just as she did, she heard a noise. A groaning. There were Others behind this door, in the pharmacy, mingling with the drugs she needed. How was that possible, that they'd be locked where she needed to go? It just was. And it figured.

Scratching her head, she tried to decide on the best plan of action. Maybe she should just call off the whole thing, head back out while she still could. After all, if there were Others in the pharmacy, they were bound to be elsewhere in the hospital as well. And she knew for a fact that she wasn't strong enough to take any on in her weakened state.

She should leave. Find a new hospital in a new town. One without zombies lurking in their medicine cabinets. But, Molly realized, tomorrow she'd be even weaker, and the next day weaker than that. Soon she wouldn't be able to leave the camp alone and then she'd be totally reliant on people she could no longer trust.

It had to be here. It had to be now.

She raised her foot and kicked in the door.

The wood cracked, the door separating from its hinges and crashing down. She still had strength, at least for now.

The razors extended from her fingers and she took up a fighting stance. As the dust cleared, she gasped. What had she done? The place was crawling with Others. There must have been two dozen of them milling about, moaning and growling. A hornets' nest of horror. Even at full strength she knew there was no way she'd be able to fight all of them. And definitely not now.

Medications sat on the shelves a few mere feet away, mocking her. So close she could almost reach out and grab them. But they might as well have been on Mars for all the good they would do her.

She turned and started running, her feet moving as fast as they could away from the monsters. She could hear them following, not far behind, making their chomping noises. Hadn't Chase told her once they didn't run? Maybe these were particularly hungry Others. It certainly sounded like they were psyching themselves up for dinner.

She whipped around a corner, then another, heading for the entrance. But soon she realized that in her haste to get away, she must have taken a wrong turn. She smacked into a dead end. Crap. She turned around. The Others were at the end of the hall, swarming toward her, slower now but arms outstretched and mouths open as they moaned. Molly's heart pounded in fear as she shrank against the wall. There were too many of them. And she was too weak. She was royally screwed.

She should have never gone off on her own. What an idiot. She'd been so concerned with being strong that she'd put herself in a position where she was especially weak. And now, after all her group had been through, after how far they'd come, she was going to die here in a hospital only a few hundred miles from Disney. In a place where no one would ever look to find her body.

Sorry, Dad. Sorry, world.

The monsters drew closer. She could see saliva dripping from their fangs. She squeezed her eyes shut, waiting for death.

But then, something inside her forced her to open her eyes again. It forced her to hold up her hands, readying her razors. She thought of Chase down in the Thunderdome. He was totally outmatched but he hadn't given up. She knew she couldn't, either. If she had to go down, fine. But it wouldn't be without a fight.

She was a razor girl, after all.

Making a few threatening sweeps with her arms, she stepped forward. It was kind of ridiculous, stupid posturing they'd laugh at if they could understand humor. But they couldn't, and they just shuffled closer, looking oh so hungry.

Here went nothing.

She charged forward, kicking out at the first one on the left, slamming her foot into its chest. It flew backward. Without stopping she whirled around, blades flashing, slicing through another's throat. The razors easily cut through, the skin as giving as rotten fruit.

She turned to the next. On and on she fought, and many of them dropped. Like a cornered tiger, desperate to survive, she was beating them one by one, forcing herself to stay focused, using every last ounce of strength.

But in the end, it wasn't enough. The zombies kept coming, endless and ready to tear her limb from limb.

This was it. The end. There would be no miracle this time around. She thought about Chase. What would he do when she didn't come back? Would he assume she just took off without them? Would he miss her at all? Would he even care?

Suddenly, the zombies stopped advancing, put their hands over their ears. Molly looked around, trying to figure out what was distressing them. She saw and heard nothing. And yet, the Others started dropping to their knees, groaning in apparent agony. Some of them turned and ran away.

She had no idea why this was happening, but she couldn't let her chance pass. Letting out a fierce battle cry, she slammed the side of one hand into a zombie's head, knocking him sideways. Another she stabbed in its eyes, withdrawing the razors only to slice another in the face. Blood sprayed everywhere as she stabbed and sliced, stabbed and sliced, praying that this distraction was her salvation.

A few excruciatingly long minutes later, she found herself surrounded by dead bodies. She lowered her hands, her arm muscles aching, and looked around, trying to discern what had happened. She felt exhausted and sick and covered in gore.

But she was alive and unbitten, and that was what mattered.

"Are you okay?"

She whirled around, shocked to hear another person's voice. A man dressed in a white lab coat stood behind the pile of bodies she'd made. He had a trim brown beard, black-rimmed glasses and some sort of strange-looking whistle hanging around his neck.

"What did you do?" she asked, leaning over, hands on her knees, trying to catch her breath. She pulled out a handkerchief from her pocket and starting cleaning her blades.

He held out the whistle. "They hate high-pitched noises," he explained. "We all carry dog whistles when we leave the Hive."

Right. She remembered Chase mentioning something like that. But . . . Hive? What was *that* about? She straightened up. Was there some new sort of society here? Hopefully they weren't as crazy as the last one.

"Thanks. I appreciate it," she said, pulling out disinfectant to wipe down her blades. She'd taken to carrying it everywhere in her jacket pockets, and hadn't had to use it much. "For a minute I thought I was a goner."

The man stepped over a zombie corpse and held out a plastic-gloved hand, then retracted it as he saw her razors. He laughed. "Well, I guess we can dispense with the formalities," he said. "I'm David. I'm a scientist here at the Hive. Where do you come from, Molly?"

"A small town in South Carolina. We're making our way down to Orlando."

"I see. How many are you?"

"Eleven. Mostly children." For some reason she had a strong sense that she could trust this man. It helped that he'd just saved her life.

"And what brings you to Florida?"

"My dad. He's waiting for us at Disney."

"I see," David said again. He stared at her thoughtfully.

A loud inhuman screech echoed through the hallway. David glanced in its direction then turned back to Molly. "We'd better get downstairs," he said. "It's not safe up here. They'll come back eventually."

"Actually, I'm on my way out," Molly said. "I just came here for some medication. I really need to get back to my friends before they realize I'm gone and send out the cavalry."

"What kind of medication?"

She explained what she was looking for. "Unfortunately, the Others were swarming the pharmacy, so I wasn't able to get any."

"Well, don't worry," David said, kicking one of the dead ones. "We have plenty of medications downstairs. I can get you what you need. Just follow me."

Seeing no other option—she really needed those drugs—she agreed, praying this society was more civilized than that of Paradise, and followed him down the hall. After a few turns, they came to an elevator. David pressed his thumb against a small gray pad to the side and, after a beep, the doors slid open. They apparently still had power. He motioned for her to join him inside.

The doors slid closed and they began to descend. "You guys live underground?" Molly asked, still feeling a bit wary.

"Yes. We feel it's safer. As you've seen, things can be dangerous up on the surface."

"How many of you are there?"

"Three hundred and twenty-three."

She stared him, shocked. She'd been expecting him to say a dozen.

"Actually, make that three hundred and twenty-four. We had a birth the other day. Cute little fella. Parents named him Joey."

"So you're like . . . a little underground town?"

David nodded. "We call it the Hive—mainly 'cause of all the twisty passages and little cells, just like a wasp's nest.

Before the plague it used to be a huge, top secret under-ground prison. A place for political criminals to live out their life sentences. But the Super Flu swept in and wiped them all out, just like everyone else. We figured it'd be a good place to hole up in—after we got rid of all the bodies, that was. Deep underground, it's safe from the creatures. And the former cells, cushy as they are, make perfect little apartments for our residents."

"That's great," Molly said. It was encouraging to hear things like this. New seeds of society developing amidst all the death. She wondered how many others there were spread over the world. Little tribes, little governments. It was enough to give a girl hope, especially if they were led by kind and edu-cated men like this one.

"We're lucky. We've been able to scout a lot of scientists and bring them here," David continued. "Together we're working on a cure. Of course, we need test subjects. Which is why we had those Others contained upstairs in the pharmacy."

"Oh." She cringed. "Sorry about that. Didn't mean to let them out."

"It's okay. Sadly, there's hardly a shortage."

"So, you're trying to cure them?" It hadn't occurred to Molly that other groups might have the same hopes and plans that her father did.

David nodded. "We're still a long way off," he confessed. "Right now we're trying to decode the creatures' DNA. Once we have that, we'll be able to see how it's mutated from that of a human. Maybe then we can do some kind of gene ther-apy to help them regain their humanity."

"My dad and his scientist friends are doing something sim-ilar," she said. "Down at Disney World."

David considered this. "That's interesting," he said. "We've been sending out radio messages for a while now, inviting oth-ers to join our research. We haven't heard anything from any-one in central Florida."

"Well, they're down there," Molly said, realizing she prob-ably sounded defensive. Still, she didn't like the implication.

David put a hand on her shoulder. "I'm sorry," he said. "I'm sure they're just not on our frequencies. Or maybe they're not using radios. I think it's great if there are others working on the same project. We need all the help we can get. When you get there, you'll have to tell them about us. Maybe we can all collaborate."

"Sure. Good idea."

The elevator doors swung open, revealing a fluorescent-lit hallway leading off into the distance. They walked down it and through a door, which opened into a large mess hall. Molly's eyes widened as she surveyed the place. She hadn't seen so many people since the Thunderdome. All hanging out, eating, chatting, as if none of them had a care in the world.

David led her to what appeared to be a head table. A group of about ten men and women sat behind it, eating their dinner. They looked up.

"I'd like you to meet Molly," David said to them. "She and her friends are heading down to Orlando. She tells me that there's another hive down there, also looking for a cure." He turned to Molly. "This is our council," he told her. "The think tank behind all our work."

"It's good to meet you all," she said, still awed by the whole thing.

While the council quizzed her on her father's work, David walked over to a serving window and spoke quietly to the man behind it. He returned a moment later with a bowl of steaming soup. Molly sat at the table, wolfing it down. Delicious. Real food. It felt a little bit like paradise here. And not the crazy zombie-gladiator-town type.

"We have a gym here and a school even," David said. "Everyone works. And everyone eats. People come here bedraggled and half-dead and we take them in. We've grown so much in the last year. It's great. We've even had four babies born! As I think I mentioned, the last one was yesterday. We're busting at the seams a bit, but everyone's happy. A few weeks ago we opened a lower level to add more housing for the families."

"That's so wonderful," Molly said, between bites. "As is, of course, your work on finding the cure for the Others. How would you distribute it if you were able to create one?"

"The hope is to build a factory to mass produce it and then pour it into lakes and rivers—places the creatures use for drinking water," explained a twenty-something bearded council member. "It'll take a lot of manpower, which is why we're gathering as many people as we can down here. And once we start curing them, we can rehabilitate and bring them here. They'll be productive members of society again, and in turn they can help cure more of their kind."

"It sounds like quite a plan."

"It's a big undertaking," said the council member at the far end, a blonde woman in her forties. "But we're hopeful. We have everything in place. Just need to discover that magic formula."

"Right. Well, I admire all the work you're doing. It's really encouraging to hear."

"We still need more people," David told her. "So if you don't find what you're looking for down in central Florida, I hope you'll consider coming back. We'll take all your people in."

Molly considered. "Even though they're mostly children?" she asked.

"Especially children," Mary broke in. "They're the future, after all. And so many of our adults here lost their own kids. They'd be overjoyed to become adoptive parents."

Molly looked around the room at all the happy faces. At all the food. And suddenly she realized what she must do.

"Well then," she said. "I think I have an idea."

"Chase, wake up!"

Chase groaned as Helga burst into his tent. He'd barely slept a wink the night before, tossing and turning and remembering Molly's hurt face. It took all his willpower not to get out of bed and find her and confess everything. Tell her he loved her and never meant to hurt her and wanted nothing more than to be with her forever.

But that would just complicate things. Because he'd have to tell her about the bite. About his impending mutation. That there would probably be no happily ever after for the two of them, as much as he wanted there to be.

"What is it, Helga?" he asked, sitting up and rubbing his eyes. He'd finally dozed off for a few minutes and now he was up again.

"It's Molly. She's nowhere in camp!"

Fear slammed his heart. Now he was wide awake. "Are you sure?" he asked. "Maybe she just went for a walk. Did you check the river? Maybe she's bathing." He crawled out of the tent. The sun was barely up over the horizon and most of the children were still asleep.

"I checked everywhere," Helga told him. "And then I noticed her rucksack was gone. She's left us." The girl looked at Chase suspiciously. "Why would she leave?" she asked.

Chase didn't bother to answer. He was already searching for his shoes. "She couldn't have gone too far," he said. "She's weak. I'm going to try to find her."

Helga rushed to his side. "How are you going to do that? It's not like there's some trail of breadcrumbs to follow."

"I just will, okay?" he growled. She backed off, looking frightened. He swallowed hard. "Sorry," he said. "I'm just worried about her."

"Me, too. I can't believe she'd just take off."

Unfortunately, Chase could. Obviously he'd hurt her even more than he'd intended the night before. Made her feel rejected and alone. And so she'd left. Left him and the children. To seek her own way to Disney World.

But she wouldn't make it on her own. She was too weak. She'd die. And it would be all his fault. More blood on his hands.

He couldn't do anything right.

"Molly! Molly!"

Chase looked up at the sudden cries from the children, his heart leaping into his throat. His eyes followed the direction they were running. Sure enough, Molly was limping toward the camp. Joy washed over him as he took her in. Thank God she was all right.

He followed the children over, wanting to throw his arms around her and hold her and never let her go. But her cold expression swept him then dismissed him as she turned back to the kids, greeting them and apologizing for being away. So Chase hung back, reality smacking him upside the head. In her mind, he had rejected her. And she in turn would now reject him. In her mind, they were finished. And he had been the bastard who had started it.

He realized, suddenly, that she was not alone. A tall, well-built man with a military crew cut was by her side. Jealousy raged up inside of him and he fought to keep it at bay. Who was this tool? Had she found someone to replace him already? He knew he should be glad that she'd found someone to take care of her, someone who could competently get her to Disney World, but the thought of being replaced was too much to bear.

"You're staying *here?*" asked the man, surveying the premises. "This isn't safe at all. You're vulnerable on at least three sides from attack."

Chase felt his hackles rise. They'd been doing the best they could. How dare this guy judge them? "We have trip wires set on all four sides," he retorted. "And we do regular patrols. The place is never unwatched."

"That's all well and good, but what happens when they hit the trip wires? You have no place to escape to."

Chase stepped forward. "The kids have been well-versed in evacuation procedures," he said. "And the older kids have been taught how to fight."

Molly stepped between them. "Whoa, boys," she said. "No need to whip them out and measure. Chase, this is David. David, Chase. David is a council member of a new society they're building just a mile or two from here. It's deep underground. They've got food and medicines and supplies. And over three hundred residents!" She related what she'd learned and seen.

Chase listened with interest. Sounded like Disney wasn't the only game in town after all. Maybe Molly could be convinced to give up her quest and settle here. Where she'd be safe. Chase would be much happier dying if he knew she had landed someplace safe.

But he knew in his heart she'd never give up before seeing her dad. She was too dedicated to her cause. After all, that had been the problem from the very beginning. When she'd left him high and dry on that last day.

He turned back to the conversation.

"We'd like to escort you all back to the Hive," David was saying. "It's a good place to settle down. We'll be able to find adoptive parents for all the kids and you can all go to school. There's plenty of food and we even have nightly entertainment. Bands, movies, that sort of thing."

"All underground?" asked Helga.

David nodded. "For now," he told her. "Until we find a cure for the creatures. Then, after rehabilitating them, it'll be safe to go back to the surface."

Helga turned to Molly, who nodded.

"It seems like a good plan to me," she said. "Kids, pack your bags. The journey is over. We're going home."

"And buckets of candy for everyone when we get there," David added with a grin.

The kids whooped and cheered and ran off to gather their gear. Helga hugged Molly and then headed to her own tent. Through it all, Chase hung back, not sure what to do. He knew he should be overjoyed. He'd kept his promise to his brother, caring for the kids and getting them to a safe place. And Molly would be safe, too. So that was good. But, of course, it was all an empty happiness, knowing that he'd lost the woman he loved and would soon, on top of that, lose his life.

If only he hadn't been bitten. One more day after six years and he never would have had to worry about it again. But, no. Fate was too cruel to allow him his happily ever after. And now that everyone else had theirs, he knew what he'd probably have to do.

CHAPTER FORTY-TWO

Molly locked the door to her room then climbed on a chair to pull her suitcase down from the top shelf of her closet. Tossing it on the bed, she unzipped it and started selecting clothes. A gnawing guilt crawled through her stomach as she packed. What would her father say when he realized she'd gone, that she'd taken his implants but rejected his plan? She'd chosen the company of her boyfriend over her father.

Was she doing the right thing? Probably not. But she loved Chris. More than anything in the world. And if that world was going to end—if they were all going to die anyway—she wanted to be by his side. Her father and mother would have to understand. They'd had their time. They'd had each other. Maybe someday, if they all survived, they could all find each other again. Maybe she and Chris could make the trek down to Disney World and see the new society her father claimed they'd create. But first they had to get through the bad times, the plague and the zombies. And Molly didn't want to face that without Chris.

Chris. She imagined him right then, packing his own suitcase. Loading the van. He and Trey, rallying their friends. Soon she and he would be together always. In the new little society they'd create up in the mountains. Maybe she'd even make love to him someday. Funny, before now she couldn't really imagine wanting to have sex with anyone. Now, having fallen for Chris, she couldn't imagine anything sweeter.

They'd live in the camp like husband and wife. Sure, they were young, but who was going to care? She'd keep house for him. He'd provide food. Just like the olden times. Maybe they'd even have children. Populate the new world. And through it all, they'd be in love. Utterly and completely in love.

A loud banging on the door interrupted her fantasy. Worried, she stuffed her suitcase under the bed and went to answer. Her dad stood on the other side of the door, his hair sticking up in all directions, his eyes wild.

"Molly, it's time," he said. "You and your mother need to go down to the shelter."

Fear gripped her. No! Not now. Not when she was so close to getting away.

"What? Why?" she asked, stalling for time as she tried to think of a plan.

Her father glanced behind him and then back. "They're here. The cleaners. They're going to make their move, take me away. I need to know you two are safe."

What was he talking about? "Dad, why would someone want to take you away?" she asked, confused and frightened.

"It doesn't matter. All that matters is that you're down in the shelter where they can't find you. I'm going to lead them away, create a diversion. They won't see you go down there. And you'll be safe for six years. That should be enough time."

"Enough time? Enough time for what?" Panic slammed through her. She couldn't go down into the shelter. Not now. She had to meet Chris.

"Molly, focus. Listen to me. When the shelter doors open in six years, I need you to head down to Disney World. It's vitally important. I'll meet you there."

She didn't know what he was talking about, but she realized she had to speak up. Now. Or for six years hold her peace. She drew in a breath.

"Dad, I'm not going to the shelter," she said, wishing her voice didn't sound so squeaky and immature.

He stared at her, disbelief on his face. "What did you say?"

She swallowed. "I'm sorry, but I've made other plans. I'm going up to the mountains with my friends. We're going to wait things out there."

"Absolutely not." Ian Anderson shook his head. "It's too dangerous. And who will take care of your mom? You know as well as I do that she's not equipped to survive without help these days."

Molly cringed. Way to make her feel guilty. He was totally right, too. Her mom was lost in a dream world of pills. She'd never survive on her own. How could Molly abandon her?

But then again, how could she abandon Chris?

"Look, Molly, I need to tell you something," her dad continued. "When I added your cybernetics, I did something else, too. I inserted a special code into your brain. It's stored in a section you don't use—you wouldn't be able to access it even under torture. But it can be extracted by the scientists down at Disney World."

Molly stared at him, hardly able to believe what he was saying. "Code?" she whispered, her life crashing down all around her. "What kind of code?"

"If I tell you, I jeopardize your life. The government will kill you to find out. But suffice it to say, my daughter, you hold the only copy of the key to rebuild the world. So you see why it's important that you make it to Disney World when those doors open in six years. We'll be waiting for you. You'll literally be the second coming. Our savior."

This was so not fair. So not fair! She felt tears cascade down her cheeks. "Why?" she demanded, grabbing him by the shoulders and shaking him in fury. "Why would you do this to me? Your daughter? Isn't it enough you turned me into a robot? Now you ask me to sacrifice everything that means anything to me in order to save the world!"

"You're my razor girl," he said quietly. "There's no one else."

"I didn't ask for this! I just wanted to be normal."

Suddenly a banging from downstairs interrupted them. Her father looked at her and nodded. "They've just broken down the door," he said. "They will be here soon." He dangled a gold key in front of her. "Decide now," he said. "Your boyfriend or the shelter. The fate of the future hangs on your decision."

CHAPTER FORTY-THREE

That night at the Hive there was a grand celebration. All the residents gathered in the main underground hall to meet the newcomers. There was a feast, plates overflowing with delicious food, and wine and spirits flowed freely. Not that Molly partook. A band thrown together by local teens, Apocalypse Then, rocked out on a makeshift stage, and everyone cleared away the dinner tables to dance. The Hive's residents were all friendly and welcoming, and for the first time in years Molly felt like she was home.

But, of course, she wasn't. And while this was a great place to settle the kids she was protecting, her own journey was not quite over. She still had to get down to Disney World and meet her father and his scientist friends. Give them the data stored in her head—whatever it was—to help them rebuild the world.

It was her mission. And she had almost completed it.

The good news was, she'd had herself checked out by the Hive doctors. They'd cycled her blood, removed her failing nanos, and she felt good as new. She was ready to take the last leg of the trek. And she didn't need anyone else to help her now. Sure, without the nanos she wasn't as strong or fast, but they weren't eating her insides, either. She'd make it somehow. Her dad was depending on her, and she wasn't about to let him down when she was so close.

She looked around the room, smiling as she saw the children

dancing and frolicking and having a grand old time. Starr and
Torn were dancing cheek to cheek: young love finally ex-
pressed in a safe place. Darla and Sunshine chatted wildly with
the couple eager to adopt them. The would-be parents looked
thrilled—they'd evidently lost their own little girls to Others a
few years back, and now they had a chance to have a family
again. And Helga was locked in what looked like a deep conversation with David. Perhaps the two would hit it off.

But, as Molly scanned the room, she realized she didn't
see Chase anywhere. In fact, now that she thought about it,
she hadn't seen him all day. At first she hadn't been sure he'd
be willing to come to the Hive in the first place, but he had
tagged along, staying mostly silent. She'd longed to talk to
him; he was the only one likely to understand she had to finish her quest. But when she'd approached him, he'd quickly
shut her down. For whatever reason—and she still had no
idea why—he had little interest in her. Nothing to say.

She decided to go find him, to at least say good-bye. She
wouldn't just disappear on him again. She owed him that.

They'd assigned Chase a small studio-type apartment at the
end of Floor 23D. In no mood to celebrate and not feeling
very hungry, he'd returned to it earlier that night, tried to
read a bit—they had actual books here—but found he couldn't
concentrate. He just kept thinking about the zombie bite. And
about the fact that in just a short time, he'd probably become
one of them.

As he did so often these days, almost neurotic, he stripped
out of all of his clothes and began a thorough body examination, searching for any mark or blemish or spot that could be
the first sign of sickness. And this time he saw it. On his inner
thigh. A small, bubbling sore just above his knee. He stared at
it, unable to breathe. It looked just like the one Spud got a
week before he morphed into a monster.

Was this it? Was he definitely infected? Had the Other
passed along its terrible germs and injected monstrousness
into his DNA? Would this boil be the first of many spreading

all over his body as his genes mutated and his hair fell out? How long would it take until his humanity fled and he became nothing more than a cannibalistic monster, a danger to all he encountered?

He couldn't let it happen. He couldn't endanger his family. The members of the Hive. His people were safe now. Molly was safe. He'd kept his promise. So that was something, at least.

He debated his options, finding it nearly impossible to think when he was so scared and upset. He could leave the Hive, go somewhere where there were few people and let the change take him, live a half life as a monster and hope he didn't run into any humans in his mindless travels. Or—he took a deep breath—he could kill himself now and get it over with. It was the best way to be sure—the only way, really—that he'd never harm any innocents. That he'd never take anyone's life.

In the end, the decision was simple. He reached for his rifle and the bullets he'd stored under his bed.

He'd really hoped it wouldn't come to this. That he'd been immune just like Tank had been. Then, once he was sure he was clean, he could have apologized to Molly. Explained what had happened and why he'd pushed her away. Maybe they'd have even had a laugh about the whole thing. And then she would kiss him on the mouth, just like she used to, pressing her full lips against his, happy and wanting. He would lay her down on the bed and make love to her all night, caressing every inch of her body, pleasuring her until the sun rose and they were both sore yet sated. They'd snuggle into each other's arms and fall deep asleep, no need to worry about monsters anymore.

That would have been perfect. A Disney ending, so to speak. But it wasn't meant to be. And in the final analysis, he realized, he needed to do what had to be done, and he needed to do it before he ruined someone else's happily ever after. He put the barrel in his mouth and reached down to the trigger.

"Oh my God, Chase, what the hell are you doing?"

Shit. Deep in thought, he hadn't heard the door open. Why

hadn't he locked it? He looked over and saw Molly, her face white and horrified, standing in the doorway. He was busted. Caught red-handed. He knew he should act fast, blow his head off right then and there before she got too close. But he found he couldn't do it. It would scar her for life, and he loved her too much to do that. Hadn't they both seen enough death?

Against his better judgment he pulled the gun out of his mouth and lowered it to the floor. She was on him in a second, grabbing the gun and removing the bullets. She threw them across the room then turned to him, her face stormy.

"Chase Griffin, you tell me what the hell is going on here this instant," she said, sounding like his mother once had.

He hung his head, trying to buy time as he struggled with what to say. Should he come clean, tell her the truth? Guess it didn't matter anymore. And maybe it was for the best. Maybe this was what he should have done in the first place. At least this way he could admit how much it hurt to push her away. How her pain was a knife, twisting inside his gut every time he looked at her disappointed face. How he loved her more than anything or anyone in the entire sorry world. And how he would love her forever and watch over her, even from the grave.

He looked up at her, his eyes heavy with unshed tears. "I have to tell you something," he said.

Everything inside of Molly was coiled like a spring, ready to explode as she waited for Chase to explain. She'd only come here to tell him she was leaving; she never in a million years expected to see him totally naked and deep-throating a rifle. Thank God she hadn't startled him into pulling the trigger.

Why would he do this? Now, when they were finally safe? After he'd kicked the drugs, got them down to Florida and fulfilled his promise to his brother? After all they'd been through, after all they'd survived, now he wanted to take the coward's way out? Was this why he'd pushed her away? Because he didn't want her attached when he did himself in?

"I-I . . ." he stammered. "I . . ." He cleared his throat.

"First of all, I want to apologize for how I've been acting. All cold and mean and heartless. That's not me, and you don't deserve to be treated that way. I'm sorry. I . . . I love you, Molly," he said, his voice cracking.

Her heart leapt. This was so not what she'd been expecting him to say. "Then what's going on, Chase?" she asked, desperate to know but thoroughly frightened at the same time. "Why have you pushed me away? And why are you down here with a gun down your throat?"

"Remember two nights ago when I killed the Other?"

She nodded slowly, trying to grasp what he was saying. Then suddenly reality hit. She stared at him, eyes wide beneath her implants. "You got bitten, didn't you?" she whispered. Suddenly everything slid together in this horrifying puzzle. "You got bitten by one of those Others. And you were afraid you were infected." It all made sense now: how he wouldn't touch her, how he kept his distance from the kids. It all made perfect sense. Why hadn't she figured it out before? She was an idiot. A real idiot.

He rubbed his eyes with his fists. "Yes," he said at last. "I was bitten. But I didn't want you to freak out. Or more importantly, to waste any time on quarantine. I'd already slowed you down too much. The last thing I wanted was for you to die because of me. I figured I'd get you guys as close as possible to Disney, and then, if I started seeing signs of infection, then . . . I'd take care of it."

She stared down at his rifle, realizing now it was the "taking care of it" part she'd just interrupted. "You've seen signs?" she asked, her voice hoarse. Her Chase, her beautiful, wonderful Chase—the first boy she'd ever opened her heart to and allowed herself to love—was going to turn into one of the pus-filled cannibal zombies? It didn't seem possible.

He stretched out his leg and showed her a small boil. "I found this just a few minutes ago," he said. "It's the first sign. I'm sure of it."

"It could just be a small infection," she argued. "A coincidence. We've all got scrapes and cuts from being out on the road. We're dirty and not eating right. Of course that can lead to infections. It doesn't mean you're turning into an Other."

"Maybe, but I can't take the risk. If I turn into a monster, I could hurt you. I could even kill you. I don't want to endanger you or the children or anyone else here at the Hive. You don't want me to do that, either."

Tears streamed through the vents in her lenses and Molly fell to her knees at his side. He backed away, obviously afraid that even close proximity would spread the disease. But at this moment she wouldn't have cared if he had a third eye and dripping wounds.

"Chase, what am I going to do without you?" she asked.

He reached over and patted her head awkwardly. It was the first time he'd touched her since he'd been bitten. "You'll be fine," he assured her. "You're safe here. You can start a new life. Maybe meet someone new, even. Start a family. I want you to be happy, Molly. I love you." His voice broke.

"Chase," she said. "Listen to me. I'm not staying here. I need to go to Disney and find my father."

"But I thought the doctors here cured you."

"They did. I'm better already. But I made a promise to my dad and I'm going to keep it, no matter what. And," she added, "you're coming with me."

Chase looked at her sharply. "What are you talking about? I just told you I might turn into a zombie."

"Well, we're close. And I'm willing to bet you still have time left. It usually takes two weeks? It's been two days. We'll get there much sooner than your deadline. You'll be fine," she said. "Look, Chase, my dad's been working on a cure since before we even went underground. Surely by now he's made some progress. Maybe we'll get down there and he'll have an antidote."

"That's a big maybe, Molly. You don't even know for sure he's still alive."

"I *know*," she said firmly. "Don't ask me how, but I'm sure my dad is still alive. I would know if he were dead. I came all this way. I *have* to believe."

"And the antidote?"

"Well, I don't know that for sure. But what do you have to lose, right?" She crossed her fingers, praying he'd see that what she was saying made sense.

He hedged. "I don't know. I don't like the idea of putting you in danger."

"You're not. Well, not for sure. A small boil does not a monster make. And you have time. We'll be there in two days. And then, if there's no antidote . . ." She drew in a breath. "Well, we'll take care of things."

He drew in a breath, was silent for a moment, then nodded. "Okay," he said, his words filling her heart with joy. "This is why I wanted to handle things away from you—because I knew you could talk me into hoping. Well, I promised to get you to Disney World and that's exactly what I'll do. But I want you to carry the gun and keep it loaded at all times. The second you see some kind of serious change in me, you have to promise you'll shoot me. Don't hesitate. I won't be me anymore. Just do it."

"Okay." She'd agree to anything just to keep him from killing himself right then and there. Still alive, they had some hope. Not much, maybe, but some. And that was all she could ask for.

"I'm serious, Molly," he said. "You have to be willing and able to shoot me. You can't think about things. Remember Erin?"

"I know." She sighed. "I remember, and I will. It'll break my heart, but I will."

He rose to his feet and pulled her close, careful not to let his knee touch her. He embraced her hard, crushing her against him, and it brought back memories of all those blissful nights they'd shared. If only they could have that one more time. But, no. A hug was all she was allowed. All that was safe.

"I love you, Molly Anderson," he whispered in her ear. She felt his hot breath and she squeezed him harder, wanting to take him inside of her and never let go. How was she going to live without this man? It seemed an empty, pointless existence. Her dad had to have an antidote. He just had to.

"I love you, too, Chris Griffin," she replied. "More than anyone ever."

He pulled away so he could find her face with his kaleidoscope eyes. "Whatever happens," he said, "it was all worth it getting to spend this time with you. I'll never regret any of it."

She felt tears dripping down her cheeks from her implants again and sank down on the couch. "Just hold me," she begged. "For tonight."

He looked torn. "It might be dangerous. I don't want to infect you."

"I'll take the risk."

He sank down next to her, looking ecstatic but also nervous, and took her in his arms. They lay down on the couch together, him spooning her from behind. He kept his leg raised away from her. Tracing the outline of her cheek, he ran his finger up to her ear, caressing gently, slowly, as if memorizing each contour. Molly lay staring at the apartment wall, praying over and over that this was somehow all a mistake. A bad dream. That it would all be okay.

Or that they'd make it to Disney. Her dad would be waiting with a cure. She would never, ever have to make the decision to put a bullet into the man she loved.

CHAPTER FORTY-FOUR

It was raining the day they packed to leave. It wasn't just drizzling, but hurricane-like downpours, gushing buckets of water down on their heads and worse, their supplies. Trey tied everything under tarps and shoved suitcases into garbage bags, but water damage was inevitable.

"What do you girls think, you're going to Europe for the month?" Trey scolded as he shoved suitcase after suitcase in the ancient Ford E-Series van they'd bought off a black market dealer for three hundred bucks. It barely ran, spilling out black goo and blacker smoke each time you turned on the engine. But it wasn't a Smart Car, so it wasn't trackable. Trey wasn't taking any chances with the food they'd begged, borrowed and stolen.

Thank God they had a sim Boy Scout like him leading things. After spending years of his life in rather unpractical role-playing fantasy sims, Chris had very little clue about real-life survival. But Trey was taking care of everything. He calculated food, supplies, even the number of people who could join them. Ten. Any more, he said, and there would be too many empty stomachs and too many fights.

"Oh no, here comes another one," Chris said, pointing through the rain to a hooded individual running up the path. Ever since the kids in school found out they were skipping town, they'd had visitors up the ying-yang. Everyone wanted to escape, and they were willing to trade fancy, high-end sim decks, mom's jewelry—anything to strike a deal.

"Useless," Trey would say. "What good will a sim deck be when there's no power, no Web?"

The figure approached, stepping under the awning where Trey and Chris were standing, pulled off her hood and looked up at Trey with big doe eyes. Anna Simmons. This ought to be interesting.

"Trey!" she cried. "I can't believe you were going to leave without me."

Trey looked down at her. And Chris could see the debate in his eyes. "I'm sorry, Anna," he said. "We're full. We can only take ten. You said you weren't coming, and just because Richard broke up with you. . . ."

Chris was surprised. Surely Trey would bend when it came to Anna, the girl he was crazy about. But, no. As she continued to beg, he continued to shake his head. He had a plan, and damn it, he'd be sticking to it. Either that or he was still a bit sore about the whole Richard thing . . .

"What if someone doesn't show?" Anna tried. "I only see nine of you."

Oh, no she didn't. "Molly's on her way," Chris interrupted. "She'll be here any minute." He glanced at his watch. They'd all switched to old-fashioned types that only told the time and didn't have standard GPS. If he'd set it correctly, Molly was fifteen minutes late. Trey was going to be pissed.

Sure enough, Trey shot him a look. "Are you sure she's coming?" he asked. " 'Cause it's not fair to save a spot if she's not."

Chris pushed nagging doubts to the back of his mind. Even though he hadn't heard from Molly after last night, when Tara was murdered, that didn't mean she'd changed her mind. It was just hard for her to get in touch, with her dad being all strict and everything. She'd said she would be here. She'd promised and sealed it with a kiss.

"Yes," he said, trying to sound as confident as he could. "She'll be here."

"Then I'm sorry, Anna," Trey said with a regretful shrug. "I've got nothing left. Maybe try Drew. I think him and his buddies are heading south sometime this week."

Tears splashed down Anna's cheeks, mixing with raindrops. "Please," she begged. "I'm scared and I don't want to die."

Trey's face softened. "We leave at ten," he said. "If Molly doesn't show by then, you can have her spot."

"No!" Chris cried. "Dude, she'll show!"

"Fine," Trey said, looking annoyed. "Like I said, if she does, she's in. First come, first served, and all that. But if she doesn't, then there's no reason to deny Anna the spot—is there?"

Chris knew his brother had a point, as much as he was loath to admit it. He glanced at his watch again, fear gripping his heart. Where was she? Why wasn't she here? Had something happened?

"Hey, Chris, can you give me a hand with this?" cried Bill, attempting to lift a heavy box into the van. Chris ran over to help, trying to force the worry out of his brain.

She'd come. She'd promised, after all. And he trusted her with everything he was.

CHAPTER FORTY-FIVE

"Oh my God, I can't believe we're actually here."

Molly and Chase pulled up on their motorcycles—gifts from the Hive council that had made the last of the trip fly by—in front of the main entrance to Disney. The turnstiles, once manned by militant cast members who denied admission to anyone without the requisite pass, stood as harmless sentinels, suits of armor without soldiers, ineffective guardians to the gates of the kingdom. Beyond? There was an old abandoned railroad station where, once upon a time, a train would pick up passengers and circle the perimeter of the park for those disinclined to walk. Beyond that? The Magic Kingdom itself. Once the happiest place on Earth. Now perhaps not happy, but one of its last refuges.

Molly slid off her motorcycle, engaged the kickstand and walked over to the turnstiles. She ran her hand along the smooth chrome then turned back to Chase. "I'm so nervous," she admitted. "Everything's come down to this."

He dismounted his own bike and approached. Put his arms around her and squeezed tight. "No matter what happens," he whispered in her ear, "I love you."

His words sent chills down her back and she squeezed him in return. "I love you, too," she said. "That's why I want this so much. That's the real reason it means something."

They clung to each other for a moment, each lost in their

own hopes and horrors, then reluctantly let go. They were still on a mission, after all.

"I guess we jump the turnstiles," Chase said with a quirky grin. "Unless you pre-purchased tickets. Hope no guards are watching."

She chuckled. "I think Walt will forgive us, under the circumstances." She placed her hands on each side of the turnstile. "Besides, I always wanted to do this as a kid." She jumped over the bars and landed on the other side. "Easy-peasy."

Chase made his jump and together they walked under the train bridge and came out into Town Square, right on the edge of Main Street USA. Molly glanced around at the once-colorful turn-of-the-twentieth-century modeled buildings, now with their faded, chipping paint. The storefronts along Main Street were battered and neglected. Some had been knocked down entirely—perhaps by a passing hurricane or two. The place was silent as the grave, and a shiver passed through Molly. She scanned the area with her implants, searching for life.

Nothing. Totally dead.

"I guess they wouldn't be concentrating on aesthetics when they're trying to save the world," she muttered, half to herself. "I mean, they've got more important things to do than paint."

Chase reached over and took her hand and squeezed. She wondered, not for the first time, how much he believed that they'd find something here. It was beginning to seem doubtful to her as well. But she pushed on. Even if the chance was small, she had to know. Chase's life depended on it.

"This place is huge," Chase remarked, as they walked down Main Street toward a crumbling Cinderella's castle with a few missing turrets. "How are we going to find anyone?"

"I'm looking," Molly told him, glancing off toward Adventureland. "There'll be signs. But nothing so far." She stopped as her lenses picked up movement. "Oh God," she whispered. "There are Others here." She zoomed in for a closer look.

"And they're headed our way." She scanned the castle. Same deal.

"They're everywhere!" she cried. "The place is crawling with them." She motioned behind her. "Let's head back to the entrance. Maybe we can find one of those service tunnels or something."

They ran back down Main Street to Town Square and found a door that said Cast Members Only. Pushing through they found a staircase—Stairway Number 18, according to the sign—leading down into the darkness. Molly checked the passage and couldn't see any signs of movement in the dim light. Chase closed the door behind them and they both breathed a sigh of relief.

"What are Others doing here?" Chase asked dubiously. "You would think if your father and his friends were here they'd have cleared the place out. Secured it."

Molly nodded. "Something's wrong," she agreed. "This isn't supposed to be like this. It was supposed to be the last safe human outpost. Not a monster-filled Tunnel of Death." She felt sick to her stomach. Was it time to face reality, that they had come all this way for nothing? That her dad and his scientist friends didn't actually ever make it here? Was Chase doomed to die because of this waste of a mission?

"Look, there were Others above the Hive, too," Chase reminded her. She felt his warm breath as he whispered into her ear. In the darkness, it sent shivers down her spine. "Maybe it's the same here. Remember your father's plan? Maybe they're down working in these service tunnels, right? We should go check it out. Might as well make sure."

She loved him for not giving up. "Okay," she agreed. "Let's head down."

As they walked down the darkened steps, Molly kept her eyes peeled for any dangerous movements. She held Chase's hand to lead him. At the bottom of the staircase they came to a long, nondescript tunnel leading off into the distance. She did a scan. Nothing. She let out a breath.

"Okay, let's start walking. I'll guide you," she said.

They headed north, probably right under Main Street if Molly calculated right. Above them she thought she sensed Others wandering the park, but maybe it was paranoia. There were no signs of human life at all. After a while, they came to a wardrobe room. Seemingly endless racks of costumes lined it. Mickey Mouse, Donald Duck, Cinderella—all the favorites were there. It made Molly sad to think that no one would ever wear these outfits again. The silly faces would never be responsible for making another child laugh.

Suddenly, her lenses picked something up northwest of them. A heat pattern that didn't match the cool blood color of the Others. She grabbed Chase's arm.

"I think there might be a human up there," she told him, scarcely able to breathe.

"Above ground?"

"Yeah." But was it her father? Was he here, alive after all?

"I'll go up," Chase said. "After all, I'm already bitten. What more can they do to me?"

"Well, they can tear you apart and eat you," she replied. "And I'm a better fighter. I have more training, and razors. I can also pinpoint his location."

"Fair enough, we'll go together," he said.

They walked up the stairs and emerged near the Pinocchio Village Haus, an old food stand long deserted. Molly scanned the area. "It's a Small World," she announced excitedly.

"It certainly can seem that way."

"No, no—I mean, that's where the human is. In the ride somewhere."

"Oh." Chase nodded. "Okay, let's go."

From the outside, the dingy white building looked like all the rest. Dead and deserted. But Molly's zooming lenses kept getting definite hints of movement inside. They walked down into the ride and came across a waterway with a line of boats bobbing in some pretty gross-looking water.

Oddly, the boats were moving, gliding through the canals just as they had years ago, when the park was open. The only thing they'd seen so far still in action.

"Weird," Molly said, glancing at Chase. She shivered. "And creepy."

"Yeah. I guess we get in."

They climbed into the first boat and let it take them slowly down the man-made canal. Soon they were flanked by dolls on either side, all eerily silent and none of them singing or dancing as they were supposed to. As a child, Molly had found the "It's a Small World" song extremely irritating. She'd give anything to hear it now.

They paddled past Eskimo children, through Scandinavia, then past little British guards. Europe, then Asia, then magic carpets signaling the Middle East. Neither Molly nor Chase spoke as they floated through. All Molly could think was of all these different cultures, all the people of the world—how they had all become extinct.

They passed through Africa. Saw Cleopatra in Egypt. Llamas greeted them at the edge of South America, followed by volcanoes and fire dancers of Tahiti and the space helmet-wearing kids of Station 13. Then, all cultural boundaries faded and the final scene of the ride spread out before them. Children of all nations together as one.

It was then that the music started. And the dancing dolls came to life.

Molly nearly jumped out of her skin as the theme song suddenly blared from unseen speakers. The dolls whirled and danced and smiled. She looked around, wondering what was going on. Then her sensors picked up flashes of movement to the left, movement that didn't seem like part of the ride. She saw heat trails that seemed human. She motioned to Chase and they jumped out of the boat. Past the dolls, into the background, behind a wall, and . . .

Found Ian Anderson.

Her father was older. More gray. More wrinkles. But it was definitely him. He was here. Alive. He'd survived. He'd waited for her. Just as he'd always said.

She ran over and threw her arms around him, overjoyed

to have accomplished her mission at last. "Oh, Dad!' she said, burying her face in her chest. "I made it. I actually made it."

He patted her awkwardly on the back a few times—he never had been one for the whole touchy-feely thing—and then pulled away. He looked at her fondly, reaching out to touch the edges of her implants.

"You've finally come," he whispered. "My razor girl. My Molly."

"Yes, Dad, I'm here." She looked up at him, a little worried. Something seemed off. Wrong.

He paced back and forth. "Not that it's not great to see you," he said, "but you really shouldn't have come."

She stared at him. "What?" she asked. "What the hell are you talking about? Of course I should have come. That was the whole deal. You needed me to bring the data you'd stored in my head, remember?"

"Right." He sounded distracted. "But it does no good now, does it?"

"What's going on, Dad?" she asked, feeling like she was missing a vital piece of the puzzle. "Where is everyone? Where are your fellow scientists? Where's the new society?"

Her father ran a hand through his thinning gray hair. "They never came," he mumbled. "They never came."

Oh God. "Who? Your friends?"

"It was supposed to be perfect, Molly. We had it all planned out: the disease wiping out all corrupt governments. We were going to start anew. We had a Noah's Ark. But it went wrong. The zombies . . . we didn't know there would be zombies. And they killed them. All my friends. All the ones who were supposed to survive and rebuild the world. They never made it here. I waited . . . I went into hiding . . . I came back . . . But never anything."

Molly's heart filled with fear as she tried to grasp what her dad was saying. "Supposed to survive?" she whispered. "What are you talking about, Dad?"

"I guess I might as well tell you the truth," he said, glancing around. "What difference does it make now?" He gave a half-mad laugh.

And then he told her. He and his friends had formed a secret coalition ten years ago to create a virus that would work to wipe out certain members of the ruling class, using the AIDS vaccine as a conduit they could manipulate. They'd planned to stage a coup, to take over the government and start fresh.

"We were going to save all the children. Rebuild the world. There were fail-safes in place."

Chase snorted, but Molly ignored him.

"Fail-safes? And they . . . what, failed?" she asked through gritted teeth.

Her father hung his head. "Yes," he admitted. "Once the plague became airborne we could no longer control who was infected. And then there were the mutants. We could have never predicted the virus would mutate some people's DNA and turn them into monsters. Suddenly those who didn't get the plague were now at risk of being lunch. Which obviously wasn't part of the plan."

"What were you thinking?" Molly shrieked. "You thought you and your friends had the right to play God? What made you think that was okay?"

"Things were bad and getting worse. We figured starting over was the best plan. We could have made it right. And we meant to save the children. . . ."

"But you didn't. You destroyed the very world you were supposedly trying to save."

Her father shook his head but said, "Yes, well, as I mentioned before, things didn't go exactly as planned."

Molly couldn't believe it. All this time she'd been thinking she was on a mission to help her dad save the world. But he was the one responsible for ending it in the first place. She felt sick to her stomach. All that death. All that destruction. It was all the fault of her own flesh and blood.

"I can't believe you!" she cried. "I can't believe you did this! You're a monster!" She turned to Chase. "Let's get out of here," she said. "Back to the Hive. There's nothing for us here." No new society, no hope for the future. And no miraculous cure for her beloved.

She was almost back to the boats when her dad called out, "That's where you're wrong."

She stopped. Turned around slowly, not wanting to listen but feeling compelled all the same. "What do you mean?" she asked.

"You still have the data in your head," he reminded her. "So there's still hope to save the world."

The data. Right. "What's in my head, Dad?" she asked through clenched teeth. "Tell me once and for all what the fuck you put in my head!"

"The recipe for the antidote."

She stared at him. "What?"

"That's what I stored in your head. The virus code. We can extract it and create an antidote. That's why I needed you down here. We can fix this. We can still fix this."

"And it can be extracted how?"

"A simple scan with the right equipment should be able to read it. Any working hospital should have the right equipment. . . ."

She nodded. "Fine." Turning back to Chase, she said, "Let's go."

"But . . ." Chase said, looking at her dad. "The cure?"

She glared at her father. "The scientists back at the Hive will be able to extract it just as easily as him. In fact, it's the information they've been looking for all this time. They have a plan in place and resources to mass produce and distribute. Together we can rebuild the world." She glared at her father. "Not here. Not at Disney World. But *in the real world.*"

"Molly, please!" her dad cried, seeming to return to himself. "I never meant it to be like this. I wanted to make things better. For you. For future generations. I did it for you!"

"I chose you once," she said. "And betrayed everything I loved. Because I was loyal to you and your mission. But now

I realize you're the cause of it all. You don't deserve to also be the cure."

Her father looked pained. "Let me make it right!" he pleaded. Then he said, "You *need* me."

"Actually I don't," she growled. "And I never will. So you have yourself a Disney Day. We're out of here."

She spit on the ground, grabbed Chase's hand and walked away.

She didn't look back.

CHAPTER FORTY-SIX

It was nine P.M. and the rain had not subsided. But still, Chris waited. Trey and the other kids, including an ecstatic Anna Simmons, had left eleven hours earlier, headed up to the mountains. But Chris wasn't going without Molly. Not without his goddess. And so he waited, praying that she'd come, refusing to believe she'd left him alone.

Headlights suddenly pierced the darkness and his pulse quickened as he wondered if it could be her, arriving at last. Then he saw it was the van and his heart sank. Trey pulled up beside him and popped his head out of the window.

"She didn't show," his brother observed. It wasn't a question.

Chris hung his head. "Something must have happened."

"Well, hop in. We'll go head over to her house and see."

Chris complied, climbing into the passenger seat. Trey revved the engine and they took off down the road. A few minutes later they pulled up to Molly's front door. The lights were out. It looked deserted. Still, Chris had to know for sure. He hopped out of the van and ran up to the front door, banging his fist on the wood.

"They're gone."

He whirled around. A neighbor stood at the bottom of the driveway, arms folded across his chest. "What?" he asked.

"The Andersons. They're gone. Went down in some fancy fallout shelter or something," the neighbor explained. "Left all the rest of us up here to die, I reckon."

Chris stared at him, wanting more than anything to call the guy a liar. "Was . . ." he started, his voice trembling. "Was there a girl with them?"

"You mean Molly?" the neighbor asked. He nodded his head. "Yup. She was with her mother. They went down together. Down there for the long haul, I guess. Heard her father say something about six years. Long time to be stuck underground is what I say. Might be better to just get the flu and be done with it."

The neighbor went on speaking, but Chris was no longer listening. So this was it. She was gone. Even after all they'd been through, all that they'd promised each other, when all was said and done it didn't mean anything. She'd left him. Made her decision to stick with her family, follow her crazy dad to the end of the world.

He couldn't believe it. He just couldn't believe it. What had made her change her mind?

What had made her break his heart?

Trey popped out of the driver's seat and headed over to where he stood. He took Chris in his arms and pulled him close, hugging him with brotherly love. "Come on," he said, releasing him a moment later and leading him to the van. "We're going to the mountains."

Chris got into the van, feeling dead and alone. He stared out the window as they pulled out of the driveway. Watching Molly's house as they drove down the street. Hoping, praying, begging he'd see some sign that the neighbor was wrong. That Molly was there. That she hadn't abandoned him.

But the house stayed silent. And as they turned the corner, he forced himself to accept that once and for all, his goddess was gone for good.

CHAPTER FORTY-SEVEN

"My goddess was gone for good. . . ."

Chase set the hand-written manuscript down on his lap and looked up. The group burst into applause and many of the Hive members seemed more than a little misty-eyed at the tragic ending to his tale.

"God, that's so sad," sniffed a blonde woman to the far left that Chase knew as Rhoda. She dabbed her eyes with a tissue. "I remember when my mom died of the plague. I felt so alone. But you must have felt even worse."

"I can't even imagine how that must have been," Starr piped up from her seated position on the floor. She was arm in arm with Torn, as usual. "You never talked about it, either."

"It's terrible!" a soldier known as Nick said, sobbing like a baby. "You waiting there, all alone . . ."

Chase laughed. "You guys!" he cried. "Remember, this is only the beginning!" He rolled his eyes. "The story obviously has a lot more to go. And it only gets better from here."

"Obviously!" Molly declared as she stepped into the conference room. "Six years later and this lucky guy not only gets the girl, but his very own happy ending." She patted her bulging stomach and grinned at Chase. "Sorry I'm late for writing club," she said. "Council meeting ran long."

"No problem." He rose to greet her with a hug, her swollen stomach in the way, as usual. She was due in less than a month and her stomach reminded him of an oversized basketball, not that he'd ever admit it to her. Even though she'd had her ocular implants and razors removed, he knew she could still kick his ass. "I was just reading my manuscript. Not a dry eye in the house. I think it could be a best seller." He laughed. "If there was any book publisher left to print it."

"You gotta write the rest," David said, cuddled up in a corner with Helga. The two of them had been married three weeks ago, and were totally in the honeymoon stage still. "I want to hear what happens when Molly comes out of the fallout shelter. It's all very *Casablanca.*"

"I will," Chase said, grinning. "I promise."

"And I'll write my side of the story, too," Molly piped up. "You'll see why I had to do what I had to do. I wasn't the total evil bitch you might think."

"We know, we know," Chase replied. "You had to save the world and stuff." He kissed her on the nose to let her know he was just teasing. She kissed him back.

"This is what got you two in trouble to begin with!" someone called out from the back. Everyone laughed.

The dinner bell rang then and the Hive Writers Club gathered their things, exiting the room. Soon it was only Molly and Chase left behind in the classroom.

"How are you feeling?" he asked, placing a hand on her belly. He looked down into her eyes, glad he could once again peer into their depths. See her expression of love when she looked back up at him. He loved the blue of her irises. Her very human irises.

"I feel great," she said. "Never better. And you?"

"I'm great, too. A little sore, but good, all things considered." As a member of the rehabilitation team, Chase spent long hours above the surface each day hunting for Others who had been cured by the antidote team. When the survivors regained their humanity, they were confused and lost and scared. It was Chase's job to round them up, give them an explanation and bring them home. A Pied Piper of sorts, just as his brother had been before.

It had been almost a year since the scientists extracted the key recipe to the cure from Molly's head. They'd cured Chase of his own infection—he'd demanded they use it on him first, as a test in case it didn't work, and he had stayed in quarantine until they were sure it had—and then started work on producing mass quantities of the antidote to be distributed above ground. Over the year they'd cured an estimated four hundred Others, integrating them into Hive society. The underground city was bursting at the seams these days and there was much talk of going back above ground. Rebuilding the world, one town at a time.

"And your father?" Chase asked, leading her out the door and into the dining hall.

"I visited him this morning in the ward before the meeting," Molly told him. "He's getting better every day. I think the meds are really helping." She shrugged. "I'm glad we brought him here. Even after all he did, I couldn't imagine leaving him there in that creepy park all by himself."

"I'm glad, too," Chase replied, kissing the side of her head. "At first I really thought you were going to."

"Well," Molly said. "I remember something about feelings. I didn't want to go the rest of my life having abandoned him. People make mistakes. We need to forgive them."

Chase fought a surge of embarrassment. He still thought about the old days, and how he'd been. She noticed his discomfort and kissed his nose.

Chase laughed and shrugged. "When he's better," he said, "your dad'll be a valuable member of the team, I'm sure of it. He may have wild ideas, but he's smart. A good scientist. He was, after all, the one who created the antidote to begin with. I'm sure he can help with other inventions in the future. He may have been misguided, but he really did want to save the world. And here, he'll have his chance. We all have another chance."

"Right," Molly agreed. "In the meantime, we worker bees will just keep plugging away."

"You never rest, do you?" Chase teased her with a grin. "What are you going to do when everyone's cured? When your mission is finally over? What then?"

"Well, Chase Griffin, I can tell you one thing." Molly smiled at him. "I'm sure as hell not going to Disney World."

LIZ MAVERICK

Author of *Wired*,
***a Publishers Weekly* Best Book of 2007**

Katherine Gibbs is engaged, popular, gorgeous, and living a life of sheer perfection. This is her best week ever. The trouble is, it's manufactured. She's lived this week over and over and doesn't know it.

L. Roxanne Zaborovsky, Katherine's best friend, is outside looking in. But there is something she can do. The barriers of time are like the walls of an apartment—or the bars of a prison—and they can be demolished. She just has to start the jailbreak.

Walter "Q" Sheffield is just the man to free Kitty. A time-anomaly specialist, he can split seconds, erase hours and make the most of a minute. The one thing he can't do? Relationships. But hate and revenge have Kitty trapped in the vagaries of time, and only love will get her out. And that love must be…

IЯ REVERSIBLE

ISBN 13: 978-0-505-52778-3